Half the
Day Is Night

By Maureen F. McHugh

China Mountain Zhang

Half the Day Is Night

Half the Day Is Night

Maureen F. McHugh

TOR

A Tom Doherty Associates Book
New York

HALF THE DAY IS NIGHT

Copyright © 1994 by Maureen F. McHugh

This book is printed on acid-free paper.

A Tor Book
Published by Tom Doherty Associates, Inc.
175 Fifth Avenue
New York, N.Y. 10010

Tor ® is a registered trademark of Tom Doherty Associates, Inc.

LIBRARY OF CONGRESS CATALOGING-IN-PUBLICATION DATA

McHugh, Maureen F.
    Half the day is night / Maureen F. McHugh.
        p.   cm.
    "A Tom Doherty Associates book."
    ISBN 0-312-85479-X
    1. Twenty-first century—Fiction.   I. Title
PS3563.C3687H35   1994
813'.54—dc20   94-21745
                                                        CIP

First edition: October 1994

Printed in the United States of America

0 9 8 7 6 5 4 3 2 1

This book is for four women:
Ama Selu, Arla, Evelyn and Pat.
And they all know why.

Acknowledgments

Thanks to the following people: Bob Yeager, who tirelessly hounded me on technical details; all errors are mine, not his. Patrick Nielsen Hayden, who gave me time and encouragement as well as cogent suggestions. Tim Ryan and Sean Barton (Information Services-R-Us); Tim for technical assistance and Sean for being my favorite fan.

Half the
Day Is Night

1

Underwater

The man in the reflection didn't have any eyes.

It was a trick of the lighting. He was looking into a window, out into the dark, and anywhere there was a shadow on his face the glass reflected nothing back. Holes for eyes. David looked up, the light fell on his face and his eyes appeared, he looked back out into the darkness and they became empty again.

Outside was ocean. This far below the surface it was always night. You really didn't have to go very far underwater before all the sunlight was absorbed. He should have realized but he had been unconsciously expecting Caribbean warmth, Caribbean sun, not this huge expanse of black. He shuddered, and picked up his bag and limped on, keeping his eyes away from the window. He could still see his reflection walking with him, a stride and a quick step, bobbing along, favoring his stiff knee. He followed signs directing him to Baggage Claim, they were all in English. That was a disappointment, he had hoped that there might be more French, because of the Haitian population in Caribe. They would be in Creole anyway, and he didn't know Creole.

He came through a security checkpoint and presented his passport and visa to the boy in uniform. The boy was a black with a long narrow face. So young, these soldiers. Like children dangling guns from their fingers. He was getting older, he thought, soldiers had not seemed so young when he was in the *militaire*. Thirty-three was not so old. He put his duffel on the belt through the security machine; a sign said that any comments or jokes would be treated with utmost seriousness. The boy studied his passport, then looked up at him, carefully comparing the im point by point. He remembered the points: eyes, chin, nose, hairline, eyebrows.

"Immigration is to your left," the boy said in a high, helium voice, "Welcome to Caribe." A cartoon voice from a soldier with a rifle.

It smelled like wet concrete and ammonia. The Port Authority was like a second rate airport: full of soldiers and pre-form furniture in bright grimy orange and aqua. A third world country underwater. He had not realized that it would be so dark.

He waited in line to get his suitcase, waited in line again to have his passport and visa scanned for authenticity by Immigration. He was very tired, it had been a long trip and his knee was stiff from sitting so long.

Finally, he was through Immigration and allowed out into the lobby. There was a crowd of people as he came out of Immigration, families waiting, leaning over the railing. His prospective employer was a woman, a banker named Mayla Ling. He didn't have an im. He straightened his stride trying not to limp.

A big tall blond man in a sweater and tights was holding a sign that said "DAI." He looked irritated.

"You are from Ms. Ling?" David said, hating the way he sounded.

"Yeah," the big man squeaked. "Jean David Dai?"

He nodded. His own voice sounded foolish enough, but a helium voice coming out of this big man was ludicrous. The big man said "Jeen DAY-vid," the way they did in the States, not "Jahn Dah-VEED." "Just David," he said, pronouncing it the way the other had. "I do not go by Jean."

"Tim Bennet," the big man said and offered his hand. David took it and Bennet made it into a contest of strength. He won and claimed David's big suitcase. David followed him with his duffel bag.

It was cold and everything seemed far away. It was not a trick of tiredness, he thought, it was the air mixture that made everything sound so distant. People around him were dressed in winter clothes;

men in sweaters and girls in bright shiny blues and golds. This city was under the Caribbean ocean, they could make the temperature anything they wanted, why make it so cold? Did he have any long-sleeved shirts?

He followed Tim Bennet through the Port, hurrying to keep up. They went down an escalator and he studied the expanse of back. Was Bennet a bodyguard/driver? Was there more than one? He looked like he could be security but David had been told that the job was a formality, for insurance reasons. Like the job he'd had at the Caribbean Consulate when he was at University, watching monitors at night, walking through the empty building while the building system switched lights on in front of him, off behind him.

The second escalator dumped them into a concrete parking garage and again he had to hurry to keep up with Tim Bennet. The car was a tiny little black thing with a sheen iridescing blue and red under the fluorescents like oil. A little toy. Julia, the city, wasn't very big, until he had read the job description for this job and seen that it asked for a driver, he had thought they didn't use cars. Cars made no sense, burning petrochemicals in a closed system. His one suitcase filled the trunk. What would they have done if he had two, he wondered, had them sent?

"Thisis th' karyewl b' dryvin."

He had thought his English was pretty good, but he was tired and he hadn't been listening and helium in the air mix made voices sound so strange. "Pardon me?" he said.

"This car," Bennet pointed at the little car, "this is Mayla's car. You know how to drive a car?"

"I have driven . . ." his mind went blank, he couldn't think of the word, "not a car, you know, in the *militaire*, they use them."

"Troop transports?"

David shook his head. "In French we say 'jeep'."

"Yeah, jeeps, that's what we call them. Cars probably aren't too different."

He watched Bennet clamber into the car and got in his side. He almost felt as if he was sitting on the ground, it was so low. Jeeps weren't like that. Clutch, accelerator, gear shift, brake: it all looked familiar. The instrument panel was different.

Bennet put the car in reverse and squealed away from the wall, shoved into gear and squealed again, then braked into a ramp that spiraled down. He acted as if he were angry. They came off the ramp, accelerated, Bennet leaned forward and flicked something on the keyboard on the panel, then took a box off the dash and started to rummage through it. The car continued to accelerate and Bennet was not watching. They went right into a tunnel that narrowed sharply and David grabbed the dash, the wall was centimeters from the passenger door—the car eased into a bigger tunnel. A four-lane highway in a tunnel, with lots of buses and a few cars.

"Audomadick guy danse," Bennet squeaked, still looking through the box.

He thought about the words until they made sense: "automatic guidance."

"They don't allow manual driving on the belt," Bennet said. This time David was listening carefully and he understood. "Takes a bit of getting used to." Bennet smiled at him, pleased with himself. "Mind if I play some music?"

He shook his head. The wall of the tunnel was still close to the passenger door and then the car changed lanes smoothly as another car came out of an entrance tunnel. It made him uncomfortable. He closed his eyes but opened them again because not being able to see was worse than seeing. Bennet dropped a chip in the player. There was a moment of silence, the open sound before a song started, and then a crack of thunder and the soft patter of rain. Ambient music. The singer started; a woman's voice, distant, howling wolf-like, then coming close to sing the first line, "When I was six my father died."

"How d'ya like it?"

He shrugged. "It is okay." He didn't mind ambient music, but he didn't recognize the song. He had the feeling Bennet wanted him to dislike it. "Do you work for Ms. Ling?" he asked.

"Yeah," Bennet said.

"What do you do?" David asked.

"Your job," Bennet said grimly, or at least as grimly as anyone could in a helium falsetto.

The sub had come in at three in the afternoon but that was ten at home in Paris and he had started with a 5:12 a.m. flight from Orly. His employer was at work. He followed Bennet up the steps from the garage into a *house*. Well, he had known she was rich; she could afford to fly him from France and she could afford a car. Maybe houses were common here the way they were in the U.S. But he didn't think so.

The living room was huge, and the first thing he saw across the furniture and hardwood floor was the expanse of window. Outside was a strip of white gravel with dead coral pieces like bushes and then black ocean. Out in the ocean was another glow like a bowl turned upside down (the neighbors) but mostly just blackness.

He didn't like it, it made him feel even colder than he was. Nothing. It didn't even look like water out there, it just looked like nothing. Who would have a view on nothing? What would be the point? He looked away, looked around, tried to take in what he saw. Lots of wood, very expensive. On the white stucco wall behind him was painted a sun with a benevolent face, sleepy eyes, full pouting lips and flames like hair. It looked back at that awful view and he did, too, drawn inexorably.

Deep and black, empty, like the space between stars. He did not even get a sense of the awful pressure that must be bearing down on this building—he realized abruptly that it was a dome, built to distribute the pressure and that was the reason for the strange curve of the glass, but that didn't seem important. He couldn't take this job, he couldn't live in this place.

"Quite a view," Bennet said. "Something that makes you know you're alive."

Know you are alive? It made him think of the absurdity of his being alive.

* * *

Bennet showed him a little flat—bedroom, sitting room and little kitchen, all as impersonal as a hotel room—and he stretched out on the bed to wait. He jerked awake when he heard voices and checked his chron. It was almost six. His head was full of anxious travel dreams and he was cold. A woman's voice he thought, and ran his fingers through his hair. His boss.

She was younger than he'd expected. He thought she was in her thirties. Ling sounded like a Chinese name but she didn't look particularly Asian, she seemed American. She had black hair cut in a helmet, it swung slightly as she turned her head. She was as tall as he was, which, he had to admit, was not so very tall. She held out her hand, "Jean David Dai?" she said, pronouncing it as Bennet had.

"Just David," he said.

"Are you Chinese?" she asked.

"No, ma'am," he said, "my great-grandparents were from Viet Nam."

She nodded, "My greats," she waved her hand to indicate a couple of more greats, "were Chinese. My grandfather is Chinese-American, but I'm a, I guess I'm a mongrel." She laughed. "There aren't many Asians in Caribe. Some Cuban-Chinese, so you can get good Chinese food, and good Cuban beans and rice in the same restaurant."

She talked fast, mostly about the ninety-day probation period, because, she said, although his qualifications were fine they had no idea how comfortable they might be with each other. Tim slouched in the background, brooding.

"It's an American insurance company," she said, "and there are all sorts of restrictions about who I should hire. There's a lower premium for someone with security or military experience. They don't consider our military real military experience. Here, we don't fight much except each other, and people who join the military tend to stay in, you know?"

He nodded although he didn't know and didn't care. He was working hard to understand what she was saying.

"Can you drive?" she asked. He told her about his experience with jeeps. "In Africa," she said. "You were an officer?"

"Because I had a degree from the university," he said. "I was a lieutenant."

"Well," she said, "you'll be a driver but you're not expected to clean or cook. I have someone come in once a week and do the cleaning." She paused. He was tired of sorting things out, tired of foreignness. "It znat really nezesaribu can you youza recike?"

He didn't understand.

"A recyc," she said, slower. "For swimming, can you swim?"

"I have swim, swam, in a pool. Not like in the ocean."

"Tim can teach you tomorrow, it's not hard. And he'll help you with driving. Tim will be with us for a while longer, until everything is settled," she said.

"Ah," he said.

Tim had his hands in fists on the back of her chair, now he leaned against the chair as if doing push-ups. He didn't say anything. She did not look at him, either. Very angry, this room.

"I don't expect problems," she said, "you shouldn't either. Sometimes Tim and I eat dinner together when I'm home," Ms. Ling said. "Tonight you should eat with us, until you get some groceries."

"Thank you," he said, not feeling especially thankful at all.

He expected that the first thing he would learn was driving. The job description had specifically mentioned driving. At dinner he admitted that he was surprised that there were cars. "It seems, it would be bad for the air?" he said.

"There aren't really that many of them," Mayla said. "The people who have them live where the air recirculation is good, anyway, like here, where the system can handle it."

"But there is the highway."

Mayla frowned. "The highway?"

"The beltway," Tim said.

"Oh right," she said. "I'm sorry. I guess it is a highway, I just never thought about it. That was built when I was a girl, by President Bustamante."

"With money advanced from the World Fund. It was supposed to improve infrastructure," Tim explained.

"Roads are infrastructure," Mayla said.

"Sewers are infrastructure. Air recirculation is infrastructure," Tim said.

"I'm not disagreeing with you," Mayla said. "Everybody knows it was a misuse of the money. I just get tired of hearing you bash the government."

"Kids on the lower levels don't develop right because their isn't enough O^2 in their air mix and the bloody President for Life wants to build a highway," Tim said.

"We get the point, Tim, you don't care for the local politics," Mayla said.

"Don't get sanctimonious," Tim said. "You bitch, too."

Mayla turned to David, "It's really probably better that you didn't talk about politics, much. Here it can get you into trouble." She looked over at Tim. "Even if you carry a foreign passport."

"Aren't we prissy this evening," Tim said.

"I guess we are," Mayla said.

David looked at his fish and wished he could go to bed.

The next morning he had his lesson with the recyc system. Bennet took Ms. Ling to work and came back with a rented diving suit. It was blue with yellow reflective stripes like racing stripes down the legs and across the flippers. "I guessed the size," Bennet said. "It'll be a short lesson so it should be all right."

He took the suit back to his rooms and put it on. The tunic part was all right, but the tights were too long and they bunched around his knees and ankles. He stood in front of the mirror and tried to decide if his bad knee was obvious. It wasn't like his good one, up above it the yellow stripe down the tights showed the kind of hollow place where it was all scarred up. And he had skinny legs, legs like a chicken.

David had trouble with the seals, it took him awhile to figure out how they worked. He pulled up the hood and decided he didn't like the way he looked so he pulled it back down. He would have liked to pull his hair back, maybe he should get it cut? Long hair was old-fashioned. Eh, not the time to think about it.

He picked up his flippers and gloves and went out through the living room to a kind of utility room.

Bennet didn't have his hood up, either. He was doing something with the recyc units. David waited a moment, not sure if Bennet knew he was there or not. "I should, ah, learn what you are doing?"

Bennet started a little but didn't look up. "Yeah, the masks are in the closet."

The two masks were hanging on the wall like faces. Above them on the shelf was an AP15 rifle. He looked at the rifle. "Why does Ms. Ling have an AP15?" he asked. He could not stop himself from picking it up.

"She has a permit. I took some security classes, they said she was allowed to have one. She's going to sell it back."

David popped the clip and cracked it to see if it was clean. The clip was full, the rifle looked as if it had never been used. "I thought they did not allow them in Caribe."

"Military issue. They're not a good idea in a dome. Crack the dome, you break the integrity and the water pressure squashes the place flat."

His head was a little clearer this morning, he had followed that. "What's the range underwater?"

"I don't know," Tim sounded irritated. "You ever used one before?"

"Not underwater. In Africa." In Namibia, Windhouk, Gobabis, and the Kalahari, David thought. Before that in Serowe, Soweto, Pretoria. Mbabane and bloody Durban. *South* Africa.

"Are you going to stand there and play with the gun or are you going to hand me a mask."

"Excuse me," David said, embarrassed. But he pulled the clip before he put the rifle back and picked up two masks. Idiot. He had promised himself he would be careful, he would make a good impression on these people. It was time to forget Africa. He should have ignored the rifle. So clean, still steel blue and smelling faintly of oil.

He'd had an AP15 but not one like this with its fake wood stock. His stock had been a metal frame with a place on it where he'd scraped it on the sidewalk in Joburg.

He could not keep this job. Too many things were not right. He had come here to start new but security was guns and fear and he did not want any of that.

"Mayla has three recyc units but the Honeywell is so old that it doesn't even have a humidifier." Bennet showed him how to put one on, how to jack the connections into the mask and hook the airfeed into the jaw. "Ever use a full facemask before?"

"Yes, and a mike. What is the setting?" He had never used one for swimming but the facemask was similar to the respirator mask they used to drill for gas attacks. He would not mention that.

"Three. Four through eight are commercial bands. Nine is official, Port Authority mostly. Most of the fish jocks use eleven and twelve, so if you need help, try those."

"Fish jocks?" David said.

"Fish jockeys. The guys that work at the fish farms. Divers. Public starts at thirteen so everything above that is crowded. Eighteen is emergency but the local police force is not very useful." Tim pulled on his flippers. "Ever swam in the dark?" Tim asked.

"No." And did not plan to do it often, thank you.

"Okay. There's a lamp mounted on your mask. The switch is a touch plate, you have to tap it twice to turn it off." He tapped once underneath the eye of the light and it came on. He tapped twice and nothing happened. Tapped twice with more emphasis and the lamp went off. "They turn on easier than they turn off."

David pulled on the mask, it was cold against his chin and smelled of metal. He tapped blindly since the lamp was on the forehead of the mask and it came on. It took him a couple of tries to get it off. Why would anyone ever want to turn one off?

"Look," Tim said, looking at the floor, "I ah, I noticed your limp. Your, ah, leg. Will it bother you swimming?"

"No," David said. "It's fine." He looked at Tim so that Tim could not look at his knee and Tim hauled the recycs out of the pool instead.

"Yeah. Ah, well then," Tim said. "As soon as we're suited up, that's it. The thing to remember when you're diving is to breathe normally. There's a telltale on your facemask that measures the amount of carbon dioxide in your blood. Just try to keep it within normal range and if you find you're having a problem, let me know."

They hauled on the recyc units, heavy with water, and David fell backward into the entry pool, copying Tim.

The water was very cold. It was a shock. The tights and suit had been uncomfortably warm but they weren't now. The pool was really a tunnel, a u-shape that dove under the ground and back up into the sea. It was about two meters across and that didn't seem like much. Tim hit an orange circle between two lights and the opening above them constricted shut. The air from the recyc had the faintest taste of the inflow valve, a rubbery taste, but it was warm. He tried drawing deep breaths to keep himself warm. The warm air in his lungs would warm his blood and that would warm all of him, but he might hyperventilate.

"When you come out," Tim's voice came clearly, "don't look straight into the lights, okay?"

"Okay." The telltale displayed amber numbers, they seemed to hang in the water in front of him about level with his left eyebrow.

They began to swim down, angling their bodies. Tim kicked lazily, David felt the water resisting his kicks. Cold, viscous saltwater. (He knew cold water did not resist any more than warm water did.) He was not sure if he was breathing properly, he seemed to be taking unnecessarily deep breaths. The telltale flickered, "26, 27, 26, 27, 28, 29, 28. . . ." What was normal and correct? Ahead was the black eye of the ocean, or was it black because the ocean had no eyes? His indicator told him his respiration was still increasing. They followed the tunnel up, no more than six meters all told, and rose out of the garden, outside the dome. They came up past the window, looking in the living room, and the benevolent sun on the wall watched them sadly.

They rose over the second floor, all dark, and their headlamps reflected off the dome. Their masks were blanks of copper in the reflection, like new smooth coins. Down the other side towards the lighted ring of garden. It would be better in the garden, in the light he would not feel so adrift.

There was no feeling of weight, they moved through space unencumbered, down past the curtained main floor to the rock garden below, where frightened fish fled silver around the dome.

Into the dark beyond. David slowed up, Tim kicked easily, moving like a shark. David followed. Light was swallowed up by ocean. He had to swim hard to catch up. He had trouble knowing which way was up and which way was down. His legs were shorter, he kicked more often than Tim, and because of his bad knee he kept veering to the left. He wasn't in very good shape, but at least he wasn't worried about hyperventilating anymore.

He wished Bennet would slow down, but he wasn't about to ask for any favors. Where the hell were they going? If he lost Bennet he wouldn't have any idea where he was, although he figured he could always double back. He glanced back, he could still see the dome. But then he had to work to catch up. Funny there weren't any other domes out this way, Bennet must be taking him out away from the city. They angled up a bit until the ground disappeared. He looked back again, barely able to make out the glow of the dome. Goddamn it was cold. He should stop right here and not go any farther. He should swim back.

Which was ridiculous, Bennet must have a reason for swimming this way. He concentrated on working his bad leg better, making his kicks more even. This would be good exercise. The therapist had told him that swimming was good, no weight on his knee. No dome visible behind them. The farther they went, the more depth the dark had, not by the absence of light so much as the quantity of dark that separated them from the lighted dome. Entropy made palpable. Entropy, quit thinking like a physics student. Besides, entropy isn't a substance, it's an absence. Disorder, not malevolent, but the slow seepage of energy, the heat leaving his body, swimming slower and slower, as Bennet, the machine, would disappear into the dark at the edge of the light cast by his mask. He would be lost out here, without even directions like up and down. He wouldn't even realize he was slowing down, but he would get slower and slower until he was empty and the heat of his body evenly, randomly dispersed among the cold water.

Particularly paranoid this morning, he thought. It was the dark, the dark always bothered him. A child's distress, maman don't turn out the light.

He was panting with the effort to keep up. Bennet wanted him to ask to slow down. Macho nonsense. So ask to slow down, you stubborn fool. Where were the other domes? What were they doing out here? How did Bennet know where they were? They could be angling up. That was dangerous, could lead to the bends. Nitrogen bubbles in the blood. Stroke.

Paranoia, he sang to himself, par-a-noi-ah. Just because you're paranoid doesn't mean that they aren't really out to get you. If he lost Bennet he would turn around and try to head back for the dome but there was a good chance he would miss it in the darkness, particularly with his tendency to veer. His recyc unit would go on taking oxygen out of the water for days, but already the cold was making his hands stiff. How long until hypothermia? He would die of exposure in a couple of hours. Very convenient for Bennet. He could say he'd thought David was behind him, and he didn't know when they'd gotten separated. In a few hours, would he find another dome?

Bennet stopped suddenly, with a graceful swirl of hands and arms, and hung. "Don't go swimming alone," he said, "It's easy to get lost."

"Paranoia," sang in David's head. "How do you know where to go?"

"I used to be a fish jockey, I've got an implant in the back of my head that tells me what direction Port Authority is. You can get one if you really want to, but you don't need it unless you plan to do a lot of swimming."

"Which way is the dome?"

Bennet pointed slightly to the right of the way David thought they had come. He peered into the dark but all he could see was the cone of light from their headlamps. Bennet's headlamp went out on his right, and as he turned, the Australian made a couple of strong kicks that took him out of the cone of David's light.

Abruptly he realized he had been moving for the space of half-a-dozen kicks in the direction Bennet had vanished. He didn't remember moving. No sign of the reflecting bands on Bennet's recyc unit, and he should have been able to see them. He halted. Was he paranoid if he was correct? He turned in a full circle to see if he caught the glint of silver off Bennet's fins or unit. Bennet could go anywhere, up or down as well as any direction. Turning had been a big mistake, without anything to orient, he wasn't sure how far he had turned or what direction Bennet had gone, what direction was the dome, from here no way to even guess direction, he was fucking well lost in the night and the amber lights of the indicator were flickering as his respiration went up; slow down, slow down, slow down. Think. He could turn off his headlamp. With his off he would stand a better chance of catching sight of Bennet's light—if Bennet's was still on. With his on he was visible to Bennet. He reached up and tapped his headlamp twice, had to do it a couple of times. His light finally went off.

Instantly, the black rushed in at him. He saw movement in the nothing, things, shapes, shells, bullets, streams coming at him, his mind making something out of the absence of sensory information, son of a bitch, he couldn't handle the dark, even if it made good sense he couldn't do it, the amber letters of the telltale going up and up, his respiration climbing, he fumbled for the lamp, cold fingers missing the plate while the only light, the amber letters of the telltale told him he was approaching hyperventilation, he used both hands and the light came on and shapes swirled only at the periphery of his vision. Panic, frigging anxiety attack, come on, he thought, be calm, you can die if you aren't calm. He whirled again, circling to find someone, nothing, but hanging there in the water his headlamp was a beacon, he was vulnerable, a still target, he had to think, think think think, think about the dark. Don't think about the dark. What would orient him? Nothing around but water, 250 meters of water between him and the sun above, below, below there was ground. Bottom. Under water ground was called bottom, swim down, folding in the water, not sure if this direction was really down but it must have been because almost instantly he saw sand and rock. The indicator said his breathing was down a little. He touched bottom, solid bottom, hard and rocky, not much sand, like the Kalahari which really had very little sand at all, groped and found a rock as big as his fist, hefted it, feeling how heavy it was, how slow he would move it in the water.

A headlamp came on close by and he turned to face it, his rock held ready, slightly behind his body, because he'd have to get real close to Bennet to use it. Bennet said matter-of-factly inside his mask, "That's exactly what you should do if you're ever lost, head for bottom."

David held the rock, waited for the other to come closer, he would be slower in the water, he would have to wait until the other was very very close. And he did not know if Bennet was armed.

"Around here you can always switch to band eleven," Tim said. "Somebody will be on the band, around here there's always someone. Of course, I was close. Sorry about that, but that's the way I was taught, you don't forget a lesson like that. You ready to go home?"

David nodded.

He dropped the rock about halfway back. Later he realized that if he'd brained Tim he'd never have been able to find his way anyway.

2

Funeral Games

Mayla did not read about Danny Tumipamba's murder in the paper because that morning she didn't get a chance to finish it.

Most mornings Mayla got into the kitchen before Tim. She made her coffee and listened for signs that he was awake. She hated to admit that she ordered her life around Tim, but there it was. She hated when he was there, and the quiet time before he came down was ruined by anticipation.

She heard his feet on the stairs from the loft. She looked at her paper.

"Morning gorgeous," he said. Some mornings he came downstairs furious, some chipper. He touched the side of the coffee pot. "Cold. Christ, Mayla," he said, "how can you drink this stuff?"

"Practice," she said. No one really drank coffee at boiling, not even in Los Etas. Tim had a special coffee maker in the loft. He didn't really need to use the kitchen but most mornings he did. Mostly to bitch about her coffee. He said he didn't like Caribbean coffee, that it was bitter and weak. She didn't like surface coffee, it tasted wrong, bland. And on the surface coffee stayed too hot, too long.

He rummaged around the cupboards while she read about Mandatory Sterilization for Incorrigibles, particularly women who were addicted to neuro-stimulation. He was looking for the jar he used every morning. "Why don't you use that vacuum thing in the loft?" she asked.

He found the jar. She kept pushing it to the back of the cupboard but he kept finding it. He poured coffee in and tightened the lid.

"One of these mornings it's going to explode," she said.

"Nah," he said. The coffee boiled almost instantly, frothing until it filled the jar. He left it, letting it build up pressure, a tiny little storm of coffee.

Mayla could sympathize with the jar. Don't, she thought. Just relax, don't let him get to you. If it breaks, then it breaks. The worst that would happen was that it ruined the flash. She could buy a new flash.

The jar didn't break, it never had yet. Jars didn't break for the Tims of the world, she reflected. If she stuck a jar in the flash there would be coffee everywhere. It would look like the scene of a murder. The flash binged and he pulled it out, opened the lid and the room smelled of coffee. He had to hold the jar with a dish towel to pour. "Ah," he said. "That's what coffee should be. You know, cold coffee is what destroyed the Roman Empire."

She nodded, pretending to look at the paper. Mandatory Sterilization, the headline she had already read. Too late, she thought, he's already born.

"Oh," he said, eyebrows quirked. "Cranky this morning."

"I've run out of things to say about coffee," she said. Her voice was flatter than she intended.

Tim just turned from her and sipped his coffee. The only way he knew how to talk to people was to joke.

She waited for him to say something. If Tim wasn't talking he was mad. "Want the sports?" she asked.

He shrugged.

Another long pause. He wasn't going to be here much longer. She could be polite. "How are the driving lessons going?" she offered.

"Okay," he said, his back to her while he fiddled with his coffee. Now he wouldn't talk in the car, either. She should just enjoy it when he didn't talk but she never could. He had all this energy in the morning—he had all this energy, period—but mornings she was murky and he was ready to fight, to be angry.

"Maybe David could drive this morning?" she said.

He shook his head. "I dunno," he said. "He really isn't ready, yet."

"Ready for what?" she said. "He gets on the belt and puts it on automatic, and when he comes off the belt he's at the bank." She certainly sounded cranky. She wanted to sound reasonable.

"He can't drive very well yet," Tim said.

"This way he could get some practice."

"Give him a break, Mayla," Tim said, sounding aggravated.

"Give *me* a break," she said.

"What is your *problem* this morning?" he said, turning around.

"I want David to drive the car," she said. Take your place, she was saying, and he knew it.

"And you don't give a damn whether he's ready or not," Tim said. "Fine."

"You wouldn't say he was ready if he could—" she couldn't think of an example of expert driving, her mind didn't work in the morning, "—if he could, I don't know, drive like a race car driver."

"Fine," he said again. "And what am I supposed to do?"

"Go back to bed," she said, "enjoy the time off."

"*Hijo de la chingada,*" he said. "Son of a bitch." Except that no one but an anglo would use it that way. When Tim swore in Spanish he sounded even more like a foreign *gabacho* than he normally did.

He would be gone in a month, she told herself. A month, at the most. As soon as David was ready to take over.

When she told David that he would be driving that morning he looked uncomfortable. He came out to the kitchen to get a coffee cup—unlike Tim *he* used the coffee maker in his rooms. He was dressed but his hair was still wet and slicked back from the shower.

"You don't have to unless you feel ready," she said. "Tim can drive me."

"Oh," he said. Which wasn't really an answer. It was hard to be sure how good his English was. He spoke pretty well but sometimes she got the feeling he was nodding without understanding. But he didn't say he wouldn't drive and he was waiting in the kitchen when she was finished getting ready.

He drove cautiously and he seemed to regard stop signs as little time outs. He got to the intersection at the end of her street, stopped the car and sighed, then carefully looked around and drove on. She wanted to turn on the news but felt that if she moved she would distract him, so she decided to wait until they were on automatic. He was all white knuckles getting onto the beltway until he could reach forward and punch 2 on the automatic guidance—preprogrammed for the bank. Then he sighed again.

The news was still talking about mandatory sterilization for incorrigibles and what a wonderful idea it was and how it would work to break the cycle of poverty. That was the only thing she had read in the newspaper this morning so she half-listened and half-watched traffic. At least David's silence was language-related, not directed at her.

"—Danny Tumipamba, an executive in a subsidiary of Marincite Corp.," the news said. The name snagged her. "Although there is no confirmation from Marine Security, it is widely believed that radical extremists are behind the killing. If so, Tumipamba would be the seventh Marincite executive to fall victim in the last nine months."

"I know him," she said, startled into speaking out loud.

"I am sorry?" David said, not having heard her. Or maybe not having understood.

"Shhh!" she said, but they were talking about someone named Ybarra who'd been killed ten weeks ago. "I know him," she said. "The man in the news. I am working with him on a bank deal." Her Marincite deal, a very big bank deal.

"He was arrested?" David asked.

"No," she said, "He's dead. He was murdered." Murdered. It seemed melodramatic when she said it. Tumipamba was murdered. She knew someone who had been murdered. Had anybody at the bank heard?

"He was a friend of yours?"

"No," she said. Not a friend at all. Danny Tumipamba had a broad

Mayan face and hook nose; a face like the Olmec man. He was hard to work with because she never knew where she stood with him, or what he thought of either her or the bank. And now he was dead. A bomb? she wondered, or shooting? She should have been paying attention.

"I'm sorry," David said uncertainly, but the car was slowing down to come off the beltway and his attention was taken by the intricacies of driving.

She didn't have the deal yet, they had still been courting. No papers signed. And now he was dead. Another dead executive in Marincite City, Christos, was it open season on executives over there?

She tried to think of how she felt. Murdered. Dead. Tumipamba was dead.

Dead was something that she didn't understand when someone told her. It was like when her Gram had died, it was the little habits of thought that made her understand Gram was dead. Like thinking that she had to call Gram, she hadn't talked to her in—and then when she started to think about how long, when she started to really think about it, she'd realized that Gram was gone.

Danny Tumipamba was dead. She didn't have a deal with Marincite yet. She needed that deal.

She would have to talk to her boss. She would have to find out who was taking Tumi's place. She couldn't call this morning, the place would be coming apart. The bank should send flowers, she should find out when the funeral was going to be.

If she was going to get the loan with Marincite Technical Exchange she was going to have to find out who would be deal making.

Maybe she could go to the funeral and see who represented the company. At the funeral she might be able to talk to someone, get a sense of how things might shake down. A couple of hours in a sub, and if the funeral was early she could go in the morning and come back in the afternoon. She would only lose half a day. David could go with her, there was no driving in Marincite. She wouldn't have to take Tim at all.

*   *   *

Tumipamba's funeral was on Thursday morning, two days after he died. Attending meant that Mayla and David had to catch a sub to Marincite City at 6:30 a.m.

Marincite was a labyrinth.

On the map it was a lot of overlapping circles, hubs with roads leading away from them, so the map looked like a drawing of bicycle wheels lying helter-skelter.

It was Mayla's experience that Marincite was an easy place to get lost in. It was older than the capital, and it wasn't a planned city at all. Once it had been a cluster of mining complexes and fish farms, each one dug into the bedrock. Some of them were a single level, some of the mining complexes had been cones going down six or eight levels. Now they were all neighborhoods, overlapping circles, and the streets ran every which way, from hub to neighborhood hub to neighborhood hub.

The funeral was at the Cathedral St. Nicolas in a neighborhood called Wallace. From the sub port they took a shuttle to a place called Sauteuse, and from Sauteuse David used her map to get them to Wallace. He was quite good with the map. Good sense of spatial relationships, she supposed.

The last moving sidewalk dumped them off at a security post manned by Marine Security. *Les Tontons*, "The Uncles." A young man in Marincite maroon stopped her and asked her business. He had that Marincite sound, slightly deeper than Julia. Not surface but different. Everybody's voice was a little deeper in Marincite because it was about twenty meters higher and the air mix was different. He checked her smart card in his reader and flicked a light pen in her eyes for a retinal scan.

David was wearing the gray suit he'd arrived in. Have to have him get some clothes, she thought. He was a skinny little Asian. With his long hair, the suit made him look like a Hong Kong hood in an outdated vid.

He dropped David's smart card in his reader. "I'm sorry, ma'am," he said, "Marine Security records show your security to be a man named Tim Bennet."

"He used to be," she said, "but David has replaced him. I'm sorry, I didn't realize I needed to let you know."

"Without clearance I cannot let him attend you," the young man said. He handed David his smart card with the air of someone finished with a transaction.

"Wait," she said, "Tim doesn't work for me anymore. I have to take David."

The officer frowned, all sharp cheekbones under his polished visor. He looked Haitian. He checked his reader, and then looked icily from under his visor. "His account is still active and linked with yours, so you're still paying him."

She hadn't known they were going to check bank accounts. Now she looked as if she were lying to Marine Security.

"He will be leaving in about four weeks," she said. "But David's account is linked with mine, can't you check that?"

No, he wasn't interested in checking on David, that would take a search which would tie up his reader for a few minutes. The trace to Tim's account was already in place from when Marincite Corp. had registered them.

He was pissed with her, too. Great, just what she needed, problems with *Les Tontons.* Security was everywhere in Marincite; sneeze and an Uncle said, "Good Health." "I really have to go to this funeral. Is there some way I can get clearance?"

"You can go," the officer said. "He can't."

Her insurance said she wasn't to attend public functions in her capacity as a banker without security. But the Cathedral was obviously secure, and who was going to tell the insurance company? Unless she did something stupid like fall down the escalator and broke her leg.

She fumbled with her purse. "Look," she said to David, "go get yourself a cup of coffee, come back in—" how long would a funeral take? An hour? "—an hour and a half."

"Wait," he said. "The problem is what?"

"Marine Security doesn't have any record of you," she said. She didn't want to be late, she wanted to get there early to see if she could maybe talk to Owen Cleary, Tumi's assistant, and she didn't want to explain all this to David. "Take this," she pushed money at him, "find yourself a place to get breakfast or something." She hadn't had breakfast, either. She could never eat when she first got up, but she was hungry now. Oh well, you weren't supposed to have breakfast before mass, anyway. Even if she wasn't Catholic anymore.

"Excuse me," David said to the officer. He pulled out a passport folder and opened it, it was full of his documents. "I have here my papers, no? I have a work permit, here, see, Ms. Ling's name? She is my employer?"

The officer shrugged.

"Also," David pulled out a flimsy, "here, it is my, what do you call it, like a permission, *autorisation,* to drive a car. See, she has insurance, you know? The insurance says she must have a driver? She, she has paid for my insurance to drive her car, here is her signature? Why would she bring me, arrange this permission to have a car, if I am not her security?"

The officer frowned.

David handed him the folio. The officer didn't want it, he held up his hands as if he were going to say no but David pushed it on him and he took it without really wanting to. Then he didn't seem to know what to do with it. He read the driving permit, paged uncertainly through the passport and ran his pen across the information band. Finally he held it up so he could compare David against the im.

He sighed and handed David back the documents. "All right, but you'll have to wear a telltale. It'll take awhile to get one up here, wait over there, please."

David nodded to the officer and to her, a crisp, know-your-place-in-the-hierarchy kind of nod.

"That was good," she whispered.

"It is like being in the army," he whispered. "If you make it easier for them to do it than not to do it, then they will do it." Then he grinned at her, a sharp little grin.

She grinned back. He was smart, she thought. Smarter than he liked to let on.

She liked that. She could live with that. Once she got rid of Tim, maybe things would work out pretty well.

The telltale was a plastic strip like a hospital bracelet. "Don't fiddle with it," the officer said, "it has a dye packet in it. If you try and take it off, it explodes. The bracelet will let us keep track of you, and it can be triggered either by a security officer or by passing a sensor."

"Where are the sensors?" she asked.

The officer shrugged. "Banks, checkpoints."

David turned his wrist over studying it, then shot his cuff over it to hide it. He didn't look happy. Mayla couldn't blame him.

They took an escalator down. She checked the time. Probably too late to get a chance to talk to someone, maybe after the funeral she could find Owen Cleary for a moment.

The courtyard in front of the cathedral wasn't empty yet so mass hadn't started. The courtyard was bordered by rows of columns etched with palm leaves and capped with cherubim. Behind them were people in dark clothes and headsets. The Uncles, watching and listening.

Too late, Tumipamba was already dead.

David was watching the Uncles, too. "Why so many police?" he asked.

"Tumi was murdered by extremists," she said. She had told him he was murdered—proof that his English really wasn't very good, he missed a lot.

David frowned, "Say again?"

"Murdered by extremists. You know, terrorists. The radical arm of *La Mano de Diós*, the Catholic Socialists." Or some other splinter group, but *La Mano de Diós* was as good an example as any, there were a lot of Catholic Socialists.

"He was a politician?"

"No," Mayla said. "He was an executive for a subsidiary of Ma-rincite Corporation. Marincite Corporation runs this city, it's a company town, so some of the radical groups have started targeting executives."

She wasn't sure how much he had followed but he was intent on her. "This man who is murdered, he is a *zaibatsu* for Marincite?" he asked.

"I guess," she said. She didn't really think of Marincite as a *zaibatsu* kind of corporation, sing the company anthem and live in a company enclave—Marincite wasn't an enclave for corporate types, it was a city.

"You are in danger?" he asked.

"Me?" she asked.

"Like this man," he gestured towards the cathedral.

She resisted the impulse to laugh. "No," she said. "I'm just a banker, not CFO for a company."

"I am not a person who can protect you," he said. "I think this is a mistake. I was security for the Consulate, but that is just sitting at a desk, watching the monitors. That is just walking around the building, closing the doors."

"It's only insurance," she said. She looked up at the church, suddenly nervous. Funerals. When she was a little girl at school they went to all the funerals during school hours. She never thought anything about them then except that they were longer than regular masses. When they were schoolchildren they attended so many funerals that they knew all the responses. They knew them better than anyone except the priest and the sisters.

"It is not right," he said.

Her Gram had been buried on a Saturday. Schoolgirls in blue uniforms had not said the responses at her funeral. Not that many people had attended: a couple of old men from when De Silva was Minister of Finance and her grandfather had been a *persona de influencia*. De Silva had come. The skin on her grandfather's hands had looked like crumpled paper.

David was looking at her, demanding more. Explain, his face said, explain.

"It's just insurance," she said again vaguely.

The church was like the churches from her childhood, white walls climbing to clerestory windows. Light angled down from the east windows, sharp and brilliant columns that marched up the center of the nave as if this were the surface and the sun were shining in. Such an unnatural hard-edged light that when Mayla was little she thought it was the light of the saints.

They were going to be late if they didn't go in and get seats. At the end of the nave the altar was outlined in tiny blinking colored lights. When she was in school in New York she only saw those lights at Christmas. The white coffin was tilted at an angle and faced from the waist up in glass, so the deceased could watch the mourners come in. She couldn't see Tumi looking at her, from where they stood the light reflected off the glass in a glare of white.

"Look," she said, "we'll talk about it later, okay?"

He stood, all tense, not wanting to let it go and for a moment she thought he wouldn't. Were the Uncles watching them squabble? But he softened and they went in.

They sat on the side, close to where the votive candles flickered in blue and white jars in front of the statue of the virgin. An Erzulie-Virgin, she noticed, a Haitian voudoun madonna in a lace veil and white dress embroidered with rose-colored flowers and hearts. She wore ropes of pearl necklaces and Mayla thought that her wedding ring might actually be Erzulie's three gold rings. The pillars that flanked her niche were striped blue and rose and white, the colors of the loa. Under the candles on the hard concrete floor were a bar of perfumed soap and a handful of wilted pink carnations.

Some woman asking for help in her love life? At home in Julia they would never allow it, never allow any of the signs of Haitian voudoun in the church. She had heard rumors that the execs who ran Marincite Corp asked advice of the loa but it was hard to imagine Tumipamba bringing rum to a mambo in a white headcloth. Even harder to imagine Tumi ecstatic, possessed by spirits.

The priest wore white vestments, like Easter. "Behold, I tell you a mystery," he read, his arms out and his head bowed. "We shall all indeed rise again: but we shall not all be changed." He was a very young man and his hands trembled slightly. The gestures of priests were always effeminate.

After the mass she got in line to pass the coffin. Owen Cleary, Tumi's assistant, stood on the left and a woman with Tumi's square face and Mayan nose stood on the right. Mayla smoothed the folds out of her dress from where she had been sitting.

Owen was white and tired. "Good of you to come," he said when he shook her hand.

"It's a shock," she said and glanced at the coffin but only saw the wash of white. She turned around and a young woman dressed casually in tights and a sweater was taking an im. For the paper? Mayla wasn't supposed to have her picture in the paper, especially not at a funeral for a man murdered by radical extremists.

But the woman had already picked up her bag and was backing down the aisle, and Mayla couldn't think of what she would have said anyway. The woman would have taken other ims. The Uncles were probably taking ims, too.

And then she was out in the atrium with its angel-headed columns and David was coming out to find her. That was it. She had come all the way from Julia by sub to shake Owen's hand. And Owen probably wouldn't even remember she had been here.

She looked around hoping to catch sight of someone to talk to, something to make this trip worthwhile, but she didn't see any familiar faces. People were clustered and the Uncles were standing against the walls like kabuki stagehands. The family would go on back to the house, Owen would probably go, too.

David was waiting for her to tell him what next.

She looked back down the length of the church, at the shafts of hard white light falling at angles. Dust glittered in the light. Imagine light so bright that dust glittered. "Let's go home," she said.

He patted his pockets and came up with their tickets for the sub and showed them to her. At least, she thought, she hadn't had to deal with Tim. And once David understood that she wasn't likely to be the subject of terrorist attacks he seemed as if he'd do the job very well. He had a sense of propriety about him, he kept his distance. In the evening she would be able to sit in her living room and not worry about Tim.

Privacy! She had built a house and she had no privacy! It was almost as bad as living with her grandfather.

Which made her think of Gram and the dust glittering. The mote in God's eye. She had never understood that before and now she'd seen it, bright dust motes in a column of light. She felt light-headed—not physically so much as her thoughts skittered around.

"Excuse me," a man said.

David came around, wary. The man was dressed like an exec, a *gabacho*, what the Marincite people called a *blanc*, North American looking with his black suit and his pale face and wavy brown hair. "I don't believe we've met," he said. "Were you a friend of Danny's?"

"A business associate," she said. "I'm Mayla Ling, from First Hawaiian of Caribe."

"Polly Navarro," he said, putting out his hand. "I didn't think I recognized you from the family."

The name sounded half-familiar and she thought she might be supposed to remember who he was. "I'm sure it must be a shock."

"I've been to too many funerals this year," he said. "Makes me wonder if one of these days I'm going to be the guest of honor." A self-deprecating smile, as if it was really in bad taste to say anything so blunt.

And then she connected the name. Not Polly, *Polito*. Polito Navarro. Chief Financial Officer for Marincite Corp. A man who had good reason to wonder if he was going to be the next corpse. Her mind went completely blank. Say something, she thought, anything.

"You were good friends with Danny?" she managed.

He shrugged. "I've known Danny for almost twenty years."

The paper had said Tumipamba was shot leaving for work in the morning. "They're saying it was *La Mano de Diós*," she said. "Does that mean that they've made some progress towards an arrest?"

"There will be an arrest," he said.

She knew what he meant, that there would be an arrest even if all the evidence was fabricated.

What was Polito Navarro doing wandering around out here by himself? Then again, the place was crawling with security, he could hardly be said to be by himself.

"They're saying the usual," he said, "that it was dissident elements, but Danny might have had some large debts. It may have been his gambling."

Tumipamba was a gambler? Quite a scandal if the CFO of a Marincite subsidiary was killed over gambling debts—not that it would ever come out. Why was Navarro telling her all this? "I'm sure Marine Security will get to the bottom of it," she said. Trite and pious.

"They should have known before it got to this," he said. And told him, he meant. Like a Medici prince, he was part of the ruling family, he should know. There might be a shakedown among the Uncles before this was all over. "Wasn't Danny working on the MaTE division business with you?"

She and Danny Tumipamba had been talking about First Hawaiian providing the funds to allow Marincite Technical Exchange to buy itself from Marincite Corp. Then as an independent company it would turn around and continue to provide services for the parent corporation. It was a complicated deal because in order to amass the capital to buy itself off, Danny had intended MaTE to purchase another company and then strip mine those assets to fund it's own independence. MaTE was nowhere near the size of Marincite— Marincite was as big as a small country—but the amount of capital it intended to borrow from First Hawaiian was more by far than any other deal First Hawaiian had ever funded.

It was more money than First Hawaiian was worth. If the buyout didn't succeed, then technically the debt would swallow First Hawaiian whole. It would be bigger than all of First Hawaiian's assets combined, including not only its capital reserves but even the building the bank was in.

But it was not much money at all to Marincite Corp. If Marincite Corp. would guarantee MaTE's assets, then if the buyout didn't succeed, Marincite Corp. would assume the loan.

"I'd like to talk about the MaTE division," Polly Navarro said. "At a more convenient time," he added.

"Oh, yes," she said. She had a card, although it took her a long embarrassing moment to dig it out. "I'd like that very much."

"I'd like to work with First Hawaiian."

"Mr. Navarro," she said, "First Hawaiian would like very much to work with you."

"It would get my good friend Enrique Chavez off my back," he said and laughed. "He's always telling me that Marincite has a duty to return capital to Caribe."

Enrique Chavez was the Government Minister of Finance. "Well, I think you should take the Minister's advice," she said.

He was amused.

"At a better time, then," she said and offered her hand.

"Yes," he said. "I'll be in touch."

He walked back towards the church. One of the big wooden doors was closed and St. Ulrique clutched his fish and looked down at them while St. Patrick thrust his hand out and snakes writhed down the center of the door. Both St. Patrick and St. Ulrique had distinctly Caribbean features.

"We are in the way," David said.

They were standing close to the escalator and people had to cut around them. Riding the escalator up, she watched for Navarro to come back out of the church. Maybe he was going back to the house with the family.

What luck. It proved she was right to have come. Not that anyone had said she shouldn't but before she had run into Navarro she had felt as if she had wasted the bank's time and money.

Milagroso. Miraculous.

At the top of the escalator David headed towards the checkpoint.

"We don't—" she started until she saw him hold out his wrist. The telltale. She had forgotten. She had been about to say that they didn't need to check out. Where was her mind?

She wished she could tell her Gram about meeting with Polly

Navarro. It was an accident, she would have said, Gram, it was just luck.

You make your own luck, her Gram would have said.

Not really. When her Gram was alive she probably wouldn't have told her about it. It was bank business and she never told Gram much about bank business. Church made her sentimental. You can take the girl out of the church. . . .

If they hurried they could catch the sub that left ten minutes after the hour and be back in Julia in about three hours.

David was still standing at the checkpoint, talking to the woman officer. Hadn't the officer been a man before? Don't walk over, she thought, let David handle it. But he looked around for her and then she had to go see what was wrong.

"The officer who put it on," he said, "he has left."

"He must have taken the deactivator with him," the woman said. The checkpoint was small, a little booth only chest high in front. "Titon must have had it on his clip, I'll call him." She tugged the mic on her headset up and stuck her finger in her ear. She spoke softly, half-turning away from them so they couldn't hear.

"The officer is in Castle," she said. "It'll take him awhile to get here."

David was waiting to see what she wanted to do. "Do you suggest we wait?" she asked. Damn it, why was it that when she hired people to take care of things for her she still ended up taking care of them herself?

The officer thought it would probably be about thirty minutes. Which meant they would miss the next sub. "Okay," Mayla said. There weren't any benches around.

"Maybe," David said, "we should get a cup of coffee?" To the officer, "Is there some place? To get coffee?"

The officer thought that there might be a place at the hub. David looked at her to see if she approved. Fine with her, she was delighted to see him take the initiative. "Lead on," she said.

"If I go past, there is no, how do you say," he held out his wrist, "it will not make it go off?"

The officer shook her head, there was no sensor in the booth.

"What trips it off?" Mayla asked again.

Places like banks, jewelry stores, shops that would have a security system.

"As long as we avoid banks we're basically okay?" Mayla said.

"Pretty much," the officer said.

Wallace was a pretty neighborhood. The fronts of the flats were clean and bright: blues or corals to about halfway up and clean whitewashed white above. The windows were covered with ornate grilleworks, metal lattices of roses and leaves or curling vines with butterflies.

They found a cafe with pseudo-wooden tables and yellow walls with fantastic clocks painted on them. Mayla sat down and found she was worn out. Traveling made her tired. Maybe she wouldn't go back to work, it was going to be late. But she'd call Alex, her boss, and let him know about the meeting with Polly Navarro.

A burro made her feel better. David seemed a little taken aback by the waitress. She wore a peasant skirt and blouse but her hair was bright red and she had ocher and green stripes that ran not just across her eyelids but from temple to temple. War paint. She didn't look very much like a peasant girl in a cantina unless perhaps the cantina was in the infamous neon district in São Paulo.

Still in all, she thought as they walked back to the checkpoint, a little lunch made all the difference in the world.

Riding the pedestrian mover she couldn't see the checkpoint. She checked the time, it was just about thirty minutes, just the time they'd been told to be back. Then she saw that it was laying on its side, folded flat. A crew of three in coveralls was getting ready to load it on a skid. There wasn't any sign of Marine Security.

"They are gone?" David said.

"I don't know," she said and started to walk down the moving sidewalk. The flats fled past them, and then she was stepping off, feeling the strain in her knees as she changed from the speed of the ped mover to solid floor. Two women in maroon coveralls were strapping the folded checkpoint to the skid and a third, wearing a headset, was supervising.

"Excuse me," Mayla said to the stocky woman in the headset. "We were supposed to meet an officer here?"

The woman looked at her. "No officer here now. We are all closed up now."

"No," Mayla said, "they told us to be here now. My security man has a telltale on and someone was going to be here to take it off."

The woman looked at David. "I don't know nothing about that," she said.

"Can you call and check?" Mayla said. She didn't want to get irritated. If she got irritated they'd never get anything done.

"The officer," David told the woman, "his name is Titon."

She looked at David as if she wasn't sure about him, then pulled her headset mic up. "This is Lupe at Sant Nic," she said. "I got two people here say they are waiting on an officer named Titon." She listened, eyes on nothing. Her hair was cornrowed, with little silver fish at the end of each short braid.

"I'm sorry," she said, not sounding particularly concerned. "We are just maintenance, my dispatcher does not know about the uniforms."

David looked at Mayla, sighed. "Maybe there is someplace we should go. Nearby is there a post, for police?"

"You mean a police station? On Tarrou."

"Where is Tarrou?" Mayla asked.

The woman waved vaguely back in the direction they came. "Down three levels at the hub," she said. To the other woman she said, "Is it secure?"

Streets radiated off hub in all directions. "Are you going that way?" Mayla asked.

"No," the woman said and turned her back on them.

David looked at the woman, looked at Mayla and shrugged. He pulled out his map and started pulling off overlays to find Tarrou.

"Not this hub," he said after a moment, "I don't think. Excuse me," he said to the woman. "Tarrou, it is not from this hub, is that right?"

The woman did not even look at the map. "I have to work," she said. The checkpoint was secured and one of the women sat down on it. The woman with the headset got in front and the third woman sat down next to her.

David said something in French which did not sound polite.

"I agree," Mayla said.

The woman with the headset started the skid and turned it in a tight circle.

There was no evidence that the checkpoint had ever been there.

"So, we wait," David said, watching the skid putter off. "How long, do you think?"

"Maybe we should call," Mayla said. She didn't see a callbox but they could probably call from the cafe where they'd gotten the burro. Of course, if they went back there, Titon or whatever his name was could show up and leave. David could with here and she could call. Or they could use the map and try to find Tarrou.

"There's a police station in the port," she said. "Why don't we just go there and have them take it off?"

He shrugged again.

"If we wait we could be here for hours," she added.

He shook his head. "They are always this efficient?"

"A lot of things are like this," she said.

He checked the map to see how they got back to the port and she let him lead.

Better than Tim, she thought on the ped mover as the flats slipped by. Tim would be blustering.

David looked surreptitiously at the telltale and then pulled his sleeve over it to hide it.

The way back to the municipal shuttle seemed shorter than when they had come in the morning. The waiting area wasn't crowded but the shuttle wasn't in, either. She fumbled through her purse until she found change for the turnstiles. Just beyond they triggered a VR ad and the air was suddenly full of electric blue butterflies. The shimmer was irritating and the focus was off because the butterfly flock was without depth. She ignored them and as soon as she passed out of range they disappeared.

She glanced over her shoulder in time to see David walk into them. He started, raising his hands against the empty air.

"They are allowed?" he said when he had gotten through. "In France, they are not allowed in a public place."

A good idea, she thought. She didn't like them and every so often she read where a tracking laser had burned someone's eyes. The walls were covered with advertisements. There were butterflies in a lot of them: women in carnival costumes with yellow gauze wings, women's faces painted with wings so their eyes became eyespots, the electric blue butterflies, this time alighting on a flash unit, wings scintillating as they settled and then flickered off, the advertisement tirelessly repeating. Why so many butterflies, were they this year's gimmick?

David sat down next to her, slouched on the bench studying his shoes. He looked very foreign in the suit. Of course he looked pretty foreign anyway. He really needed some new clothes. She should say something but she didn't want to insult him.

The people in the waiting room were the flotsam of midday. There were women who worked the evening shift, old women with their shopping bags, old men in old sweaters and tights that bagged under their knees and around their ankles. A group of boys who should have been in school stood by the door talking and laughing. They wore divers' vests that bared their long ropey arms. A crew. One had a leather demon mask hanging from a seal by a leather thong. The mask was supposed to mean something, it was some kind of rank. At least according to the vid.

David was watching the boys, too. "Why aren't they cold?"

"Pyroxin, probably."

He looked at her sideways, he didn't understand.

"It's a drug. Makes your metabolism burn higher. Divers take it."

He sort of sat up. "You don't get cold?" Interested. Surface people were always cold.

She shook her head, grinning. "It's illegal. Don't even think about it."

He gave an exaggerated sigh and she laughed. She liked him. He could be funny when he wanted to. Once his English got a little better he'd do fine.

The metal door was the size of the door on her garage. As it pulled up, the boys ducked under, but everybody else waited until it was all the way up. The embarcadero was lined with advertisements and she could smell seawater from the surfacing pool.

They walked through the door and there was a sharp crack and David shouted, a hoarse startled shout.

"What—" Something red, bright arterial red, spattered the floor and her side. She shrieked. David crouched, one arm across his eyes and his whole front and left side was covered in red. She thought, *Diós mio,* he's hurt. He's been hurt, there was so much red, so much blood, all over him.

This is bad, she thought.

There was an acrid, eye-watering smell.

Astoundingly he was crouching there, not fallen, but there was so much blood she didn't want him to turn around. There had to be something bad if there was that much hurt and she didn't want to see it, and she stepped back a bit more and her back was against the wall.

She started coughing, David was coughing, still holding one arm over his eyes. Her eyes were watering furiously, tears blinding her.

Pinche tear gas. It was the telltale. He had his right arm held straight out away and behind him. The telltale had gone off. It wasn't a bomb.

People in maroon were running towards them shouting at them in English and Creole. She saw a gun drawn. Mother of God don't let them shoot, she thought, it wasn't her fault. "It's a mistake!" she wheezed. Her throat hurt and she kept coughing. David was shouting in French, still holding his right arm over his eyes, and three Marine Security officers had their guns drawn on him. But he was all right, she thought, as long as they didn't shoot him he was all right.

"It's a mistake," she said and coughed again.

"Shut the fuck up!" an officer yelled, wheeling on her with gun drawn. Just like the vid, she thought, and shut up.

David's wrist was burned where the telltale had gone off, and his eyes were bloody red from the gas. His suit was completely ruined. The Uncles gave him a pair of maroon overalls to wear and gave him his suit in a sealed plastic bag. He came out to the waiting room with his hair slicked down from the shower and his eyes on the floor.

"Are you okay?" she asked.

He looked up at her with his red eyes, furious, but didn't say anything.

"I'm sorry," she said, thinking, it wasn't really her fault. What could she have done? The Uncles had just lectured her for an hour on how they should have waited for the officer to come to the checkpoint. Her dress was ruined. She'd buy him a new goddamn suit.

"They said we can go now," she said, her voice small.

He nodded. His left hand was still faintly red from the dye.

Maybe she should have said they should wait, but the woman at the checkpoint hadn't said anything about sensors at the shuttle ports, just banks. He could have insisted they wait.

Outside the station they stepped on the ped mover. He didn't say anything the entire trip to the port. He glanced up at her once, with his red furious eyes. They looked ghastly. Her eyes ached, too. But his eyes hurt to look at.

At the sub port he had to open the plastic bag and find the tickets in the wreckage of his suit. Her eyes started watering. The tickets were red and stank. "I'll take them," she said.

He waited while she explained to the ticket clerk what had happened, and the clerk ended up punching her another set and throwing out the ones she had.

She came back and sat down beside David. "Are you all right?" she asked.

He nodded. Then he sighed. "It was a mistake," he said.

She asked him what he meant, but he just shook his head and wouldn't explain any farther.

3

Probation

On Saturday David drove Mayla to see her grandfather.

"I am thinking," he said in the car, "I am not the person to do this job for you."

"I think you're doing fine," she said. "I expected it all to take some time to settle in."

He thought of the telltale going off. The burn, the shock. For a moment he had felt the dye and thought it was the moment before one knows one is injured, when there is only the shock and the feeling of something wet. "No," he said. "I think it is not a good idea."

She did not say anything and he stole a glance at her. She was looking out at the road. "I'm sorry about the business in Marincite," she said. "That was my fault."

Yes, he thought, it was. "That is not it," he said anyway, "I think I am just not the right person."

"Is it Tim?" she asked. "He'll be leaving."

He shook his head.

"You haven't even been here thirty days," she said. He put the car on automatic and they accelerated smoothly onto the beltway. "Try it another sixty days," she said. "It'll get better."

"I do not think so," he said.

"I can understand your feelings," she said. "Tim is being a prick. And what happened in Marincite, that would shake up anybody."

He shrugged. It would not get better, but sixty days wouldn't really make a difference. "All right," he said.

"Thank you," she said.

She directed him off the beltway and they dropped down to the second level of the city, then onto residential streets.

The street was a great deal like the street Mayla lived on. Just featureless garage doors, no sense of the residences behind the concrete. She had him stop, and she got out and palmed the sensor next to the garage door. For a moment he thought it wasn't going to open, and then the door lifted.

He expected a garage like Mayla's with space for a couple of cars but this space would have easily held twenty. A public garage, like at the bank. He had not thought much about where her grandfather would live in the city. He guessed he had imagined a place like Mayla's, not this huge residence for many people.

There were only two cars: a long car like Mayla's boss rode to work and a sedan. "Park next to the Benare," she said and pointed to the sedan. Her voice echoed off the concrete. Why were there only two cars in the parking? It wasn't a workday.

At the back of the garage were wrought-iron doors on a lift. The iron was worked into figures, tall birds like cranes and palm trees and flowers. Like an ornate bird cage.

They went below the floor of the garage into a lobby. Concrete walls painted white, black and white tiles on the floor. Dusty Greek busts on pedestals like garden statuary. The space felt cold and disused, even colder than the usual lobby. This whole country seemed built of concrete.

She folded the lift door back and the iron crashed. He followed her across the black and white tiles into a carpeted hallway. The doors were big heavy wood, and set into each one like a porthole was a Chinese blue and white plate, blue willow plates depicting a girl and her lover fleeing her father the angry mandarin. Some of the doors were open. An office that looked unused—so this was not just residential flats. Then a storeroom full of old furniture. Then a bedroom. Just one room, with a bed. Like a hotel room almost except there was bric-a-brac all over the table: glass harlequins on a lace doily, feather masks on the wall and a handful of medicine bottles on a glass dish. An old woman's room.

Bedsitters? Rich daughter letting old grandfather live in poverty—although the place didn't feel impoverished, just empty and ugly and full of old people's used things.

He followed her down five steps and across a large room with dining tables and chairs draped in white cloths. The walls were mirrored, reflecting back white-shrouded furniture. Community dining?

"Jude?" she called.

The place made him uncomfortable, with its empty concrete rooms. Maybe it was being closed down or something? She had not said anything about having to move her grandfather, but then she hadn't said anything at all about him.

"Jude?" she said again, and he followed her through a door into a kitchen. Just a kitchen, good sized, with a wooden table and chairs and a shiny yellow tile floor. The black man mopping the floor said, "Don't you step on my floor, miss."

"Jude," Mayla said.

The man leaned the mop up against the counter and tiptoed across the clean floor and gave Mayla a hug. "Where you been?" he asked.

"I've been busy," Mayla said.

"He's an old man." "Old mon," Jude actually said, in helium falsetto.

"I know, I know. How's his cold?"

Jude shrugged. "The man, he's eighty-two."

"Is he in bed?"

"No, he's out on the spring court."

"Is Domingo with him?" she asked.

The man shook his head. "There's nothing wrong with Domingo. You just feeling guilty, knowing Domingo is taking care of him and you don't get out here often enough."

"I didn't say anything," she said, throwing her hands in the air. They both laughed, as if this was an old thing between them.

"You both staying for dinner?"

"Oh, Jude, this is David Dai, he's working for me. David, this is Jude."

"Where's that other one?" The man's voice was carefully neutral.

"Tim is going back to Australia. We can't stay for dinner this time. Next time, I promise."

David suddenly understood, this was all one house. This was all Mayla's grandfather's house. The lobby, the parking, all the rooms. The dining room draped in white. All empty.

"I'm baking potatoes," Jude said, "not in the flash, neither."

"With real sour cream?" Mayla asked.

"What do you think?"

"Next time," she said. "I promise."

All one house. Huge and ugly and cold.

He followed her again, back out across the empty dining room and up another five steps to a room with mirrors like windows and tables covered with lace and picture frames. Another wooden door with a blue and white plate set in it. Mayla pushed the door open and yellow light spilled out.

The room was full of light and he blinked. The bright air was damp and misty, no, it was misting. Raining. Like rain. Space went up and up; twice, three times the height of the kitchen. There were clusters of plants and in the center of each clump stalks of tall bamboo, four or five meters high. The floor was terra-cotta tile, glazed Indian red with artificial rain. All around the walls, tall mirrors like windows. And in the center was an old man in a wicker chair and a young man holding an old navy blue umbrella.

"Hello," Mayla said, her voice too loud and too cheerful, "over your cold?"

"Nearly," the old man said. He was a flat-faced, long-boned ugly old Chinese man with dyed black hair. At least David assumed it was dyed. "How is the bank?" the old man asked.

"The bank is doing well," she said. "Can you turn off the sprinklers? We're getting wet."

She took the umbrella from the young man—Domingo?—and held it while he went to turn off the sprinklers. "I just got back from

Marincite," she said. "Did you read in the paper about Tumipamba's funeral?"

"Jude said your picture was in the paper," her grandfather said.

There had been an im in the paper, of the coffin with Mayla standing at the foot, facing out of the picture. Mayla's presence in the picture was an accident. Crisp black-and-white im, the cliché of
funerals. Tim had said she looked like "a frigging presidential
widow."

"I went to the funeral." She sounded defensive.

"That was stupid," he said.

"I was working with Tumipamba," she said. "I thought I should
go to the funeral."

"And get your picture in the paper?"

"I didn't even know they took the im," she said.

"You were working with this man? In Marincite?"

"We're negotiating an agreement," she said. "With Marincite."

She offered that as a kind of gift, her voice hopeful. The old man
was silent, considering.

The rain stopped. David found he'd been hunching his shoulders.

"What kind of agreement?" her grandfather asked. Like his own
father, David thought, this was a man who did not trust gifts. Who
had to turn them over and over and who always suspected either a
bribe or a catch.

"Marincite Technical Exchange is going independent," she said.
"Marincite is spinning them off. We may do the financing. A lot of
money."

He didn't help her, just waited for her to go on. After a bit of silence she said tentatively, "I offered short-term notes with an automatic rollover. It would have been a better deal for them, but they
wanted five-year fixed, something about the way they do business."
The terms meant nothing to David but he listened to the sound of
her voice. He could hear things better now, through the strangeness
of language and the shrillness. He could hear her nervousness, and
hear how she got a little less nervous as she talked. She chattered on

about buying some buildings and leasing them back to the company, while the old man sat silent, his eyes on the Indian red tile.

"Short term?" he said suddenly, and coughed, a bark. "Why'd you push short term if they wanted fixed?" He had a hard, flat, American voice, David could hear that, too.

"The U.S. market is falling," she said, her voice gone sharp and defensive again, "it's got to correct, and then interest rates will drop. We thought with Marincite we'd have to give them short term. The bank will take short term," she said and shoved her hands in her pockets.

The old man looked up at her. "You didn't do your homework." The old tyrant looked pointedly at her hands and she took them out. "A client shouldn't have to be sold," he said.

She didn't say anything, just took her dressing down. Maybe she knew that nothing would make any difference. Better than himself, every time he saw his father they ended up screaming at each other. When was the last time he had seen his father?

Mayla's grandfather looked at him. "You're new," he said.

Mayla promptly introduced her grandfather, "John Ling," she said. John Ling leaned forward in his wicker chair and held out his hand and for a moment David thought he was supposed to help the old man stand up. Then he realized the old man wanted to shake hands.

Loose dry skin over fragile bones.

"What happened to the big blond . . . Tim?" the old man asked.

"He's going back to Australia," Mayla said.

"Are you American?" John Ling asked.

Nobody had ever thought he was American before. "No sir," David said. "French."

"Southeast Asia?"

"Yes sir," David said, "Indochina."

"Speak any Chinese?" the old man asked.

"No sir, my grandmother speaks Vietnamese."

The old man sat back. Nodded. "I went to Chinese school after regular school for a couple of years, but I never learned a bit." His attention went back to Mayla. "What are you wearing?"

She had on a red silk blouse belted over tights, something simple and bright, David thought. Although what did he know about how people dressed?

"You spend a lot of money on clothes," he said. "Your grandmother never spent so much on clothes."

She sighed.

The old man stared out at the plants. Was his vision bad? The silence hung.

"So how are you feeling?" she said, trying to fill the space.

"Old," he said. "And helpless."

She looked up at Domingo and then at David, looking for help or for something to say. Her face was pink.

David found he could not meet her gaze, so instead he looked at the bamboo.

"I was thinking," she said in the parking, "maybe we should go someplace for dinner." Her voice was bright, working hard at it. She dug in her purse. "I think, I looked up restaurants . . . but I think the best place . . . wait," she found a piece of paper. "I thought maybe a French restaurant, you know, I thought you might like some food from home."

Food from home. Chicken. Pasta. Something other than fish. "It does not matter," he said. Homesickness washed over him in waves, all he could think of was bread and butter—not tortillas and not that bland stuff from the U.S., just a decent piece of bread. He wanted to go home. Sixty days, he had promised. At the moment it seemed an immeasurable wait.

"I went away to school," she said, "I remember what it was like. Besides, after that business in Marincite, I wanted, you know, I mean I can't make you forget that but—"

"It doesn't matter," he said again.

"It does," she said. "I don't know what to say about it. It was horrible. It was horrible for me, and I wasn't wearing the telltale."

Blind. He had thought he was blinded. The memory was bad, he slid away from it and shrugged.

She looked down at her hands.

He meant only to pass it off, but she looked as if he had shrugged her off. She looked the way she had when she was standing in front of her grandfather.

"I would like to go to a restaurant," he said.

She smiled at him, grateful. How easy to make her happy. "Well," she said, serious again, consulting her scrap of paper, "there are a couple of places but everybody says that the best place is Botticelli's. It's in Aphrodite, that's a casino." She looked down at her piece of paper. "Actually, it's not French, it's Continental. But they have some French dishes and some other things, too. Italian, and Spanish."

"Okay," he said, and was rewarded again by her smile, so he smiled, too. "Okay," he said, to make her smile, to feel his own face mirroring hers.

"Okay," she said.

He nodded, and because he didn't know what else to say, he said it again. "Okay." And it sounded so inane, this dialogue of "okays" that they started to laugh, grinning at each other like idiots. A couple of emotional cripples, he thought. Grinning at her in her grandfather's parking.

Botticelli's was in the middle of the casino. It was dark and each table sat in a little pool of light. For a centerpiece each table had a stand and a live parrot: blue parrots, green parrots, gray parrots, all with heavy bills and strong ugly feet. He looked and was relieved that at the tables where people had food there were no parrots.

The prices made him still. The chicken, the beef dishes were 45cr and 55cr. He looked up and the blue parrot flipped down to hang upside down. A little sign said that they nipped.

"Poor things," Mayla said, "they don't do well in the air mixture, the cold gets them. Most of them don't live long."

He supposed they didn't fly because their wings were clipped, but what kept them from climbing down the stand and onto the table? The parrot turned and twisted its head, snake fashion, then clambered sideways and righted itself, flapping its wings. It opened its beak when a waiter walked by and its tongue was black. It stared at David, flipped upside down again.

A waiter stopped at their table and the parrot righted itself again. The waiter asked if they were ready to order.

He had no idea what he wanted, he hadn't even decided if maybe he should order fish—it was the cheapest thing on the menu.

The waiter said he'd be back and fed the parrot a peanut. The parrot craned its head and fluffed out its feathers. It raised its wings and made a "ding" exactly like the sound of a flash unit signaling "ready."

Mayla looked up from her menu.

"It was the bird," David said.

She laughed and the bird stared at her. "They're distracting, aren't they? I think we should get a bottle of wine, but you have to order, I don't have the nerve to order wine in front of a Frenchman. The chicken dishes are famous."

There wasn't much on the menu he had ever eaten before but he didn't tell her that. He ordered *coq au vin* and she ordered some kind of chicken with garbanzo beans so he got a Chardonnay. White with chicken and he liked Chardonnay. Growing up his family hadn't drank wine often, and when he did buy it he usually just got a *vin de table.* He really didn't know much about wine.

The waiter came and got the parrot, whisking the thing away, stand and all. David was relieved.

The food was good, and even if it tasted a little different, it was not fish. It tasted so good he wolfed it down so it never really had a chance to get cold. The bread wasn't bad, warm crusty rolls wrapped in a big napkin, and he sopped his plate clean. He thought the wine was all right and Mayla seemed to think so.

Coffee after dinner, not-hot-enough Caribbean coffee. Then they walked back through the casino.

"Blue and whites," Mayla said suddenly.

He looked at her, not understanding.

"There's been a bomb threat," Mayla said.

David looked around. He saw people at the slot machines, heard the muted whir and chime of gambling, nothing out of place, everything seemed normal. Then he saw, at the door, six in police blue and white.

She sighed. "We could end up standing here for an hour if they've just started a sweep."

The boy who stopped them looked maybe nineteen, with the smooth skin of a young man. Under his lifted visor he had the look David associated with the military: youth and exercise and steady food. Like the young people at the security check in Marincite, except that this boy wore crisp blue and white fatigues rather than maroon and cream. "Excuse me," the boy said, "can I see some identification?"

They passed over their smart cards and the boy dropped them in his reader, then used the image to check, im against face, all six points. Like the port, David thought, so thorough. He consciously loosened his shoulders.

"Is it a bomb threat?" Mayla asked.

"No ma'am," he said. "An arrest. But we don't know if the suspect is here to place a bomb or not, so we are being very careful. Could you stand over there for a moment?"

Mayla seemed to find it normal. This country was crazy, David thought. They stood over at the side of the entrance. How could these people live this way? he wondered. He watched as two men and a woman saw the team and hesitated. It was obviously irritating to have to stand around and wait. He wished they could wait outside, particularly if they thought that someone might be placing a bomb. Then it occurred to him that in a structural sense there really was no outside in Julia. The doors didn't make so much difference. The three people stopped and the woman said something to one of the men. "What can I do about it!" the man said. The third man hung back a bit.

They came down and presented their IDs. The woman was tiny

and dark, with a triangular face. African, he thought. Maybe she was Haitian, some Haitians were as dark as Africans. Just because he had been in Africa he thought she looked African. She was angry about something, refusing to talk to the man she was with except in clipped monosyllables. "How long will this be?" she asked the boy in blue and white and he shrugged. He thought she sounded African, but he still had problems with the way the air mixture distorted everything.

"You'll have to wait over there," the boy said, pointing at where Mayla and he were standing.

"I wasn't even supposed to be here tonight," the woman said.

Northern Africa, he thought. She didn't look like the blacks he'd fought with in Anzania.

"Over there," the boy said.

She still wanted to argue but the boy shrugged his rifle around and clicked the safety.

He looked at the rifle and then at the woman. The rifle didn't seem to matter to her, but she grimaced and let the man she was with pull her towards the side.

It did not feel dangerous, exactly, surely the boy was just trying to put her in her place, and yet it did. Africa, and rifles in the hands of very young men. After the way things had gone with the telltale, Caribbean Security forces made him nervous.

"Identification," one of the blue and whites said to the man, who had not really been with the couple. At least, now he did not seem to be with the couple, but before, when David first saw them, he thought that they had been. Not because they were talking, or even walking exactly together, but not walking separately. But now it seemed that they did not know each other.

This country, it made him see plots everywhere. Like Tim's diving lesson.

The man handed the blue and white his smart card and the boy dropped it in the reader. David put his hand on Mayla's arm and pulled her further back. He didn't know why, perhaps it was the sound of the safety on the rifle when the boy had been talking to the woman, perhaps it was thinking about Africa, he didn't know.

The boy grabbed the man's arm and wrenched him around, letting the reader swing on his belt, "DON'T MOVE! NOBODY MOVE!"

The young man said. *"There's been a mistake—"* Always, the same thing they say, he thought, mistake.

"AGAINST THE WALL, MOTHERFUCKER!" the boy shouted, and the other officers were shoving him, too, and the man panicked, swung out. One of them slammed his head against the wall, it made that hollow melon sound, and then they hit him in the kidneys with their rifle stocks.

The young man's nose was bleeding and he was dazed. Blue and whites came running. Blue and whites everywhere. David was backing up, pulling Mayla with him. The young man disappeared in a crowd of blue and whites. At the edge of the blue and whites stood the African woman and her man. They were not backing up, they were watching, their faces blank. The woman had the man's arm, her fingers straining the fabric of his sleeve.

She looked away, looked back at them. She looked at Mayla, who was watching the blue and whites. She looked at Mayla a long moment. David wondered what she was thinking, maybe she did not even realize she was looking at Mayla.

He looked at her, and she glanced at him and looked away.

It was almost an hour later when they finally got their smart cards back. A different officer dropped them each in readers, "Ms. Ling," he said, and handed her hers.

"Mr. Dai."

To the African woman he said, "Ms. Clark?" Odd name, David thought, maybe they are married? But the man's name was James.

They walked back to the parking, to the shining little black car. He was edgy. Paranoia, he thought. The sound of the safety, the age of the boy, the African woman.

"Clark," he said. "Is it a common name, in Haiti?"

Mayla was not paying attention and he had to repeat the question. "Not that I know of," she said.

So the woman was not Haitian, he thought. Maybe she was from a different island. Maybe she was not African, he had trouble with voices here.

The car park was not very big and it was only half full, most of the vehicles were motor scooters, parked all in a row. The Skate was parked beside a delivery skid, invisible from where they came in. But it was there, snug and polished. David found the keys and heard a cry. Small and animal, nearly soundless.

A child, an infant, he thought, and looked up at Mayla. She was looking at him, waiting. "Did you hear it?" he asked.

Before she answered he heard it again. Not a baby, a kitten, from close by. The sound was so helpless it hurt his chest.

He crouched.

The kitten was tiny, hunched next to the wheel. David clucked with his tongue and it mewed again.

"What is it?" Mayla asked.

"A kitten," he said. He wished that it would come out, if the driver of the skid didn't hear it, it would be crushed. "Where are your people?" he asked.

"What?" Mayla said. She crouched down. "I don't see it."

"There," David pointed.

"Ah," Mayla said. *"Pobrecito."*

Yes, poor thing, stuck down here. Caribe seemed an unnatural place for a kitten, never able to sit in the window in the sun.

It took a few tentative steps, its tail a bottle brush. Out in the light it was gray with dirty white paws and belly. It was skinny and filthy. Little refugee. Its eyes had little tiny sores, flea bites? Suddenly it sat, scratched its ear vigorously and shook its head. Ear mites, he thought.

"Where does he come from?" Mayla asked.

"Nowhere," David said. She stood. The kitten scuttled sideways and went back under the skid.

"Is there someplace we can take him?" David said. "You know, people who take care of animals with no people? A *société* for animals?"

Mayla didn't know of such a place.

David clucked again and the kitten mewed. It came a few steps and mewed again, tiny teeth and an astonishing pink mouth. He clucked and wiggled his fingers.

Stiffly the kitten approached him. He coaxed closer, moving his fingers just out of reach, and the kitten stretched to sniff, stopped nervously, came another step—David snatched it up. It grabbed his jacket.

"You'll probably catch something," Mayla said.

"I already have," he said and grinned. He felt absurdly pleased with himself. The kitten clung and mewed.

"What are you going to do with it," she said.

He shrugged. "Maybe I will find someone to take it. A *société* for animals."

She shook her head, "You keep him in your apartment," she said.

"Just for a few days," he said.

"Right," she said.

But she held the dirty little thing on her lap while he drove home.

"What will you call it?" she asked.

"I should not give it a name," he said, "I want to give it to a place where they will take care of it." They would probably kill it, he thought, but that would be better than leaving it to die of neglect. He could not keep it, he was leaving.

"You have to call it something," Mayla said. She was teasing, she was saying that she didn't think he would give it away.

"Call it Mephistofele," he said. "From the opera," he added.

"Well," she said, "he probably will turn out to be a little devil."

He was pleased that she knew the name. "Ah, non," he said, "I was thinking, he will never see the sun."

She looked at him oddly. Foolish thing to say, she lived here, she didn't see the sun much either.

* * *

At Mayla's request, Tim took him to get some clothes. They went into a part of town where he had never been. Here the traffic was all motor scooters and bicycles, and they had to park the car and take escalators and walk.

The air was damper here and didn't smell right. David found he kept taking deep breaths. The shops were all small. The shop where Tim took him to buy clothes was a deep narrow place that had once been a restaurant. The flash unit and grill were gone, but the counter and stools were still there and the counter was piled high with stacks of sweaters. The Indian who ran the shop bobbed along behind them.

"Tights," Tim said, "for him."

"Sirs," the Indian said, "what size?"

David didn't know, sizes were different here. He gave his inseam in centimeters and the shopkeeper turned to the wall of shelves and rifled through neatly folded stacks of tights. "Sirs, will you be wanting the new colors? I have bright colors, all very popular."

He gestured towards the wall opposite the counter where shelves were stacked high with neatly folded pairs of tights. Two columns of tights were vivid rainbows: rose madder and cobalt blue and bright hard yellow.

Tim grinned. "No, I don't think so. Just black and gray."

Three pairs of black, three pairs of gray. And sweaters.

David went into the dressing room and tried on tights. They looked cold, the outside was some slick, rubbery-looking material. But the inside was soft, like chamois, and warm. He found a pair of gray that fit. They were wonderful, so much better than pants.

He eyed his reflection. The dressing room was barely big enough to turn around in, but he could still see the effect. Embarrassing. He had not really paid much attention to the way other people looked in divers' tights. Except for at the bank, where the men wore suits, most everybody on the street seemed to wear them.

He had legs like a chicken. Tim did not have legs like a chicken, Tim had broad, strong legs like tree trunks. He did not relish the idea of wearing these around Tim. He considered critically, did they show his bad knee?

Probably, he thought, and sighed. Still, they were warm. Vanity or comfort? Everybody wore them.

He bought a gray pair and a black pair. And four sweaters: a dark green, a navy blue, a kind of olive green and a red one. The last because the red looked so warm. He also bought a pair of sandals. Nobody wore shoes, shoes looked foolish with tights. He stood there in his new tights and the olive sweater, feeling foolish, and tried to sort through the maze of Caribbean currency.

So Tim was amused, he told himself.

Still, on the street with his purchases he felt a little less conspicuously foreign. Tim walked fast, took long strides, and he had to work to keep up. The sandals had no backs and there was a knack to keeping them on; if he wasn't careful he would walk right out of them.

Silly to buy clothes when he wasn't going to stay here. Which made him think of the kitten. It was a bother. He had looked in the directory for a place for animals but there was nothing. But he couldn't take it back to France. It would cost so much. He supposed he would have to have it put down.

Poor little refugee.

Tim would be pleased to know he didn't plan to stay although mostly Tim ignored him. Even walking down the street, Tim paid no attention to him. Like the way he used to ignore his little sister when he was a kid. Or when he was in Blacksburg, and he and Thieu used to run around and ignore his younger cousin. Maybe he could fly to Blacksburg when he left Caribe, see his aunt and uncle and run around a bit with Thieu. Thieu was married and had two, or maybe three children. He would like to see his cousin's children.

It might be awkward. He would write his aunt and ask for Thieu's address.

"To call the United States," he asked Tim, "is it so expensive?"

"I don't know, I've never called the U.S. Why would you call the U.S.?"

"I have family there," David said. "I thought I would like to go see them."

"It probably isn't that expensive. Have you talked to Mayla about time off?"

"No," David said. He didn't think he should say to Tim that he was leaving, he didn't think Mayla wanted Tim to know. Then again, Tim might be a little easier to live with if he thought David was leaving.

Silence might be best.

He did not like secrets. "I do not know if I will take the job," he said. "You know, this is a probationary period. Maybe at the end I will leave."

Tim frowned. "What's wrong with the job?"

"I am not suited, I think," David said.

"It's a good job," Tim said. Which was beside the point.

They got on the escalator. The escalators were awful, dirty and graffitied and this one smelled of smoke on top of a strong odor of urine. At the top of the escalator was a shed that sold sausages. Coals glowed in the bottom of the grill. David thought that fires were illegal in Caribe because they ate up oxygen and put a further burden on the air purification systems.

A whole family seemed to live in the shed: father, mother, a girl about six or seven, and a naked, potbellied little boy no more than three. The little boy had a dirty cord tied around his ankle to keep him from wandering. Flat mestizo faces watched people get off the escalator. Nobody seemed to buy. The little boy alone seemed unconcerned, he stood on a pink blanket gone gray with grime and cooed and crowed to himself.

This country could not take care of its people, there wouldn't be a *société* for animals. Maybe not even veterinarians. What to do with Meph? He could not just abandon him, it would be cruel, but if there was no vet. . . . Could he kill the kitten himself?

There would have to be a vet. Some people, like Mayla, they would have a pet, wouldn't they?

"Is it Mayla?" Tim asked.

"What," David said.

"Why don't you like the job?"

"I don't like this country," David said. A half-truth.

Tim seemed to relax. "Yeah," he said. "I can see that. The place is a mess, isn't it. But Mayla is all right. Sometimes she doesn't know what she wants, you know."

David didn't know, but he nodded.

"Sometimes, she gets me so mad I don't know what to do with her. She changes her mind. One minute she likes you, the next minute she doesn't. I think it's because part of her is North American, like her family, and part of her is Caribbean, and the two sides are at bloody war half the time."

"Why do you stay?" David asked. The question he had been wanting to ask.

"I don't know," Tim said. "I went to Belize and was there for awhile, and then she asked me to come back and she offered me this goddamn job. And then she decided she was mad at me and she wanted to get rid of me. I figure she'll change her mind again."

David did not think so but he didn't see any need to voice an opinion.

"Besides," Tim said suddenly, "Sometime in your life you gotta stick to something, you know?"

A strange statement that left as many questions as it answered. How had he known Mayla before he went to Belize? Why had she asked him to come back?

If David stayed, would she change her mind about him, too?

One more reason why he did not want this job.

It was the easiest job he had ever had. He took Mayla to work, picked her up in the evening. Sometimes he did the grocery shopping. Most of the time he spent in his room, with the kitten, Meph.

In the afternoon, when she wasn't working late, he got to the bank half an hour early and sat in the Skate in the parking, reading. He should have been reading English, to improve. But he didn't like reading English, he read it slowly. The university bookstore had some French novels: Camus, Sartre, Gide, Heureaux. He found a copy of *L'Etranger* (which struck him as an ironic book to sell in a foreign country). He couldn't say he really liked the book, but he had spent over a month in a hospital in Algeria after he had been wounded in Anzania and he liked the descriptions of North Africa, even though he had been in In Salah, in the middle of the desert, rather than Algiers, on the coast.

Someone tapped on the glass. Two people were standing there, a man and a woman. He opened the door wondering if he was late? But it was not yet five, not quite time to go upstairs to get Mayla. Something was wrong with Mayla?

The woman said, "Are you Jean Dai?"

"Yes," he said. She said "Jean" the way they said it in France, not the way they said it in the States. Nobody ever called him "Jean," except people who didn't know him and got his name off of records, like in the military or on the first day of school.

"Could we talk to you?" she asked.

"Is something wrong?" he asked.

"No," she said, "but we would like to discuss some business with you." She was familiar, but he couldn't place her, from the bank, maybe?

"Ms. Ling gets off at five—"

"It won't take long," the man said. He sounded as if his first language was Spanish.

"Would you come with us?" the woman asked. She was tiny, with a narrow face in which all the muscles and ligaments stood clearly on the bones, just underneath skin so dark it almost looked blue under the lights in the parking. "There is a place up the street, a restaurant." She leaned forward and the shiny black plastic crucifix she was wearing dangled between them, the Christ twisted in exaggerated agony.

"Are you with the bank?" David asked. No, not the bank, where had he seen her?

"I think it would be more comfortable to talk elsewhere," she said.

"Perhaps we could talk here," David said. "I would be late." He thought of the handgun in a sling underneath the seat. He had thought it was foolish when Tim showed him.

The man looked at the woman, she lifted her shoulders fractionally. The man sighed and pulled a paper out of his jacket, opened it on the hood of the Skate and leaned on the car. "Is this your employer?"

The paper was a copy of the im that had appeared in the newspaper after the funeral: Mayla in her black dress, looking off the page.

The hood of the car was flexed under the man's weight. "Please do not lean on the car," David said. The man straightened sharply.

"You do not mind if we speak French?" the woman asked. Her accent was clearer in that language, even in falsetto. "It is much more private that way."

He didn't mind. (But he did, she was trying to use him. "We are the same," she was saying. When he did not even know who she was.)

"Your employer's family came to Caribe before the 'liberation'." She said *"liberation"* fastidiously, her teeth delicate white. "The liberation was supposed to free this country, but the unemployment rate is now higher than it was when Bustamante took power. The housing shortage is more severe than ever, and the construction of the new sixth level is progressing so slowly that by the time it is finished we will need even more housing than we do today. And do you know why? Because of the corruption of high officials who pretend to buy first rate materials and pay labor, when in fact they buy third rate materials and create phantom companies with no real employees and line their own pockets with money. But you work for Ms. Ling, who is a tool of these people, so surely you know this? I am boring you, I am afraid?"

No, she was not boring him.

"You are the woman from the casino," he said, "Clark." She was the woman who had been there when the man was arrested.

The tiny woman clasped her hands together. "The man who was arrested, he is innocent of any crime except the desire for justice for all peoples. Are you aware that almost half of the households in Julia with children under six are single parent households? That forty percent of all the children in Caribe go to bed hungry? That the average family's major source of nutrition is yeast substitutes? And the government lines its own pockets, and banks such as this one loan them the money to do so. They mortgage their own people."

Namibia. Woman and children lined up clutching enamel bowls, waiting for boiled corn. That was mortgaging one's own people and going bankrupt. He didn't like politics; the woman was telling the truth, he thought, but he couldn't be drawn into that just now. He had to think. He was fascinated by the black plastic crucifix swinging between them. It was as long as the palm of his hand, the features of the Christ's face a clearly defined rictus of pain. He had seen crucifixes like that before.

"Here, the rich get clean, dry air. Go down a few levels, Mr. Dai. The air is damp and impure. There is not enough oxygen because the recirculating equipment is old, insufficient for the population and not maintained." She covered the crucifix reverently with her hand, tiny wiry hand with beautiful nails, pink and paler than her skin. "Please come and talk to us, Mr. Dai," she said in English, "we need your help. Our brothers are held in prison with no chance of due process or escape, if we are to free them we must bargain with the government. You can help us turn their own tools against them."

"Êtes-vous Catholique d'Afrique del Sud?" he asked. South African Catholics. She was, he recognized the Christ, but what would a member of the South African Catholic and Apostolic Faith be doing in Caribe?

"Divisions within the world church are artificial in the eyes of God," she said. "For centuries the Church has allowed itself to be schismed by internal politics while neglecting the very people it should serve. And now the official church has no more to do with God than this bank." She gestured towards the entrance to First Hawaiian. "But God is in the world, Mr. Dai. God is with us. We are his instrument, and we will set in motion powerful forces. You know, Mr. Dai, that the world is a complex web, and that not one of us draws a breath but that it affects the rest of the world. But God sees the pattern in chaos, and he shows us where to strike. We are God's surgeons, Mr. Dai."

This woman was violence. Here he was, in a city under the ocean (when he pictured Caribe he always thought of an atlas, blue oceans, the Atlantic and Caribbean with the arrows of currents sweeping great circles); here he was, and *Afrique* had followed him on one of those arrows. *Afrique* was making demands on him.

She was still talking. "You are inside, Mr. Dai. You can bring us inside. If we are to free our people, we must place our scalpel in precisely the right place. You can be our hand."

He nodded. Go away, he thought, leave me alone.

Her eyes were huge, hungry. The face of the South African Irregular Forces, who sometimes fought with the Republic, sometimes with the Prots. And now that the war was over and the Republic had won, the faces of the people who had lost most of all. "You could help, you could strike a direct blow. I wish I were in your place." She did wish it, her face said desperate things, "help us." It said, "help *me*." It said, "I am hungry."

He looked at her and she looked at him, holding her black plastic crucifix folded in her small hand with its clean pink nails. This woman wants to die, he thought.

"We are friends," the man said, taking the woman's arm and pulling her back a step, holding her next to him as if to dampen the intensity of her wanting. The weight of their wanting.

David glanced around, checking the exits. Through the Skate's window he saw the book, *L'Étranger*, open and upside-down on the seat. "Excuse me," he smiled, "my book, that isn't good for them." He opened the door and the man tensed, but before they could really do anything, David rested his knee on the seat, closed the book and dropped it between the driver's and passenger's seats. In the mirror he saw the man waiting. David reached under the seat, expecting them to lunge, and for a moment his hand did not find anything but still they did not move. He found the handle of the handgun, smooth and cool, and straightened up. "Please go now," he said, holding it on them.

They stared at him. What was he going to do now, shoot them? Once he had shot a South African Prot less than ten feet away, close enough to see the other's face dissolve. But that was with shooting going on all around, running, the incredible noise of battle. That was a different kind of fear, larger, but less complicated than this fear. He did not know what they would do. He could see the terrible betrayal, the terrible sadness in the woman's face. The man's face was blank and that was worse because he did not know what feeling was behind it, what the man might do.

Should he shoot the man?

Then the man backed up a few steps, pulling the woman with him. She looked as if she might say something.

"I have been in *Afrique*," David said. "I have already paid. Please, just walk."

And then they turned and walked away. Just like that.

He waited, rigid, until they had left the parking, gone across the street, walked out of his line of sight. The im from the funeral—Mayla in her black dress—was still sitting on the hood of the Skate. He picked it up, locked the car and went into the bank.

In the elevator up from the parking he had to figure out what to do with the handgun. He tucked it in the waist of his tights and felt foolish pulling on his sweater as the door opened. "Hello Max," he said to the receptionist. "I have to talk to Ms. Ling."

Max called. She was on a call, just a moment.

"Tell her it is an emergency," David said. Max looked at him and nervously adjusted the cuffs of his suit before calling. David was afraid that in a moment the shaking would creep from his knees to his hands. Max pointed down the hall.

It was the first time he had been in her office. Books, real books, a whole wall of them, and leather chairs. There were overhead lights, but on her desk next to her console was a gooseneck lamp with a green glass shade. "I'll get back to you," she was promising and then she cut off the call.

"Two people in the parking, they just tried to, what do you say, make me join their organization. Politics. They wanted me to do something."

"What two people," she said, "what do you mean?"

"What two people! I don't know these people! They have this, ask me if I work for you!" He thrust the paper at her and she took it, frowning.

"They gave you this?" she asked.

"They left it," he said, "I held the gun on them, told them to leave!" He pulled the gun out of his waistband.

She did not look at it, she looked at him. Like the woman with the crucifix, the weight of her look, wanting something from him. Then she keyed the console. "Police please, Corinne Street District."

He was cold. It was so cold here. It was what came after the adrenaline. He crossed his arms thinking, this is it. This is not the army, I do not have to stay. If I want to I can leave.

"Are you okay?" she asked.

"Cold," he said, furious with her. When she had hired him she did not say anything about this.

She called Max, asked him to bring two cups of tea. "What happened," she said, "what did you do?"

"I told them to go away," he said. He put the gun down carefully on her shiny black desk. She blinked.

"Who are these people," she asked. Looking at the gun.

"A South African Catholic," he said. "The people from the casino, from the arrest."

"From the arrest?" she said. "You mean blue and whites?"

"No! I do not mean policemen. I mean two people like us, who are leaving the casino when the man is arrested! You did not tell me this job was like this!"

She said, "Nothing like this ever happened to me before."

Like the man arrested in the casino, saying *There must be some mistake.* "Insurance," he said. "You did not say anything about terrorists, South African Catholics who think they are instruments of God!"

"La Mano de Diós," she said. "Were they from *La Mano de Diós?"*

"I do not know, they did not introduce themselves. I am not an assassin, I do not shoot people, do you understand? I do not know about security, I was a soldier, that was different! I was not even a very good soldier, just so-so. I do not know about politics! This is a mistake, I am not what you think I am!"

Max knocked, brought in tea. "Good night Ms. Ling."

"He should wait," David said. No sense sending the young man out alone. "Maybe people should wait until the police come."

"Max," she said, "someone approached David in the parking, threatened him. Maybe you better have people wait until the police get here, then someone will see you to transit or take you home, all right?"

Max looked at David. Angular face, skin the color of sandalwood and wiry hair that grew close to his head. A sleek young secretary with a job that might get him into the middle class. He didn't look frightened, just wary. It wasn't real for him. It wasn't real for Mayla, either.

"Make yourself a cup of tea, and don't let anyone else up or down the elevator until the police get here. They'll be able to access."

Max didn't want to leave, didn't want to stay. "Yes ma'am," he said finally. He closed the door softly, as if he might waken someone.

"I think I am not suited for this job," David said.

She did not answer.

"It was a period of probation," he insisted. "So I think I should go back." Meph, what to do about the kitten? Stupid to stay in a country because of a kitten.

"All right," she said. The color was bright in her cheeks. She is angry, he thought. But he didn't care.

"I need to hire someone else," she said, her voice low enough that it sounded in the upper registers of normal even in the air mix—or was he just getting accustomed to the way people talked? "I need to replace Tim, can you at least stay until then?"

"Tim can stay," he said harshly. Tim did not seem to want to leave. Tim would probably like all this macho shit about guns and terrorists.

"I really don't want Tim to stay," she said. She was not angry, she was embarrassed. The color in her face was embarrassment.

"What difference does it make, Tim or me?"

"There is a problem with Tim," she said. She wanted to avoid this.

"What?" he insisted, because he was angry and he wanted to push her.

She gestured to the air, not looking at him. "Tim and I, Tim thinks he is . . . that we are having a relationship. You see, I knew Tim before I hired him, we went out a couple of times."

Her discomfort was a palpable thing.

"It is my mistake, really," she said. "I should never have hired him. He said it was only for awhile, that he was going back to Australia. Now he says that he never said that. You see, he came back to Belize to clear up a problem I had with a bank suit, he did me a real favor. I feel like I owe him . . . something. But I'll talk to him, have him arrange the date to leave. Then you can leave. Only a couple of weeks, I promise."

"What about your insurance?" he said, goading her.

"Oh fuck the insurance! I don't care about the insurance. I'll tell them you quit unexpectedly and that I'm trying to replace you. It must happen. A few weeks," she said.

He shrugged.

"Please," she said—pleading like the woman in the parking— "don't mention quitting to Tim."

He wanted to laugh, he had already mentioned quitting to Tim.

But he felt tired, tired of these people and their wanting. It was easiest not to explain he had already said something to Tim. Easiest just to go along.

He sighed. "All right."

4

A Few Simple Things

At the police station, David was seated in front of a pale screen, empty of everything but light. Mayla closed her eyes and the after-image of the pale screen was a red square. She could hear the hiss of the air-circulating system. "We will be monitoring your pulse rate, your eye movements and pupil contraction," the blue and white told David. "We will be showing you ims. If you can identify them, please name them for us."

"This is the same equipment that they use for interrogation?" David asked.

She flinched at the word "interrogation" but did not open her eyes.

The blue and white said, "You are not being interrogated Mr. Dai."

"I understand," David said. "But these—" in his pause she imagined him searching for the English, "I was in the military, they use these things."

She thought of Tumipamba's white coffin and it was there in her mind's eye, tilted up, with Tumipamba watching her from behind the glare of light on the glass. She couldn't get it out of her head so she opened her eyes. The screen was empty and bright, and Tumipamba's coffin was whited out.

People had sat in this room and been interrogated.

If it had been an interrogation, how would they make someone look at the screen? How would they keep someone's eyes open? Cut off their eyelids?

She blinked.

"Have you yourself ever been a subject before?" the blue and white asked David. "Conducted a session?"

David had not.

"Fine. Just relax. You won't feel any discomfort."

The first im was her own face in a less than flattering image. Oh God, it was from her driver's license.

"Mayla Ling," David said, "my employer."

Another im.

"Mr. Talsing, I worked for him in France."

Tim's. A woman he didn't know. Another woman. "Not familiar," David said.

Another woman.

"The President of France," he said, sounding amused.

Mayla let out her breath, not aware until that moment that she had been holding it.

A man.

"Familiar, but I cannot place him."

A square-faced oriental with deep lines around his mouth. "My father, Philippe Dai," he said so softly she leaned forward. Where did they get these images?

More people, some he knew, some he didn't.

Then they told him it was not necessary to talk although he could make any comments he chose. The system would measure the way he reacted and build off of the features he found familiar or resonant to construct her face. He should not try to picture the woman.

David frowned. "Do not picture her?"

"That's really a bit of a trick," the blue and white said, friendly. "It's like the old recipe to turn water into gold. Put it in a big pot on the back of the stove and stir it and stir it, all the time not thinking about a white rhinoceros. After I say it, all you can think of is the white rhino. Now eyes on the screen, Mr. Dai."

Ims began to flicker in front of him. Faces: some light, some dark, and most (but not all) female, shifting in a plastic blur, liquid chins and noses and cheeks and foreheads brightening and shading. They began to show certain characteristics: black eyes looked out, arrested, became fixed, while features shifted around them, melting and moving. Some alchemy measured the way David looked at things, how his pupils expanded, how his eyes moved when the face was familiar, what his heart did. *This* is familiar, their measurements told them, *that* is not.

Voudoun, she thought. Technological voodoo.

He started to turn his head and the blue and white said, "Eyes on the screen, Mr. Dai."

The features became less plastic, solidified. David was leaning away; in the light reflected from the screen she could see his shoulders and hands tense, pushing against the arms of the chair as if he were pushing up and back, over the back of the chair, getting away from the image in front of him. A woman's face was drawn out of him. Pulled out of him. It did not seem possible that they could do this. It did not seem right, or fair.

The ims flickered, slowed, stopped. There was a woman's thin black face with hard round apple cheeks and great dark eyes. David said, "It is the woman at the casino." He turned in his seat to look back at Mayla, "When we had dinner at Aphrodite."

The blue and white looked at her but she could only shake her head.

She couldn't remember the woman at all. Was the memory hiding somewhere in her unconscious? Could they have pulled that face out of her, arising, all unknowing? What else was down there that someone could pull out?

Stir and stir and stir, and at no time think of a white rhinoceros.

They wanted David to register for a course in defensive driving and a course on personal security. She wished he could have stayed while she talked to the blue and whites about what she should do now, but they wanted him to do some ID for their records; retinal scans, DNA samples.

An officer, a blue and white with sergeant's bars on the sleeves of her uniform told Mayla that she had to continue with her life, that she must not allow terrorism to keep her from functioning. The phrases the officer used were phrases from the paper and the vid, so familiar that Mayla heard them in capitals. "If you Allow yourself to Succumb to Fear," the officer told her, "They have Succeeded. They have Disrupted Society. The Only Way to Fight Terrorists is make them Powerless."

On the other hand, she was supposed to take certain precautions. She was supposed to do A Few Simple Things. "Vary your schedule. Leave for work at different times, change the route you take." She lived on a dead-end street, she worked at the bank, no matter how she varied her routine she had to start at the same place and end at the same place.

There was a Delicate Balance between disruption and Normal Common Sense. What, Mayla wondered, would Abnormal Common Sense be?

"Who was the woman who approached David?" she asked.

"Her name is Anna Eminike, she is wanted for a number of charges both here and abroad. We are conducting an investigation and we are closing in on these people. In the meantime, just be a little careful."

Be a Little Careful, Mayla thought. "Is she part of *La Mano de Diós?*"

The blue and white said, "I'm sorry, this matter is under investigation, that is not information I can give out."

"Why is she after me?"

"I'm sorry, Ms. Ling, but during an investigation we cannot talk about the particulars."

Had this woman singled her out because of the im in the newspaper? Or because they had seen her in the casino? But when they'd seen her in the casino, how did they find out who she was? David had told the blue and whites that the woman had said she was an instrument of God, that she was God's surgeon. Wasn't that what *La Mano de Diós* believed? That God told them what to do?

That there was providence in the fall of a sparrow? That God selected them to be the instrument of the sparrow's fall?

"Ms. Ling," the blue and white said, "your dossier indicates you travel quite a bit on business. It might be a good idea to go somewhere for a few days, perhaps the U.S. or Marincite?"

"Mayla," Polly Navarro said. "I'm sorry to hear about your trouble, but glad Marincite could help."

"It's actually a wonderful opportunity to work with your people on the MaTE restructuring," she said.

Polly's office was as formal as a royal court. The door was tall and wooden, like the doors of the Cathedral St. Nicolas. The whole right side of the office was virtual window. The scene was a city.

A secretary brought them coffee. He was a young man in a vanilla suit with amethyst cufflinks and buttons. He had amethyst slips in his eyes, too. He was absolutely silent, like a good waiter. Her coffee tasted like surface coffee. She glanced at the window again, not meaning to, and saw Polly follow her eyes. "Hong Kong?" she asked.

He nodded. "Hong Kong, 2038."

Okay. Although why he would want to look at Hong Kong in that particular year eluded her. "Quite a display," she said.

"Thank you," he said. "I like it." He tapped a little brass control panel set in the desk. "Clear," he said, "orchids."

The window dimmed and came bright, and this time the wall looked into a greenhouse of orchids.

"Clear, Hokkaido." Twisted pine trees and mountains, mist and stone. At least they weren't as bright.

"Clear, Serengeti."

Desert at dusk and below them a muddy drinking hole.

"Impressive," she said. Voice activated. The money spent on this office would probably buy her a house.

"Set," he said. "I like the space in this one."

Lots of it, the plain falling away in a long sweep, darkening to blue in the dusk. Tim would like it, she thought, but it wasn't exactly her taste.

"I wonder if you would be willing to talk to someone here regarding a loan for a city project," Polly said.

For a moment she was surprised. Not that she should have been, deals usually required favors. "Certainly," she said. "Mr. Navarro, First Hawaiian would like very much to establish presence in Marincite in any way possible."

"I'll have him call you. Watch a minute," Polly said, "the lions will come down."

She looked at the window. And after a moment they came, bellies swaying and lean hips rocking, to crouch at Polly Navarro's waterhole and drink with long pink tongues.

Polly Navarro's "someone" came calling. Saad Shamsi was a gazelle-eyed Pakistani. "Just Saad," he said, and added, smiling, "rhymes with 'odd'." He was an aide with the Marincite City Department of Education and Health (he gave her his card). Aide could mean anything. His job may even have been a real job, although aide could mean anything.

He wanted a loan for a nursing school and clinic to be built in an area of town called, whimsically, Castle. "Are you familiar with Castle?" he asked, convincingly sincere. "It's not a very good part of the city. This way we can address two problems at the same time, the need to educate young people and provide jobs, and a way to increase health care."

Politician talk. She dropped the chip into her reader and looked at the figures. She could structure a loan proposal, it wasn't even a very complicated loan. "I don't foresee any problems," she said. There was no reason for Polly to send her this loan, it was a nothing loan.

There was nothing to be understood from Saad-rhymes-with-odd Shamsi, either. He was about her age. He spoke impeccable English, sounded North American rather than Caribbean. Maybe slightly British in his diction but it was hard to say. His suit was appropriate, that kind of neutral gold color that meant he could have bought the suit yesterday or five days ago. Not too expensive, so if he was skimming, he wasn't making big money, or at least not spending it on clothes. Not flashy.

"It looks straightforward," she said.

"Good," he said. "I mean, I didn't expect much problem."

"So why are you working with me?" she asked.

"What do you mean?"

She shrugged. "Anyone could do this loan."

"Mr. Navarro suggested you," Saad said. He was not evasive. He looked at her clear-eyed, his face open.

Maybe Polly really did just want to send some business First Hawaiian's way. This was a token, easy enough.

"Who knows why Mr. Navarro does anything," Saad said. "He sits in the middle of his web and pulls us all together." He shook his head. "Have you spent much time in Marincite?"

"Business trips," she said.

"Maybe I could take all of you around the city some evening?"

Then it will come, Mayla thought, whatever the secret cost of this loan would be. A loan for his mother at low interest. Financing something. "That would be wonderful," she said.

"Do you like jai alai?"

Tim loved jai alai. Terrific, Saad would get some tickets and they would go see some jai alai.

Saad Shamsi collected the three of them that evening after dinner. He didn't seem put off by having to take her security, seemed in fact to get on very well with Tim. He had tickets for good seats, although Mayla didn't know, she had never been to a jai alai match.

Jai alai players leaped, arms top-heavy with *cestas* like flamingo beaks whipping the ball. The games were fast, the slap of feet against the floor, an explosion and a yell. The odds changed constantly and she didn't understand the betting. A player leaped, flicking the ball across the court. His gear was brilliant red and he looked like a barbarian in armor covered at the vulnerable points: head, knees and elbows. He had silver streamers like tinsel tied around his biceps on his *cesta* arm. She wondered if that meant something, but not enough to ask.

It was hard to concentrate on the game. She didn't feel tired, not physically; fatigued, maybe. Eventually he would ask for it: a loan for a company run by a friend or that the administration of the monies for the construction work be handled by another company—selling the loan to him so he made half a percentage point a year.

If he'd just get it over with, then she could be done with this nonsense of jai alai and evenings of entertainment and get on with the MaTE loan. More meetings with Polly Navarro.

She wanted to see him again, wanted to talk to him, the way he had started to talk at the funeral. About terrorists. About security. What would it be like to work for Polly Navarro?

The red player with the silver streamers scooped the ball, whirled and fired it, streamers tracing a fluid arc. Tim went to his feet, he had money on the game.

She felt out of touch. She thought of *La Mano de Diós* and suddenly she could not manage to care about the jai alai game or about Polly Navarro or MaTE.

She glanced to her left just as David looked her way and their eyes met. Nothing in his face. Her face felt the same way, nothing. They were just here, not part of this place at all, two people for whom the game and the excitement meant nothing. And then he quirked a tiny smile and shrugged ever so slightly, just a little gallic twist of his shoulders. "What can you say?" his shoulders said. And she felt herself smile back a bit.

"Secrets?" Saad said, catching her off guard.

He was watching her, too.

Tim looked down, puzzled, and in that moment something must have happened on the court because the crowd around them erupted. She stood up and cheered, too, sliding out from under Saad's gaze. The player in black and green walked to the side to pick up a towel and wipe his face—stage business that athletes use when they are in the spotlight. Off to the side stood the player in red, streamers hanging motionless. He looked bemused.

She knew how he felt.

* * *

Saad was back two days later to talk about the hospital and clinic loan. She had the loan of an office by then, and was started on the business of the MaTE deal.

"Hi," he said from the door, "just who you wanted to see, right?" She rolled her eyes in mock disgust and he came in and sat down. "Ms. Ling," he said, "my most favorite person in the whole world."

"Not because I'm going to give you a sizable chunk of money," she said.

"Of course not," he said.

His office had received quotes from construction firms and he had a change in some of the figures. She plugged the figures into the system. It wasn't a complicated loan at all.

Saad sat in a chair beside the desk, craning a bit to watch her. "Is that all?" he asked.

"That's it," she said.

"That's slap," he said. American slang, she knew it from the vid.

"What can I say?" she said.

"You're amazing," he said, mock serious.

"Your English is amazing."

He shrugged. Apparently he knew his English was good. It was casual and fast, and he always caught what she was saying. Bilingual. She wanted to know where he learned.

"I studied it at home, in Pakistan, and I lived in the U.S. for awhile," off hand, slightly embarrassed.

"Oh yeah?" she asked, "where did you live?"

"Cincinnati, Ohio," he said, and she laughed at the unexpectedness of it.

"That's funny?" he asked.

"Why Cincinnati, Ohio?"

"Actually," he said, "I lived in Los Angeles for a year, and then the company I worked for transferred me to Cincinnati. I liked Cincinnati." That sounded a little defensive. But he was smiling, he knew she had expected him to say someplace like New York or Miami.

"I'm sure it's a lovely town," she said.

"It is," he said, emphatic. "Believe it or not, I want to go back there. I want to go back to Cincinnati, Ohio, marry a blonde American girl, and have three perfect blonde daughters."

She shook her head. "Genetics are not on your side."

He sighed. "Biology is destiny, I know."

"So why did you leave?" she asked. "Did you get transferred here?" Marincite could have a subsidiary in Cincinnati, Ohio.

"No," he said, "the U.S. Immigration Department informed me that my presence in the U.S. was no longer an asset."

That surprised her, since he'd had a job.

"The U.S. says that you can't take jobs from American citizens. You have to be an engineer or a scientist or something, then they let you stay because there are never enough of those people. But not an administrator, a manager of a finance department." He looked down at his hands, now made pensive. She was sorry she had asked.

"Well," she said, "if those are the only changes to the loan you have, then we're still on our way. I'll have papers any time you want."

"I'll take them now," he said. "I can bring them back tomorrow with signatures."

She hadn't expected that, it was too easy. "You want them now?" she asked.

"Sure," he said. He sounded so American.

She printed them out and handed them to him. That was it? No catch? Saad Shamsi *was* odd if there wasn't a catch.

He looked through them and she felt her shoulders tense, waiting for him to say casually, "I have a friend. . . ."

"Looks good," he said.

"Do you foresee any problems?" she asked.

"What do you mean?" he asked.

"Getting signatures?"

He looked puzzled. "It's a pretty straightforward loan, isn't it?"

It was. Of course it was. Or would be in a place like the U.S. where people didn't pay each other to do business. "Unless someone wouldn't be in or something," she said.

"Oh," he said, "no, no problems. We've got a meeting tomorrow on the clinic so I can get this taken care of then. If I can't get all the signatures tomorrow I can bring the papers back to you Friday, can't I?"

Of course he could.

That was it. All this time she had been waiting and that was it. The jai alai, reading motives into everything he did and said . . . he was just a nice guy. Oh, *Madre de Diós*, was she blushing? It wasn't her fault. It was the way business usually happened in Julia, she wasn't accustomed to Marincite. She had always heard Marincite was worse than Julia, but maybe that wasn't true at all, with the Uncles around keeping watch.

He stood up and buttoned his jacket. "Hey," he said.

"Hey," she echoed. "What?"

"Would you like to go to dinner with me, tonight?"

Would she like to go to dinner with Saad-rhymes-with-odd Shamsi? Well, sure. Why not? She hadn't been exactly fair to him. "Okay," she said. "That would be nice."

"Great," he said, "absolutely slap."

She laughed. What a decent, nice guy, she thought when he left. A date. How long had it been since she'd had a date? Months, maybe over a year. Not that she expected anything, she couldn't expect anything, he lived in Marincite and she lived in Julia and a relationship would be impossible over that distance. Besides, it was stupid to even start thinking about a relationship when he had just asked her for dinner.

It would solve all of her problems with Tim if she were dating. He would give up and leave. David wouldn't care, and he wanted to leave anyway.

Insane, all these thoughts running through her head, worrying about the equation of Saad, Tim and David. It was just a dinner date. Nothing more.

It would be wonderful to be out on a date.

* * *

Mayla was unprepared for how she felt when she saw him at the door to the suite. She smiled too much, she was too happy. "Hi, come in a moment." She wished this were over with, that this were the second or even the third time they were going out. It would all be easier then. "I'm sorry, David has to go with us," she said. Quickly, "He doesn't have to eat with us, just go—" Saad looked taken aback, "—because of the insurance and all of that."

"No problem," he said. Sweet relief.

Still awkward, though, to go out with Saad and have David in tow. She had never had to worry about that before because until she had been promoted she had never been required to have security. At least David wasn't Tim. David was quiet.

David stood just behind them on the people mover, his body angled away, watching the bright shops—in Central the lights were dimmed at second shift to simulate dusk.

She wished Saad Shamsi would take her hand. She wanted a hug. It was too soon, and if he had taken her hand then her longing would be destroyed because he would be forward, he would be pressuring her into an intimacy that didn't exist yet. He would destroy all trust. And besides, David was behind them, a chaperon carefully not watching them. She was too lonely, it was dangerous to go out to dinner with this man when she was so lonely.

She was thinking about what if something developed between her and Saad. She was thinking it was possible, he was in some ways so North American. Not a Caribbean male who would be threatened by her own success. And she liked him, he was funny and smart. She hadn't been fair to him at first. Some day she would tell him that. He would come to Julia some weekends and stay with her, she would come to Marincite some weekends and stay with him.

Maybe she would move to Marincite. She could imagine living here, and she could probably get a job with Marincite Corp.

She wondered what kind of family he had back in Pakistan. A gaggle of doe-eyed sisters in saris who spoke no English? Was he a cultural stranger to his family? Were they cosmopolitan?

She knew they were just going out to dinner.

She wasn't really having these thoughts one at a time, they were kind of all jumbled up with standing here next to Saad, who was quiet because her bodyguard was standing behind them, pretending not to pay attention to them.

The restaurant was American. She wasn't really surprised.

"I will wait there," David pointed to a bench on the street. He showed her his book, something in French.

While they were waiting to be seated Saad said, "Isn't he allowed to eat?"

"He ate before we came," Mayla said.

Saad nodded.

"It's his job," she said.

"That's why there are two of them?" Saad said. "Days and evenings?"

"Well, no," she said. "Tim is quitting. David is taking over."

"Tim is getting a different job?"

"Tim isn't really security. It's complicated," she said. She wasn't going to explain Tim to Saad, certainly not now.

The dinner lurched along. They neither of them seemed to know how to conduct a conversation. It's a first date, Mayla thought. How could they save this? Through the menu bound in hunter green, and the too-expensive chowder and her glass of wine and his beer and crippling onward. He wasn't funny or quick and her head was empty.

It was her, he was usually different. Things had started wrong by having David come along. She should get things back to the way they had been in the afternoon when Saad had been easy to talk to but she didn't know how.

"Do you like Marincite?" she asked.

"It's all right," he said.

"It's not Cincinnati, Ohio," she said.

"No," he said. That was all, just "no." No quip.

"It's not like Julia, either," she said. "In some ways it's more like the U.S."

"How do you mean?"

"Well, it's sort of better organized. There's less bribery, maybe." Like you, she thought, although she didn't dare say it. He didn't understand, how could he? "In Julia, everything is paybacks and kickbacks and somebody has his hand in someone else's pocket. I know that happens in Marincite, too, but Marincite is different."

"I don't think Marincite is like the U.S."

"It's not, really," she said. "It's run by Marincite Corp., you're really not allowed to breathe without permission—"

"Air tax," he said, grinning. The old joke, in Caribe you even had to pay for the air you breathe.

"But Marincite keeps everybody running by company regulations, which is kind of honest. Julia's not like that."

"Sure," he said, although she couldn't tell if he really agreed with her or was just being agreeable.

"I was thinking of moving here," she said, "you know, getting a job with Marincite Corp." Which was stupid, because if she moved here, she would have to have a job with Marincite Corp. "I've been having some trouble in Julia, I've become a target of some, you know, political people."

"You?" Saad said. "I mean, not that you don't have a good job, but, I mean. . . ."

"I'm not important," she said. "Don't worry, I'm not insulted."

He grinned. "I mean, I think you're important, after all, you're doing this loan for me."

She felt her face crinkle with pleasure at his joke. "Well, my grandfather started First Hawaiian, that's the only angle that the police can come up with. But I guess that Marincite isn't really any safer than Julia. Look what happened to poor Tumipamba."

Saad had to think a second. "Oh, yeah. Right, the guy, the CFO."

She nodded. "If politicals could get to him. . . ."

"If it was politicals," Saad said.

"Yeah?" she said. "I heard something about gambling debts."

"I didn't hear that. But I think there's a shakedown going on at the upper levels of Marincite Corp."

"You think they're killing their own execs?"

"Hey," Saad said, "I don't know. And the walls have ears."

Another dead space. Too serious, she thought. She should have kept things light.

When dinner arrived she was grateful for the business of putting sour cream and butter on her potato. For the occupation of eating.

"I ah, I hate to bring up business at dinner," Saad said, "but I have a friend and he and I are trying to get something started and I was wondering if we might be able to talk to you about a loan?"

"A loan?"

He nodded.

"What kind of loan?" she asked, gone still inside. Suspended and waiting.

"For a business," he said. "I was wondering if maybe you could come with me and meet my friend, we could talk about it at the shop."

Not an answer, she thought, which was a different kind of answer. "Why don't we talk about this at the office tomorrow?"

"The shop isn't far," he said.

"I don't usually do business away from the office."

"We could get it over with."

"When?" she said. Maybe she wasn't being fair again. Maybe he would say Saturday or Monday, after the papers for the clinic loan would be signed.

"Tonight?" he was eager. "Would that be all right? It wouldn't take long."

No, she thought. No no no. "How about Friday?" she said. Hoping he would say "sure."

"Really," he said. "Tonight might be a better time."

"Or there might be trouble getting signatures on the loan papers?" she said. Rude, angry with him.

He didn't say anything, but it was true.

"Goddamn you," she said. And then, "Goddamn you, you have a lot of nerve."

"Yeah," he said. No explanation, no apology.

"Why did you wait until the night before the papers were signed!"

"Because the loan would almost be in your hand and it would be harder for you to say 'no'."

"What makes you think I need this loan? Do you have any idea how big a deal the Marincite loan is, and how really tiny your piddling clinic is?"

"It's all Marincite," he said. "This whole city is all Marincite."

Then she remembered that Polly Navarro had sent Saad.

She sighed. "Okay. Let's go see this friend."

There were lots of young people out on the street. She was glad of the noise, glad to have David behind her because it all kept Saad from saying much, just things like "cross here."

Mayla was so angry at herself. So stupid. All that fine speech about how Marincite was different. People don't borrow money from stupid bankers.

Saad took them down one of the hubs a couple of levels. "We have to take the chute," he said.

"Public transportation," Mayla explained to David.

The walkway back to the station was tiled in Marincite maroon and cream and they stood on the platform in silence. David looked at her, a silent question. "We're working," she said.

"Pardon me?"

"Bank business," she said.

Saad stared down the tunnel, at the concrete platform, anywhere but at her.

Served him right, she thought.

The chute was a string of seats, like an amusement park ride. Each pair of seats had a smoke-colored canopy. The one that came into the station was almost empty, only a woman with a string bag full of groceries near the front. Mayla waited until Saad started to climb in and then sat down in the seat behind him. David frowned but got in with her.

When the canopy came down the dome light came on. Saad

glanced back, his face distorted by the plastic. She should have smiled but she looked down at her hands until the chute jerked forward. When she looked up it was at the back of Saad's head.

They went into the dark of the tunnel. In front of them was a string of dome lights, each made hazier by the succeeding layers of plastic canopies. The chute curved down.

"What is wrong?" David asked.

"Nothing," she said. "It's just business."

He looked at her a moment and then shrugged. "Okay."

"In my business," she said, "in this country, if you're going to do a loan for someone you have to do them a favor."

He smiled. "I think that when you get a loan, the bank does you a favor, no?"

"Maybe for regular people," she said. "Not for businesses."

"Ah," he said. "What kind of favor?"

"He wants a loan for a business he is starting up. Either it won't have any credit or it'll be illegal," she said.

"You do that?" he said, surprised. He regretted it. "I mean, it is not my affair."

"No," she said, "it is your affair, in a way. I mean, considering your job."

He didn't seem to care for that.

The string began to slow and curve upward and for a moment the dome lights in the front seemed to brighten as they curved above the canopy behind them. Then they leveled off. The dome light flicked out and David grabbed her arm, but then they came into the lighted station.

David laughed nervously, embarrassed.

The tile looked green and yellow through the plastic but when it lifted she could see that they were actually blue and white. Saad stood up, "This is our stop," he said.

On the wall it said "Cathedral."

One of the overheads was out at the exit and the tunnel beyond it looked dark. The tiles on the wall were cracked and scratched and painted with angry graffiti she couldn't read. David balked a moment, "Are you sure we are in the right place?"

"Why don't we do this in the office?" she said to Saad.

"We're almost there," he said. "You can meet my partner this way."

A few feet farther and the light was back, although dim. The tunnel smelled of urine and mildew. Then a flight of stairs and they were outside on the street. Mayla's shoulders were hunched and she had to make a conscious effort to loosen them.

There were lots of young people here in this hub, lots of couples. The kids were all dressed slap, some of the girls shining as if they were wet, looking like the pop singer, what-was-her-name, DanHe. David was tense, watching everything.

Saad seemed at home, although he was dressed too well to fit in. Following, watching the bare-armed boys standing corners, who were watching them, Mayla felt painfully obvious.

"It's not far," Saad said.

Two streets over and he stopped at a heavy, industrial looking door and opened it with a key. They followed him up narrow, badly lit stairs to what looked like a manufacturing loft, mostly empty except for a couple of workbenches against the wall. At the end were a couple of offices, one with a light on.

Saad knocked on the door and then opened it without waiting. There were two people waiting. One was a young black girl, street pretty and feral, with a mane of tawny hair tipped in black. The other was an anglo, thick and middle-aged, with a moustache. "Saad," he said, "this is your banker?"

"Right," Saad said.

"Okay," Moustache said, "go get yourself a cup of coffee. *Café*," to the girl, and then to Mayla, "decaffeinated?"

"No, thank you," she said.

"Antoinette will take care of Saad and your friend," Moustache said.

"No," Mayla said, "this is my security, he has to stay with me."

The girl took her feet off the desk and stood up. Moustache thought about it a moment and then shrugged. "Okay," he said. Then to the girl and Saad, *"Vamos."*

"I don't think—" Saad started.

"That's right," Moustache said, "you don't think. Go on."

Saad hesitated and the girl laughed, *"Viene chico."* Mayla didn't know if Saad understood Spanish or not, but he gave in and followed her out of the office.

"So you are a banker," Moustache said. "Pretty little blanc. What bank? The chico told me but I don't remember."

Moustache had brown hair and was fairer than she was—she thought he might be Argentine. "First Hawaiian," she said. David was behind her and she was glad he was there.

"Did the chico tell you about the business?" Moustache gestured at the office. "It's a little manufacturing concern. We need some working capital to get started."

"What kind of manufacturing?" she asked. As if it mattered.

"Jewelry," he said.

Jewelry, she thought. Right. Who gave a damn about jewelry? "What just exactly is the problem?"

"Eh?" he said, frowning.

"With the loan," she said, impatient, wanting to be out of here. "What's the problem? Do you have a credit statement? Or is it *en la sombra?"*

Moustache flinched. Apparently anglo women bankers weren't supposed to say things like *en la sombra,* "in the dark." Or maybe he just didn't expect her to come out point blank and ask if it was illegal.

"There is a problem," he said in Spanish. There was always a problem. With papers, he explained. Her Spanish wasn't good but she could follow him well enough.

"¿Una problema con Los Tontons?" "A problem with the Uncles?" she asked. If Marine Security wasn't in on it she didn't want anything to do with it.

Oh, no no no, Moustache said, the Uncles were fine, everything had been arranged with the Uncles.

In English she said, "Do you have a front?"

"*¿Qué?*"

"A front," she said. "A business statement, balance sheet, for whatever this company is supposed to be. Something I can use as a credit statement at the bank."

"Ah!" Moustache understood, "*¡La barba!*" "The beard." "*Sí, yo lo tengo.*" He had a chip and hard copy and passed it to her. The hard copy was the paperwork for a concern that made facsimiles of Incan and Aztec jewelry pieces using the lost wax technique. The facsimiles would be sold in the United States. Each piece would be made by hand.

She wondered what the business was. Caribe was an open gold market, like India, so there were no restrictions on buying and selling gold and the price wasn't regulated. Maybe fraud? Gold labeled fourteen carat when it was really eight? Or the pieces would be sold as the actual items rather than reproductions? Or maybe nothing connected to jewelry at all.

"How much?" she asked.

"200,000cr," he said and started to say more but Saad was in the door. "What is it?" he said, brusque.

"Nothing," Saad said. "I'm just your partner, remember?"

"You have done your part," Moustache said. "Now let me do mine."

"I'm not going to say anything, I'm just going to listen, okay?"

"I tell you everything."

"So if I'm here, then you don't have to tell me."

Moustache was irritated. Mayla glanced back at David, he looked very tense. "Okay," Moustache said to Mayla, "this is how the money will be handled."

He wanted the money to come through a numbered credit account, and the mailing address to be a mail drop. Two-bit, crooked little game, she thought. What was she doing here? She didn't handle legitimate loans this small. She didn't like Moustache, she was royally sick of Saad-rhymes-with-odd Shamsi. And she was offended.

Bankers were not supposed to be offendable. The credit committee wouldn't have any trouble with this, as long as the credit statement checked out—and she knew it would. With the papers for the front, the bank could pretend ignorance in the event something happened, could even claim fraud.

"I have to put this through the credit committee," she said. "I won't know until the bank approves it. But it should be fine."

"Excellent," Moustache said. "Thank you for coming. If you need to get in touch with me, you may do so through Saad."

She didn't have any intention of getting in touch with him. She had done some strange things to get loans, but she had never sat in a manufacturing loft in the wrong part of town. If Saad had wanted to buy the loan that would have been fine. People did that. People came to her office. But this was two-bit, shoddy, appalling.

The girl was sitting on one of the bare work tables in the loft, swinging her legs. She was dressed like a pop vid star; lynx-haired, black industrial nonskid top, rainproof boots. Too much makeup. Not much jewelry, though, just a plain bracelet. She was leaning back on her arms and the bracelet was turned around so the flat black plate was pressed against the inside of her wrist. The bracelet struck Mayla as odd, but she wasn't up on industrial chic. The girl looked at Mayla, looked down at her own wrist and laughed. *"Un otra pollo,"* she said to Moustache. "Another chicken."

"Shut up," Moustache said.

"Hasta luego, hermana," the girl said, "See you later, sister," and laughed again.

"Yo no soy tu hermana," Mayla said. "I'm not your sister."

"Va a la oficina," Moustache said, the way someone would tell a child to go to their room, but the girl didn't move. She was still sitting on the table, watching them, while Mayla promised she would get back to Saad when she had heard from the credit committee.

Saad took them down to the street. "Go straight for three blocks, then turn left." He pointed, not looking at her. "That'll take you to the chute." At least he had the decency to be embarrassed.

David was still, looking up and down the street.

The boys were still on the corner, watching, and there was a swirl of Indian dance music from the Indian restaurant across from them, light spilling through the beaded doorway. A little street cleaner swished up the street, leaving a black trail that reflected the overhead lights.

"The girl," David said, "she was wearing a bracelet, how do you say it, retro-action, ah, you know, stimulation neural." His inflection was French.

For a moment it didn't mean anything to her. Stimulation neural, neural stimulation. Then it did. A self-stimulating system, a neuro-feedback bracelet. It set up feedback to stimulate the wearer's own nervous system, banish fatigue, increase awareness and induce a mild state of euphoria.

A goddamned slave bracelet.

That was the jewelry business, making slave bracelets. Extremely addicting. "Christ," Mayla said. "You're sure?" But as soon as she understood him she knew it was true.

"I have never seen one before, except on the vid," David said. "Maybe that is not what it is."

"Did you understand what they wanted?" Mayla said.

"They want money, for this business, yes?"

Yes. Oh yes. Oh Christ. Oh *Madre de Diós.* It wasn't illegal for her to cut the loan because they had never told her what they were going to do. And their papers would check out. Oh, sure, they would check out.

"What are you going to do?" David asked.

"I don't know," she said.

"Ah," David said. Nothing else, just "ah." As if she had told him something.

The beads clattered across the street and out of the restaurant came two boys and a girl, her bright hair burgundy under the light. She was stumbling and the boys had hold of her arms. They were laughing and she was laughing, but hers was a high, nervous laugh, the sound of a drunk who didn't quite know what the joke was.

"You're okay," one of the boys said, a delicate-looking Indian boy whose bare arms were smooth and muscled.

"I'm fine," she said.

"Oh yeah," the other boy said. "You're *fine*. Come on."

"I have to go home now," she said. "I have to go home." The boys were laughing. She flicked her hair back and the red dot of her caste mark stood like a stigmata on her forehead, the color of her dyed hair. "I have to go home now," she said helplessly.

"You're okay," the first boy said, looking over her at the other boy.

The boys on the corner were still watching Mayla and David. But then an intoxicated girl wouldn't be very interesting to them.

David was waiting, his face neutral, the way it had been in the jai alai game. What did all this look like to him? Down here in the wrong part of Marincite, making loan deals with people who fabricated illegal neural-stimulation devices.

She had never done anything like this in her life.

"We should not stay here," David said quietly.

Her boots were meant to be worn to a nice restaurant, not for the streets of Cathedral in Marincite. They clicked as she walked. David's sandals were noiseless. David was mostly noiseless. Carefully unobtrusive.

"The boys are walking behind us," he said, *sotto voce*. "Do not turn around. I think they are just bored."

"Okay," she said, but her voice was too small for him to hear. Not that it mattered. Click click click click. Her boots were so damned loud. A target. Why hadn't Saad arranged the loan in her office? An amateur. It was all just too wrong. Slave bracelets.

What was she doing here?

In thirty minutes she would be back at her room, and this would all be over.

She wanted to go home. She wanted to sleep in her own bed. She was afraid of this place. She hated Marincite.

It was a longer walk than the way they had come, but at least they didn't have to go through the tunnel the way they had come out.

"Are they still following us?" she asked.

"I do not think so," David said. "I think, you know, they are just bored."

White tile on the walls with blue letters—Cathedral.

What the hell was she doing here? It's your job, she thought. She didn't want to get pulled into this. What if they wanted more? The bank would love it, a foothold in Marincite. As long as they could keep their paperwork clean. But she didn't want it, didn't want Saad Shamsi or Moustache in her office. It was too easy to imagine, a couple of years from now, being in bed with these people. If she continued in A&M, if she kept getting larger loans, what kind of people was she going to get into bed with?

Danny Tumipamba in his coffin. Who had he been in bed with?

"It isn't worth it," she said. And as soon as she did she felt a faint trembling through the soles of her feet. The chute coming to take her out of here. A sign, a portent, a reward from on high. God played dice with the universe, generating random numbers, or maybe only almost random numbers.

David looked at her, curious.

"I'm not doing the loan," she said.

"Ah," he said, not surprised.

"What kind of problems?" Saad said. "With the paperwork? I can call someone, get it cleaned up, whatever it is."

"No," Mayla said. "It's not that. I just think you need another banker."

"What's the problem?"

You lie down with dogs, you get up with fleas, she thought. And yet, she could make up a problem, something small, and he could go off and get it fixed up and then she would make the two loans, Moustache's and the clinic.

"You think it won't pan out? It'll be fine," Saad said. "The bank is clean."

"I don't like your business partner," Mayla said.

"And what is that supposed to mean?" He sat down in a chair, his knees wide. "It's some kind of popularity contest? He has the strings and the expertise. You think I know anything about manufacturing that stuff?"

"How did you get into this?"

"Everyone has a racket in this city. Everyone."

"So you had to have one, too," she said. "Don't you realize that once you get into bed with these people they mark you? You never get out again?"

"Wrong," he said. "One time is all I need. Three million in U.S. dollars. Then I qualify for resident alien status."

"Oh, right," she said. "A blonde wife and three blonde daughters in Cincinnati, Ohio."

"That was a joke," he said.

"Well, I'm not going to emigrate to Cincinnati, Ohio, Saad. This is my home. And I don't have any desire to crawl between the sheets with your partner."

"So you're clean," he said. "Everything you've ever done is clean."

"What difference does it make," she said. "Whether I'm clean or not, right now I'm telling you to find another banker."

He ran his hands over his hair. "Okay," he said.

She waited for him to say more.

"What else do you want me to do?" he said. "If you won't touch the deal, you won't touch the deal. I'll take my clinic loan to someone else. Someone in Marincite."

She wanted to go home. The longing for her own house, her own kitchen and living room and bedroom, drowned her, and then washed off her. Time to go home, she thought.

"I'm sorry," she said. "I hope you get to Cincinnati."

He looked at her, a gazelle-eyed Pakistani, Saad-rhymes-with-odd. "Polly Navarro will hear about this," he said.

The MaTE loan was big, too big for Polly to jeopardize it for something like this, wasn't it?

"Let me think about it and get back to you," she said.

"Don't take too long," he said.

The secretary ushered her in to Polly's office. This time the suit was cinammon and the cuffs and slips in his eyes were tourmaline green. Polly had his back to her, working at a console, and he glanced back over his shoulder, his face flat.

"I'm sorry to bother you," she said.

He didn't let her off the hook, didn't say it was all right, just wheeled his chair around.

"I need to get back to Julia," she said. Work piling up there, and she needed some of the bank's resources to work on the MaTE loan, too.

Hong Kong was out the window. If it had been the lions coming down to drink then she would have been worried, but didn't Hong Kong just mean "Business is business"? She waited for him to bring it up, obliquely. Something about how were her other leads in the city going, or was First Hawaiian picking up some business in Marincite.

"We'll see you soon, then," Polly said.

It would be all right when she got home. Things would be normal.

So she went back to work. Up the elevator, gray, bone and red tweed reflecting in the polished elevator door. She ran the paperwork through for the renewal of a note for Asset Corp., talked on the phone about the possibility of upping a line of credit and ran it through to see what the credit committee would think of the numbers. With one thing and another she was there until after six, and when she came down the hall she saw David sitting in reception, reading.

He stood up as she came down the hall, sticking one thumb in his book to mark the page.

"Good evening, David."

"Good evening, Mayla."

Max was gone for the evening, but the elevator recognized David so he palmed it and they waited. So ordinary. Onto the elevator.

"I'll get the car," he said when the door opened.

She didn't want to wait so she said, "Don't bother."

"Busy this afternoon?" he asked.

"Not so bad—"

He shoved her behind one of the concrete supports. She hit it with both palms, holding it and he kept pushing, pushing her down. She didn't even realize she'd heard the shot. In fact, what she heard first was the shattering of the back window of the car behind them and she thought—there's a bomb in the car.

Everything was so normal and she had the insane desire to ignore it, to step backwards, into normality.

The heel of her hand scraped along concrete, the air tasted of dry concrete dust. His hand was between her shoulder blades, holding her down. He sprinted to the next pillar, his run liquid if uneven with his bad knee, and she could still feel his hand between her shoulder blades, although when she concentrated she could feel that it was gone, that her skin just remembered it. Time to think of all this, but outside of time. She watched him flatten against the concrete support, he had a gun, where had he been wearing the gun?

He held the gun out, aimed, it jumped twice, and then he dropped but did not fall. Afterwards she could not remember hearing the sound of those two shots. It must have shattered that concrete garage, echoed. An engine hummed, whined into high gear, she heard that. The headlights flashed across the wall and towards the exit. The car was gone.

Then she ground her teeth. She could make a noise and she tried, and for a moment nothing would come, but then she managed, "David?" And she was back into time. Then she was afraid.

David stood from his crouch, unhurt. Until he stood up it hadn't occurred to her that he might be. He came back, looking over his shoulder, around the garage.

"You are all right," he said.

"Yes," she said clearly, and then realized that she was, and that this had happened to her. She didn't know what it meant that it had happened to her. "Yes, I am."

He stood and looked at where the car had disappeared.

"Are you?" she asked.

"What?"

Every sentence hung in the air, unconnected to the others. "Are you all right?"

"Yes," he said, standing above her, tension making him all cord and wire. His eyes followed the walls of the garage all the way around and if she tried it was as if she could see where he was looking. He held the gun pointed up and away in a manner that made her think he knew how to use a gun, the way cops do on the vid. Then he looked down and frowned and helped her up, looked at her hand where she had scraped it. His fingers were cool, cradling her hand.

"I didn't do anything," she said, apologizing. "I just sat there."

"You did fine," he soothed.

"I didn't even know what was going on."

"Nobody does the first time." He smiled. "It is like sex. But it is all right now." Still watching he put his hand in the small of her back— like we're dancing, she thought—and walked her to the car.

"Looks like you're earning your keep," she said, trying to joke. Grace under pressure and all that.

He opened her door. "I did not do right," he said.

"You did fine," she said.

He slammed the car door, surely that was not as loud as those two shots, but she couldn't find them in her memory. "I did not go get the car," he said. "I should get the car, not walk with you."

"I told you to do that. I did that, and I didn't do anything at all when they were shooting. They could have done anything." They could have killed her, the stupid bystander in the background of the im, the one with her mouth open, not running, not ducking, just standing there, the one that she always looked at and thought, "I wouldn't be like that."

"Mayla," he said, "you aren't supposed to do anything except stay out of the way." He put the car in gear.

"Oh God," she said.

He put the car back in park and leaned across the gearstick. "It's all right," he said, putting his arm around her shoulders. His shoulder, even leaning across the gearstick, was bony and solid. "It's over." She wanted to be reassured.

His heart was beating, she could hear it with her ear against him. "You're scared, too." That was a relief, maybe she could learn how to know what to do even when she was scared, although she hadn't been scared, she hadn't been anything.

Anna Eminike did this, all the time. What kind of person would have a life like this? What kind of person would willingly be this afraid?

Anna Eminike was probably in that car. She felt sick.

"Don't worry," he said, "we'll go to the police."

She wanted to say that nothing like this had ever happened to her, she wanted to protest the outrage. It sounded so banal she didn't say anything.

5

Mephistofeles

The police station was as cold inside as it was outside on the street—but every place in Caribe was cold, David just always expected it to be warmer. At the high front desk the uniformed sergeant was talking to another officer in tan and the console was chiming a call. The sergeant gestured as he talked, "I've got five people on it already, but they're telling me to send another team out, what am I supposed to do?"

"I hate that son of a bitch, Claude," the uniformed officer said, "I told you, I don't want to work under him."

The sergeant raised his voice over the chirp of the console. "I know, I know, but if I don't send you out, Mardalin will."

Goddamn frigging third-world country, David thought. He was still full of the anger that came with adrenaline.

"What am I supposed to say?" Mayla asked softly.

"Tell him there was a shooting," David said.

"It sounds like we fell out over a pachinko debt or something." Her voice quivered on the edge of control. He thought about putting his arm around her but that would probably start her crying. He wished the sergeant would answer the call.

"I'll explain," he said.

She shook her head. "I should."

Maybe it made her feel more in control. She stood at the front of the desk until the sergeant waved off the man in tan. "Officer," she said, "My name is Mayla Ling, I'm an executive with First Hawaiian, and someone just shot at me."

"I'm sorry," he said, over the insistent call, "What did you say your name was?"

"Mayla Ling."

David wondered if the call was an emergency. Why didn't they have someone else answer?

"Can you spell it for me? Last name first." He keyed her name into his console and picked up the call while he rifled through screens.

"He's checking my credit record," Mayla said. David smiled back. She was trying. His smile was a crocodile smile to hide his anger.

One of the walls was broken as if it had been kicked in and there was a piece of plastic and some tools on the floor. The color scheme was a kind of grimy institutional rose. He'd seen army bases in Africa that looked better than this. The sergeant transferred the call.

"Ms. Ling," the desk officer said, "Someone will be out in a moment."

No maintenance. No sense of urgency. They stood. David's knee ached. A shooting, he thought, and these people are unconcerned. Terrorists were shooting at people, and he and Mayla were waiting, as if they were at the doctor's office or something. Too much violence, these people were so jaded by violence they didn't even respond. Like Africa, this rundown police station and the feeling that there was too little money and no energy.

It was fifteen minutes before a woman in street clothes came out and introduced herself as Sergeant Andre-Baptiste. She took them down a hall lined with old plastic filing cabinets, then through a maze of cubicles. The big room full of cubicles was the same dirty rose as the front. Most of the desks were dark. Well, it was after six. David counted aisles, they turned right at the fourth and hers was the first cubicle. Her name-sign was stuck on top of the chest-high wall of the cubicle. The 'p' in Andre-Baptiste was missing.

She didn't look Haitian, even if she had a Haitian name; her hair was fine, pale brown, crinkly, and her skin was the color of her hair. Her eyes were spaced too wide. She motioned towards the chair by the desk and Mayla hesitated, then sat down. Sergeant Andre-Baptiste flicked through screens and said (apparently to the screen),

"This interview is being recorded, do you understand that a rec is being made of everything you say? Please answer vocally."

"Yes," Mayla said.

"You just had an incident, didn't you?"

Incident?

"Yes," Mayla said, "two people approached David in the parking at work, what, a week ago?"

Ah, an "incident" was something reported to the police. Was a shooting an "incident" or was there some sort of scale? Maybe it was an "occurrence"?

The sergeant looked up. "You're Jean David Dai?"

"Yes ma'am."

In island-accented French she asked. "How do you like Caribe?"

"It's all right." For Mayla's benefit he added in English, "But cold."

"Do you speak French?" the sergeant asked Mayla.

Mayla shook her head.

"I was just asking your bodyguard how he liked it here."

"Your family is Haitian?" Mayla asked, her voice polite, faintly artificial.

He looked around the cubicle as they talked, wishing he could sit down. Caribe, it was insane. Except he thought insane was actually a legal description that meant unable to distinguish between right and wrong. It was possible to be quite crazy and still know that what you were doing was wrong. As a diseased society, did Caribe know it was wrong?

Were they going to do that business of identification, as they had done with the woman? He hoped not, he had not seen anyone. It made him uncomfortable to have reactions he could not control tapped. It was strange, to sit there and watch that face form. A kind of theft. Was it the !Kung, the bushmen of Africa, who had once believed that taking an im would steal the subject's soul?

Africa. He wasn't going to think about Africa. This was not Africa, this was Caribe, and he was going to go home in a few weeks.

"Can you tell me what happened?" Sergeant Andre-Baptiste asked Mayla.

"David saw more than I did," Mayla said. "I cowered."

"That's good, people who cower live longer. I'll ask Mr. Dai what he remembers but I need your answer, too."

She should separate us, David thought. Compare our answers and see how our stories are different: not let us prompt each other, not let me tailor my story to fit Mayla's. Basic military procedure with disciplinary and criminal matters and prisoners of war.

"I don't remember anything, really," Mayla said. "I got off work and went down to the parking—"

"What time did you leave work?"

"A little after six?" She looked at him to confirm. He kept his face blank and waited for the sergeant to say that she wanted Mayla's estimation, but she didn't. She just typed two-fingered and they waited for her.

"Sergeant," he said, "are you going to send someone to the parking?"

The sergeant shrugged. "They're gone now, I'll send someone down but they won't find anything."

"Someone tried to shoot Ms. Ling," David said.

"Probably *La Mano de Diós*," she said conversationally. Of course, it's just a terrorist organization, he thought. These people! "So," she continued, "you finished work at a little after six, is that the time that you usually leave?"

"Sometimes, sometimes earlier, sometimes I work late. I don't really work an eight-to-five job, and you, I mean the police told me to vary my schedule so I have been."

"Wait," David said. "What are you going to do? I should not be here while you have her, what do you call it, *deposition*."

"You're not being accused of anything," the sergeant said.

"But it will not be clean," David said. "I will hear her story."

Sergeant Andre-Baptiste frowned. "I'm aware of procedure. I don't think that kind of formality is necessary under the circumstances."

"You are not sending anyone down there. These are terrorists."

"Mr. Dai," the sergeant said, "I know these are terrorists, and you are frightened but this day the Deputy Minister of Finance's home was blown up and eleven people died. This department is strained trying to deal with that. You were not hurt so they intend to frighten you, not to kill, or you would both be dead. If I made a fuss every time some group decided to harass an executive I would tie up this entire police force and that would be doing exactly what these people want."

"So you treat this as if it were adolescents drinking, or a skid stopping traffic?" David asked. He would start to shake. He always did this, after he got angry would come the shakes.

"We will check it out and make a note in the file," she said, coolly. "If you are contacted by this group, please, you tell us."

"Third-world country, third-world police force," he said in French.

The sergeant looked at him for a moment. "Mr Dai," she said in English, "if you want to get a cup of coffee, or use the restroom, they are that way," she nodded her head towards the hall. "You take a little walk and come back when you feel better. Now, Ms. Ling, how many ways are there to get from your office to the parking?"

David stalked down the hall until he found a machine that dispensed lukewarm Caribe coffee.

In the morning David had a vague sense of being hung over, a metallic taste in his mouth, a fatigue almost like an ache in all his joints.

"Are you still quitting?" Tim asked. He was at the end of the hall, filling up the opening to the living room.

It was early in the morning, too early to deal with Tim. David shrugged. "Why?"

"Well," Tim said, "someone ought to, you know, be taking care of things, since I'm leaving and you're quitting."

"Maybe a professional," David said. "Excuse me, I need a coffee mug."

"I was thinking," Tim said, "you sounded pretty professional back there. Why don't you stay for awhile?"

"I am not the person for this job," David said. "Excuse me."

Tim stepped back but followed him into the kitchen. Coffee was made, that meant Mayla was up. He wondered if she wanted to go to work at the regular time.

"Don't you feel bad about leaving her like this?" Tim asked. "What if something happens?"

"Something has already happened," David said.

"Yeah," Tim said, "something has happened. And you and I are running out on it."

David shook his head, poured his coffee.

"Don't you feel any obligation?"

"I cannot stay here," David said. "Do you understand? I have done what I could do, in Africa. I have already paid."

He would have to buy a coffee mug, even if he was only going to be here for a few more weeks. Maybe he could just forget to bring this one back.

Tim was standing there still, watching. Or thinking, David wasn't sure which. *Obligation.* There was no *obligation.*

"You shot at the car," Tim said.

Shot at the car? Ah, in the parking. "Yes?"

"What were you trying to do?" Tim said. "I mean, were you trying to shoot the people or disable the car?"

What was he trying to do? He had to stop, think a minute. When he shot at the car, what had he been aiming at? Just the car. So why shoot at the car? If he had somehow stopped it, then he might have had to worry about the people in the car getting out and shooting at him. And he hadn't really thought about the people in the car.

"I was just shooting," David said. "They shoot at me. I shoot back so they will leave so we can escape." To be honest, he had not thought anything. He had just shot, because he was being shot at and he had a gun. He had not even thought about firing in a concrete parking, about ricochets or wild shots or how crazy this all was.

"I've never shot a gun," Tim said. "Except on a range."

Tim was still watching him. Like he was crazy? No, maybe with a funny kind of respect. Stupid, just because he had shot a gun at some people. People did not understand. Tim did not understand. Any thickheaded idiot can walk into a liquor store and shoot at someone. "That's good," David said. "I hope you never do shoot one. I wish I never had."

There was no one in the parking that morning. Or the next morning.

Saturday he wondered how he was going to fill the day. Maybe Mayla would need errands done or would want to go see her grandfather. He wondered what her grandfather thought of the shooting. Old man in his chair, sitting there like a relic of colonialism.

The cat got out when he opened the door to go get his coffee. Getting out was the reason for Meph's existence. He chased the kitten down the hall and it went under the couch in the living room. Mayla was looking up as David came by the kitchen. "I am sorry," he said. "He is like a child, you know?"

She laughed. "Let him roam around a bit, he won't hurt anything."

"I can get his food, he always will come for food."

"Get your coffee first," Mayla said.

Saturday morning, she was in a sweater and tights. The casual Mayla. Easier to be around, not so serious as when she was a banker. At the bank, Mr. Morel's driver Luis called her "Princess Ling."

He poured coffee. "Did you get the paper?" he asked.

"The *Journal*," she said. She got two papers, a financial paper from New York and a local paper.

"I'll see if the other is in," he said.

"Don't bother, it's all fiction," she said. She didn't like the Julian paper, she always said it was third rate.

"I would miss my serials," David said. She shook her head. "How can you read those things?"

"They are easy, even for someone with my English."

"Written for people with the reading skills of ten-year-olds."

David nodded. "Yes, like me."

She laughed.

The paper came with the mail, in the living room near the garage door. Meph followed him. Julian mail was delivered by forced air. There were a couple of letter cans and a cylinder and the paper. David picked up the paper. Trouble in the Colombian Republic (underneath the headline in smaller print, "American Support Insufficient to Buoy Unpopular Regime"). He stopped, looking at the headline rather than the cylinder, ready to scoop it up, and glanced down at the address. The address read Ms. M. K. Ling. He stopped, hand still out.

He stood someplace else in his experience, looking at the cylinder. It was about the length of his hand from the tip of his longest finger to the heel. The front was dirty translucent plastic, filled with oily liquid. The base was a pressure trigger for explosives, a dull beige disc that was sensitive to vibration. There was a bomb in Mayla's house.

The bomb must have been dropped nose first into a mailing chute so the pressure-sensitive trigger would be spared the slight stresses of acceleration and friction. That could have been done anywhere; on the mall, in the mailchute at the end of the street. The air in the chute would catch it and cushion it; maybe it was tampered with so it would not be so sensitive, to insure that the steady acceleration would not disturb the trigger and that was why it had not gone off when it landed in Mayla's living room. Or maybe it had just managed to land in the way that would not set it off. Maybe it was dead, a dud, or meant to scare. Maybe it wasn't. If it wasn't, and it went off, besides killing whoever was standing close by, it would breach the integrity of the dome. The dome would implode around them. They would be dead before they knew it.

Except of course, himself, he would be dead but he knew it already.

He couldn't do anything about the bomb, he didn't know if the trigger was working or not and if it was and he touched it he could set it off. If it was unstable from tampering it might just go off by itself. So he must do something about his people.

Time was moving so slow, blue time they called it during the war. He thought all these things in the time it took him to read the cylinder, then straighten, unconsciously hiking his shoulder to keep a nonexistent rifle strap from sliding.

"Tim, Mayla," he called.

"What?" Tim called down from the loft.

"Listen to me. There is a bomb in the mail." He didn't know any other way to say it.

"What?" Tim said, "What the hell?"

"Did you call?" Mayla asked from the kitchen. She came to the door with a cup in her hand.

"I said," he was talking to his people, he must impress them, move them with his voice, "there is a bomb in the mail. Now you must leave."

"David—" she said.

"Now!" he snapped.

"Did you say a bomb?" Tim said.

"Wait on the street, walk softly. Go on." He was standing as still as he could.

"Can you do something," Tim asked, "can someone defuse it?"

"I am doing something. This is not the vid. Go on. Walk softly, it may have sensitive."

Mayla did not believe, he could see. It was not doubt, she just did not comprehend. She stood in the kitchen entrance, still holding her coffee cup. "My things," she said.

He shook his head. "Come on, Mayla," he coaxed. "We must leave or perhaps we will all die."

She looked at the cylinder, then came towards him, putting her feet down carefully, as if they were sore. She was wearing sandals. She had long feet. Gingerly, she opened the door to the garage. For a moment she looked at the button to open the big, outer garage door and he knew what she was thinking, it might set the bomb off. She looked at him. Tim, standing and waiting for Mayla to go first, looked at him. He shrugged, it was the way out. So she tapped it and the door went up smoothly.

"Son of a bitch," Tim breathed.

"Okay," he said, and she went down the curving steps.

Tim walked with his eyes on the floor as if walking a line. Like a drunk walking for a policeman. He stopped and looked at the cylinder for a moment. Then back at David. He did not believe, David thought. Not really. In his head he understood, but he did not believe.

"Go on," David said.

Tim shook his head.

David followed him onto the steps. He looked back at Mayla's pretty house. The kitten was at the mail, sniffing the edge of a capsule.

"Mephisto, non!"

The kitten looked up and his tail twitched.

"Venite! Maintenant!" he called the kitten.

"What are you doing?" Tim looked up the curve of the stairs down into the garage. Blue eyes.

"Calling the cat," David said, "go on."

"Fuck the cat," Tim said.

He should, he knew. Mephisto decided to go back towards his rooms. Little cat, he would never see the sun.

"Mephistofeles! Venite," he called. Insolent, the kitten walked to the hall. He could go to the kitchen and get out a food packet. Sifting through the rubble of the dome, he thought, police find his remains clutching a cat-food packet. He followed the kitten back across the living room, walking carefully, feet falling smoothly, rolling to minimize his weight although it probably didn't make any difference. The big orange and yellow sun beamed benevolently, oblivious to the black water. It was a tiny warmth; it, Mephisto, himself, they would be smothered, extinguished in an instant. If the trigger was still active. If the bomb would still go off. The cat disappeared into his bedroom. He remembered when he had first been in Afrique, a corporal had carried a dead shell as a good luck piece. They'd all been told not to pick up anything, but they did. One time, the corporal had taken it out of his pocket and left it sitting on the tailgate of a

transport and it had rolled off and exploded. All the time the corporal had carried it in his pocket nothing had happened and then, at that moment, it fell and went off. Or maybe it did not, maybe the corporal had carried his all through the war and that was a story he had heard and gotten confused. He'd seen a shell go off but he couldn't remember when.

The shoulder patch of an American Air Force Observer had a sword through a heart and emblazoned underneath it the word "DILLIGAFF." He said it meant "Do I Look Like I Give a Flying Fuck?" Funny thing to think of.

Half crouched, David stalked the cat down the hallway.

In the bedroom the kitten watched over its shoulder and when it saw David it flattened its ears and went under the bed. He crouched by the edge and it slunk out of reach. David clucked his tongue against the roof of his mouth. The kitten hissed, back against the bottom of the bed.

Don't be stupid. Leave him.

"David!" Tim must be standing at the top of the stairs.

He lay down, chest against the rug, and reached under the bed. His hand fell short. *"Mephisto, Mephistofeles, venite."* The bomb was going to go off, the water was going to come in and the cat was going to get them both killed. He reached again, Meph lashed out and scratched the back of his hand. The cat was panicked. He should go now. He reached again, palm up. Meph lashed again and he caught the cat's paw. Meph reflexively sank his claws into the meaty base of David's thumb. David hauled on the kitten who squalled in terror and anger and tried to dig claws into the rug. He yanked the kitten out, Meph grabbed his shoulder, still screaming.

"Jesus fucking Christ!" Tim said, watching him come down the hall. In the living room he thought it felt colder. Of course that was crazy, the room wouldn't be colder until the water came in and then it would be very cold.

He limped down the steps, counting them, the cat craning around to see the garage. At the base of the steps he palmed the door latch and the big safety door creaked and closed off Mayla's house as he watched. It would have to be opened by the security company now that it had been manually closed. It probably wouldn't stop the water from coming into the garage. He looked at the Skate. There was a lot of money in that car. He wondered if it should be moved, but hell, the insurance would pay for it. He shifted Meph to one arm and sprinted the last distance. Tim palmed the big watertight garage doors and they slammed into place, powered by the water force they were built to withstand. David winced, expecting explosion.

But there was nothing.

He looked at Mayla and Tim and grinned. Adrenaline made him suddenly, furiously happy.

"What the bloody hell were you doing?" Tim asked.

"He wanted to play with it. I thought maybe he would explode it before we were outside. We should call the police." He put his arm around Mayla's shoulders and squeezed. She was still holding her coffee cup.

"What kind of bomb is it?" she asked.

"Not a very good one," he said. "We should go and call the police. I can explain to everyone once."

They walked to the next house. David kept his arm around her shoulders and did not allow her to look back. He kept expecting the explosion behind him, kept waiting for it to go off, knowing it would startle him. Each minute it didn't go off made him think that maybe it wouldn't; that Mayla's house, the yellow sun, the black car, the music chips, Tim's vacuum coffee maker, his clothes, everybody's clothes and toothbrushes—he wished he had brushed his teeth—and the pots and pan and the groceries would all be all right. That they could go back inside and forget it.

David pushed the buzzer. A woman's voice said, "Yes?"

"Hello," he said to the air. "My name is David Dai, I work for Mayla Ling, your neighbor? May we make a call from here?"

"Step back please?"

He assumed they were being surveyed.

"Ms. Magritte?" Mayla said.

"Oh, hello Ms. Ling." Then nothing. David looked at Mayla, wondered what was going on. Then he realized Ms. Magritte had to come down and let them in. So they waited and he ignored Mayla's house and the big steel doors.

Ms. Magritte's garage door opened. The domes on this street didn't have front doors. Or sidewalks or windows on the street or any of the other places and ways that neighbors were neighbors. "Hello, Ms. Ling," Ms. Magritte said, smiling. She was a tiny dark woman who spoke American-accented English. "Is there a problem with your system?"

"No," Mayla said, "there's a bomb in my house."

That struck Tim as funny.

Ms. Magritte did not know what to say.

"We have to call the police," Mayla said.

"Oh my God," Ms. Magritte said. She looked up and down the street as if she might see someone, and then at Mayla's garage doors. "Who—" Ms. Magritte started and then closed her mouth.

"I'm not political," Mayla said. "It's because of my position at the bank, I think."

Ms. Magritte nodded as if this explained something and led them upstairs. David relinquished Mayla to Tim's arm. He handed the cat to Mayla and was amused to realize that it was good there was no one else who needed watching because he was working against the law of diminishing returns. "Careful," he said, "he scratched me." Welts stood on his hand. Mayla nodded. Like Xhosa refugees, he thought. She would be all right as long as he could keep telling her what to do. Tim would be fine as long as he did not allow himself to realize. And he would be all right, he reflected wryly, as long as he had to keep telling her what to do.

"I have a Steuben glass bud vase from the 1900's," Mayla said to Ms. Magritte. "It was my grandmother's from Hawaii. I was afraid to take it to work because I was sure someone would knock it off my desk. Isn't that ironic? Of course, David says it may not go off. I guess I should have put it away where it would be safe but I always felt what's the use of having those kind of things if you don't leave them out where you can see them and enjoy them?"

Ms. Magritte licked her lips. "I think you should sit down and have a cup of coffee. Then after your man calls the police maybe I should call Girardin. Girardin is my husband, Ms. Ling, I'm sure you remember him?"

David made the call. He wanted to relate things crisply, not wasting words. Unfortunately the officer kept interrupting him, asking him about things before he'd gotten to them and then making him go back to explain. But he had been through this kind of thing before; people who did not know how to take a briefing. "No sir, I don't know when it got there . . . yes sir, a pressure trigger . . . yes sir, I've seen them before, in the war in South Africa . . . no sir, I'm not a citizen, I work for Ms. Ling . . . no sir, I've never seen one like it . . . the trigger, just the trigger, I've never seen liquid explosive . . . I don't know, it could be nitroglycerine for all I know, it looks transparent . . . nitroglycerine . . . no sir, I didn't say it was that. Nitroglycerine is something people used to use, like dynamite, a hundred years ago. It could be anything, I don't know . . . I was a chemist before the war . . . no sir, I don't know, I was just making the point that I do not recognize it, you see? I do not think it is nitroglycerine . . . no, I did not touch it, it would probably explode . . . yes sir, everybody is out . . . we will be waiting outside . . . yes sir, the watertight doors are shut. Good-bye—what? . . . David, David Dai . . . D, A, I . . . the records might be under Jean David Dai, that is my whole name . . . yes sir, that's right, Mayla Ling . . . yes, French . . . yes sir . . . thank you sir . . . good-bye.

David took back the cat and they thanked Ms. Magritte and went outside, standing together. They watched the door and looked up the street at the direction the police would come. The cat clung, curious and frightened. David's hand hurt where Meph had scratched him. He realized he was tapping nervously on his hip and made himself stop.

"This is crazy," Tim said to no one in particular. He kept shaking his head, as if this were some sort of amazing entertainment.

The sound of sirens set David's teeth on edge. It was a scream that bounced around stone tunnels and made it impossible to tell where the noise was coming from. It was unsafe under the artificial lights. Of course, lights were confusing for pilots in the old night-vision goggles the Prots used. Not like the new German goggles that compensated. He realized he was thinking they would use the lights to call in strikes. The first car rocked around the corner, a blue-and-white Julian patrol car. They turned the siren off but left the blue-and-white lights flashing and shifting across the walls and the street, glancing off the metal doors. Far off another screech was colliding with the walls and corners. Doors slammed, an officer pointed at them, he straightened up. He identified himself to the officer and said that he was the one who had called. The officer was black, one of ours, he thought. He told the young officer—whose eyes kept disappearing behind the polished visor of his cap when the light reflected off it—what he'd found and what they'd done (leaving out the part about the cat) and which doors they'd shut. While he was talking, a third and fourth car parked next to the first two, cutting off the back half of the street. He had to wait until they shut off their sirens to finish speaking. They left their lights on. It bothered his eyes. He wondered if he'd ever be able to stand the sun again.

The officer walked over to Mayla who was standing by the first car. He stopped, nodded respectfully. There were white officers and that seemed strange. In Africa he had worked with mostly black troops.

The cat squirmed. David relaxed and scratched his ears, but Meph laid them back and mewed, his eyes slitted against the flashing lights. A lower siren set Meph squalling, a skid pulled up, lights flashing blue and green. Men in combat beige overalls stepped out and began to pull out equipment. Explosives Unit.

He shifted his shoulders and then realized he had no rifle. An officer came up and told him to move back behind the cars, out of the way. Of course, here it didn't matter what color the officers were, this was not Afrique. People had begun to collect and a civilian crew pulled up and took out vid equipment. Mayla was talking to someone, her hands were in motion as she explained something. From where he stood her eyes were hidden by the shadow of her hair except when the light from the cars swept across her face. Then the blue light made her face perfectly white, and her eyes, hair and mouth were as black as water.

"Lieutenant," someone said to his left and he turned but it was an officer talking to one of the men from the skid. Meph mewed and he realized he was squeezing too hard. Relax, he told himself. He was waiting for the explosion and he knew when it came he was going to start, he was wound up tight and there was nothing he could do except wait.

"Is this like the bomb on Esperance?"

"I think. Nobody's seen it yet. One of her staff described it," the lieutenant said.

"They usually go off."

"Either they do when they come in or they don't at all," the lieutenant said. "Usually once they've fucked with the trigger it either works or it doesn't."

"What about Desalines?"

"That one had been there awhile. Usually, though, they go off or they do not."

The officer nodded, "This one probably won't—"

The explosion was a thud-thump, the watertight doors into the garage held for maybe a tenth of a second and then there was the hammer blow of the water hitting the main doors. The water immediately muted the sound, giving it an odd, flat quality.

Then silence.

David raised his head. He was behind a car with the cat shielded by his body. The force of the water hitting the big garage doors had warped them, bowed them out, but they must have been built to do that. The lights slid down one wall, across the street, angled up another wall and across the warped doors, meeting and forming and splintering again, back down the walls. He was the only person who had ducked, everyone else stood staring. He tensed for the firing to begin, or for the mortars to start elephant walking down the street.

Somebody whistled appreciatively.

David got up. This was just his job, no one was going to start shooting. He looked at Mayla, standing next to an officer, staring at the doors, and she was not anyone he knew.

Screw it. Someone else was handling it. The walls rose up, more sharply than the spine of the ridge of highlands behind the wash, where Namibia and Kalahari almost met, about Rehoboth. His knee ached, remembering Rehoboth. He cradled the cat who was too frightened to complain. Nobody was looking at him. They were walking to the doors, or reaching into their cars to call the station.

An officer told the crowd to disperse. It was only a dozen people but David stepped back through them, became part of them, walked down the street trying to give the impression of purpose. He kept his head down and did not look back. At the end of the street he waited. The tunnel buses ran fairly often, although he'd never taken one, he'd seen them. He hoped he didn't have to wait long. He counted slowly, in French, and at 512 one coasted around the bend. He looked back.

Tim Bennet was tall enough and blond enough to stand out in the group. He was looking at David. Even from the distance David could tell.

He didn't know what to do. He expected Tim would shout, say something to someone. He put his foot on the step.

Tim Bennet was watching him, but he didn't move.

David got on and paid with change out of his pocket, "The cat is a problem?" he asked, hoping he would not have to get off and let the cat go, or walk.

"No problem," the driver said.

He hadn't even looked at the front of the bus to see if it said where it was going. He knew where he was going.

Away.

6

House Arrest

The blue and whites brought her home in a patrol car. She had to stand on the street and use the intercom to ask Jude to open the door. Then she had to go to her grandfather who was eating soup and tell him, "Someone blew up my house, sent a bomb in the mail and it blew up."

Her grandfather looked up at her, holding the spoon in his shaking hand. "What did you *do?*" he demanded.

He wasn't asking her what she did when it happened, he was asking her what she did to cause it.

"I don't know," she said, honestly. And then, to her great embarrassment, she felt the heat in her face and the threatening tears. She cleared her throat to explain that she thought that she was just in the wrong place at the wrong time, but when she tried to speak, her voice shook and broke. "I don't know," she managed again and he looked away.

He wanted her to stop crying. He didn't know what to do when she cried. He hated crying, it made him nervous.

He waited, and she looked at the vid. The vid was sitting on the counter where he could watch it while he ate. Jude had put on the mute when they came in, and a man and a woman were standing in a jungle, speaking intently and soundlessly to each other.

Finally she said again, "I don't know."

"You stay here, Mayla Lee," he said gently.

Just that. But it made her cry and Jude put his arms around her and told her it was all right, that she was safe now. Her grandfather stood up and patted her back awkwardly. She thought she was cry-ing from gratitude. He was telling her that he loved her enough to bring her trouble into his house.

Anything could happen. And if anything could happen, then true love was trusting, wasn't it?

David Dai had disappeared. The blue and whites thought that it was possible that there had been collusion between David and Anna Eminike. An officer sat on the sheet-covered couch in Mayla's gram's sitting room. "It explains why he runs, and why he is hard to find. Because he has help to hide, you see?" The blue and white was a chubby young island boy with big eyes and an air of earnest help-fulness.

It didn't sound right to Mayla. If David were working with *La Mano de Diós* then why had he still been in the house when the bomb arrived?

"He was a dupe," the officer said. "*La Mano de Diós* used him. They didn't tell him the bomb was going to come."

"Why would he go to them for help to hide if they used him?"

"Maybe they had made a plan, not expecting him to be alive to use it. To make him think they would help him. And now he is using it."

She pointed out that David came to her immediately when he was approached in the parking.

The officer thought about this. "These people, anyone connected with *La Mano de Diós*, they all are under constant surveillance," he said. "Maybe they were afraid that we would find out that he was working with them. They met him in the parking, and to divert the suspicions of any watchers he pretended to turn them away." He nodded to himself, warming to his own theory, liking the taste of it in his mouth. "And when you were shot at in the parking the gun-man had intended to miss. They were establishing Dai as a target."

"What was the point, the profit," she asked. "Why plant a spy in my house? There wasn't anything for them to learn, I don't have any information."

"Connections." He rolled his eyes. *"La Mano de Diós* looks for patterns."

God's surgeons. One event has innumerable ramifications, ripples in Mandelbrot patterns of chaos, and God told Anna Eminike the things to do to initiate God's patterns. Murder this person. Bomb that house. Sense in every moment, divine inspiration in every random action. God alone saw whole.

"We aren't saying that he is working with them," the officer said. "We're just considering the possibility." He made this qualification without real conviction. The sheet he was sitting on had a pattern of pale washed flowers in pink. Her gram had liked pink. Mayla's sheets were gone. She had not had any pink sheets in her whole house and now she was back sleeping on pink sheets.

"He'd only been here a month," Mayla said. "It's not very likely that they could recruit him and convert him in a month."

"Maybe he met Eminike in Africa," the officer said.

"That's pretty thin, isn't it?" she asked.

"Why did he run?" the officer asked.

She didn't know. That was the simple truth, she didn't know why he had run. She didn't know why her house was gone.

"I think he'd had it," Tim said. Tim had watched him get on the bus. He said David had just walked to the end of the street, waited until one came and got on.

"And you didn't think about stopping him?" The blue and white asked.

He just sounded curious but Tim squirmed. "I figured," Tim said, "if he wanted to tell somebody he would have. I wasn't thinking about him being a possible terrorist, I mean, he kept talking about how he wasn't the right person to work for Mayla and about going home and he said how he thought that this country was crazy. I just thought that enough had happened that the guy should be allowed to leave if he wanted to. I was beginning to wonder if it wouldn't be a good idea to go somewhere else, you know, standing out there."

"Where did you think he was going?" the officer asked.

"I don't know," Tim said.

"Did you think he would come back, get in touch? That he was going to see friends?"

"I wasn't thinking about anything," Tim said. "You know, Mayla's house had just been blown up." But then he shook his head. "No, I guess I wouldn't say he'd come back."

"Why not?" the officer said.

Tim stared at his hands. Finally he said, "If you'd seen him. Just the way he looked, you know."

"Try to explain," the officer said. He was smarter than he acted, more patient than Mayla has suspected and she suddenly felt a chill.

"I don't know, purposeful, I guess. Like . . . I don't know."

The officer prompted, "Purposeful. Like he knew where he was going?"

"Of course he knew where he was going," Tim said, "it's a bloody dead-end street. And no, I'm not saying he was going to meet some frigging terrorists."

"What are you saying?"

Tim shook his head. "If you'd seen him, you'd know what I mean."

"Ah," the blue and white said.

Oh God, Mayla thought, they were going to pin it on David.

Mayla's grandfather's house had breath—cool air moved in the rooms and the tall peacock feathers drifted—but no life. By Caribbean standards it was old. It had been built when the first and second levels of Julia were the only levels, sixty years ago. It was, in its way, a frontier house: built in a big square and starkly simple, just a concrete warren of blind rooms and corridors closed in on itself.

Her gram had tried to make it pretty. She had put mirrors on the walls to create windows and had filled the rooms with spindly wooden tables covered with lace and tall red and yellow Chinese vases filled with pale fronds of pampas grass and peacock feathers. When she was a girl Mayla had loved her gram's things.

The mirrors reflected mirrors on the opposite walls so that the tables covered with knickknacks and pictures of cousins and family and the Virgin in silver frames were reflected in infinite progression. Sometimes, from the corner of her eye, Mayla thought she saw movement in the rooms at the backs of the mirrors.

Paranoia. Or just plain fear.

She was back in her old room. The bed was still pink, the walls the palest rose. In the drawers were old things she hadn't bothered to take with her when she moved out: clothes ten years out of date, a bracelet with a little wirework horsecharm dangling off of it that was supposed to be a voudoun sign—they had been big when she was in school—and a box of hair solution to streak her hair metallic silver because Terez, who was her best friend, had streaked hers gold. She threw them out.

"What are you doing?" Jude asked her in the hall.

"Cleaning up my room," she said. Strange behavior, she thought. Here she was, reduced to almost nothing but the clothes on her back, and she was throwing out whatever else she could find. She threw out everything in all the drawers. There were a couple of dresses in the closet that she could still wear to the bank. Her gray dress, the cliché of the banker gray dress, without style or taste but perfectly functional, she could wear that. Her oyster-colored dress. It had the funny Egyptian linen collar that made it look dated, but she would only wear it until she could get some more things.

In the top of the closet she found a shoe box with a rubber band around it. She slid it off the shelf thinking it was full of letters or something, but when she opened it up, it was full of picture cards. On top was a card of a conical volcano, perfect as a film set, not real.

She turned it over.

> *Hi Princess,*
>
> *Things are beautiful in Bali! It's hot hot hot! I'm going to be here awhile, maybe in a few months I can bring you here for a visit.*
>
> *Love, Dad.*

She looked at the date, she would have been eleven years old. When she was eleven her parents had been gone for five years. They had left when she was six.

When she was six. She closed her eyes and thought of being six. What was six? Her parents gone to see her grandfather's family in Hawaii. Cousins. Caribe had still been part of the U.S. First Hawaiian of Caribe was still connected to First Hawaiian of Honolulu and the Lings of Hawaii.

When she was six, Enzalo Estaves y Otoya launched a violent independence movement. She could see her gram filling the bathtubs with water in case it was shut off—although she pictured her gram as an old thin-legged lady in tights and a cardigan. When she was six her grandmother was, what, in her fifties? Her hair wasn't gray, she kept it blonde. With effort the blonde gram from ims could be superimposed. They grew algae in buckets and plastic tubs and they had an old-fashioned air recycler sitting in the kitchen, all in case the air was cut off. All of the house staff left except Jude, who cooked for them and ate with them. If the air went bad they planned to shut off most of the big house and live in the kitchen, bathroom and dining room, all four of them including Jude—but in their part of the city the air stayed good.

Her grandfather was home all of the time. President Enzalo Estaves y Otoya nationalized the bank. He sat around dressed like it was Sunday afternoon, in tights and shirts and alpargatas, sandals like slippers with cotton soles. He was angry all the time.

"Be quiet," her gram would say, "your grandfather is worried about a lot of things."

Her mother and father sent cards, first from Hawaii, then from Spain. The cards came in bunches wrapped in string, some of them sent three or four months before and some only two weeks old. Then nothing for a few months. The mail was "interrupted." Like someone speaking.

Her mother wrote that they had tried to call but couldn't get through, or that she had gotten a card or letter. When the calls did get through, her mother's voice was a foreign voice now, deep and rumbling, deeper than her father's voice had been at home. A stranger's voice like voices on the vid.

Her father sent picture cards with little notes on the back addressed to "Princess" or "Mayla Lee." The underwater mall complex financed by First Hawaiian U.S. at Waikiki. Mauna Loa. The Kamehameha Island Causeway. Then Moorish architecture of Grenada, a woman in a black lace mantilla, great expanses of golden field and narrow streets. Mayla kept the cards in her shoe box, rubberbanded together in packets the way they came. She sat on her bedroom floor and laid them out all around, some propped up against her pink bed, some on the floor, making up a vast, sundrenched landscape. All the cards were full of such space, such light.

She stayed in her bedroom a lot. She remembered pieces of things. Her grandfather shouted at Gram that she was a weak, hysterical woman and Gram cried. She and Gram had packed cases with underwear and a change of clothes and Gram had sewn her engagement ring and her pavé cockatoo pin with the clock and the big ruby into the hem of Mayla's poncho. She connected her grandfather's shouting with the packing although she wasn't really sure they happened at the same time. She didn't remember ever actually leaving, where would they have gone? What was her Gram planning they should do, try to get to America? There were no subs running. Maybe her Gram meant to go to friends—but she couldn't think of who that might have been.

Her mind went back to playing on the floor of her bedroom, laying out cards, making landscapes of the woman in the lace mantilla dancing in front of Mauna Loa. The woman in the black lace mantilla was the only real person in any of the cards her father sent her. There were little people, far away—bent over in the fields, strolling through the streets of Grenada—but they were too small to be someone. The woman in the black lace mantilla had shiny black hair, and Mayla had black hair. The woman danced through the sunny bright places all by herself. She hoped her father would send her a postcard with a picture of another person, a friend for the Spanish lady.

She tried to remember more, but what came was later, when she was older. A memory of the yellow kitchen full of young men in black jackets, laughing and talking in Spanish. Waiters, sent by the caterer for big parties. She was older then, her grandfather was back at the bank. President Enzalo Estaves y Otoya had been arrested by Colonel Bustamante, who everyone called the Argentine. The Argentine became President-for-Life Bustamante. He declared the Revolution a failure, denationalized the bank, and her grandfather put on his suit and went back to work. Her grandfather became *una persona de influencia*, good friends with people from the government. Old men like De Silva and Chavez.

The parking was full of government cars again. That must have been when she went back to school. (She knew that Gram taught her at home, but what could the lessons have possibly been? Vague memories of workbooks.) She was enrolled in *La Escuela de las Órdenes de Los Desaparecados*, a Catholic girl's school where despite the name, no Spanish was spoken. She got letters (from her mother) and picture cards (from her father) one at a time, not in bundles. From Tenerife, from Hawaii again, from Los Angeles, from Spain, and then the letters came from Madrid from her mother, and the picture cards came from her father in Barcelona. The letters finally started coming from Barcelona, but by then the picture cards were coming from Majorca, from Morocco, from Corsica, from Crete, then from Bermuda. The letters never moved from Barcelona, but the picture cards ranged farther and farther. And every time a letter came from Barcelona, her Gram frowned.

Her father called. She got to talk to him for a moment. She was accustomed to the way his voice sounded, so deep and foreign. Jimmy Ling was very tan, not very handsome. He didn't look Chinese like her grandfather, or American like her gram. He didn't really look like anyone she knew. "How are you, Mayla Lee?" he asked. "Are you studying? Did you get my card from Bermuda?"

She said she had.

"What did you think of that, pink beaches? They really are pink, isn't that amazing? Would you like to come and see a pink beach?

Your Dad is going to make money, a big real estate deal, and then maybe you can come to Bermuda."

The picture card from Bermuda had shown green hills, a big white building with tiny figures in red coats in front of it. No beach.

Her Gram said, "Jimmy, don't promise the child things you might not be able to do."

"Marceline is still in Barcelona," he said to Gram. "She's staying in Barcelona, I'm getting a divorce. I don't know why you get that look, mom, you always bitched about Marceline. I can't please you, I can't please dad. I'm damned if I do and damned if I don't."

"When are you coming home?" Gram asked tightly.

"I have a business," he said, his voice climbing although not high enough to sound like a Caribbean voice. "Things are busy right now. As soon as I get this thing wrapped up in Bermuda. You'll see, it's really going well, not like Majorca. I didn't know enough about the market in Majorca, and besides, that was all that European old-boy network. I'm working with some local people here, it's going very well, mom. Tell dad I'm doing very well, I'll call you."

The second picture card from Bermuda arrived two days later. The beach was pink, but so was the sky. Skies were supposed to be blue, which made the whole picture suspect anyway. She put it in the shoe box with the other picture cards.

The card on top of the Bermuda beach was dated four or five months later and came from Tenerife, a picture of yellow birds. She had never gone to Bermuda or Bali.

She sat on the pink bed in her grandfather's house and looked at the picture card from Bali. Had it been the last one? Or had he continued to send them for awhile and she just hadn't bothered to put them in the shoe box?

She put the rubber band back around the shoe box and put it back in the closet. She didn't throw anything else out.

7

Dedale

David sat down on the bed. Yesterday when he'd taken the room he'd declined to rent the vid, but today he'd gone back and paid for a week. 2cr a week, that brought his rent to 37cr a week. He didn't have any chips to play on it so he was forced to watch Caribbean broadcasts or American imports—sometimes dubbed in Spanish or Creole. He didn't like soap operas or news, but at least it was noise.

He and Meph were living in one room, with a tiny flash unit, a cooler about a meter high and a sink. The walls were painted bluish-green, the color made it feel colder. The walls were visible all the time because he couldn't sleep without the light on. The bed didn't heat properly either.

"In a couple of weeks, we'll go home," he told Meph. Meph, who was sitting by the door gazing off into space, mewed to be let out. "To a place where there is sun and we can get warm. It is summer there, you know?" He added hours, ticking on his fingers. "It is late in the morning, in a little bit it will be lunchtime."

It was 6:30 p.m. here, he'd have known even without the vid because his neighbor in number three was just home. He heard him come in and then he heard crowd noises and the voice of the sports announcer. He couldn't hear clearly through the walls but he could tell that the sports announcer was speaking Spanish. A soccer game. David flicked through the offerings. Nicaragua and San Salvador. On the other side the neighbor in number five did not get back until midnight. Not that time mattered in Caribe, there wasn't any daylight, day shift, night shift, it was all the same. When number five got in at midnight he apparently started dragging plastic chairs all over his room. At least that was what it sounded like.

The dehumidifier clicked on. It was noisy, but outside the air was more humid than it had been on the upper levels where Mayla lived and worked.

David watched Nicaragua beat San Salvador.

Sometimes the cat would come crawl in his lap. He clucked his tongue but Meph was ignoring him, crouched by the door, staring at the wall as if he could see through it and watch number three's soccer game. Abruptly Meph flicked his ears back, then looked at the back wall, listening. David listened, too. After a few seconds he heard the rumbling. A freight line ran in back of them, tunneled through rock. He didn't hear it so much as feel it, but he was getting accustomed to it.

This morning the Sunday paper had a little story about the bombing. Terrorists. Political elements. Linked with the bombing of the minister's dome. It said Ms. Ling's driver had left the scene and was currently sought for questioning. He did not think he should be any part of "wanted for questioning."

Hide. And wait. Eventually maybe it would get quiet and he could leave. Maybe a month, two months. He did not have a passport anymore. He had money. When he got on the bus the morning the bomb went off it had taken him to the central terminal and when he got off he saw the row of bank machines. He tried the bank machine there and his funds had not been frozen so he took out everything. It had taken almost ten minutes; the system had done a retinal scan and then asked him to wait and he had waited and waited, wondering if a blue and white was going to show up. But finally it had given him the money. At home the machines would not do that, they would only give a certain amount.

Then he had tried to decide where to go. The buses were all different. Good buses were clean and had company names on the side; *L'Exprimier* and *Garrara Transportation Company*. The worst buses were the *taptaps*. Psychedelically colored rattle traps. People waited patiently in line for the good buses and most got seats. When a tap-tap pulled in the disembarking passengers had to force their way though crowds of middle-aged women with shopping bags and young women with too much makeup and metallic colored hair. They forced their way on, shoving, while young men in jackets the shimmering blue and green of dragonflies waited leaning against the wall.

So he got on a taptap marked "Dedale" because he knew he couldn't hide in a neighborhood like Mayla's. What would he do, knock on garage doors until someone like Mrs. Magritte called the blue and whites? Besides, *dedale* meant "labyrinth" in French. It had seemed like a good place to hide.

And here he was.

He fixed dinner and he and Meph ate. Meph seemed to get a great deal more out of the tile fish than he did. Maybe if he had mustard he could hide some of the fish taste; it wasn't that he hated fish, he just got so tired of it. Then they watched the vid. Then he got up and did some exercises, calisthenics and isometrics using the door frame and stretching exercises. And then he flopped back on the bed, listless. Doing nothing all day was oddly tiring, but he didn't feel ready to sleep. Meph was curled up on the pillow. He watched more vid, a movie from Brazil dubbed in English about a man whose wife and lover poisoned him with fugu fish toxin, but the man only went into a coma and his friend the doctor realized and substituted the corpse of an indigent. Most of the movie was about the husband's revenge. He was supposed to sympathize with the husband but he found everybody in the movie unlikable.

Eventually the neighbor in number five got home and started dragging the plastic chairs around.

After that stopped, nothing to do but try to go to sleep.

The walls bounced the light back at him. They were bluish-green, low-rent lacquer glossy, chill. Maybe if he turned off the light it wouldn't seem so cold. It was ridiculous for a grown man to sleep with a light on. He settled Meph and turned off the light.

He lay on his back. The bed was underneath him, he could feel it firm and steady. There was no light except a faint line around the curtains in the window because the corridor lights were on all the time. Like the lights around Mayla's dome. It was so dark he couldn't see the white of the sheets. He concentrated on the bed. He would build the room in his mind, then he would not feel as if he were drifting. A frame, a mattress that would only get warm on the left side and in one patch in the upper right corner. The cat asleep under the blanket against his waist. On his right. Very important to be oriented. He wondered which direction he was lying in, he knew north from south when he was driving on the belt. The belt was a circle around the first level of the city, the only level of Julia aboveground, and Julia was mostly inscribed within it except for a couple of arms thrown out like the part that Mayla's house had been in. He tried to orient this street within that circle but he didn't know how it was. He should be able to remember the bus route, orient that way. In his head he could construct the route of the first bus he'd taken, from Mayla's house to the city. Then he'd cleaned out his account and taken another bus, a 1 Center St. to 6 Sphinx Rd., a bus from the first level to the sixth level. But he couldn't remember the whole trip, couldn't get all the turns. Laying in bed he didn't know if his head was pointed north or east, south or west. He could feel his heart pounding. Why should it matter that he didn't know if his head was pointed north or south or east or west? People went their whole lives not knowing which direction they were lying when they slept. (His heart was pounding anyway. Foolish heart, there was nothing to be afraid of here. He felt so disoriented.)

Forget it. The bed was parallel to the road. The road was to the right. He was lying in bed on his back. The cat was on his right side. Even though he couldn't see it, the vid was at his feet. His feet were pointing at twelve o'clock. The door was about two meters away at about two o'clock. The sink, etc., was at his left, at nine o'clock, the bureau with the blue metal lamp on it was at eleven o'clock. And the other blue metal lamp was on his right, on the bedside table.

At ten o'clock was the door to the bath. Hold it in his head, hold the room. Cup it there. Even if it was not visible it was looming, solid, surrounding him. Now he knew where he was, relative to the room. Relative position was the best anyone could ever do anyway. He had studied science, he knew that. Absolute position was a myth. Heisenberg. The Uncertainty Principle. What was his spin?

He took a deep breath to try and calm himself. It was the dark. Stupid for a grown man to be afraid of the dark. Orient himself. The ceiling above him was dark. Above that, the fifth level and the fourth, and so on, all the way up to the ocean. And then two hundred meters of saltwater, then warm air, and stars, and he imagined a big silver moon. Closing his eyes he found it easier to imagine that than the room. His bed floating on a warm ocean. Ursa Minor, Ursa Major, Cassiopeia, Orion, Draco, the Pleiades. . . .

Could they see Draco this far south? Ursa Minor? They weren't far enough south for the Southern Cross, they were north of the equator.

But once the Cross had entered his sky he couldn't get it out. It hung there, brilliant, not quite symmetrical. Perhaps because in the time he'd spent south of the equator he'd been outside at night, he'd considered the African sky. Now that sky—or some sky he had imagined containing the Southern Cross—spread broad and vast above him. He turned on his side. He was not under that sky, he was in a room a couple of hundred meters under the ocean. He touched Meph whose breath swelled his tiny belly. So fragile. David clasped his hand over Meph's belly, imagining what he could do, how vulnerable Mephisto was. He tried to feel those tiny ivory ribs. Tried to feel even fear in that to bring him back to the room. But the sky was still above him. He made himself feel the bed that was only warm on the right. His heart was pounding, he was sweating. His body was doing all the things a body did when it was terrified, but he didn't feel any fear. Oh God, he hated this. His heart pounding. Maybe he was having a heart attack? No, he knew he was not having a heart attack, just afraid. Afraid of the dark. Give in to the fear, let the fear swallow him, maybe he would come out the other side? The bed was perched on a *kopje* in the Transvaal, night-colored bluegreen, under the Southern Cross. Around him, miles of dry grass, the *bandu*, and twisted *enkeldoring*, dry branches rubbing and whispering in the hot

January wind. He opened his eyes but it was so dark it was as if they were closed. The stars were distant, white, cold. So far away, so old. He was so small. He couldn't do anything with the fear.

He sat up, Meph mewed, he fumbled until he found the touch-plate on the lamp. Light. A room with cold, bluish-green walls. He pushed back the blankets, scooped Meph up and held the sleepy and irritated kitten against his chest, crooning to him in French and English.

"You son of a bitch," he whispered to Meph, "you sweet fucking bastard, *Mephisto, ma petit merde.*"

By Monday morning he had to get out. Meph tried to get past him but he got the door shut. The curtains stirred and Meph was on the windowsill watching, mouth opened soundlessly, pink and demanding. It was not fair. If he felt cooped up, then Meph felt cooped up, too.

"Life is not fair," he told the kitten. Meph wailed again, eerily silent behind the glass, and then batted at a drop of condensation running on the outside of the window.

It was so damp, air he could smell and faintly taste. Musty, old socks air. The air wasn't as good as it was on the upper levels. The man who rented the rooms was walking the length of the pink concrete hall, spraying fungicide again. The smell was faintly sweet. "Good morning, Señor Park," the man said.

David nodded and smiled and walked the other way. He had registered as Kim Park. He had said he was Korean—Park was a Korean name—but the man probably didn't know a Korean from a Zulu.

He had to decide what to do.

The smartest thing to do was to do nothing, to lie low and wait. To be invisible. But he didn't have a passport and if he was going to get out of Caribe he'd have to come up with one. Somewhere he thought he could buy a passport—but then he suspected he didn't have enough money to buy a black market passport. He did have enough to pay for passage to the U.S. If he could get to the U.S. he could explain to his uncle in Blacksburg and maybe they could help him get home?

Maybe if he waited the Caribbean police would arrest Anna Eminike and he would be cleared.

Then again, maybe he would win the national lottery.

Best to lie low for a few days and count on the inefficiency of the blue and whites. They would lose interest. Although they would probably flag his name so if he tried to buy a ticket for a sub they would be alerted.

There was a street name painted on the wall at the corner. Bestinata. Nothing was level here, streets did not feed into one another but were all on different levels. The whole area was haphazard: a true, three-dimensional maze. At the corner he climbed five concrete steps to a broader gray corridor going left and right.

No reason to choose left or right, so he went left. Cracked concrete "street," children playing crouched between plastic trash bins. They had a flowered rag on a string to make a wall, making smaller spaces in the narrow corridor. Some of the lights didn't work and he walked through a dim place. The air smelled of garbage and old socks. A little girl looked around the rag to watch him walk by. Her hair was in tight braids against her head. Her eyes were solemn and she rested her tiny hands on her dirty knees, her elbows stuck out like wings. Her sweater had faded blue and gilt butterflies on it.

That street emptied onto Plaza Del Malabarista. He had to go down three steps to get to the Plaza, it was about the width of a regular city street, and ran about six blocks.

The air smelled even worse here: unwashed bodies and curry over the dirty sock odor. The Plaza was rimmed with shops and the streets were full of vendors with vegetables set out on tables, homemade clothes on blankets, stalls that sold Indian food. He couldn't shake the feeling that he wasn't getting enough oxygen. He looked in shop windows; a pharmacy advertised antibiotics in bright foil envelopes, chrome and red and blue. Textiles piled like a still life, bright gaudy fabric patterned in gilt butterflies for saris and lamé for dance dresses.

Two girls and a boy were leaping into a square of walkway and leaping off, giggling. The littlest girl looked about five, she leaped and looked up at something invisible to David, shrieked and covered her mouth and jumped away. Some advertisement activated when they came within range. The boy said something to the littlest girl and she hesitated, tortured by her desire to test again. She was at the stage when children are all legs. She leaped again—an exaggerated jump where she kicked up her red plastic shoes—and stood for a moment, watching. The oldest girl looked at David coming towards them. For a moment he wondered if he should cut through the vendors in the square, but the older girl called, "Aloka!" and they all ran.

He almost walked around the square where they had been playing; he didn't like VR advertisements. At home it was illegal to have them on a sidewalk or street. Here he figured that the lasers that tracked the viewer's eyes to feed the visuals weren't calibrated or maintained very often. He knew they were low power and that people didn't really get blinded in freak accidents. . . .

What had the children found so fascinating? He stepped onto the sidewalk and looked up at the shop.

Marquesa Mariposa. Was it a beauty parlor? A teenaged girl appeared on the sidewalk—or rather, not quite on the sidewalk, the image wasn't angled precisely and her feet were a little above the ground. She crooned something to him in Spanish although she was wearing a robe more like a kimono, gauzy blue with veins of gold and silver in some sort of pattern. She opened the robe, and it spread like wings, butterfly wings, ah yes, *mariposa* meant butterfly—

She was nearly naked under the wings, just a gold g-string and a kind of silver bikini top that was more like two strands of fabric in an "x" across her chest barely wide enough to cover her nipples.

It was a VR peep parlor. *Mariposas,* "pretty girls." He almost jumped in his hurry to get off the square and looked around to see if anyone had seen him standing there like some old man looking for a thrill. He couldn't tell if anyone had been looking at him. His face burned.

Go back to the room, he thought.

But he couldn't face that, either.

Stairs cut up to his left between two shops so he headed up them, a long narrow flight of concrete stairs that left him breathless. Another street of residences. He was afraid he'd get lost, but if he just headed straight he figured he could always turn around and get back to the Plaza. The streets weren't ever very long here, anyway.

This street felt different, the flats were mostly whitewashed instead of blue or yellow and the people were Creole rather than Indian. He felt foreign. Women leaned on windowsills chattering in Creole, but they stopped talking when he passed and stared. Children stared at him, too.

This street emptied out on another shopping plaza, smaller than the first. Painted high on the wall it said *Parish Jeramie.* Nothing here he hadn't already seen except that the street vendor sold coconut bread and stew. Maybe he would walk around once and then he would go back to the Plaza and buy some tortillas and beans for lunch. Maybe some rice. And catfood.

The storefronts were whitewashed or pale blue, some with rainbows and snakes around the doors. The paint peeled from the damp concrete. He wished he were home. The homesickness came overwhelming and sharp and his eyes watered with the intensity of it. He wanted to go to the port, buy a ticket and get on the sub, be home in a day, have his life back.

Foolish thing to do, but he wanted to so badly. Maybe he could just go to the port and see what tickets cost. He could apply to the French Consulate and get his passport replaced, maybe the police would not notice, they were so sloppy here—

All it would take was one flag in the system.

Plazoleta D'Imagen. Reality Parlor. Naive illustrations leaped around the door, green men carrying blazing guns, little more than stick figures, women with exaggerated breasts swooning in lovers' arms. He was not interested, he would go home and watch the vid.

He turned around to head back to the stairs and saw the blue and whites, three of them, coming through the crowd. Just walking, purposeful. Without a thought he stepped into the reality parlor, pushing aside the black curtain. The girl behind the counter looked up.

"How much for a booth?" he said, because she was looking at him. Because he had come in here.

She stared at him, too. "One hour? Three hours?" she asked.

"An hour."

"Six cerciorcados," she said holding up the requisite number of fingers as if he might not understand her.

He gave her the money and she pulled a cardboard box out from under the counter and found him a pair of gloves that fit. She gave him a cotton haircover, too. The exit was at his back, he was listening for the blue and whites to pass, but the street sounds were muted by the curtain. He didn't think the blue and whites had been looking for him since they had not acted like they saw him or cared. He should have just walked past them. He pushed through a second curtain—almost running into a tall, long-armed boy who looked about sixteen.

The booth was small, three walls made of plastic partitions and the fourth the concrete back wall of the building. There was a worn, black plastic visor, the padding and the forehead was split and stuffing bulged out. And there was a treadmill and a set of handlebars hung from the ceiling.

What was he doing here? He sat down on the edge of the treadmill. Maybe he would just sit here for a few moments. He was just nervous, that was all. He would go back to the room.

He could try the games here, see what was on the network.

The visor was too big and felt heavy, he wondered how many people had worn it? He was glad for the cotton haircover. He stepped onto the treadmill and grabbed the handlebars suspended from the ceiling. He pulled the visor down.

Then he saw a room. Most of the room was a sketchwork of line, not a real room. He could see his schematic hands glowing like phosphorescent bones. Hanging in the middle of the room were the glowing words CREOLE, ENGLISH, SPANISH.

He raised his glowing hand and pointed to English with a bony finger.

"Welcome to the Parish Jeramie Reality Parlor. Please give your system name." The voice was female, cool and husky, American.

His system name when he was a kid had always been Lezard because that was the name of a character from the vid. "Lezard," he said.

"That configuration is new to this system. Do you have another name for this system?"

"No," he said.

"Please enter your personal information on the index." A schematic keyboard appeared in front of him and a form. Name: he typed "Kim Park." The gloves had feedback so he could feel resistance when he typed, as if he was hitting keys. Age: "34," Sex: "Male."

Address: He skipped that. Body Configuration: At the top of the form it said he could ask for a catalogue so he did.

The room suddenly fleshed out and the cool, female voice said, "A catalogue requires full system, this time will be counted as part of your hour."

He didn't care, he was just killing time.

The catalogue was the size of a magazine, and the gloves were too clumsy to turn the pages so he had to press the icons at the top. There was an icon for male—circle and arrow, an icon for female—circle and cross, an icon of a doctor's caduceus, an icon that said ZOO, an icon of a gear, and an icon of an arrow pointing to the right to page through. He pressed the icon for males.

And laughed at the first body. Big, black, broad-shouldered, immensely handsome body-builder type. Not interested. He paged through the stock bodies pretty quickly; a couple of vid stars and some model-looking types, a Haitian street boy, a Latino street boy, a white street boy, an Indian street boy, a Native American street boy, an oriental street boy. A soldier in camouflage, sports figures, a wizard in robes, a knight in chainmail, cliché after cliché. Then exaggerated types, metal bodies: chrome, silver, bronze, aluminum white, matte black, metallic red, blue, green. Leather bodies, neon bodies, negatives.

He ran completely through the males without finding any image he could imagine assuming and found himself in the female section looking at Denise Deren, the American VR star, who he admitted was very pretty with her green eyes and pale hair but who he also could not imagine wearing, so he pressed the caduceus.

A doctor looked at him out of an American-style surgical p-suit. "Normal human or other?" the doctor asked.

He didn't want to be chrome so he typed "yes" and for gender he typed male. Gave a height of 1.8 meters—hell, he might as well be tall. A weight, and a schematic of a generic male body appeared. He increased the weight by five kilos, decided that made the body look a little like the body builder on the first page and took it off. He was presented with a range of skin colors. He thought a moment, chose something dark. It would be nice to blend in. That meant curly black hair, close to the head. A presentation of eyes and noses and mouths and he chose pretty quickly. Then clothes and he just picked a sweater and tights. Normal, just look normal.

"Save this body as Lezard?"

"Okay," he said. And he had a body. The gloves were gone.

"Continue browsing?"

He started to say no then thought of the zoo. That would be interesting.

The first page was a dragon, sea green with red eyes and huge wings. He laughed again. No, he did not want to be a dragon. Not a demon with a face like leather and batwings. Not a winged horse, either. A whale, a green-tailed mermaid, an angel (luminous and quite pretty in an androgynous way but certainly not him.) A tall elf with long silver hair and green eyes and pointed ears. Alien creatures, part human, part leopard, or lizard or horse. A snake with beautiful scales like bright green and copper glass. Funny figures, fat old men and Charlie Chaplin and cartoon people. Then traditional animals.

An animal, that was appealing. He would like to be an animal. Not a lizard, despite his choice of names. He paged through thoughtfully. An owl, a hawk, a bat, a gazelle, a lion, a horse, a number of kinds of dogs, a wolf, a cat. . . .

A cat. He had never really thought of himself as catlike, but maybe a cat. But then he would have no hands. Maybe not.

The next section was all machines: planes and tanks and cars. He did not want to be a car, either.

He sighed and closed the catalogue.

Now there was a door in the wall. He grabbed the handlebars and took a step, the treadmill activated with a slight lurch and he was walking towards the door. The door opened.

It had been a long time since he did anything like this, maybe since the militaire. He had done simulations in training, there, but most of those had either been at consoles or in body suits. It was a little strange remembering that if he turned the handlebars he *turned*, even though his feet kept going straight on the treadmill.

The door opened on a playground. It didn't look real, wasn't supposed to. Everything in it was geometric, smooth, perfect in silver and red, surrounded by water and plashing with fountains. The pillars reflected his image in curving chrome. It all looked dated, like something that had been popular when he was a kid.

It was crowded but places like this were always a little crowded. If there weren't enough people the system generated a crowd. He looked up and the top of the fountains were crowned with blue gas flames. He sighed.

Actually getting here was a lot less interesting than picking a persona. In picking a persona there was so much potential. Like getting dressed for a party.

He looked until he found the access portals in the pillars in the center of the playground. (They had huge red metal balls bouncing up and down on top of them.) He could probably leave now, he had only ducked in because of the police, who were not even looking for him. Paranoia. He could go back to the apartment and Meph.

And do what?

"Time available?" he asked.

42.27, 42.26, 42.25, 42.24, 42.23. The time left blinked in front of him for five seconds and then disappeared.

Might as well play a game or something. He started forward and the treadmill started under his feet. Strange sense of being two places at once, in the playground *and* in the cubicle wearing the visor and gloves.

The systems available were listed at the access portals and there were people standing there reading. He had to kind of peer around. Some of the titles were dark, he supposed those were either not up and running or required membership. Flight simulations, adventure games with wizards, romances, combat games, after the eco disaster games, mysteries, a pirate simulation/adventure that had been popular when he was a kid. . . .

"We need a sixth," said a beautiful Latino woman with an eyepatch. The fact that she was beautiful didn't mean anything, anybody could be beautiful. "Is there anyone here interested in making a sixth?"

"Everything here is chaff," said a tall blond American male with a distinct Caribbean accent.

"It all looks system generated," the woman said.

It was easy to pick out the five users, once he knew there were five; besides the one-eyed woman and the American blond there was a tall, saturnine-looking fellow with an earring and an alligator tattoo on his arm, a woman with silk-white hair like fine egret feathers, and a fey-looking young man with copper hair and green eyes who probably spent too much time playing wizard adventure games. The copper-haired young man was looking at him. "He's not phantom," Copper Hair said.

"Sure he is," the one-eyed woman said.

"No he's not," Copper Hair said. "You're not, are you? You want to play?"

David shrugged. "I do not know the games, and I only have forty more minutes left."

"How the fuck you do that, Monode!" Alligator Tattoo said.

"He don't act like a phantom," Copper Hair said. "Phantoms don't stand still when you look at them, they have to do something."

"I'll pay for some extra time," One-Eyed Woman said.

"I got change, too," Alligator Tattoo said.

"It is not a problem," David said, "I can pay. What do I say to get out?"

"System," said Alligator Tattoo and flickered out of existence. In a second he was back. " 'Recommencer' will bring you right back to here."

"System," David said, and the world went black. He lifted the visor and went back out to the counter and bought two more hours. The five were still waiting when he came back.

They were in a virtual adventure league and they were playing a war-game simulation called *Zone of Fire.* Somebody hadn't shown up and if they hadn't found a sixth they'd have had to forfeit. "You don't have to do nothing, I mean, unless you want to," said Alligator Tattoo. Alligator Tattoo was clearly much younger than his persona. They all called him Chaco, except for the copper-haired boy, who called him Santos.

The portal opened and they stepped into an arid landscape, a field of dry grass. Almost, but not quite, the landscape of the Transvaal. The light was bright and hard and under it he felt himself expand. "Where are we?" he asked.

"Argentina," the one-eyed woman said.

Behind them were hills, in front of them was the long flat expanse of wheat he supposed was the pampas. The wind bent down the grass but he couldn't feel it. The light! The light was so wonderful. He blinked, his eyes watering. Driving out the darkness, the dimness of Caribe. He could sleep in a light such as this, he could live in a light such as this.

"Base camp is there," the blond said. In the strong sunlight David could see that the blond was cyborged with a delicate tracery of chip at the temples, like a vid character in bad American science fiction. What was it supposed to do, make him faster? Make him see in the dark?

He thought of the look he had chosen and smiled to himself, he really did look plain.

The base camp was not what he had expected. There was a tent, a tank, a collapsed glider and enormous amounts of ordinance. No mess, nothing for living. It wasn't at all real. People knew what they were doing; the blond American clambered into the tank—he must have been sitting at a console rather than using a treadmill—and Alligator Tattoo started handing out rifles. The rifles looked familiar enough, AP30s, cousins to the rifle he had carried in Anzania. When he took the rifle the glove tried to simulate weight by locking up and contracting. It didn't really feel as if the rifle weighed anything. David wondered how he was supposed to shoot and keep one hand on the handlebars. He tried to shoot the bolt, but the action wasn't smooth.

Alligator Tattoo—what was his name? Santos?—said, "What are you doing?"

"Checking the," how did you say it? "ah, the barrel." He shrugged. "Just trying to do something." He turned it over and looked at the clip. "How much ammunition?"

"I don't know," Santos said. "You don't have to reload."

"Ah," David said, "that is convenient."

"You ever shoot one before?"

"An AP30, only a couple of times. I have shot an AP15."

"Yeah?" Strange but the look, the tattoos, the body language and voice and expressions all fit a man older than David but Santos sounded young, maybe eighteen or nineteen. "Were you in Brasil?"

"No," David said.

Santos didn't know what to say. The one-eyed woman was looking at them, and the copper haired boy.

"I was in Anzania," David said into the silence. He didn't know if they would believe him or not, he couldn't remember any Central or South American troops in Anzania. This was a mistake. He should not have done this. He was aware of standing on the treadmill, his knee was starting to ache a little.

On the other hand, these people didn't know who he was. There was no way they could ever find out what he looked liked. He was free to relax, to tell them the truth as long as he didn't tell them his real name. "I am Lezard," he said. "You are Santos?"

Alligator Tattoo frowned, "Santos or Chaco. My call name here is Chaco. That's Monode—"

"Cobre," the boy corrected.

"Si, Cobre or Monode, whichever. The chico who drives the tank is Jack Stomper, the sarge is Amazon Lil," the woman with the eye-patch, "and that is Gin." Gin shook back her egret hair and smiled.

There was a crunch and the landscape around them shook, although the feeling was not translated into sensation. "Ay, cabron!" the blond said and yanked the hatch down. The one-eyed woman clicked on a communications port and called coordinates. The tank pivoted, treads reversing and churning up grass—that was a nice touch, David thought—and moving out.

"Lezard!" Santos shouted, "come with me! Touch that Kessler!"

David obediently touched the big Kessler gun and it rumbled to life.

"Follow me!" Santos said.

Santos' Kessler was following him like a big dog. As David followed, "his" Kessler trundled docilely behind him. He couldn't help it, he started to laugh.

Santos glanced over his shoulder and grinned. "Do like this," he tapped his headset—where had he gotten a headset? David reached up and low and behold, he was wearing a headset. When he tapped it suddenly he heard Amazon Lil talking in his ear, "Santos, you and Lezard head up around 14.5 and see if you can get a little mortar action on that ridge." Talking like a movie, he thought. Around him he could see red digital readouts, like looking through a heads-up display.

This was nothing like a real battle he thought. Thank goodness.

* * *

David called his Kessler "Fido." Fido was behind him while he and Santos planned what kind of fire to lay down. They were "lying" behind cover. It didn't feel as if they were lying because he was still standing on the treadmill and his knee was aching enough that he couldn't forget it was there. Still, he was having a very good time.

"They are there, I think," he told Santos. He didn't really know, but Amazon Lil thought that a team like him and Santos would be there. He picked over the land. He could make decisions about where they might be if this were real, but the restraints on the system made different things work.

"We'll lay down fire," Santos said.

"Okay, you want we should elephant walk the shells?"

"¿Qué?" Santos said.

"It is a pattern, better than just a grid, because it forces your enemy to fall back behind the fire. You lay a diagonal line of fire, and then another line behind it, and then another line behind it. See, they will go back, away from the line up towards 13.4, 13.3," he pointed to the coordinates. "Then after they learn our pattern, say five, six rounds, we fire on their position, where we think they have run, where we gave them to run. Then if we have enough shells, we can do again."

Santos nodded. "Okay. Okay. This, this is what they do in real war, right?"

"Yes," David said. Of course, in a real battle he would probably prefer to set the gun emplacement and fall back, so when the firing started they would not be targeted. But that wouldn't work if Fido was going to follow him around. Santos told him that if they got up, the Kesslers would stop firing and follow them.

Santos showed him how to set the guns and key in the pattern.

"Once we shoot, they will shoot back at us, no?" David said.

"Si, they'll have our position."

It was only a game. It didn't matter. Still, it made him uncomfortable, knowing he was going to be exposed. Maybe they would get lucky, take out the other team's guns. "Okay, Fido," he said, "it's time."

The sound from the Kesslers was startlingly loud. The sound deafened him and he closed his eyes, feeling the handlebars, the treadmill, the visor resting on his forehead. "Fuck," he said to nothing in particular.

The krump krump krump krump of the mortars across the grassland was pretty realistic, too, he thought. But now the others had their range. His only hope was that they were too busy running to stop and fire. Krump krump krump krump. Krump krump krump krump. Elephant walking. He'd seen the fucking elephant, like the Australians said when someone got wounded or killed.

It *was* nice not to have to worry about ammunition.

Krump krump krump krump. And then the pattern changed to angle the other way, to catch a team in retreat. Krump krump krump KRA-THUM-krump.

"We got a Kessler!" Santos shouted. "Come on! Vamos!"

"One more walk," David said. Krump KRA-THUM-krump, the sound of the exploding gun swallowing the motor sounds.

"Two of them! Slap, man! Now we split so they can only get one of us! Down the hill and watch for the glider!"

Down the hill. It didn't feel like down the hill, the treadmill didn't tilt, the ground wasn't uneven. David just walked, pushing the handlebars to indicate speed, but he and the Kessler zoomed downhill, it bobbing and swaying as if traveling fast over uneven ground. In his headset he heard Santos reporting, "Two Kesslers, Sarge!"

"Clear," Amazon Lil said. "Fallback Al."

Fallback Al? What did that mean?

"Ah, fuck!" Santos said. "Lezard! I didn't tell you the fallback patterns!"

"Ears on the line! Com clear!" Amazon Lil said sharply. Vid army talk that said the channel wasn't secure and the enemy was listening.

"I just keep my nose clean then," David said.

All he needed to do was hide. Although that was hard to do with the Kessler rumbling along behind him. He tried to keep close to the ridge, on the flat grassland the Kessler would stand out like an oil derrick. Camouflage nets would help, heat reflecting nets. Break up the signature of the Kessler. He should ask Santos if they could get any.

The grass swished around him, he wished he could feel the wind. Still, the sunlight was so nice. And he was sweating from excitement. He was, he had to admit, having a hell of a time.

Were there mines?

Nothing to do if there were, he couldn't get the Kessler to go in front of him. He should have asked more about the rules. Next time.

Too late he caught a glimpse of something and looked up. "Watch for the glider," Santos had said. Although what he was supposed to do when he saw it—

"Glider above me at 15.4," he said, just as a woman with a banner of black hair leaned over the side and dropped something. He tried to push the handlebars out to go faster and there was this tremendous noise, the world went red, then black—

And he was in the playground. His ears were ringing. Around him stood phantoms, talking and laughing. He caught his reflection, a tall black man in a green sweater looking back out of the curving chrome of the pillar. He laughed a shaky laugh.

The playground was darker than the simulation, like being inside rather than like being in strong sunlight. Like being in Caribe.

Of course. When you died you went to Caribe.

The day was half gone, time eaten up by the game. That was something, it was even fun. He stood on the treadmill, absently rubbing his knee, wondering what he should do next.

He should leave a message for somebody. He put the visor back on and went back to the playground. If one of them got killed while he was leaving the message then he'd run into them. He didn't want to do that. He didn't know why, but it just seemed easier to just leave a message and get off the system, not say anything about getting killed in the game.

He told the system he wanted to leave a message for Santos.

The system didn't recognize the name.

Shit. What was the other name they had called him? Something like chico. Chaco. Leave a message for Chaco?

The system pulled up a phantom of Chaco and it was Santos, alligator tattoo and all.

"Okay," David said. "Thanks, ah, tell everyone thanks. It was very interesting. Ah, and I have a good time. Sorry I get killed and all, I hope you win. Fin."

David pulled the visor and was back on the treadmill. Stupid message. He could never leave very good messages. And he knew his English had been bad. He thought about going back and changing it, but every moment he was in the playground increased the likelihood that one of the others would pop out.

Enough. It had been a nice time.

Now all he had to do was remember how to get back to his room. And maybe pick up something to eat. He was kind of hungry.

David didn't plan to go back, it just used some of his money and he should be saving. He didn't know what he was saving for, he was pretty sure he didn't have enough for a passport and every day he was here he spent a little on the room, and on food for him and Meph. Bleeding to death a drop at a time.

"I should get a job," he told Meph. A job would be nice, pass the time, bring a little money in instead of the money all going out. But he would have to have identification.

Maybe he should sell something? Make something? What could he possibly sell or make? If he didn't do something, sitting in this room was going to drive him crazy.

Meph was sitting on the windowsill, ignoring him. Meph wanted to go out. Every time he opened the door he was afraid Meph would get out, if the kitten got away he thought he would never see him again.

When he stood up Meph mewed, hopeful. "No," he said. "I am just going for a walk. You stay here."

Sure, just going for a walk. Well, he would just see if Santos had left an answer to his message, see if they had won.

He didn't have to go back to the *Plazoleta D'Imagen*, but he didn't know of any others, so he went that way. The square was full of peddlers, but there were no children playing in front of the peep show, so the butterfly girl had no audience to activate her. He was careful not to walk near.

People still stared at him. How was he supposed to hide? Maybe he could get surgery? Change his face? He didn't even know who to ask to find a doctor who would do it. And he didn't want to change his face. He wanted to goddamn well go home.

Maybe if he cut his hair he would look more like these people. Not many people wore their hair down to their shoulders anymore. He would do that, see if it helped.

He shoulders ached from tension by the time he got to the Reality Parlor. At least it was the same girl. He paid for an hour. Just an hour. If he met anyone he could always pay for more.

There was a message for Lezard, the system told him as soon as he hooked in.

Santos, of course. David felt himself smiling, Santos' way of talking was so boyish, so completely at odds with the sinister-looking revolutionary persona he wore. "Hey, Lezard, you should have waited around! We won, five to four. You were the only person to get killed, but that was my fault because I didn't tell you where it is we fallback. And I did not tell you how to hide the Kessler. The thing you did, elephant walking the mortars, that was great!

"Anyway," Santos went on, "We play again on Saturday. Zanaza is supposed to be here on Saturday, so we have the six, but maybe you can show up and if someone else can't come then you can play, you know?"

No, he really shouldn't. He couldn't. It was a waste of money, playing games when he should be planning what to do, figuring out a way out of this country.

But where was he going to start finding a way unless he talked to people? Through the system he could talk to people and they would never be able to tell anyone who he was, never be able to betray him to the blue and whites.

So he might, after all.

But maybe he should look more like the others? In a way, he was more obvious than if he were somehow, how could he describe it? Flashy.

He asked for the catalogue again, called up the doctor. What could he do, strange-colored eyes? He tried blue eyes. No. Green eyes. Eh. Not so much difference unless he made them really green, and that felt foolish. Red, orange, yellow, purple, metallic, stone and other. He couldn't even imagine trying purple eyes, metallic gave him the obvious choices (with or without pupil). Featureless bronze eyes seemed very distracting and rude and when he looked at his own image they made him uncomfortable. He looked, he thought, dead. Other was very strange. Pupils shaped like hourglasses, hearts, circles like snakes, shattered eyes, tiger eyes, goat eyes, lizard eyes (which was kind of funny), eyes that were hollow as if there was nothing in there except darkness, and to take that further, empty eyes that were like windows on galaxies.

He wiped that as quickly as he could.

One of the options for yellow eyes was a dark amber, almost like brown eyes but not quite. He liked that. It was a little different, but not something anybody would notice unless they looked close.

Then he changed clothes. Something a little stranger, maybe like a commando would wear? Sweater with a shoulder patch to rest a rifle butt, boots.

It looked a little foolish. He almost switched back. No, save now, he thought, before you change your mind.

He saved and then wandered into the playground. He stood at the list of games trying to decide what to play. He could go to Tokyo, go diving, be a spy, be lost on a spaceship . . . but nothing would take him to Paris. It would have been nice, even if it was a synthetic Paris.

Eventually he tried being a spy for awhile. There was an international module but if it took him to Paris he couldn't get that far. He stopped playing before his hour was up.

On the way back to the room he stopped and got his hair cut short. But he still felt foreign.

8

Mindgames

Mayla and Tim settled in to her grandfather's house and her grandfather had Jude open up the rooms and take the dust covers off the furniture. It raised dust and in the dry, carefully maintained air of her grandfather's house the dust hung, fine as fog. Mayla couldn't see it but she could feel it, cottony tasting, coating her tongue and the inside of her mouth. It dulled the mirrors, dulled the fabric of the furniture, dulled her sense of taste and smell and made her feel tired and thick. She ran her finger across the mirror and left a line. The service came in and cleaned and the mirrors looked as clear as windows, but the next day the dust was back.

Two men from the insurance people came out and sat on the pink flowered couch where she had sat while the blue and white asked Tim why David wasn't coming back. The older, shorter man had a gray unhealthy face. Mayla supposed he had good insurance, though.

"Will you be staying?" he asked.

"No," she said, "well, yes, for awhile." She wasn't going to rush into buying a place and it would take awhile for the insurance money to come through.

"You will move to the United States?" the gray-faced man asked.

"Pardon me?" she said.

"If you are not staying."

"Oh, no. No. I thought you meant would I be staying here, with my grandfather. I'm not leaving Caribe."

"Ah," he said. "You see, a lot of people do, after something like this."

Leave home.

He told her she needed to hire some security.

"I will," she said. "I plan to. As soon as things get settled, right now I don't have a place of my own."

"You need someone now," the gray-faced little man said.

"It's not like I don't have someone, Tim is still here," she pointed out.

Tim sat, listening, his empty hands loose on his knees.

"It has upset everything," she explained. "I have to tackle things, one at a time. There are some things at work that I have to take care of, and then I have to find a place to live. And since Tim is here, I have security."

"Ms. Ling," said the gray-faced little man, "if you are going to stay, we believe you need to hire someone professional."

"Okay," she said. She could understand why they didn't exactly consider Tim a professional. "As soon as I can." First, she had to settle the MaTE deal. If she settled the MaTE deal, everything would fall into place; she could think about things, she wouldn't have to worry about being a banker, about work. "It might take me a few weeks, right now I don't have any place where someone could live, do you understand?"

They did not understand, or rather, as they made clear, she did not understand. Her insurance rates were going to triple, no matter who or what she hired.

"Triple?" she said.

The house had been bombed seven days ago. And if she did not hire someone within the next fourteen days, her insurance would be canceled. She was now in a "high risk group."

"Because you have been targeted, Ms. Ling." The little gray-faced man seemed sympathetic. "And your security is compromised." He said "promised," as if she had been promised something. "Because your staff is involved."

"David wasn't involved," she said, from habit more than conviction.

"Yes," the man said, "but he ran away. So, we insurers, we are conservative people, we have to assume the worst. I have a list of agencies," he checked his briefcase, but it was his partner who handed it to her, "ah, yes, there it is. They can send you people to interview. These agencies, they are approved, you see?"

"Yes," she said. She held the list and read the names and when she was done she couldn't remember what she'd read.

Tim sat with his hands on his knees and the two insurance men sat on the dusty flowered couch, all of them looking expectant, looking at her.

"Thank you," she said. And then, much to everyone's surprise, including her own, tears welled up in her eyes. She blinked and blinked, but she couldn't stop them.

"I need to go back to work, to establish a routine, but I'm unfocused," she explained to Tim. They were almost in Marincite. She was working again. Or she would be, just as soon as she got to Marincite and started. "I can't seem to put my attention on the things it's supposed to be on." The house had been gone for nine days and she had twelve more to find security. "I suppose it's normal, but I'm worried about the Marincite deal. I am not very focused, you know. I can make mistakes, say the wrong thing, because I'm not sharp. People don't make loans with stupid bankers." When she got back to Julia, she was going to make an appointment with a counselor.

"Somebody else could go," Tim said.

"No," she said. "There's this Saad Shamsi business, I have to die about that."

"What?" Tim said.

"It's *en la sombra*," she said.

"No, what you said, you'd have to 'die about that'."

"Decide," she said. "I said 'decide about that'."

"No you didn't," Tim said, "you said 'die'."

"I meant 'decide'." She shook her head. "Don't go analyzing, Tim. That business about Freudian slips isn't true. It's medieval psychology."

"I didn't say anything about Freudian slips," he growled.

The sub lurched, lousy docking. At the subport in Miami, she thought, the docking system was automated and it was always smooth. Everything in Caribe was inept. Would she have been able to make it as a banker if she had had to in the U.S.? Or was she inept, too?

She didn't want to come back to Marincite, but she had to. She would stay for two days, then go back to Julia and hire some security and start thinking about a place to live. Routine. Establish a routine. Then she'd be fine. She was a competent person, she was just unsettled.

The first class waiting room was quiet. A dark-haired man in a business suit was standing at the gate, waiting, and she thought, that person looks like Saad Shamsi. She was worried about that, seeing Saad Shamsi everywhere like a guilty conscience.

It was Saad Shamsi. Her luck, just to happen to come in at the same time as Saad was supposed to be meeting someone.

Then he saw them and waved. He bent his head to talk to the woman at the gate, then handed her his smart card. She passed it through a reader and he came through walking towards her with purpose.

"*Madre de Cristo*, I'm not ready for this," Mayla said to Tim.

Tim frowned.

She smiled at Saad as if she was happy to see him.

"Mayla," he said. "Mr. Navarro thought maybe it would be better if someone you knew met you." He held out his hand and she shook it.

What did that mean? Was Polly Navarro telling her that she should give Saad his loan? Or was he thinking that after losing her house she would feel better recognizing her escort?

Saad was with the city government, what was he doing at

Navarro's beck and call? Because Marincite Corp. *is* Marincite City. Not sharp, Mayla, she told herself, she was not sharp at all.

She couldn't very well leave Saad to chase their baggage, so the three of them all stood waiting for it to rumble up from the depths of the port. Saad was quiet, was it awkward for him to be standing here? He would say something about her house. Everybody always did. She waited for it. He didn't say anything.

Finally she said, "How's business?"

"Pretty good," he said.

"Have you secured a loan with someone else?"

"Not yet," he said. "You said you'd think about it. Mr. Navarro suggested I talk to you about it before I went to Caribbean Securities."

"I see," she said. If it was true, didn't that mean that Polly Navarro wanted her to make the deal with Saad? She wished she could ask Mr. Navarro, but that would be stupid.

"We don't have to talk about it now," he said. He was uncomfortable.

"MaTE will put me in a conference room, we can talk there."

"It would be better if you came out to the loft," he said.

"No," she said. No. She didn't want to go to the loft. Didn't like it there. People came to her office, she wasn't supposed to go to places like that.

"My partner can't very well come to MaTE," he said.

She almost asked why not. Her mind, where was her mind? If Saad said his partner couldn't come to MaTE he couldn't come. She was going to make a mistake, say or do the wrong thing. She could feel the shakes, creeping around her hands, loosening her stomach. Think this through, she told herself. Why couldn't he come to MaTE? She couldn't think because she was anxious. "He said everything was all right with the Uncles."

"It's okay," Saad said. "The Uncles are no problem."

He wasn't explaining. He looked at the luggage claim rather than at her. She didn't think he was lying but she didn't know. He wasn't going to tell her what was going on.

"Why can't you and I negotiate this?" she asked.

He shook his head. She knew the answer there, she had met his partner, seen how things were between Saad and Moustache.

Dead end. Everything was a dead end and her mind wasn't working. Meet somewhere else? She didn't know places in Marincite, one place was no more safe than another. Tim's duffel rumbled up and he reached between her and Saad to pluck it. It was good to remember Tim was there, big blond Tim.

What to say. What to do. She couldn't very well talk about it now. She had to collect herself, she had to be calm. Take a deep breath, she thought. This anxiety, she thought to herself, it is mindless, it is reaction to stress, you can handle it. Once she had collected herself she could talk to Saad.

"Look," she said, "I need some time to think about this, why don't you call me this evening?"

"I'm sorry," Saad said, "I don't see how that's going to make any difference. The loft is the best place to meet."

"Earlier," she said. "Like about six-thirty."

"I'll call and confirm," he said.

Her hunter-green garment bag rumbled up. "That's mine," she said and Saad leaned to pick it up but Tim said, "I'll get it." Saad took a short step back but Tim just looked at him for moment before bending over and picking up the bag. It was the kind of look Tim had given David when David first came to work for her. Territorial, she thought. Alpha male, squaring off.

Tim, taking care of her. She shouldn't have wanted him to, but Mother of Christ, she did.

Tim didn't like going to see Saad and his partner, and unlike David, he made it clear. He had heard of the part of the city called Cathedral. He said it was a pit, a ghetto, a *budayeen*. He didn't trust Saad Shamsi.

"You liked him well enough when he took us to see jai alai," Mayla pointed out.

Tim didn't bother to answer.

"In and out," she said. "I'll just get a signature on the papers and leave." Polly wanted the loan, then she had to do it.

Tim scowled and hunkered down next to her in the chute. He filled the space in the bubble, overwhelmed it. She had forgotten just what a physical presence Tim could be. Put your arms around me, she thought, I want to hide. Not that she would, it was completely inappropriate and she knew the consequences. His hands looked small compared to the rest of him.

Tim was imposing, if you didn't know him. He would make Saad's partner think twice. He was better than David, that way. Maybe she should remember that when she hired security, hire someone big.

Or maybe she was supposed to hire someone inconspicuous. She didn't know. She didn't know enough about any of this. The men from the insurance said she had been targeted. Once she was a target, what was she supposed to do? Get protection? Emigrate? Half the people she went to school with seemed to have emigrated. Emigrate where, the U.S.? Follow her mother to Europe? Not to Europe. She didn't like Europe. When she was fifteen she visited her mother in Barcelona. She had embarrassed her mother because she couldn't adapt, couldn't get used to sunlight and weather. She tried to think of something else. She wished she could take a pill right now that would make her think clearly, that would stop her thoughts from skittering around.

The chute rose into the station, into the light. Cathedral. The humidity hit her when the chute opened. The refresh was not as good here as it was in Central and the air was clammy. Poor man's air.

The loft was empty when they got there. "He's coming," Saad said. "He said he'd be here." The loft smelled like aldehyde, chemical sharp and sweet. "He'll be here," Saad promised. "You want some coffee? A soft drink?"

"Nothing," she said. She didn't really want coffee or something to drink, not with that smell.

Tim glowered. Saad looked uncomfortable.

The loft had long tables in it now, and newspapers in bundled piles in a corner, edges curling in the damp, and a huge plastic drum with a tube and a siphon. There were dirty footprints all over, perfect prints of soles with circles, zigzag lines, and makers' marks, as if the floor had been mopped and then walked on.

Nobody knew what to say.

"I guess coffee sounds good," Mayla finally said. She didn't have to drink it but it gave Saad something to do.

Where was Moustache? She didn't like that he wasn't here. Things weren't going right.

Saad brought coffee for her and Tim. It seemed to her that it smelled chemical, the same sweet-sharp chemical she smelled in the air. The surface of the coffee iridesced, like oil, under the light.

Saad went back to get another cup for himself and she heard the door open at the base of the stairs. Moustache came up the steps, followed by the tawny-haired girl, who kept her eyes on the floor. Moustache barely glanced at them. He stomped to the back of the loft and started talking to Saad, speaking low and fast. "What?" Saad said. And again, "What? I can't understand you."

The girl stood in the middle of the loft. She sniffed and rubbed her nose as if she were going to cry.

Moustache struck the table with the flat of his hand. The girl started as if struck. From the way she was standing, Mayla couldn't see her wrist so she didn't know if the girl was wearing a slave bracelet or not.

Saad looked back at them a couple of times, but Moustache talked on and on, words tumbling out, thick with rage. Was he drugged? Mayla thought he had to be. Saad looked back again and Moustache grabbed his shoulder roughly. "¡ESCHUCHA!" Then his voice dropped down again, a rumble of consonants that Mayla couldn't decipher.

Maybe she and Tim were supposed to leave? All she wanted was to say to Moustache that she'd give him his damn loan and then she could leave here, and worry about these people later.

The girl shifted her feet a little, as if she would like to sit down.

Moustache looked around and said, "What do you want?"

Mayla looked at the tawny-haired girl. The girl looked at Mayla. And Saad said, placatingly, "About the loan. She is here about the loan."

"Big anglo," Moustache said. "Your boyfriend?"

He was talking to her, not the tawny-haired girl at all. "No," Mayla said, her voice rising in surprise. "No, he's not my boyfriend." Did Tim act like her boyfriend? She hadn't even thought Moustache noticed them there.

"Who is he?"

"Her security," Saad said.

"I thought her security is the little rat-faced *chino*."

"He doesn't work for me anymore," Mayla said.

Moustache didn't like that answer. He scowled at her. *"Chinga,"* he said.

Tim scowled back. Don't, she thought, don't start anything. It doesn't matter.

"What is your problem!" Moustache shouted at her. He strode across the room, into her face, so close she took a step back. "You play mindgames with us, what? WHAT IS YOUR PROBLEM, BITCH!" He was standing so close that spittle flicked her face and his breath had a strange odor—almost fruity like aftershave—and the whites of his eyes looked yellow. She flinched, and he grabbed her arm. She pulled away and Tim grabbed for Moustache.

Moustache jerked away and the tawny-haired girl shrieked.

"Hey hey hey," Saad said. "Easy. Everything is all right."

"Don't touch her," Tim said. "You hear me? Don't touch her."

"You think you own everything? This is Marincite," Moustache said, ignoring Tim, "you are in my city now. Here, I could have you both disappear. No one would find you. Anglos, no one here likes anglos. No one likes an anglo *chinga*. No one would care. Here, this is not the capital, this is Marincite."

"Hey," Saad said, his voice smooth and placating, "nobody is talking about disappearing. We are going to make a loan, that's all."

"Shut up," Moustache said, not even looking at Saad. "Listen, I just want you to understand the rules. We are not impressed by *las norteamericanas* here. Your big country may be rich, but it's far away. So don't play mindgames anymore."

She wasn't North American. She knew better than to correct him, don't explain, it would only make him angry if she explained. But she wasn't from the U.S., white skin or no white skin, she was Caribbean. He was crazy, he was toxic. What did it matter what he said? The tawny-haired girl was watching, watching. Not moving at all, even her breath invisible.

He was looking at Tim, and then he started to grin. The tawny-haired girl covered her mouth with her hand. *Madre de Diós,* Mayla thought. The tawny-haired girl looked scared and that was bad. This is bad, Mayla thought, the words in her head. He's going to hurt Tim.

Tim didn't look scared, Tim looked furious. "What's funny?" he asked.

"Tim—"

"*Estupido,*" Moustache said, grinning. Behind him, Saad looked scared, too.

"What is your problem?" Tim asked.

Moustache turned around and walked away a few steps. Turned around again and he had a gun. A little gun, the size of his hand, all graphite gray. Not like the handgun that Tim carried under the seat of the car. Small. Illegal looking.

Nobody said anything. Please God, Mayla thought, let it be all right. Just let this be over. In a couple of hours this will be over.

Moustache was full of contained energy. He was looking at Tim and she knew not to move because if she moved he might look at her and she didn't want Moustache to think about her. It was awful, hoping that he wouldn't notice her, being glad that Tim was his target. It was sinful. But she did, she couldn't help it. Don't notice me, she thought. Don't move, she thought to Tim.

Tim did not move. Like the tawny-haired girl, he did not even seem to breathe.

"*Bueno*," Moustache said. Then he looked at her and she felt her breath stop, a pain in her chest. His eyes were brown, the whites yellowed; his eyes were diseased looking and he was watching her with his rancid eyes. She didn't know what was going to happen.

He aimed the gun at her and she could not imagine what she should do. Move, leap away like the vid. But the truth was she couldn't think. If she moved he would shoot her. Maybe if she didn't move, he would not shoot. But if he was going to shoot she should move. She could not think, could not make herself move. How would she know when he was going to shoot? How would she know when to jump? Please, God, don't let him shoot. She was afraid of the pain. She was afraid to die. She couldn't. She couldn't. Please.

Nobody did anything.

She could not even look at the gun, just his rancid eyes. The way the irises looked as if they were not sharply round, as if the edges were breaking down, melted looking.

It went on and on. How long had she stood here like this? A minute, five minutes? Ten minutes? She had to do something. She wanted to just be still, hope it went away. She had to do something. Breathe. The veins in his yellowed eyes. Maybe he had a medical condition? Jaundice? People didn't get jaundice anymore, did they?

She opened her mouth, but nothing happened.

Be still. Don't startle him, if she startled him he'd jerk, he'd squeeze, he'd fire.

"Hey," she said, so softly, because that was how her voice came.

He didn't jerk, didn't move at all. Now he was going to kill her.

"*Oye, eschucha*," she said. "Hey, listen."

He didn't answer her. She would make him angry. Just a little push and he would shoot.

"Hey," she said. "We're here to make you a loan. We're here to do a little business."

Moustache watched her with his yellow eyes.

"Everybody is here to do business," Saad echoed. His voice

sounded smooth, soothing. His voice made her hopeful. His voice said everything would be all right. But maybe that wasn't true. Some times when you thought everything was going to be all right, it wasn't.

"We want to talk," she said.

And Moustache turned and aimed the gun into the office. The gunshot was a little sound, just a blurt.

The tawny-haired girl shrieked and Tim started. Moustache laughed. "No mindgames," Moustache said. "You see? No mindgames."

Mayla was suddenly aware of the sweet chemical smell again, so strong she felt dizzy. "No mindgames," she agreed. She would go through the motions, she would say anything he wanted, and then she would get away.

Moustache looked around the loft. Looked at Saad and grinned. They were all standing around watching him, waiting for what he would do. Mayla could feel the individual tickles of perspiration on her ribs. Her jacket would be perspiration stained, maybe ruined.

"Maybe," Moustache said, "we should show the lady what we make?"

"I don't think that's a good idea," Saad said, soft.

"Fuck you," Moustache said conversationally. That struck him as funny. "Fuck you," he said again, liking the sound of it. "I think we should."

Humor him, diffuse the situation. "Okay," Mayla said.

Saad looked startled. Moustache rounded on her, delighted. "You see? *La norteamericana* wants to see."

"I don't think—" Saad said.

"That's right," Moustache said, "you don't think. Go get some bracelets."

Saad went back into the office. Mayla found she didn't want him out of sight, she felt better when he was right there. He could talk to Moustache. Tim was just watching, very still, his face blank. She didn't know what he was thinking, or what he was planning. Don't do anything, she thought, just don't be crazy.

She heard the jingle of keys, loud in the loft. Moustache was looking at her, and he still had the gun in his hand, although it wasn't aimed at her. It wasn't aimed at anyone, as if he had just forgotten it. She tried not to look at it, so she wouldn't remind him he had it, but she didn't know what to look at. Should she look at Moustache? She couldn't look away, she needed to watch him, she had to know what he was doing. He could do anything.

If she kept looking at him, would he get mad? She couldn't look at his eyes, so she glanced away, but looked back at him, in his eyes. Away, across the loft, at Tim. Back at Moustache, back down at the gun, back up at his strange eyes. She didn't know what to do with her gaze.

Saad came back out of the office and she could look at him. Then she could watch Moustache again because *he* was watching Saad.

"Let's see," Moustache said.

Slave bracelets. They didn't look like anything, just a plate of dull metal on a strap like a watchband. He had six or seven of them and he held them out to Moustache, who selected one and held it up, dangling it like the strap was a tail.

"You try one before?" he asked.

"No," Mayla said.

"Go ahead. I think you like it."

"That's okay," she said.

"No, really," Moustache said. "It's good. You try."

"I," she swallowed, "I can't."

"Are you playing games?" he said, conversational, and she felt the prickle on her neck.

"Let me look at it," she temporized. She held out her hand to take it but Moustache took her hand and turned it over. Tim gave a little start.

"Enough," he said.

"Shut up," Mayla said, sharply. That startled him. Moustache laughed and the color started in Tim's neck. Be embarrassed, she thought, just don't be stupid.

Moustache's hand was damp. Like the air. She wanted to wipe her hand off. He held her hand a moment, as if he was going to tell her fortune, looking at her palm, at her long fingers. Maybe he was, maybe he was making her future. She thought, she would be changed by this, by the slave bracelet. Like losing her virginity.

Moustache turned her hand back over and put the bracelet on so that the flat metal plate was against the pale inside of her wrist. Then he did the flat catch.

She expected a jolt, like an electric current, but it wasn't like that at all. No spike, no high. But her head felt clear. Her thoughts weren't all skittering. She felt calmer. Still scared, but calmer.

"See? Is not so bad." Moustache smiled at her.

And well. Not tired, when was the last time she had not felt tired? She realized that people felt tired all the time. The only time people didn't feel tired was when they were really angry, or really happy, or really frightened, and then they couldn't appreciate it. Now she could feel what it was like not to be tired. It was wonderful, as if something had been lifted off her. This was the way people were supposed to feel.

"She likes it," Moustache said.

She did like it. Very much, she liked it.

"Now we will discuss business?" Moustache said.

"Okay," she said.

Tim shook his head.

"It's not like that," she said. "It doesn't make your head muddled." It made it easier to think, because her mind wasn't dragged down by all those feelings and tiredness. She felt good.

She could weigh the pros and cons. She dug out her papers and her chips. Her hands were shaking a little. She was still afraid; if she thought about it she could find it, her fear. It was a thing in her thoughts, like a rock in a river, and she could flow around it. Because of the bracelet. Good to be afraid, just not so afraid that she couldn't act.

Maybe she couldn't trust her thoughts? Bracelets were illegal. She laid out her papers and Moustache started reading. But they were illegal because of the degeneration they caused in the nervous system. Because of prolonged use. And they were addicting because they really did enhance. So she should take advantage of this one time. Lucky, because this was the one time she really needed it.

While Moustache read she looked around the loft. People were amazing. Tim was amazing. His skin was amazing, flushed with capillaries in his face and neck, so smooth over his forehead. Tim was so handsome. But so was Saad, with his high temples and his beautiful, neat hands. Dark and almost manicured looking. People were extraordinary, and nobody realized it except maybe for a few great artists and poets. How completely artificial it was to divide people into beautiful and ugly.

Moustache handed each paper to Saad as soon as he had read it. Mayla looked at the tawny-haired girl. She was strained and tired looking, but beautiful, too. Youth was truly astounding. No wonder they all worshiped youth. Even through her tiredness she glowed, and Mayla felt the pang of loss. And she never knew it was hers to lose because she never realized she had it until she looked in the mirror one morning when she got out of the shower and saw the skin of her collarbones and neck and realized she was thirty years old and it was gone. It wasn't fair.

Moustache signed, Saad signed. She took the papers. "That's it," she said.

"So when do we get the money?" Saad said.

"It'll take a couple of days to process, it has to go through the credit committee for approval," she said. "I'm not in Julia, so maybe four days, and then it'll be in your account."

"All record keeping comes through me," Saad said.

All record keeping was by numbered account, no names. "Your PO," she said.

"Perhaps you would like to buy a bracelet," Moustache said. Pleased with himself.

She could not. She fingered it, not wanting to take it off. That was why it was addicting, because it just made people more human, more themselves. Enhanced them.

The tawny-haired girl smiled. *"Hermana,"* she said. "Sister." A smile like Moustache's, pleased with itself, and Mayla wondered if she had misunderstood. Was the girl Moustache's daughter?

Mayla unbuckled the clasp and the weight of twenty-one atmospheres fell on her like an ache. She shuddered. For a moment she didn't want to move. The tiredness swallowed her up. Every day she felt this way, for the rest of her life, she felt this way. Oh, God, she couldn't bear it.

"If you want to buy," Moustache said, "you let us know."

"Let's go," Tim said.

And Saad, what did Saad think? Had he ever tried it? Could he see that she was hooked? She handed the bracelet to Moustache. She wanted it back. Moustache looked at her with his yellow eyes and she thought for a moment, now that he had what he wanted he would kill them.

But the loan wasn't through committee yet.

Her mind started to go in different directions. She thought of the house, of hiring security, of the fact that now she was bound to Moustache by this loan.

"Come on," Tim said, urgent. Tim was scared.

Oh, God, she was so tired and so scared and so unhappy. She gathered up her papers.

"Be in touch," Moustache said. "We can do business again."

He was crazy. She had bound herself to a married man, married to him by the bank and Polly Navarro. She didn't know what to do. She couldn't think at all, could do nothing through her misery except follow Tim down the hollow steps, her heels clicking on the empty steps as if they were drums, all the sound bouncing.

"What the hell did you do that for?" Tim said on the street.

"What?" she said.

"Try the thing on? It could have done anything, you didn't know if it was wired right or not! It could have fried your nervous system!"

"It didn't," she said.

"Are you sure?" he asked. He grabbed her wrist and started down the street.

She wanted to run away. She wanted to go somewhere where she didn't have to act, didn't have to think. "After neural stimulation, there's a bottoming," she said.

"What?"

She was mumbling. Louder, she said, "After neural stimulation, people bottom out. I've read about it."

"Great," Tim said.

She didn't want to see Saad Shamsi ever again. She most certainly didn't want to see Moustache.

She wouldn't put the papers through. She'd burn them. It was illegal, a signed contract was a binding document and destruction of it without the other party's consent was against the law. But what were they going to do, take her to court? She didn't care about the Marincite loan, it wasn't worth dying for. If she got the Marincite loan then she might eventually get promoted and then things would get even more complicated.

She wanted to go somewhere and live, maybe Del Sud. Buy a flat, live by herself, watch the vid. Have a simple life. Quit the world. Anything was better than her life now.

She sat in a conference room, waiting to talk to Polly Navarro about the Marincite loan, about the takeover target to finance MaTE's independence. She had a list of likely candidates. The air in this room was clean and dry. The window looked down on Manhattan. As far as she could tell, it was modern Manhattan. She had lived in Manhattan, she probably should have known whether it was a modern view or not.

The hard light reflected off the wood conference table. She didn't know if she should tell Polly that she wasn't going to make Saad's loan or not. She knew she'd have to find a way to let him know, but she didn't know if she was supposed to pretend that Polly didn't know what the company was or not. She knew she wasn't supposed to tell him.

Whatever happened, she had to think about being a banker.

She was either going to have to deal with people like Moustache and Anna Eminike or emigrate. Or just wait for something to happen. And she couldn't deal with Moustache or Anna Eminike, they were not people one dealt with.

Emigrate.

At one time in her life she had wanted to leave Caribe. More than anything. When she was fifteen she had finally gone to the surface for the first time when she went to Barcelona to see her mother.

When she was fifteen, she thought she was maybe the only person at her school who had never been to the surface. It couldn't have been true, but she remembered it seemed that way.

As a girl she thought that she was really a surface person. She knew she would love weather. Wind; wind would be exciting, wind was like *Wuthering Heights,* she couldn't exactly explain how but it was. And once she got there she would be with her mother.

The sub was boring, Miami was strange. She had done five days of decompression in decomp at Port Authority and she was reacting to the change. It was night, but the lights in the terminal were too bright, the lights on poles outside even brighter. And the air smelled funny, organic: like food and garbage; potato and carrot scrapings. Plants. Grass. Nobody had ever told her that the surface smelled funny—even the ocean was loud and over the familiar briny smell it stank.

She landed in Barcelona jangled and tired. Her mother was waiting with Gabriel, her four-year-old half-brother, and her mother's second husband, Tito. Her mother's hair was blonde instead of brown and she spoke lisping Spanish to the four-year-old and the husband. Mayla understood a little Spanish, but not very much.

The sunlight was too bright, her head ached and her eyes watered. Barcelona was loud. They got on a tram and her half-brother stared at her with round black eyes, and her mother's husband smiled too much. She couldn't think of what to say. Every time she looked at her mother who was silhouetted against one of the blinding windows, she got afterimages when she turned away. The husband got off before they got home, he had to go to work. He worked in one of the blinding glass towers, unnervingly high. There was too much space, the sky was so blue, it seemed impossible that any stretch of space would be such an obvious, unnatural color.

She was afraid she'd get a sunburn. Food tasted strange, salt wasn't as salty and everything had a funny, metallic taste. It's just adjustment, her mother said. At dinner, her mother kept speaking in Spanish to Tito and Gabriel. Tito tried to talk to her, but she didn't understand him, even when he said things she knew the Spanish words for.

"Mayla," her mother said, "I wanted to bring you here for so long, but Jimmy's mother—" her mother pursed her lips. Her mother wasn't going to talk about Gram. Mayla didn't talk about Gram either, but it made conversation oddly disjointed. Her mother kept saying, "Tell me about your life." But after she had talked about school, Gram was in everything.

Her mother took her shopping, bought her expensive things, with collars of eyelet lace, a sleeveless silk top, a quilted jacket. She tried to play with her half-brother, but he made her nervous. He liked to be tickled and he liked to wrestle, but pretty quickly he got rough, hitting her leg with his fist and laughing, and she didn't know how to make him stop.

The third day she was there they went downtown again and shopped. They were on the bus coming back from the city, and for the first time since she had arrived, she felt as if she could look out at the street without her eyes watering. "It's cloudy," her mother said. "You don't need your sunglasses, Mayla."

But she liked them. "I can see better," she said.

There were trees and they pulled in the wind. It was like the vid, watching the trees. Mayla felt as if she wanted to be outside in the wind. She felt afraid, but it was a good kind of afraid—excited. Water started dripping down from the roof of the bus, condensation maybe, streaking her window. Streaking all the windows. Darkening the street. It wasn't from the bus, she thought, it was rain.

"Oh no," her mother said, "I don't have an umbrella. We'll have to run." Her mother leaned forward and put her hand against the window. She looked excited. When they got to their stop, her mother took her hand, and pulled her down the steps, out into the rain, running.

The rain was pounding down, and just as they jumped to the ground there was a crack, like an explosion and she started because an explosion at home meant the sea was coming in, an explosion at home meant you were dead. Her mother pulled her, running. Mayla's face was wet and she was afraid to breathe in; the air was full of water, it was unnatural, it was cold and awful, she couldn't breathe, she felt that if she took a breath she would drown. Her mother dragged her, and she saw white sparks, things around her got black until she could only see what was in front of her. Her mother kept pulling and pulling, until they were under the overhang at her mother's house. She heard herself gasp and instead of just breathing she was crying in great, shaking sobs.

"Oh baby," her mother said, "You'll be all right. I'm sorry baby, I'm sorry." Her mother wanted her to stop crying, she could tell, but she was scared and she hated this place. It hurt her mother, her crying, but she didn't care, she didn't care at all, and she kept right on.

That was when she knew that she wasn't a surface person.

She looked back over her list. Owen, Tumipamba's successor at MaTE, got there before Polly. Of course, Polly would be late. He was the CFO, he could be as late as he wanted.

"What have you got?" Owen asked, and she passed the list over to him.

She watched him read. Owen was from the U.S., Pennsylvania or something. She wished she'd been born in the U.S., then she wouldn't have to worry about adapting.

Owen was still reading when Polly walked in. "Morning Mayla, how's it going?"

"Okay," she said. "Oh, Polly, about that clinic loan, there's been some problems." Her heart was beating hard.

"What's wrong?" Polly seemed genuine, not accusative. As if it didn't matter to him.

"There's a rider on the loan, with a partner. Normally I wouldn't have any trouble, you know . . ." she faltered.

Polly nodded.

"The partner. I can't work with the partner," she said. "Nobody could work with the partner."

"Oh," Polly said, "I'm sorry to hear that. I'd hoped it would give First Hawaiian a little presence. But it's really pretty small anyway."

"Yeah," she said. "I mean, I'd have liked the business, for, you know, presence, like you said." She took a deep breath. "But I can't. The partner . . . is a problem. I can't get around it. I can't do the loan."

"Right," he said. "Well, if anything else comes up, I'll try to steer it your way."

It sounded all right. Even though Polly had sent Saad to meet her at the subport. Maybe Polly really didn't care about the loan, maybe he didn't even know about Saad's partner. Maybe he really had been trying to do her a favor.

Maybe it was all right. Maybe she really could still make the right banking decisions.

She wanted to escape. She wanted to go to Del Sud, get a flat, a pretty little flat, and live an orderly existence. Find a different world, a simpler place. Any world was better than this.

9

Virtual Weather

Soldiers came right down the street," Santos said. "My grandmother told my mama to buy rice so we bought twenty-five kilos of rice. And water, we bought a lot of water. You couldn't buy air. But it wasn't the same as a war. It wasn't the same because there was only one side. There was the soldiers and there was just people. And it was in the city, not on a real battlefield." Santos was talking about the Liberation.

They were hunkered down in the high grass, watching for the other team. This time they were on patrol, waiting for an unnaturally accelerated twilight and darkness.

"You weren't born when it happened," David said.

"Yeah, but I heard about it." Santos' pirate face was old enough to remember the Liberation. "I know it wasn't like war."

"Sometimes war is in cities," David pointed out mildly.

"You can't have a real war in a city like Julia, there's not enough space. You know, no tanks, no planes," Santos sounded nostalgic. Was nostalgia the right way to describe it? Nostalgia for a reality built from vids and films.

The sky had just started to darken. Around them stood yellow grass, waving a bit in the wind. It should have been scratchy and smelled like sweet straw but he couldn't even smell the helmet anymore. David put his hand out and felt a tickle across the palm of the glove that was not quite like reality.

Santos didn't know it was not quite like grass because Santos had never been in real grass. Just like Santos didn't know that all that had to happen for something to qualify as a war was for events to total a certain quantity of anarchy and death.

It would be maybe ten minutes until darkness. He hated to wait, he didn't like maneuvers in the dark. He was wasting money, sitting here in virtual grass, waiting to do something he wasn't going to enjoy. If he'd known they were going to be doing a run in the dark he would have begged off.

Something chirped in the grass. The sky was blackening perceptibly. They would start moving before it got dark, as soon as it got gray enough to blur the edges of things. Maybe he could get killed quick. "Santos," he said, "when you are shot, is there a loud noise?"

"Yes?" Santos said, not understanding.

"When the bomb was dropped on me, there was a loud noise. When I get killed, last time. If you are shot and killed, there is this noise?"

"Sometimes," Santos said.

Shit. Well, maybe after this he wouldn't play anymore, it wasn't worth it. Spending money to do something he didn't like, that was stupid.

There was a crack of lightning and he jumped.

"Fuck," Santos said.

The twilight was plum colored, but David didn't know how much of that was storm. He hadn't known it was part of the scenario. "What is it?" he asked.

"Thunderstorm," Santos said.

"I *know* it is a thunderstorm. Did we pick a thunderstorm?" He couldn't imagine why.

"No," Santos said. "Sometimes the program just does it. You know, weather."

If he had wanted weather, David thought, he would not be playing virtual wargames.

"I like it when it rains," Santos said. "It's more real." Santos had never been in the rain.

The rain came towards them. He could just see it as a darker curtain in the plum-colored darkness. It was like watching a vid, there was no heavy pre-storm calm, no shock wave of cold air riding before the rain, no pregnant scent of weather on the wind. He couldn't smell anything. He could feel the handlebars, feel the treadmill he was sitting on. And then it washed across them and the sound of rain was all around them and he could see nothing at all.

In the blackness he closed his eyes and concentrated on the treadmill, on the weight of the helmet on his cheeks and across the bridge of his nose. His hairnet was messed up by the strap around the back of his head. He was sitting on a treadmill in a cubicle, listening to the rain drum all around him while he himself remained curiously dry. The shapes on his eyelids were green at first, then red Rorschach blots, random retinal firings.

He could pull off the helmet. He could quit. He could get up off the treadmill and walk away. Meph was waiting in the room. David would find a job, waiting tables, unloading skids, something. Earn a little money instead of spending it, like a teenaged boy, on pseudo-experience. Santos had never seen anything but a virtual construct called Lezard, and if they met on the street, Santos wouldn't know him and he wouldn't know Santos. "He purged," Santos would say, "we were just sitting there and he just cleared the tanks, you know? Gone. Nothing. Me and the fucking rain."

He felt Santos' hand close around his wrist and his glove pulled slightly. "It'll give us cover!" Santos shouted in his ear.

The treadmill jerked and shuddered. It was a little like walking on slick ground, but not much. The ground wouldn't really have been wet yet anyway. He couldn't see. They could walk right through the enemy's camp and not even know it in the darkness. This was foolish. They couldn't even use the mine sweep to watch for mines, they couldn't read it in this rain. Did they even have mines in this game? Well, they had the sweep, and mines scared him to death, so he supposed they did.

Lightning, and the landscape flashed around them, overexposed. It was gone before he got a sense of anything and the thunder was a painful crack that jolted him so much he went to his knees. The treadmill stopped for a moment and he heard, below the sound of the rain, his own ragged breathing.

Santos pulled on his hand, a phantom tug without real weight behind it. "Come *on*."

Fuck. He got to his feet carefully, not trusting the treadmill. Night goggles. Why didn't they have night goggles? In real fighting everybody used them. But at least the rain seemed to be slowing down, it was less noisy although he still couldn't see anything. Nothing made sense, they should have been waiting for the rain to stop. They couldn't see anything, they were stupid to be moving in weather like this. If they had been moving against a real enemy, that enemy would have been on his home ground and they would be blundering around in the rain and dark. He thought he could make out shapes, a bluff to his left, or maybe a big piece of equipment. He strained to make out the shape, maybe the turret of a tank? He should be able to see the gun—

Lightning again and the left fell away down a gentle slope, no bluff, no tank, but farther away black hump-shapes hunched in the rain—

He crouched and pulled on Santos' hand. He thought the shapes were tents, tents or vehicles. "What?" Santos said. The rain was less, Santos didn't have to shout.

"Wait," David hissed.

They waited for the lightning. He wanted to quit, he wanted to go home. How long had he been here? Not more than thirty minutes, that meant they had better than an hour, maybe ninety minutes left. The darkness was making him crazy and he was getting a headache. Had someone from the tents/trucks seen them outlined in the lightning? He was pretty sure it was a camp. If it was, Santos would alert the rest of the group with a remote and then would they sit in the dark and wait? This was not like real weather at all. If it were like real weather then there would have been more lightning by now.

His knees were aching so he eased into a sitting position. (It was hard to shake the feeling that he was going to sit on wet ground, but the treadmill was reassuringly dry.) If the enemy had seen them, they'd probably be crawling towards them now, coming up the slight rise. No lightning. Was the program monitoring? Maybe they weren't getting lightning because they needed it? Maybe the weather programming was particularly sadistic?

The sound of rain was less. It was much harder to keep track of virtual rain than of real rain. Santos sighed next to him and he wanted to shush him. If the enemy was crawling towards them they might hear.

Kill me, he thought, kill me and get it over with. Santos didn't know that fighting a war consisted of long periods of anxious boredom punctuated by intense short periods of terror.

The rain, if it was still raining, was down to a fine mist. Now what were they supposed to do? It was still too dark to see, and now they wouldn't even get lightning. And for all he knew, around them was enemy.

The sky grayed a bit, suddenly faintly luminescent. Dawn? Already? There was the feeling of movement in the sky, of wind. Then he saw edges, illuminated pale, and the clouds seemed to tear. The moon shown through a rip in the clouds, bright and defined—not dawn but moonrise—and then disappeared. Then the tatters of cloud cleared the moon again and he could see an empty landscape that seemed positively flooded with light. Below them the black shapes of enemy tents, but no soldiers around them.

His shoulders were aching with tension. Santos fumbled with the remote and David saw it blink red before Santos set it face down in the grass. Just a tiny thing, a little smaller than the palm of his hand.

Santos leaned over so he was close to David's ear. "Let's take them."

"Shouldn't we wait?" David whispered back.

"Nah," Santos said, pointing at the camp with his chin, "most of them will be NPC." NPC: Non-Player-Characters. Great; even if they were fake people on automatic pilot they still outnumbered David and Santos.

Santos slung his rifle around and David felt his irritation rising. Stupid kid, always in a hurry, not thinking. He had half a mind to let Santos go running in alone, get himself killed if he wanted to.

It was a game, he told himself. They had been playing for almost half an hour without any combat. The point of this was to "go in." He sighed, and reached back and tapped his shoulder so his weightless rifle would swing around. Once he had it in his hands it at least felt solid. No heft, just the solid feel of it. Maybe if they played some sort of space game then the weightlessness wouldn't matter.

In an hour and a half this would all be over. He could go home. Next time he would check whether the maneuvers were in daylight or at night and if they said night he'd claim he was busy.

He was a grown man. This was a game. He could separate reality from game. He should be fair to Santos, let him have his fun.

"Okay," he said.

"Ready?" Santos said.

Not exactly, but he nodded.

Santos ran half-crouched towards the tents. Best would have been to wiggle through the grass, but that would have been stupid on a treadmill. David blindly grabbed the handlebar and tried to follow. He couldn't run crouched the way Santos had because all this sitting and kneeling and falling had his knee aching, but he hunched.

Santos lobbed a grenade and as the grenade launched through the air someone opened fire from the camp, a sharp ta-ta-ta-ta-ta-tat. David checked, cringing, waiting for something, and then made himself run. He was running heavily, he could feel his feet thumping on the treadmill. No element of surprise. Of course, the people in this camp had been sitting around in a thunderstorm for half an hour, waiting to be attacked.

The lights went on, the grenade exploded, and Santos lobbed another one. David tapped his belt and then he had one. (The hardest part of this whole game was remembering the gestures that accessed his weapons.) He tapped the pin and lobbed it, grateful that he had the sense to activate it before throwing it. It was true, an overhand throw from training years ago that he didn't know his arm remembered until he'd done it. The concussions were slightly staggering, but very satisfying.

Soldiers came boiling out of tents. A woman soldier with a long tail of swinging hair came out of one tent, crackling faintly with a blue glow like St. Elmo's fire. Some strange weapon from the game? A program glitch? He checked again, looked at Santos. Santos had seen her and turned his fire on her. "A PC!" he shouted.

David was firing, and she was firing back at them. The air was full of noise and he wanted to fall but he was on the treadmill, so he was looking for cover, ducking behind tents as if canvas would protect him. The soldiers were all around, the NPCs, the program-generated people, they were like chaff. He aimed and sprayed, blindly firing and the three in front of him jerked and fell. So easy, he thought, not like people at all. They ran and shot and pointed and shouted but seemed ineffective. He aimed at one of them and squeezed the trigger (the trigger was a little soft on this thing) and the soldier fell, shots stitched in a seam across his chest. He ducked behind another tent, always moving, always keeping himself from being too much of a target.

The woman crackling with faint blue fire (no brighter than a gas flame in sunlight) she seemed immune to their shooting. Maybe the blue was some sort of protection? Santos kept trained on her, so David worked on her too, ducking, firing, ducking. She turned and ran, evidently not trusting her own equipment and David kept trained on her, a steady stream of bullets, there was still firing around him but he ignored it, keeping his gun on the woman, it should have been heating up, he should have at least emptied the clip by now but it kept on firing, die, you goddamn bitch—

Something huge lurched to his right, but it wasn't anything, he had lost part of his view, he could only see out of his left eye. Stupid goddamn moment for the helmet to screw up. Cheap equipment. No maintenance. He fired, the world suddenly flatter. He couldn't focus out of his left eye as well. The woman turned to fire, pausing, and he and Santos trained on her. She went down, finally, and he felt the rising surge of triumph, and the blue flickered all around her like lightning and was gone.

Santos whooped, adrenaline joy.

The rest were running, easily cut down. And then the little camp was in tatters. Bodies everywhere. It was an astounding amount of destruction for two people. Animated violence. "Great job," Santos said, standing there, looking around. "We got to get out of here, they have reinforcements coming, you know?"

Only seeing out of one eye was really annoying. He could hear out of both ears, all right. Maybe he should exit the game and see if he could get another cube? But how would he get back in the game?

"We should go that way, I think," Santos pointed and glanced back to confirm. "Oh shit, Lezard."

"What?" David said.

"Why didn't you tell me you were wounded?"

"I am?" David said. Of course, he was penalized.

"Can you see?"

"With one eye."

"Cristo," Santos said, "you have a medikit?"

A medikit? It had never even dawned on him that they would use a medikit in virtual. "No, I don't think so."

"I got one, wait—" Santos fumbled a moment, tapped his pocket, didn't like what came up and fumbled some more. Then he had a blue kit box in his hand. He peered at the cover in the moonlight. "Yeah, it's still all right."

He opened the box but the gloves didn't allow fine manipulation so he took out a packet and waved it in David's face. The packet disappeared—used up, David assumed. "Okay," Santos said, "now you won't bleed to death or die of infection."

Die of infection? In an hour and a half? Virtual infections, like virtual weather, must be accelerated.

"I want to check the tents," Santos said. "Only for a minute."

He still couldn't see anything out of his right eye. Seeing out of only his left eye was strange. He looked around, trying to focus, found himself looking at a corpse. Well, there were a lot of them.

The man lay flopped on his back, his chest, abdomen and groin bloody but not ruined. His blood was black and wet in the moonlight and his fatigues looked genuinely soaked (David thought if he touched the body his fingers would come away black) but it was curiously cosmetic. He was flopped there convincingly enough, abandoned the way corpses look, but he looked bland. Features too regular, somehow. Not particularly handsome. He had an insignia on his shoulder, a chess piece. It was a knight, with an arrow superimposed, pointing forward. He had a moustache but his cheeks were mannequin smooth. David couldn't put his finger on what was missing, but maybe it was that only the minimum details were there and that wasn't enough to give him humanity.

That made sense. In a game the casualties couldn't be too real or it wouldn't be fun.

"We got to go," Santos said.

They passed the body of the woman with the strange blue fire weapon as they left. She looked different, more real than any of the others, although her appearance was exaggerated. She had long hair that was black in the moonlight. Part of her face was shattered but her fatigues were open at the throat and she had full, perfect breasts filling her undershirt. Her skin was dark and smooth.

"What was that blue?" David said.

"What?" Santos said.

"This woman, she had some sort of weapon? Blue, like electricity? It made her hard to kill?"

"Oh, no. She's a PC, you know, like us. When she looked at us, she saw the blue glow, too. It's in the game."

David shuddered, a feeling that came out of nowhere and ran through his system like lightning and was gone.

Being one-eyed was making his head hurt.

Away from camp they climbed a bit. The treadmill made him have to step different, accelerating in a way that felt a little as if he were going up. Santos tapped on his cheek and was suddenly wearing a headset. David did the same thing. The set was open, he could hear the wash of a live mic, but no one was on. Where was Amazon Lil?

They were supposed to maintain com silence, but he didn't know why. Maybe Amazon Lil and the leader of the other team could trace locations through the coms. Maybe it was just the rules of this particular game.

None of it particularly made sense. He wondered how much longer until the game was over.

He sighed.

"You okay?" Santos said.

"Yeah," David said. He could hear the lack of enthusiasm in his voice.

"It makes you kind of crazy, being wounded," Santos said. "I get wounded all the time, you know? Only I always get it in the leg or something, then the treadmill messes you up, like to make you limp."

"It is not that, so much. I should not be doing this," David said.

"Why not?" Santos said. "It's just a game. Pass the time thing."

"It is a waste of money," David said. "I do not have a job."

"Oh," Santos said. They climbed a bit more and then the land seemed to level out. Some sort of plateau, David thought.

"Nothing up here," Santos announced. "We should go back down."

He took them down a wash where the shadows were pitch black and they had to watch their footing. The treadmill couldn't simulate climbing or rocks but it could jerk around a bit. The land around them was dry, but sometime it had rained enough to make this wash. Virtual rain. They had had a virtual thunderstorm, why wasn't this full of runoff now? Because it was a game, he told himself.

"Are you looking for a job?" Santos said.

"There is a problem," David said. "About the work card. I lost mine."

"Politics?" Santos said carefully.

"No," David said, "nothing like that."

Santos was silent. David wondered what he was thinking. Probably that David was a criminal of some sort. The whole bottom of the wash plunged into blackness ahead of them. David thought to himself that he just didn't want to do it. He didn't want to deal with it.

Santos paused, too. Studying the wash he said, "They are hiring people to do construction work at my fish farm. You ever been a fish jock?"

"No," David said. "I did construction work." A summer job in Blacksburg, Virginia, when he was in high school there.

"Maybe," Santos said, "I can talk to the super, you know—"

Sharp crack. From the wash, someone opened fire.

There was nowhere to go. He unslung his rifle, backing up, but the treadmill made it hard, jerking him to unsettle his footing and he kept having to grab the handlebar, groping blindly, afraid that he would miss and fall, unable to fire, and he could either stand and fire into the shadows or back up but he couldn't do both. Grenade. He stopped and pulled a grenade. He only had four, how many had he used at the camp, one? Two? Tap the timer to arm it and wait a second, he didn't want them to toss it back. Sharp, small ta-ta-ta-ta-tat, a curiously nothing noise, and him standing there in the long blue moment, waiting to throw his grenade.

The world went dark. Cloud over the moon? He threw the grenade, blind, and crouched down. Blind. He was blind.

The grenade made a satisfying concussion and then he didn't hear anything except his own breathing. Shit, was he deaf, too? Blind while the enemy probably rushed at him, mannequin soldiers with chessmen on their shoulder patches. And him, glowing in the enemy's eyes like St. Elmo's fire. He didn't know if they had stopped firing or if he was deaf, too. Maybe he had died and the system had failed to dump him into the park—sharp crack, and someone called out *"Madre de Diós."* He fired blindly in the direction of the sound, and someone fired, either at him, or it was Santos. Why didn't Santos say anything? If he didn't hear anything from Santos then Santos was dead. He fired again, a short sharp burst, blindman's bluff. Maybe they would kill him. Maybe they were crawling towards him. They couldn't torture him, he wasn't really here, it wasn't like the blue and whites, no virtual cell, no electrodes in the genitals, but still they might be coming for him, and he couldn't see. He couldn't stand it, couldn't, and didn't have to, so he reached up and just as he grabbed his helmet he heard Santos say, "Lezard—"

—then he was sitting on the treadmill in his own cubicle, breathing in great, satisfying gasps. He was never going to play again, the game sucked, and he didn't have to play. He was going to sit here a moment because his knee ached and then he was going to go back to the room and feed Meph or something but he wasn't doing this again.

He had left Santos in the wash. Although what the hell he was supposed to do blind he didn't know. The helmet was red, with cracked padded forehead and cheek rests. He fingered where the gray foam stuck out through the crack. If they played something else it would be different, some sort of spy thing maybe. Just not wargames. Or maybe sword-and-sorcery kind of wargames, that would be all right. Then if he got wounded the wizard or someone could do some sort of spell and make him all right.

Santos wouldn't have known he was completely blind from looking at him, would he? He might, Santos had seen he was wounded when he used the medikit on him.

He tried to decide what to do. He could leave Santos a message. He did that the last time. He could just forget it and go away. Walk away. It was easy to walk away. Back to the room with Meph. Look for a job in a neighborhood where everybody stared at him because he was foreign. He was really just going to fit right in, get a job where he made enough money to buy himself some fake papers and then just go home. Sure. Even assuming he somehow came up with the money, how was he going to find someone who could do fake papers? He was stuck here, and he wasn't going to get out and eventually they were going to arrest him. Beyond that he couldn't think. He was lost.

He thought about getting up, but couldn't think of why. He didn't want to go back to the room.

If he had the nerve to kill himself and be done with it. There was no logical reason to live, eh? He laughed, he couldn't even handle a fake death in a virtual wargame, what made him think he'd have the nerve to really kill himself? What would he do about Meph? He could send Meph to Tim, Tim would take care of the cat. At least until he left.

Empty thoughts. Brain white noise. He sighed and put the helmet back on and found himself in the park. Nothing to do here, either. His knee ached and he didn't really want to walk around. He had a sudden picture of himself, standing up on the treadmill and fishing blindly for the handlebars. Well, people in p-suits looked worse, wandering around in gyms, gesturing to the empty air. He walked across the park to the program listing, read down the list.

He felt paralyzed.

Oh, he ached inside. He wanted to go home.

He waited, read the program listing. He sat down, not knowing how long he might wait.

He was thinking about Meph, about having Meph on his lap, when Gin appeared, shaking back her egret hair. "Hi, Lezard," she said.

"Hi," he said, "is Santos coming?"

"Should be," she said, "time is up."

The cyborg, Jack Stomper, was next, and then Santos. "Hey, Lezard," he said, and David's stomach tightened, but Santos didn't seem upset. "You been sitting here waiting?"

"Yeah, I am sorry about leaving," David said.

"No problem," Santos said. "You couldn't see anyway."

Amazon Lil appeared, then Cobre. "Good job," Amazon Lil said to Cobre, who smiled, embarrassed, and shrugged.

"I should not leave you like that," David said.

"You couldn't see," Santos said. "It is not like you could do anything. Don't worry. Next time will be better."

"I don't know," David said. "I should not spend the money."

"You need money?" Santos said.

"I have some saved," David said, "but I should not waste it, you know, on a game." He didn't want to play anyway, but he couldn't tell Santos that.

Santos frowned. "Look, there is this place on Saucone Street, called Ramanathan. It is a bar where the fish jocks all get a job. My super, he'll be there hiring on Friday night. You come on Friday night, I'll introduce you. Maybe you can get a job, you know?"

He would lose his anonymity. "I have never been a fish jock," he said.

"You said you have construction experience," Santos said. "You can dive?"

"I have learned," David said, uneasy.

"It is construction work. Just temporary, until the job is finished, you know? A couple of months. But you can get experience. I will be there," Santos said. "If you don't come, I will wait all night for nothing. My dive vest is purple and red, and lots of people know Santos. Is Lezard your real name?"

"No," David said. "Kim. Kim Park."

"See you Friday," Santos said, and reached up. Somewhere the real Santos was grabbing his helmet, pulling it off.

The park chimed, David was running out of time. The others were gone, too. He pulled off his helmet and ran his fingers through his sweaty hair. At least it was short, now.

He hadn't even thought to ask whether or not they'd won.

Saucone Street was not in Dedale, it was up on the first level, where the bank and the oldest, established parts of the city were. He found the street in a map of the city he bought in the plaza. It was incomplete, the upper levels were all drawn out in careful detail but the third level was vague and Dedale was just a cross-hatched area. He wasn't sure how anyone could draw Dedale, it wasn't in neat levels. The fourth level was even more vague and the fifth and sixth levels, both still under construction, weren't shown at all. Leaving Dedale scared him. He stood in the plaza, trying to figure out the nearest bus stop.

There was no bus stops in Dedale proper, it wasn't accessible to buses or skids or cars. Dedale was a mapmaker's nightmare, full of steps and narrow passages. Streets were more like the holes in swiss cheese than the careful grid of a city.

He found a bus stop out on the edge of the neighborhood, on a street that seemed uncomfortably wide and loud. The bus was painted in a kaleidoscope of colors, with names overlaying names. The present owner had painted a huge yellow rectangle and lettered "Bonamie Transport" in mostly even purple letters. It didn't seem to burn petrol, maybe methane? He didn't understand these people, internal combustion stole the air that they breathed.

The bus had trouble climbing to the next level, rumbling slowly up the ramp and grinding gears while traffic collected behind them. A motor scooter shot around them, squeezing between the front of the bus and the curving concrete wall while the driver swore. They rumbled around on the third level for awhile and then had to climb to the second level, grinding and shuddering. The woman sitting next to David was huge and carried her groceries in a string bag—breadfruit, rice, infant formula and coffee. When the bus turned, she leaned against him pressing him into the window.

They entered the bus terminal on the second level and everyone got off. David found a bus schedule. His bus was on the first level and the bus station seemed about as complicated as Dedale but he finally found people standing in line to climb an escalator. The escalator wasn't working so he climbed.

He had just missed the bus he wanted. He hoped Santos waited. When the bus finally came he paid twice the fare he had for the Bonamie Transport and sat down. Wide streets, businesses (closed for the evening). He wondered why the fish jocks came to a bar on the first level.

The first level seemed clean. The air was dryer and smelled better and the buses were new. He thought at one point they were close to the bank, but he wasn't sure. The driver turned on to a side street, like a service street, and looked up into the mirror and called "Saucone." When David got off he felt the ground rumbling beneath his feet, the way it rumbled in his room in Dedale. Saucone Street was connected to the freight system. A little like the service entrance for the first level.

The bar was crowded, men were standing out front, leaning against the wall and talking, but none of them were wearing a red-and-purple diver's vest. Inside was dim and the bare walls were concrete painted yellow. He smelled the sweet sour odor of spilled beer. The only decoration were pictures of girls cut out of magazines— blonde American girls, mostly, in risqué bathing suits—pasted on the wall behind the bar. He craned, looking for the red-and-purple diver's vest.

There were a couple of people in red and purple. One was a woman, and for a moment he tried to imagine if it might really be Santos. Funny that he might have been so completely fooled, people did that in VR, but he didn't think it was true in this case. Santos was too young, too obviously adolescent male. So he looked for a kid, and found one: about twenty, twenty-two, he thought, a short stringy bare-armed Latino, standing with another diver, a dark, smooth-faced, slightly overweight young man.

David pushed through the crowd. "Excuse me," he said, "I am looking for a diver called Santos?"

"Yeah?" the kid said.

"I am Kim Park, but he knows me as Lezard?"

"Lezard?" the kid said. "No shit?" He grinned. "I thought you were Haitian!"

"No," David said, "I am not." It was a stupid thing to say but Santos nodded.

"Okay. Yeah. Ronald," he said to the other diver, "this is *Lezard!*"

Ronald grinned and bobbed his head.

"This guy knows about war."

David smiled, nodded, and they were all smiling at each other. Santos was wearing nothing under his diver's vest and looking at his bare arms made David feel cold.

"You want a drink?" Santos said. "I get you a drink, hey, it's no problem, you wait here, I get you a drink, beer okay? They have

American beer here, but I think it is too expensive and the beer from Mexico, I like it better, you know? How 'bout a bottle of Cinco de Mayo, okay?"

David took a deep breath, looked around. Ronald was still smiling at him and David smiled back at Ronald. It occurred to David that Ronald wasn't too smart.

And then Santos was back with three bottles of beer, condensation already forming on the outside. The beer was flat—everything carbonated was flat in Julia, because of the air pressure—and it had the too-sweet taste of the beer in the bottom of the glass. David had had homebrew beer in a township in South Africa and suddenly the taste was there for him, sharp, bitter beer, the way beer must have tasted for centuries. And he could see the shanty bar, with its blue-green metallic siding, industrial cast-off, and the deep darkness inside where a man sat next to an ancient cooler, waiting for customers.

Being with Santos always brought back South Africa.

"Did we win?" he asked Santos.

"What," Santos said.

"The last game, did we win?"

"No," Santos said, "we lost on points, because only you and the woman knocked out. You and me, we scored most of the points for our side, the others, they didn't do nothing. It was really dry out there, really dry, everybody circling around, if we did not find those tents, nothing would have happened, you and me, we were the only ones who got *wet*, you know? Good beer, huh? Ronald, this guy is natural out there, is like it is real for him, you know? He makes it so real. You don't know."

Santos was talking so fast that the end of his words seemed to disappear, "tense" for tents. Grinning and talking as fast as he could. Maybe it wasn't that Ronald wasn't quick, maybe he was just overwhelmed.

"You see, the guys at the bar? Right. Those are the agents for the farms. The guy in the dark blue? He is the agent for my farm, I told him about you."

Santos' agent was wearing a dirty bowler hat and a blue-black

diver's vest. Under that he wore what looked like thermal underwear, with the sleeves pushed up to leave his forearms bare. There
were four drinks in front of him, all amber-colored like whiskey or
scotch.

"You buy him a drink," Santos said. "You buy him a Cutty Sark, I
know that he likes it. You say you a friend a Santos, that you are
Lezard, and you just want to buy him a drink, that's all. Okay?"

"Why?" David said. "He has too many drinks now."

"Is an introduction," Santos said. "Is the way things are done."

David pushed to the bar. It was strange to be in such a crowd of
people and still be cold. It took awhile for the bartender to get to him.
"For the man in the hat," David said, "a Cutty Sark. Tell him it is
from a friend of Santos, from Lezard."

The Cutty Sark was expensive. The bartender poured it and put it
in front of the agent, leaning across the bar to make himself heard.
The agent looked down the bar at David, nodded, and then looked
away.

A friend of Santos, David thought, pushing back to Santos and
Ronald. Was he a friend of Santos? He had never even seen Santos
until just now.

"He nodded," David said.

"Keep watching him," Santos said. "You know which one is your
glass?"

David shrugged. He hadn't really paid any attention.

"Shit," Santos said. "Okay, I was watching, I'll tell you."

This bar was on the first level, David thought. He was still surprised that the fish jocks would come to a bar on the first level. "Do
you come here a lot?" David asked.

"Yeah," Santos said. "When I need a job. This is the place where
you get a job. People always come here. My Dad used to come here."

One of the agents at the bar—not Santos' agent, another one—
picked up one of the glasses in front of him. He tipped a little of it on
the floor and then sipped it. Without looking around he slid off the
stool and headed out the door.

Nobody took the stool. A couple of people went out the door after him but David didn't know if they were leaving or following the agent.

"Hey," Santos said.

Santos' agent splashed a bit of Cutty Sark on the floor and sipped some out of the glass.

David looked at Santos, not sure it was his drink.

"Go outside," Santos said.

Outside the door the silence was like fresh air. Santos' agent was leaning against the wall, the other agent was squatting a ways away, talking in a low rumble to a fish jock.

"Lezard what?" Santos agent asked.

"My name is Kim Park, Lezard is the name I use for games," David said.

The agent frowned. He was not very tall, a little taller than David, about David's age. His cheeks were pitted with acne scars. "Are you Cuban?" he asked.

"No," David said.

"Santos said you were Haitian but you're not," the agent said. "When I see you I thought maybe you were Cuban. I know there are Chinese people living in Cuba."

"I am Korean," David said.

"Oh," the agent said. David thought Korean was good, the agent had probably never seen someone Korean, wouldn't know a Korean from a Xhosi. Besides, Park was a Korean name.

"You have dive experience?" the agent asked.

"I know how to dive. And I have worked on a construction crew, but never as a diver."

The agent frowned.

"There is a problem," David said. "I do not have a work card."

"Santos said that," the agent did not look at him. "Santos said it is not political."

"It is not."

"Santos is all right," the agent said. "He is young. But I knew his father. He'll settle down."

"He is a nice kid," David said, not sure what else to say.

"Maybe, until you get this work card straightened out—"

David started to say that he didn't think he would get his work card straightened out but the agent didn't stop.

"—you can work on probation. No contract, just to try you out, you know? It is a favor, to Santos. I cannot offer you as much money as I pay the other divers. 82 a week. No rent for your bunk, it is an honest farm. And they take back twenty for your food. You take it or leave it."

"Okay," David said. He could try it. If he didn't like it he could quit.

"You know where to catch the sub? Santos can tell you. Be at work on Monday morning, no late, or I have you cut before you even get there, understand?"

David understood.

"This work card nonsense," the agent said. "If I find out it is political, if I find out you bringing politics to my farm? I feed you to the sharks, you understand? So if you decide to change your mind, if you think maybe it is all more complicated than you say, then you do yourself a favor, you don't show up on Monday morning."

"Yes sir," David said.

With an air of finality, the agent poured the Cutty Sark onto the rough concrete. It ran towards the center of the street, the scent of the scotch whiskey rising strong and clear like an offering.

And David was hired.

10

The Sorcerer's Birthday

Marincite went in circles, everything spiraling down into old mining holes.

Paul was the admin assistant assigned to Mayla at Marincite Corp. He was a dark, small, neat young man. When she stepped off the sub from Julia on Monday morning, he was there, waiting in his dark red suit, holding a white wax paper bag with his breakfast of beignets. When he found out that she liked them, he started buying two for her on Monday mornings. Instead of "good morning," Paul always said, "And the night?"

"Not bad," she always said, feeling a little silly. Tourists thought everyone in Caribe talked that way, because that was the way they talked in vids like *Horsemen*. Tourists thought everybody in Caribe followed voudoun.

Paul fell into step beside her and La Merci dropped back a discrete two meters. "You remind me of my sister," Paul said.

"How so?" she asked.

"Because you are tall and you walk like a man."

She laughed and he shrugged, smiling a little. She didn't know what to say, not so much because of Paul as because of the listening ears. La Merci never gave any sign she was eavesdropping, neither did Joe or Hermione. And yet, Mayla could imagine any one of them reacting, reacting like a snake strike, all the feigned indifference gone in an instant. Not like Tim who would be caught openmouthed when the gunman struck. Guns out, instantly dangerous, La Merci catlike—

Maybe she would move here. Maybe it would be safer than Julia.

Real life was not the vid. The truth was she didn't know what would happen. And other than the vid images, her mind refused to imagine.

They walked into an ad. It was The Sorcerer's Birthday, there were signs all over proclaiming it, broad painted words on what looked like sheets. A man in a dusty top hat and maroon tails stood on the sidewalk with his back to them and a goat stood beside him on the street rolling its golden eyes. He half turned, neat and quick, as if she had interrupted him. His look was unknowable. And then she stepped out of the ad.

She decided she liked the ad, even though she didn't know what The Sorcerer's Birthday was.

Paul stopped at the newstand and she dug into her bag and handed him money for a *Wall Street Journal* and two coffees. He looked at the front page for a moment, then folded the paper under his arm.

"My sister is a powerful woman," he said.

"What does she do?" Mayla asked.

He thought a moment. "She gives advice," he said, with a note of finality.

Mayla wondered if he couldn't think of a way to describe what she did or if the words were for Marin Security. Although it was difficult to imagine Paul's sister doing something illegal. "Is your sister married or does she work?"

"She is married," Paul said. "Maybe you can come and have dinner and meet my sister."

She said that sounded nice. Nothing would come of it, but it was sweet of him to ask. She wondered about how it sounded to La Merci. What would they do if she said she wanted to go visit Paul's sister? Would she be away from their ears? Would they tell her not to go? Could they listen to her anywhere in the city? Surely not.

They walked through Marincite maroon-and-cream corridors up to the checkpoint where the guards just glanced up as she and Paul went through. La Merci turned around at the checkpoint without a backward glance. Mayla had been delivered. She was behind the wall. Now the gunman could not follow, could not come out of a side door or down the corridor towards her. She was safe. She yawned, passing the half-open doors, the offices with bright windows and sunlight on gleaming wood surfaces. She always started yawning when she got into the complex. She felt sleepy. She wouldn't dream if she could sleep here, wouldn't wake up in the night listening and seeing shapes in the dark. If she could she would stay here at night, sleep behind the checkpoints.

Paul sat down at the desk in the front cube, but she had a temporary office—no window, but a desk that looked as if it might really be wood. If not, it was an excellent fake. She put some figures on the screen and drank her coffee, and ate her pastry. The beignet left a dusting of powdered sugar on the maroon carpet. She hummed to herself. What did it sound like to the listeners? It would be pleasant, wouldn't it? To hear someone humming to themselves, at peace with themselves and the world. Did the Uncle listening nod?

She sat with International Regulatory and Legal half the morning to go over what papers had to be filed when they started the bid. It was a teleconference, the Regulatory and Legal people from First Hawaiian attended by screen. She didn't like teleconferences, she found she spent all her time looking at the screen rather than the Marincite Legal and Regulatory people. Everybody did, conditioned by all those years of vid watching. By the time she was finished it was time to think about lunch so she took the elevator up to the commissary and got a surinami salad to take back to her desk. Small pleasures, she thought, eating. She tried to think of what other pleasures she had these days. The elevator stopped at the main floor—it usually did—and Saad Shamsi got on.

"Mayla Ling," he said.

"Saad," she said.

He stood beside her in the elevator, eyes on the display.

"Did you get your money?" she asked.

He nodded. "From another Julian bank. Caribbean Securities."

Caribbean Securities was her competitor. "Who did you work with?" she asked.

"Aristide Mendoza." Saad glanced sideways at her. "We're meeting Mr. Navarro and Owen Cleary of MaTE now, I arranged the introduction."

Bringing Caribbean Securities in to take a crack at her deal. "I'm glad everything worked out for you," she said, mechanically. "How long before you go to the States?"

He glanced up reflexively, and she realized too late that he probably was afraid that security was listening. He certainly didn't want Polly Navarro to know that he wanted to skip out on this.

She didn't know what to say, she hadn't been thinking. Saad would probably think she had meant to say that, paybacks being hell and all that. If she'd been thinking fast enough she would have.

The elevator halted and they both got out. Owen Cleary and Aristide Mendoza of Caribbean Securities were standing at the far end of the hall in front of Polly Navarro's door.

"Take care," Saad said.

"You, too," she said. "How goes, Aristide?"

Aristide smiled back at her, a crocodile smile.

She took her salad to her desk. For once she wished her little temporary office had a bright window so she could look out on a waterhole in the Serengeti and watch the lions come down to drink. Just because Saad and Aristide had a meeting didn't mean anything. Polly was just covering all the bases. Caribbean Securities would be starting from scratch, she had four weeks work behind her.

Things were so far along that Polly had to realize he'd lose money if he changed in midstream.

What if Marin Security had been monitoring their conversation? It couldn't hurt that she had mentioned Saad's plans.

Don't second guess, she thought. Just keep working and do the best you can. What could she do? Maybe the targets for takeover weren't attractive enough? Don't get flustered, she thought. Don't just start doing things. She called up the deal, went over the rows of numbers. Maybe First Hawaiian had been too conservative about their own exposure—they were in over their head anyway.

Don't start doing things, she thought. If Polly likes what Caribbean Securities offers, he'll let you know. It was in his best interest to let the jackals fight it out at the waterhole.

But she should be ready. Tonight, after work, she would start repackaging the deal, have something ready to take to the credit committee at First Hawaiian.

She dreamed but in the morning she could only remember bits and pieces about blue and whites and her grandfather's house. Something about not being able to go into her grandfather's house because something would happen, there was a disease or radiation or something in the air mix.

She woke up with a pounding headache so blinding that she thought she'd been dreaming because there was something wrong with the air mix. Tim didn't have a headache. He called Security anyway and they came out and checked but the mix was fine. They told her that it was good she had called. Right, they had nothing better to do than humor women with migraines. Well, one nice thing about having a blinding headache was that she was too stupid to feel embarrassed.

She stuck a painkiller behind her ear and then nearly yanked the transdermal off with a comb, and the damn thing didn't do anything, anyway.

She waited for Tim to tell her not to go in, although she had to go in, but he seemed to assume that the patch was working. Or maybe he didn't assume anything, maybe he assumed she was an adult and she could decide for herself whether or not she should go to the office.

Fooled him.

So she sat in her cubicle and tried to pull together information for Polly. She tried to figure out what Caribbean Securities might do, but she couldn't think of them doing anything she hadn't already done, which would put them behind her in terms of presentation. Unless Polly was pissed at her about the Saad Shamsi business, in which case it wouldn't matter how good her presentation was.

So she might lose the biggest deal of her career. There was no reason to worry about it now, she'd done what she'd done. But she worried anyway, her thoughts running and running and getting nowhere, until she told Paul she was going home. (Well, not really home, home was gone. Home was blown up and squashed flat.)

"I think you should meet my sister," Paul said.

She didn't know what he was talking about. "Pardon me?" she said.

"I think she can help."

"Your sister can help my headache?" Mayla said.

"My sister can help," Paul said.

"Thank you," Mayla said, "but it'll go away on its own. But it's nice of you to worry." It *was* nice of him to worry.

Paul pursed his lips.

"Really," she said.

He was a sweet young man, she thought. With his beignets and his concern. He liked her and she didn't know why, but his concern was reassuring.

"Can I tell my sister about you?" he asked.

"Well, sure. Why not?" she asked. "I mean, I don't think she'd find me very interesting or anything."

"She will ask about you," he said.

"Oh," Mayla said. Paul was serious, it was important in some way that his sister would ask about her. Mayla had gotten the idea that his sister was a spiritual reader/advisor, he said she "gave people advice."

"She will ask about you, you don't mind?" he said again.

"No," she said, "I don't mind."

"Okay," Paul said, relieved. "I'll tell her about you." He nodded pleased. "I'll tell her about you and she'll ask."

It would be interesting to hear what Paul's sister the spiritualist would say about her.

She turned down the corridor towards the elevator and ran into a group coming out of a conference room. The man at the front of the group was wearing a dark red coat, Marincite red, cut long and conservative and for a moment she tried to think what he reminded her of. He turned and looked back at her, and it was Polly. Polly wasn't usually down on this floor. He didn't smile, he just glanced at her. More than glanced, looked at her, but didn't acknowledge her.

She didn't get on the elevator, just kept walking as if she were heading somewhere else. It didn't seem like a good idea to let Polly know she was leaving early, although he probably didn't care, she wasn't on his payroll.

What did his look mean? Not that he looked so much, but that he had looked angry. Cold angry. Maybe it was just the meeting.

She went back and waited for the elevator. It wasn't until she got to the street that she connected what it had all reminded her of: the ad for The Sorcerer's Birthday, the young man in red tails and a top hat that she had seen in the street. The one with the goat.

Just a flukey thing. Polly was a blanc, his broad back has just connected to the figure, they hadn't even been really dressed alike because the magician in the ad was wearing tights, not a suit. Funny how the mind worked, particularly when hers was functioning so badly this day.

On the third day of the headache from hell, Mayla left work at two and spent an hour waiting for a doctor to look at her. In the waiting room she sat obsessively thinking about brain tumors, but the doctor found nothing wrong but the kind of imbalances associated with stress. "Have you been under stress?" the doctor asked.

Oddly embarrassed she said, "Uh . . . yes. I've been under stress in my job."

The doctor gave her a prescription and sent her home. The medication didn't seem to do anything to the headache but it sent her to sleep, a thick sleep full of dull ache.

"Mayla?" Tim said. "Mayla? Are you awake?"

The room was dark and she had no sense of time. "Do I have to go to work?" She had been asleep, but she had felt as if she wanted to turn over and couldn't, as if the medication had immobilized her.

"No," Tim said, "someone is here to see you. It's evening."

"I can't see them," Mayla said, but there was a black woman dressed completely in white standing behind Tim saying in a strong voice, "Mayla."

It was an authoritative voice, so strong it almost sounded as if the woman were on the surface. The woman was wearing sunglasses.

"Hey! Wait a minute, would you!" Tim said.

Mayla tried to think of who this woman was—*La Mano De Diós?* Had she finally been found? Her head was so thick she couldn't move, couldn't think, and it was just that as she had always suspected, Tim was completely useless.

"Ms. Ling?" That was Paul, from work. What was he doing here? Maybe this was some sort of headache dream?

"Ms. Ling isn't feeling well," Tim said, "you'll have to leave."

Right, Mayla thought, throw the terrorists out. Let's just be polite about all this, you'll have to come back and shoot Ms. Ling later when she's feeling better.

"Mayla," said the woman again. "Come out." Mayla sat up and grabbed a robe.

"Ms. Ling," Paul said, "my sister has come to see you."

Oh shit. The floor was cold under her feet. The room was cold, and her face felt hot. She held her hands to her hot cheeks. Then she put on the robe—they were all standing in the doorway, but she didn't care. The room was full of heavy air, but she didn't feel as if she had to take very deep breaths. The medication made her body very calm, very still. She didn't need much air. "I am sorry, Paul," she said, standing at the door to the bedroom. "I really don't feel very well."

"I know," he said, "so I brought my sister."

If she concentrated, Mayla could feel the floor under her feet, but if she stopped concentrating, she forgot it was there. She didn't feel at all light or insubstantial, but it was as if all the signals of her body were below the level of conscious recognition.

"Excuse me," said a man from the door.

Everyone looked at him; Tim, Mayla, the woman with the sun-glasses and Paul.

"Ms. Ling," said the man, "we are here to see if everything is all right?"

She didn't know who *he* was, either. "Everything is fine," she said.

"Perhaps these people are bothering you," he suggested. He was a smooth-faced, innocuous-looking sort of person with thinning hair.

"No," she said. She almost said yes, except she didn't know who the man was.

"You can tell me who these people are?" he asked.

"This is Paul, who works for me, and this is his sister."

The man studied them.

"Who are you?" Paul's sister asked.

"I am a friend of the family," the man said by way of good-bye, and reached out and pulled the door closed.

"Your uncle," the woman in sunglasses said to the closed door.

It sounded like an insult. Her uncle. Oh, right, Marin Security, keeping watch. Well that was reassuring, even if it proved that the flat was monitored. She hoped they'd enjoyed listening to Tim's soccer games.

"You keep strange company," the woman said to Paul, shaking her head. Then briskly to Mayla, "My brother says you have troubles." She took off the sunglasses.

"I don't really feel well," Mayla said, "but I appreciate your coming all this way."

The woman said. "You have to think about your life, girl."

Her head hurt, she wanted to lay down again and try to sleep.

The woman stepped up to her and raised her hand. Mayla flinched away, but the woman laid her palm against Mayla's fore-head. Her skin was cool and Mayla closed her eyes. The woman took her hand away and when Mayla opened her eyes the woman handed her the sunglasses. "Legba will not mind," she said.

Legba, voudoun loa, guardian of the gates and crossroads, maker of great *coups* or spells. A magician, but not like the one in the street, the one in the ad. Papa Legba was an old man. Mayla put them on and the world was removed, dim and distant. Not as dark as she would have expected, they looked almost black from the outside but wearing them just made everything less bright. She should have realized that the woman was a mambo when she saw the sunglasses. Only voudoun and corner boys wore sunglasses, except in Del Sud where the light in the Del Sud dome was bright enough to need them.

"Ah," the woman said, "it's nice, isn't it." She was older than Paul, a little older than Mayla, and she had fine wrinkles around her eyes that crinkled when she smiled.

Paul smiled, shyly. Tim frowned. "Ms. Ling really isn't feeling well," he said.

The woman didn't pay any attention. Poor Tim, people tended to not pay any attention. "The sunglasses, they allow you to look at things without pain," the woman said. "I think you need to look at things."

Actually, the glasses helped. The world was dim and her eyes didn't hurt. "What do I need to look at?"

"Why do you have a headache?"

"Stress," Mayla said. "The doctor said I am reacting to stress."

"So you have problems, too many problems, and you cannot deal with them. So you have a terrible headache and the world is simpler, you have only one problem. And there is only one thing you can do, go to bed. But the problem is that your other problems do not go away, you see? So now, you have to hold the problems off, so they are small, and look at them."

"Okay," Mayla said.

"That is what the drugs do, is it not?"

"Yeah," Mayla said. She thought she understood. She wasn't sure she could explain it to someone else, but it made sense.

"The thing is," Paul's sister said, "you cannot tell what is important and what is not."

Mayla nodded.

Maybe you need help.

Mayla thought Paul's sister had said that but she wasn't sure.

Maybe you need help.

"You can come and see me," Paul's sister said. "But for now you can keep the sunglasses. Tomorrow morning your headache will be gone. Papa Legba will take care of you."

"Okay," Mayla said. Her hair felt as if it was wrong way against the part, tousled from sleep. She felt disordered. It would be nice if her headache would be gone the next morning. "Papa Legba," she said, and then stopped, because she had wanted to ask something but she wasn't sure what.

"Yes?" said Paul's sister.

"Papa Legba, he's an old man?"

"Papa Legba is not a man, child," Paul's sister said.

"I know," Mayla said, "I mean, he's not young, like the man in the ad, the sorcerer." God, she was so confused she wasn't making any sense.

But Paul's sister understood. She looked stern. "That is Carrefour, he is not for you. He is *petro*, he is the short way to power, the young man's way."

"I know," Mayla said, which wasn't true, she meant that she knew he wasn't for her.

"You come see me," she said. "You let Papa Legba take care of you. The other, he is not for you."

She watched them leave through the smoke dim light of the sunglasses. Then she got something to drink and went back to bed.

When she woke up at five a.m. the next day, the headache was gone.

The headache stayed gone until almost three the next afternoon. Then it crept back, glinting at her off the polished surface of her desk. It hurt through her eyes first, sharp little shards that left residual ache.

She closed her eyes and the ache stopped building.

She could take a headache pill, but that would leave her stupid. She didn't believe that Paul's sister had made her headache go away, after all, she had gone to the doctor.

She had the sunglasses in her briefcase to give to Paul. It would be stupid to put them on. Sitting at her desk wearing sunglasses. Either they would think she was very odd or they would think she was involved in voudoun. Being involved in voudoun would be a career limiter, it was unsophisticated.

Maybe not here in Marincite, there had always been rumors about voudoun. Of course, all she had to do was picture Polly Navarro in sunglasses and she could guess how much substance there was to those rumors.

She took them out, thinking to give them to Paul. They were plain sunglasses, very dark. Anonymous. Always appealing, anonymity. The plastic felt cold. She put them on for a moment and they stopped the glints from the desk from being painful.

She had to brighten her monitor, but then she could see well enough to work.

If someone came in she'd feel very stupid. She looked like an adolescent from the wrong level, the kind of girl who dyed her hair extraordinary colors. But then, Paul would buzz her and let her know if someone wanted to see her. So she kept them on.

Paul caught her with them on, but he wasn't going to think she was silly. "Paul," she said, "what is your sister's name?"

"Layte," he said. "Ms. Ling, when are you coming to see her?"

"I will, as soon as I get a chance."

"She says you should come on Friday night."

Tomorrow night. "I can't, I go back to Julia tomorrow night."

"You can go Saturday, can't you?"

She almost said she had appointments on Saturday, but she really didn't. On the other hand, did she want to go to see his sister? She had never been really attracted to voudoun. Being Catholic had been more than enough.

What would his sister say to her? She had said some pretty wild things the night before. "Okay," Mayla said. "Friday night."

"I will come and get you, around six-thirty. Okay?"

"Sure," she said. Through sunglasses he almost looked green, as if he were underwater.

"Bring a little money, for the donation," Paul said.

* * *

"Great," Tim said. "Just great."

Paul's sister, Layte, lived in the section of the city called Kikuyue. It was a dark part of town, coming up from the chute people walked in and out of pools of shadow where the light strips were torn away. The air was wet and had that smell she associated with the lower levels of Julia, a mildewed, stale smell. The air didn't seem to move at all.

It made her skin crawl.

"See scenic Marincite," Tim muttered.

Her sunglasses wouldn't have been too out of place here. There seemed to be a lot of boys about upper-middle-school age just hanging around at the entrance to chute. They all wore jackets with demon faces on the back or they had bare arms, long roping muscles exposed to the cold air. Pyroxin. Why didn't security just arrest anyone who didn't wear sleeves and test them for drugs? Except where would they put them all?

Layte lived about fifteen minutes from the chute. Her place was part of a long row house, just a doorway and a couple of windows in a long row of doorways. But light spilled out the doorway, bright and yellow, not like the cool lights of the street at all. There were a lot of people standing outside: women in old-fashioned dresses of shining white jacquard and head scarves and men in thin white pants. Like something out of another century.

"That means this is a traditional *houngoun*," Mayla said to Tim.

"So what are they going to do," Tim said, "Slaughter a chicken in your honor?"

"No," she said, irritated. Although after she said it she didn't know. Did they sacrifice animals? They did in historicals on the vid, but surely they didn't anymore.

There would be drums and dancing and people would be possessed. She was both curious and apprehensive about possession. Possession wasn't real—or it was real, people actually believed it, and they went into an altered state—but it was a form of hysteria. Like speaking in tongues. Spirits didn't take over your body.

People were looking at them standing there in the street. She hadn't even thought about what color clothes to wear so she was wearing gray leggings and a black sweater. Oh well, maybe they wouldn't be allowed in.

One of the men by the door cocked his finger, beckoning her. "You have been invited," he said.

"I'm sorry we're not wearing white," she said.

He shrugged. "Are you a child of Guinee?" he asked.

She didn't know. She didn't even know what the question meant.

He shrugged, "Papa Legba won't mind."

Someone took them inside. The front room was filled with people, and across the back was a long table with bread and covered dishes on it. She could smell sweet yams. There were rum bottles, too, she counted eleven. She wondered if the number meant something.

"What did he mean?" Tim asked.

"What?" she said.

" 'Papa Legbo won't mind?' "

"Papa Legba," she corrected. "Papa Legba is a loa. He's the one that opens the gates."

Tim shook his head. "All I know about is zombies."

"Didn't you ever see like the vid, *Horsemen?*" she asked. Everyone had seen *Horsemen*. But Tim hadn't. "Do you know anything about possession?" she asked.

"Yeah," he said. "I've seen vids about exorcism and demons. This isn't like Satanism, is it? I thought it was different."

"It's not like Satanism," she said. When she was growing up, the nuns had always said it was, but everybody knew it wasn't. "The loa are like spirits, and they come and mount people's heads, you know, they take over their bodies. But they're not demons. They don't hurt people."

"So we're supposed to be possessed?" Tim asked.

"No," she said, "not us. We're not, you know, like part of it. They don't come to everyone."

"Okay," Tim said, uncertain.

Someone touched her on the arm and she looked around. A tiny woman was standing next to her. "It is good you came," the woman said. It took her a moment to realize that the woman was Paul's sister, Layte. She was smaller than Mayla had realized.

"I have a donation," Mayla said. She pressed the money into Layte's hand. She had brought 50cr. She hoped it was enough.

Layte nodded. "That's good. Come with me."

Should she have given the woman that much money? Paul hadn't said how much.

The flat had two bedrooms, but the smaller bedroom was completely bare except for a little square table set in the middle, with a post from floor to ceiling behind it. The floor was painted dark red. Marincite maroon. "This is the *sobagui*," Layte said. "Here, when I nod, you should take the jug, you see, and offer it to each of the four directions. Okay?"

"Okay," Mayla said. The post was dark, speckled with white paint. On the wall on the back there were three painted *veve*: a pattern of lines like wicker or ironwork; an elaborate cross, something like a grid or a gate with asterisks like flowers; and one quite clearly a ship.

Veve were roads or gates, things the spirits used to come into this world. When she was in middle school they had been popular as jewelry. She'd had a little wire horse, a cheval, but they had to take them off when they got to school and hide them or the sisters would confiscate them.

She wished she knew more about voudoun. "What are you going to do?" she asked.

"Ask the loa what is wrong, why your life is like this," Layte said. "I am sorry, there are three people we have to ask the loa about tonight, and there is the usual Friday night, we must get ready now."

Mayla didn't know if she should go into the other room or not, but people started coming in and standing next to the walls. Paul pulled her back, so she was standing against the wall, too. All of the wall space was taken up, and Layte came back in. Behind her, people crowded in the door. Three men came in with drums and three-legged stools and sat down on the side.

Layte nodded at her. She felt awkward, and the jug was heavy, but she picked it up and carefully offered it in each of the four cardinal directions. Then she handed it back to Layte and went back to stand by Tim. Another woman came up and took the jug, offered it in four directions, and handed it back to Layte. Finally a boy, about sixteen, took the jug in shaking hands, and offered it to the four corners, his movements jerky with nervousness, his dark face shiny with sweat. Layte went to the door and poured a little water on the floor: once, twice, again. Then she poured a fine stream of water from the door to the *sobagui*. Then she wet at right angles to the first line of water and poured another thin trickle from the walls to the *sobagui*. Mayla expected her to go to the back wall, but she didn't.

Layte knelt down and reached inside a cotton drawstring bag tied around her waist. She pulled out a handful of white powder, like chalk or flour and traced lines on the dark red floor.

Tim whispered, "What are they doing?"

"They're drawing *veve*, like the ones on the walls, spirit gates. That's how the loa come, through the *veve*."

People around her started singing, *"Fait un vever pour moin."* Mayla expected the drums to start, but they didn't. The singing was full of rough bits and untrained voices, women singing in little girl voices. Did anybody sing much anymore, except when no one was listening? Or in church?

Layte drew carefully. Everybody watched. Some people sang but a lot of people looked around, not really paying much attention.

There was a bit of commotion at the door, and then three people backed in, two men and a woman. One of the men and the woman carried flags made heavy with spangles of white and silver buttons. They were white or silver on white but they made swirling patterns like waves and lines and spirals. The other man carried a saber. Except for the fact that they were walking backwards they looked almost like a flag corps. The room was so small and there were already so many people in it that the flag brushed Mayla as they backed past and Mayla could see the sweat mark under the arm of the woman's dress. They came slowly and deliberately around the room, sweeping to end up with a flourish right in front of the altar, just at the time Layte stood up. Layte said something in Creole, a strong statement, and the people answered back. She said something else and the people answered back. It took Mayla a minute, but then it became so familiar that she felt goosebumps on her arms. She couldn't understand the Creole but the response sounded like church.

Saint Barbara, she heard that, she thought. *Les morts,* "the dead." Bits and pieces, but she didn't even understand French.

The prayer finished. People stood with their heads bowed. There was a moment of silence, and then *"Ave Maria . . ."* Layte began and the rest of the congregation followed her in the Hail Mary, and then, in Creole, the Our Father. Monotonous drone of recited prayer, as familiar to her as school. They said the Our Father three times and then there was a silence and everyone stood with their heads bowed.

Mayla wondered what the next prayer would be, maybe the Apostles' Creed? Voudoun wasn't anything like she had expected. It was like a storefront church.

Layte shook a shell rattle and Mayla jumped. The rattle was a gourd covered with cowrie shells laced together and Layte shook it, a sound like a rattlesnake's tail, and shook it, and shook it and shook it and stopped.

Silence.

Everybody clapped and the drums boomed and Layte struck the ground with the rattle. The sound in the little room was intense. In unison: the clap, the drum, the thump of the rattle, one, two, three, pause. One, two, three, pause. One, two, three pause. Like knocking on a door. Bam, bam, bam, breath, bam, bam, bam, breath. Steady and slow, a demanding rhythm, relentless. The tension in the room was building, too. Everyone was waiting, watching the drummers. Or each other. Some people were starting to perspire. The room was warm, because of all the bodies, but not warm enough to get people sweating. One, two, three, and then beat-beat-beat-beat-beat-beat for what, half a minute? And then it stopped. Everybody seemed to wait, listening.

In the silence she could hear the echo of the drums in her ears, in her pulse.

Then it started again. One, two, three, pause. She could feel the impact in the bones of her skull. What if her headache came back, here? This was a foolish idea.

But it didn't seem to be starting her headache. Light caused her headaches. But the light here didn't bother her, even though it was just a bare fixture over the altar in a concrete room painted white. Bam, bam, bam, breath, bam, bam, bam, breath. It felt as if the sound drove the air out of her chest and only in the pauses could she breathe. She was clapping, although she couldn't even hear the sound of her own claps.

And then it ended.

What next?

Everybody stood for a moment and then, as if a plug had been pulled in a sink, people began to drain through the door. Was that it? The loa hadn't come? She had paid a donation, had she been taken advantage of? "Paul's employer, she'll pay money, we can tell her the loa didn't come and then she'll go home, anglos don't know anything."

She let herself be towed along, pulled into the front room. The table had been put against the wall, although nobody touched the food. The drummers came out and Layte followed, backing, pouring a thin stream of water on the floor.

No, it was rum, Mayla could smell it.

Most people weren't even paying any attention. A girl was looking for her handkerchief, she had laid it down. Someone produced it. People were chattering, mostly in Creole. How much longer until she should leave?

The drummers were sitting by the table, setting up as if they might play, but nobody seemed to pay much attention. The door opened and a couple came in. Somebody called, "Ramise!"

The woman waved.

A couple of people had little folding stools and they settled them around the walls but everybody else stood around the room. It was only a little after seven-thirty. It had been sort of interesting, but Mayla wasn't sure she wanted to stay for the party after.

Then Layte called out and everybody answered again. People turned around. Layte called again, and the chorus answered. (In the space between the answer and the next call, she heard someone talking.) Layte poured rum into a little metal bowl and lit a match and dropped it in. There was a flame, nearly invisible.

The drums started again, a more complicated rhythm, and some people came away from the wall and started dancing. Simple steps, two steps forward, one stomp. Mayla felt someone tugging on her sleeve, Paul, pulling her.

She looked up at Tim, pleading, come with me. Tim followed them into the thick. One-two one. One-two one. Simple. An easy motion. They flowed around the room, around the bowl of burning rum. The dancers rolled their shoulders, a sensuous motion that Mayla couldn't duplicate. She felt stiff, anglo. A dumb, awkward blanc. Not my culture, she wanted to say. But everybody was looking at the floor, dancing to themselves, hypnotizing themselves with the rhythm. So she tried staring at the dark floor, rolling her shoulders. After a few turns around the room she felt her shoulders loosening up, rolling like the women around her. She looked up and smiled at Tim, who couldn't isolate the movement and shook his whole chest, but he smiled good-naturedly back at her. Good old Tim, she thought, always ready to go along.

Maybe it was more her culture than it was someone like Tim's.

Her mind kept going and going, her thoughts running like a mouse wheel. What if she could be possessed? What would it be like? It would be great if it were true, if there were loa. She probably couldn't be possessed if she didn't believe in them—and there was something strong in this room.

The drums kept going. Her calves were aching. You probably had to do this a lot to be in shape for it.

She let the drums propel her around, left-right LEFT, right-left RIGHT. Easy steps, and her mind wandered. Like doing exercise, where there was nothing to occupy her. Maybe that was the major benefit? Just letting her mind go, letting the rhythms take her, tiring her body out and not concentrating. She should empty her mind. She glanced around. Some people seemed to be concentrating, some didn't. A few were looking around.

The drums stopped, and everybody looked around. The faces were mostly blank. The drums started again, a different rhythm, a different dance, a kind of step and glide.

She didn't like it, she liked what they had been doing before, the shoulder roll thing, and she couldn't do this glide thing right, but she liked the dancing. The drums were wonderful, calling her, pushing and pulling. She tried to let herself glide into the drum beat and for a moment she thought she had it, if she could just not think she would have it, but she lost it almost right away. She had to sort of think, but she had to just know she was going to do it, and she didn't know that, she was thinking too much, she had to just go with the drums. Maybe if she came on Fridays after awhile she would be out here and she could just go with the drums—

The big drum changed rhythm and everybody broke, the drum just went *thump thump thump thump thump* while the other two drums kept going under and over each other as if the big drum were still playing with them, and everybody took long steps, stride stride stride stride stride, and then the big drum was drumming again and they were all dancing again.

She felt wild and startled, it seemed like a hallucination, that break, with everybody dancing as though the women had not thrust their hips down, the men thrown their legs out and everybody taken those long strides, like giant steps, take three giant's steps, Simon says, or really, the big drum says. Listen to the big drum.

She liked it. She liked it a lot. She liked the dancing. It felt good, heating her muscles up and moving around. She'd be sore tomorrow, but that was okay.

Around the invisible center, a constant motion, a current of water, her legs were getting tired and then the big drum broke again and in that moment a man stumbled, caught himself and went rigid, falling backwards so that the man behind him, who was just in front and to Mayla's right, had to catch him. The other dancers strode past. A woman stumbled away as if struck and then her leg seemed to root to the maroon floor and she pitched forward, as if a current had come from the man. People behind Mayla were pushing her forward, so she went on, craning her neck. The man who had stiffened and fallen backwards had been as rigid as someone turned to wood, but now he suddenly jerked left and right, breaking away from the man supporting him. The woman was still pitched forward, another woman holding her arm. She looked terrified, her eyes wide. *"Merci!"* the woman shouted.

They are having seizures, Mayla thought. It was as if she had caught it from him, or as if the ground had suddenly conducted an electric shock. And then the man, and then the woman, straightened up. The man began to pace in harsh staccato movements, but the woman began dancing. Gliding, dancing, beautiful smooth movements, her face an alien mask.

The man went over to the table and appraised the food, and then Mayla lost sight of him, swept by the current of dancers. In a moment she could see him through the people again, and she could see he had a roll and was chewing on it. Nobody else was eating, but nobody seemed to find his actions odd.

Two people standing by the table nodded to him, respectful.

Then Mayla was swept past him again.

She stepped on the heel of the person in front of her, a woman in white satin. She murmured sorry, although the woman did not look around and could not have heard her.

She could see the man again, and he was looking at her. Someone came up to him and he turned his head and smiled, let the woman take his hand. Then he gestured, telling her something, his palms flashing pale.

Think about the dance, not the man. He was all right.

But she couldn't get back the feeling. She looked back at the man and he was wearing sunglasses, the shining black glass turned towards her, and she knew he was looking at her even though she couldn't see his face. *Papa Legba.*

Step and glide, step and glide. People possessed by the loa weren't supposed to remember what had happened afterward. They were supposed to have amnesia for the time of possession. She wondered what was happening to the man, did everybody have hidden personalities that only multiple personalities and the possessed got to use?

She stepped on the woman's heel again and embarrassed she found her way out, through the people. From the wall she turned around and caught a glimpse of Tim. He was grimacing and his eyes were closed and he was part of the river. She could see it, even though he was awkward in the dance, he was caught up in whatever the rest of these people felt.

And she wasn't.

"Lady," a woman touched her arm, speaking loudly to be heard over the drums. "Papa Legba, ask you come."

She looked over and the sunglasses were watching her.

"Papa Legba say come," the woman—really a girl—said again.

She followed the girl around the edge of the room.

The girl did a kind of bob in front of the man with the sunglasses. He touched her head and nodded, a paternal gesture. The he held his hand out for Mayla. She took it, he clasped her hand loosely, his was hot, and she felt a tension in all her body at his touch. The drummers were playing some sort of intricate over and under, filling the air around them with sound she could feel buffeting her.

The man in the sunglasses beckoned her to follow him in the room with the pillar and the altar, where everything had started. She wondered what she was going to be talking to. How had he known that she had paid a donation, had he been in the room when she saluted with the water jug? Probably. Of course, she was a blanc and she wasn't wearing white. It was easy to guess she was here for something.

It was not so loud in the room with the altar. "Girl," he said and stopped. Paul came around the edges of the crowd.

The man—or Legba if she was supposed to believe all this—nodded at Paul and spoke in Creole. Paul held out his hand in ritual salutation and braced himself, standing with his feet a little wide as if for a blow. When the loa took his hand he rocked back on his heels a bit, as if a current of electricity had passed through him.

The power of the loa, she had heard of that. Did the loa pass from the man to Paul? No, the shock didn't mean that, Paul was still Paul.

She expected Paul to be deferential, but while he was respectful, somehow he was less unnatural with the loa than he was with her. He wasn't friendly, the way he was with her, but he was relaxed.

"Papa Legba asks how you passed the night," he said. Which was odd, that was how you said good morning in Creole, *"Et le nuit?"*

"One gets along," she said, puzzled.

"Papa Legba says you do not have such good night vision, but he sees you have glasses," Paul said.

"I don't understand," she said.

"In your bag," Paul said. "He means the sunglasses."

"Oh," she said.

"He says you need to develop your night vision. You need to see in the dark."

Fortune-telling talk, vague horoscope kind of things that could relate to anyone. But she couldn't help it, she could feel tears welling up in her eyes. Sometimes, when people told her nightmares, her eyes would water, she didn't know why. Ghost stories made her want to cry. She had that now, too much feeling, she didn't want to see in the dark.

"Tell him, sunglasses don't help you see in the dark," she said.

Legba grinned yellow uneven teeth before it was translated.

"He says it will make you practice," Paul said. "If you can see with the sunglasses, then it will be no problem to see without them."

"Girl," said Legba, "this isn't your home."

"You mean Marincite?" she asked. What did he mean, that she shouldn't think about trying to get a job with Marincite Corp?

"You are not a child of Guinee, you don't belong on the sea. You must find another home." He had no trouble with English. "It is a good ceremony," he said, and then something to Paul in Creole. She wished she had studied Creole.

Legba paid no more attention to her, it was as if she had vanished. He walked away, taking another piece of bread off the table and then passing unerringly through the crowd of dancers until he found Paul's sister, the *houngoun*. He talked to her for a moment. Then he shook himself, kind of shook his shoulders, and then was shaken as if by some terrible spasm, and fell, limp. People grabbed him, held him like a puppet by the arms, and he was all elbows and joints. They pulled him to a chair, and sat him down and took off the sunglasses. Layte folded them into a pocket of her dress.

The man raised his head, his face slack as if exhausted, and looked around, blinking. He raised his hand to his chest and rubbed it slowly, not as if it ached, but as if to reassure himself.

"What is a child of Guinee?" Mayla asked Paul.

"We are all children of Guinee, anybody who listens to the loa," he said.

"Why did Legba say I'm not a child of Guinee?"

"Maybe because you have not been initiated?" Paul said. But he didn't sound as if he believed it.

"He told me to go home. Maybe I should leave."

She half expected Paul to shake his head, but he just dropped his eyes, his face blank. "I will take you home," he said.

Something changed in the dancing, something in the rhythm. Not the drums, but something. She thought it was a possession, and she craned to see, but all she could see was that people had stopped. People didn't stop for possessions.

It was a possession, a middle-aged woman standing in the middle of the room. She stood with her shoulders back. Mayla didn't know any female loa except Erzulie, loa of love. Was this woman Erzulie? It was hard to see around people.

Mayla could see Layte come out on the floor and talk with the woman. The woman's voice was deeper than Mayla expected, almost male sounding, although maybe that was the air mixture in Marincite. The woman shifted and there were people in the way again, and then the woman had sunglasses on. Mayla was pretty sure that Erzulie didn't wear sunglasses. Legba? The woman was different from the man, when he'd been Legba, but maybe that was just the personality of the person coming through. It wasn't supposed to.

Paul sucked on his lower lip.

"Who is it?" Mayla asked.

"I don't know," Paul said.

Whoever it was was demanding something.

"I think it's Carrefour," Paul said.

Carrefour? The sorcerer? "Why is he here?"

Paul shrugged.

Not for her, she hoped.

"I'll take you home," Paul said. "Wait, and I'll get your friend."

"What will happen?" Mayla asked.

"My sister will take care of him," Paul said. "Don't worry. He is just powerful right now."

By rights, Mayla thought, a company with a name like Robit ought to have been in robotics, but of course it wasn't. It did some sort of solar cells.

The deal was this, MaTE needed to buy itself from its parent company, Marincite Corp. To raise the money, it was going to buy another company and then borrow against that company. The company they were going to buy was called Robit. It was something of a financial shell game, but it was all legal.

She was working with Owen Cleary of MaTE. He had been Danny Tumipamba's assistant. She told him her banker joke. God was thinking of expanding heaven so he was checking out real estate. He found a great patch of land, sunny, elysian, wonderful, and was surprised to run into the devil who was thinking of purchasing the same piece of land.

God said to the devil, "You can't be serious, there's nothing devilish about this place, if you brought people here they wouldn't be suffering the torments of the damned."

The devil shrugged. "It would take a lot of work, I don't know if it's worth the time and the financing. I'll have to think about it."

God said, "Aren't you worried about it being gone before you decide?"

The devil looked at God and laughed. "Like you've got any bankers?"

Owen laughed politely.

To buy Robit, they needed to get more stock on the market. So they bought what stock was available, and that made the price go up.

She waited for the big investors—the pension plans and the mutual funds—to read the upswing and start to release shares to the market. MaTE had to buy enough of Robit to make the price go up about five points. A lot of the stock was in trust portfolios—pension plans, money markets. If the stock went up, the software that controlled the buying and selling for the trust would release a little into the market.

So the big investor funds would make enough available to allow MaTE to keep buying and to keep the price artificially inflating. Then they would profit take, selling a little more and a little more. Robit was regarded as an undervalued stock, a good growth stock, but it didn't pay much dividend. She figured when it reached twenty-one there'd be a number of large sell orders. Then the price would dip as MaTE held off buying. At nineteen MaTE would buy again.

They were playing against the big computer-monitored investment programs, carefully manipulating the stock to put a lot of it on the market. If MaTE got 35% of the Robit stock today it would be enough of the corporation that MaTE would control the board. Then they'd use that equity to pay Marincite Corp. for MaTE.

The trick was to spend enough money to pry open Robit but not to spend so much money that Robit was too expensive.

At one-thirty in the afternoon while she was eating a bagel Owen Cleary of MaTE said, "It's at twenty-one and an eighth."

"It should start to fall," she said. Although he knew that.

At two o'clock the stock was holding at twenty-one even. There wasn't a lot of activity, but a few people bought takeover stock, hoping it would continue to go up. Surely by two-thirty it would start to go down.

At about a quarter to three it started to climb. "Someone else is buying," she said. She felt sick. Who would be buying?

A white knight maybe? Somebody out to protect Robit? By now the street would know that MaTE was making a move, Robit might have appealed to someone to buy them, a friendly buyer.

She called Singapore and established a link with New York to increase Owen's credit. Owen started buying at twenty-two. That meant that MaTE would start its life as a new company heavily indebted, but that was a risk they had already decided to take.

The stock went to twenty-five. This was not good, this was a worst-case scenario. They couldn't afford to go on. The New York Stock Exchange was querying, the loan was now larger than the assets of the bank, did First Hawaiian have a guarantee?

Polly Navarro was her sugar daddy, he would use Marincite Corp. money to guarantee the loan. "Owen, call Polly," she said. "New York is going to shut down our funds."

It had all been agreed on, Polly would step in if things went wrong.

After a moment Owen said, perplexed, "I can't get Polly."

"What do you mean?" she asked.

"I've got his tickler number," Owen said, "but there's no answer. He's not answering."

"Call his secretary," she snapped.

The secretary said Mr. Navarro was not available and he didn't know where he was.

"Owen," she said, "What the fuck is going on?"

"Maybe he's in the john," Owen said.

She had an image of Polly in the john, pants around his knees. Once it was in her head it was stuck there, hard to think around.

She queried someone in New York, a broker she had worked with, could he find out who was buying Robit?

Yeah, he could find out, give him a moment.

While she was waiting, New York suspended credit to First Hawaiian pending a guarantee. Singapore followed suit.

The loan was at $172,000,000 more than the worth of the bank. First Hawaiian was technically bankrupt. At this moment, on paper, her company was worthless.

Her broker came back. "Marincite Corp. is buying Robit," he said.

"Who else?" she said, exasperated.

"Just you," he said.

That made no sense. If no one else was buying, the price shouldn't be going up. First Hawaiian was burning down.

"I'm going to look for Polly," Owen said.

In the john? she wondered.

Robit was bleeding, she could see the shares spilling into the market and someone was buying them. The stock was at twenty-six. And First Hawaiian couldn't give Owen any money to buy stock because First Hawaiian's creditors had stopped giving money.

She watched the stock fluctuate, twenty-five and seven-eighths, twenty-six, twenty-five and three-quarters, twenty-five and five-eighths, twenty-six and an eighth.

She couldn't do anything, she was locked out. First Hawaiian was calling her through her console, they wanted to know what was going on, and she didn't have an answer. She didn't even bother to answer, they could see as well as she could. She called the broker in New York again. "Who else is buying Robit?" she said. "I've got to know."

"I told you," he said, "It's all Marincite. It's two Marincite accounts. What's going on?"

Two Marincite accounts? Marincite was a big company, was it bidding against itself? Somebody in investing didn't know about the takeover and saw a chance to make some money? "Some sort of communications fuck-up," she said to the broker, "Thanks for the info."

That was okay, they would just transfer the stock. Her heart was pounding. She just had to tell Owen when he got back, he'd tell Polly, he'd find Polly.

How could someone be spending that much money without Polly knowing? Polly would know about the takeover, he wouldn't okay this kind of buying, this was big money, as big as the deal she had set up with them.

It was the deal she had set up with them, only First Hawaiian wasn't running it.

Polly had to be doing it.

Why would Polly be ruining her deal? First Hawaiian was burning down. Why was he doing this?

Owen didn't come back.

She called First Hawaiian and told them that the money was coming from Marincite, but she didn't know what was going on. They were screaming at her, and she didn't know the answers, so she cut the call. And then she watched the numbers.

Robit bled, and First Hawaiian burned. First Hawaiian couldn't meet its debt, and in a few hours the creditors would call the money in, and then First Hawaiian would cease to exist.

Her grandfather's bank was going to close. Well, at least it was all in the family.

Singapore called first.

Then New York suspended First Hawaiian and froze all assets in the U.S.

The numbers kept flowing. Someone in Marincite appeared to have acquired sufficient assets in Robit to spin MaTE off, if they wanted to.

That was when Polly Navarro walked into the conference room in his Marincite maroon suit, cut long, like the Sorcerer in the ad except, of course, very classy. Polly knew what was going on, she could see that. And he wasn't going to save her company. "Mayla," he said. "I'd like to talk to your people."

"What's going on," she asked.

"I'm going to offer to buy First Hawaiian," he said. "When Marincite Corp. guarantees the debt, New York will release assets and business can go on as usual." He sat down one seat away from her, which was good. She didn't want him sitting next to her.

"You burned my company down. What did you do?" she asked.

"I needed to acquire a bank," he said reasonably. "I wanted a Caribbean bank. It was either First Hawaiian or Caribe Securities, and you made the best pitch."

"You made the best pitch." As if that were some sort of compliment. "You had inside knowledge," she said, wheels spinning but nothing going anywhere. "You broke a verbal agreement. We'll sue." But she was just making noise.

"I'm sure you will," he said pleasantly. "But I think the Caribbean courts will side with me."

She thought he was probably right.

11

In the Dark

The pyroxin hit while he was pulling on his gloves. The gloves were lined in something like chamois, soft and warm. The chamois was a wonderful surface, friendly as stroking a cat, embracing his hands, trapping warmth. It felt good to put his hands in something warm, and he felt good. The diver's suit he was wearing felt good. Since he'd left France he hadn't been warm, really warm, except in bed. His muscles relaxed, no longer tense from cold. Pleasant ache of relaxing. Pyroxin made you warm. Pyroxin. It even sounded warm.

Santos was grinning at him. "You look like a cat in cream," Santos said. "My mama is always saying that, 'you look like a cat in cream,' but you do man."

David grinned back. Hard to reconcile this Santos with the pirate face from the reality games. Santos had a narrow dark hatchet face, cheeks pitted with acne scars. An amazing face. David could see Indians, Mayans in that face, protein-starved generations of Native Americans. And Spaniards in that face. A face that was a type, that perfectly summed up Santos, what he was, what his history was, all the generations of his family coming together in that face.

It felt good to be warm. Pyroxin was a wonderful substance.

"You don't want to get too hot," Santos said. "It's not so good then, you sweat and then you get too cold, too fast. Go on down and stick your legs in the pool, I'll be suited up in a minute."

David picked up his facemask and his recyc unit. It was an old Travis unit with stripes of reflective tape across the back. A couple of the strips were gone. The newer units had reflecting bands painted on. Santos had told him to use the Travis. He said it was better for shorter guys to use a Travis, the Honeywells hit in the small of the back if you weren't tall.

He wandered down to the pool and sat down on the side and dropped his legs in. A couple of the other jocks were sitting there, too. The water was deliciously cool, and he could feel the cool creeping up and meeting with the warm in a most pleasant way. He imagined his heated blood circulating down through his legs and picking up some of that cool, then bringing it up into his body. The light was breaking off the water in the pool and little brine shrimp were collecting in the light. Like insects drawn to a lamp.

He was noticing everything. Pyroxin made him alert, too. He had been worried that someone would call him Kim Park and he wouldn't be quick witted enough to respond, but the pyroxin took care of that. Made him notice, made his mind work, allowed him to sort out the noise and notice the substance.

He shrugged into the recyc. The webbing was a little strange and he fumbled a bit awkwardly with the straps but he got it set right.

One of the other jocks pulled his legs out of the water and then turned around and fell back into the pool, holding his facemask. David pulled his own facemask on and the air was silent. The mask smelled of polycarbons and the black padding of the seal felt strange around his face. Then the mic clicked on and he could hear open air. *"No esta aqui,"* someone said. The mic brought their voice intimately close, as if they were whispering in his ear. He pulled his legs out and stood up, then crouched and fell backwards, too.

The water churned over him, a circle of light, a ceiling, with legs sticking through it and blurry unfocused figures on the other side. He floated backwards, looking up, looking into the circle. The figures on the other side seemed to be looking back at him. People in the yard were chattering. *"Pas plus mal."* Creole, but the same as French except for the island sound. "Not too bad."

He felt himself adrift, unmoored, the figures could be below him instead of above him, he had no sense of weight. And then in his mind they were below him and he was drifting up, slowly away, helium filled and awash in the ether.

Then another jock fell through and he realized he was awfully close, that he better get out of the way so other people could come through.

He kicked over and swam down into the yard.

"*¿Quién?*," a woman barked in his ear. Not a voice like the others and he stopped, waiting for the regular chatter to come back. "Who is it, who's in? Parks, is that you?"

Facon, the yard boss. Everybody said "Parks" instead of Park. "Yeah," he said, "it's me." Easy, keeping on top of things.

The water was cold, but he still felt good. The lights and chatter in the yard made it warm.

And this was his *job*. To feel this good. He would like doing this, he never wanted it to end. He was happy here, he wouldn't need much, just be allowed to do his job. All these years he had been looking for his place and here it was.

He felt himself clicked in place like a puzzle piece and knew he had quit running. He would become Kim Park and spend the rest of his life this way.

After awhile Santos swam down into the yard. "You need a bike," he said.

There was a rack of "bikes," they were nothing more than a motor with handles. Santos grabbed a bike from the end, and David took the next. Santos showed him where the little thumb switch was, and David thumbed it on. The bike was pointed down and it almost smacked the bottom before he wrestled it back up. They didn't steer well, he had to force it with his arms and wrists, but he got it pointed after Santos and let it pull him out of the yard.

The construction site was well away from the main farm, away from the pens. They passed a few lighted pens and then they were out in the dark. He heard Santos' bike grinding louder as Santos thumbed the engine higher and he copied. Ms. Facon, the yard boss, had told him not to go over medium speed, but he had to put it as high as it would go to keep up with Santos. Maybe he had gotten a slow one? He streamed along behind the bike, his legs just loose and dangling. The water was colder, like wind, at this speed.

He would have to be careful and not lose Santos. They weren't going far anyway. He could see the lights of the construction site in front of him.

He didn't think about the dark, didn't think about the cold. The pyroxin helped him, helped him look at the lights and think about the lights, as they got bigger and bigger, until they were at the construction site, which was a slab with girders rising in a superstructure all awash in a cloud of silt. The water was heavy with silt, so that the lights were fogged and the color washed out of everything only a few meters up.

The site boss was MacKenzie, a woman with a hard North American accent.

"Santos," she said, "you're working with Lemile. Park, you'll be working with Patel, spot welding, as soon as she gets her skid."

"MacKenzie," Santos said, "I think maybe I can work with Park? You know, show him around and stuff?"

David could hear her grinning, "Like I'd get any work out of you? Forget it."

"No, really, we wouldn't goof off—"

"Forget it, Santos." She kicked sharply, one, two, three, and rose above them.

Santos shrugged and grinned. "Lemile'll run my ass off. Nothing ever good enough for him. Someday the fucker be yard boss. Mama Patel'll take good care of you, though."

The silt wasn't like fog, it didn't swirl. It was just there, suspended by their construction. He wondered if it clogged up the filters on the recyc unit. He was cold after the ride out. He waited, thinking that the warmth would come back now that he wasn't being dragged behind the bike, that the water wasn't rushing past him, absorbing all the heat.

"Park?, I'm Patel."

Patel's faceplate reflected one of the lights, a blinding mirror for a moment. He looked away, unnerved by talking to a faceless person.

Indian women seemed to use the deeper parts of their voices when they talked.

She took him up on the superstructure, where the silt ate a lot of the light. There were footholds stuck to the girders, like handles. He took off his right flipper and she showed him how to slide his foot under the handle to keep himself from drifting off the girder.

His job was to drag a kind of pallet along the girder. (It had a kind of clip that made it easier to balance on the girder). It had pieces of something like right-angled ductwork stack on it. He couldn't figure out why they would be putting ductwork on this way, but he didn't know anything about construction under water. He figured he'd find out eventually.

The pallet was awkward, he slid it along the girder to a foothold, then he had to look down to find the foothold. Looking down meant looking into the murk-obscured light. He mostly found the foothold by touch. Then he'd unclip a duct (keeping the pallet steady with one hand) and Patel would do some sort of spotweld to secure it against the girder. Then they would jimmy the pallet around the foothold and secure it to the girder again, Patel would swim to the next spot and he would slide the pallet along while she got ready for the next weld.

In twenty minutes he was even colder. He couldn't remember what it felt like to be warm. He could tell it was twenty minutes because the telltale glowing green on the facemask included a chron. He could watch the time creep.

His foot cramped from using it to hang on. He wasn't much accustomed to arching his toes up to hold on. Patel was patient. "No," she said, "lift it towards you, swing it up, like a lid, yes, that is the way." He couldn't see her face, there wasn't enough light.

He lifted and jimmied the pallet awkwardly, eased it along the girder to the next two holds where Patel waited, stocky and opaque, balanced on the beam. It hurt to curl his cramped toes under the foothold, he tried twisting his foot to give the aching tendons a rest and could kind of float while he unclipped the duct thing, but in order to jimmy the pallet onward he had to square his foot and hook on. He grit his teeth and jimmied the pallet. His foot cramped.

When he got to Patel he stopped for a moment and tried to rub the cramp out. His foot hurt no matter which way he bent it.

"What's wrong?" she asked. She didn't sound angry but he couldn't be sure she wasn't irritated. His earlier clarity was gone.

"It has a cramp," he said.

"Give it a minute," she said.

It was the cold as much as the unexpected exercise. Cold hurt muscles, made them strain easily. Dancers wore leg warmers. He was so goddamn cold.

Stupid job. Why was all this labor done by hand? There had to be a smarter way to do this.

"Okay?" she said.

No, he wanted to say, so he said nothing, just caught the foothold and unclipped another duct thing. Resting seemed to have made it worse.

After awhile he tried using his other foot, but that was awkward. Still, it gave him a chance to rest the cramped one. They worked for three hours, attaching the duct things to the girder. And then finally it was time to find his bike and follow Santos back to the yard.

Facon had to call his name three times before Santos said, "He's here. Hey, wake up, man."

"Sorry," he said. He was so cold he was stupid. They would think it was just because he was cold, they wouldn't think he had a different name.

The water in the shower was hot, thank God. Then he just wanted to go to bed until the two-hour shift in the afternoon.

"No," Santos said, "you got to eat. Pyroxin make you empty. You feel better after you eat."

He didn't want to eat. But he hobbled after Santos. His foot still hurt.

As soon as he smelled food his stomach contracted into a hard knot. He was so hungry he couldn't think of anything except the smell of tomato. The jocks got enormous amounts of food, huge plates of rice and beans and spaghetti and rolls and cake and dough-nuts rolled in sugar. "Carbohydrates," Santos told him, "That's the best." Skinny Santos had rice and beans and curry. "You like chapa-tis?" Santos asked. "Try some. Indian food, I never have them before I come to work at the fish farm. I really like the Indian food."

Chapatis looked like tortillas. David got spaghetti and two big soft rolls and found himself going back for white cake with pink frosting. He could not remember when he had ever eaten so much in his life.

After lunch he was so full he could barely move, but Santos chat-tered like a maniac. David just wanted a nap. Santos was going on, something about Big Andre, one of the other divers, who was Hai-tian and who did voudoun. Santos hung around while David sat on his bed and wished everybody would leave him alone.

"It's the pyroxin," Santos said. "At first, you know, you are not used to it, and it just wipe you out, man. But after awhile you get used to it."

And then it was two, and they had to go back to the lockers and suit up for two more hours in the dark and the cold.

Santos handed him another pyroxin. David looked at the tiny white pill in his hand. If it made him feel as bad after the second dive as it had after the first, maybe he should skip it.

"Are you crazy?" Santos hissed. "You can't stand it out there, you not take a pyroxin."

He had made a mistake. He should never have taken the job. But what else was he going to do?

"Hey," Santos said, "don't worry, you get used to it. Everybody does."

He spent the weekend on the bright sunlit grasslands. He didn't like the shooting, but if he couldn't escape into the light he didn't know how he'd have stood it.

But after that it was Monday.

In the yard on Monday, MacKenzie said that someone would have to take samples on Wednesday. There were only three people in the yard but the air was full of voices volunteering.

"What kind of samples?" David asked Santos.

"For the project, in Miami," Santos said. "She never take me."

"What is so good about taking samples?"

Santos shrugged. "It's different, you know? You take the sled out, and this drill. And you work around the site, see, and when you are done, you go back, even if shift is not over."

He wouldn't be picked. Of course not, why would they pick someone who was so new? Who didn't know how to do anything?

Still, on Tuesday he was helping mix the stuff they used like cement, turning the bag and wondering about the properties that allowed it to harden underwater the way it did. MacKenzie swam over to make Inez go up on the structure and he said, "This is interesting stuff."

MacKenzie swung towards him, but the site was full of silt and they were close to the lights, so there was glare on her faceplate. He couldn't see a thing. She probably thought he was crazy. Or mouthing off.

"I have studied a little chemistry, see," he said. "I am thinking about why . . ." his English failed him, not so much because of his lack of vocabulary as because he just went blank, could not manage the effort of thinking in English.

"You've studied chemistry?" MacKenzie asked, her clipped American voice made him feel as if he should stand up straight. "Is your chemistry like your construction experience?"

He managed to laugh, not sure if she was ribbing him or not. "No," he said, "my chemistry experience is more."

"My chemistry experience is *more*"? "*Better*," he meant *better*.

MacKenzie said, "Okay." Nothing else. And then she was moving off, shouting at someone for stirring up more silt.

At shift end on Tuesday he swam back to the yard, shivering and tired. He felt bruised from the cold. The jocks would all climb out, lips blue from the cold, like when children swam at the beginning of the year and the water wasn't warm.

"Park," MacKenzie said, waving him over.

He didn't know for a moment if he should put his bike away or not, the cold made him stupid.

"Didn't you say you had studied chemistry?"

"Yes ma'am," he said.

"You take samples, then."

Around the yard there were groans. "Fucking Parks?" someone said, but it didn't sound really angry.

Wednesday after lunch he took a nap. He was dozing when the cat jumped onto his bunk. Meph stood a moment and then curled up in his face.

"Non," he said. Cat hair in his nose. He moved the kitten. Meph stood up and looked over the edge and David assumed that he was going to leave but he climbed over David's knees instead and curled up against the back of David's legs.

He was still there when David woke up and watched David get up but didn't move. "Is comfortable, eh?" David said.

The kitten stuck his leg into the air and started grooming.

When David left he assumed that Meph was still on the bed, but the kitten suddenly ran down the hall ahead of him and stopped. The locker room was damp and proved too much, Meph sat down in the hall. Lemile, one of the other jocks, bent down and petted him and Meph stood up and arched under his hand.

When he left, he thought maybe he could leave Meph here. Someone would see he got fed.

"Kim Park? You're taking samples? I'm Naranji, I run the lab. Are you familiar with the instruments?" he asked. He was small and neat and very dark, the palms of his hands very pale when he spread them to make a point. There was quite a bit of equipment and he went through it carefully, explaining what David should do. "If you have trouble," he said, "I will be in the booth with Facon, just give me a holler." Naranji smiled, "You know the phrase?"

Like Virginia. "I'll give you a holler," he said.

He suited up. The pyroxin cleared his head, woke him up.

Out into the yard. He was the last jock out because of the time he'd spent with Naranji but Ms. Facon just said, "Park?" without reprimand.

He went out to the site and set up the little drill to take samples. He took water samples, which he thought would be full of sludge. He took a series, moving farther and farther from the site until he was surrounded by the dark and the cold, the work lights a yellow haze. The instruments steadied him, having a purpose made it easier to be out here. But it took longer than he would have thought and he wasn't done any earlier than the work crew. It was still cold. But he liked the work better than construction, liked folding up the drill and putting it on the sled. It would have been easier if his fingers weren't clumsy in the cold.

"You took a long time," Naranji said when he got to the yard.

"I am sorry, it is the first time so I think I'm slow," David said.

"It's okay. You took the samples away from the site? Good."

"He was thorough," MacKenzie said, startling David.

"Good job," Naranji said and grinned. "I like thorough."

After that it was just the same thing, day after day. A job.

Two of the jocks were arguing in Spanish, their voices hard off the concrete walls of the locker room. One of them was new. Fish jocks disappeared, new faces replaced them.

It was the second dive of the day, and this week they were diving two hours in the morning, three in the afternoon. It made for a long afternoon. David preferred to do three in the morning. He could face the cold better in the morning.

But it was pyroxin that made it bearable to suit up. He could dread the dark water but still anticipate the heat. The precious heat, starting with the chamois lining of the divers' gloves—sometimes it started in his chest, but mostly it was like the first time he suited up, and he put on the gloves and his hands were warm, and the warmth was all through him waiting for him to notice. He liked the pyroxin, but that was dangerous, no matter how much Santos told him it was not addicting.

Santos told him to just take one, but sometimes the divers took two. Big Andre almost always took two. Santos said sometimes he took two, but with Santos it was hard to know how much was truth and how much was exaggeration.

The problem was that the pyroxin didn't last three hours. He dreaded the cold, dreaded the water. The best thing would be if he could take the pyroxin halfway through the shift, just as one was wearing off, start another. He would be tired after the shift, but that was okay, he could just sleep it off. If the warmth lasted the whole shift, then it wouldn't be so bad. Maybe two would make it more bearable.

So he popped two and finished suiting up.

The divers called the surfacing pool *la luna*. It was pale blue-green, lit by a circle of light and it cast a clear cold light up under the faces of the jocks standing around it, getting ready to dive. Last night he had dreamed about the moon pool. It had been the kind of dream where he had just deal with the unpleasantness, just done what he had to, walked down to the pool and dove in, and once through the pool he was a soldier again, fighting an underwater battle, swimming through the dark. The dream did not jerk him awake but eventually became unpleasant enough that he woke up. Lying there in his bunk, staring at the dark ceiling, surrounded by the barracks snores of the other divers and wondering who the hell the cat was sleeping with, he had tried to resolve the dream, tried to think of what he should have done instead, and afterwards he had gotten more and more disturbed, until lying awake thinking about the dream was more frightening than the dream itself had been, because the feeling of the dream wouldn't leave him.

He had the aftertaste of the feeling now, looking at the pool. He needed to quit. Even the hotel room was preferable to this. Meph would be pissed, Meph liked the fish farm. Maybe he could just leave the kitten here.

Any fool who would come here and establish dependents deserved what he got.

He sighed again and sat down beside the pool. Cool water. He pulled his facemask down, worked it a moment until it felt right against his cheeks and forehead. Isolation, and then the mic opened and he could hear the chatter from the yard. Nothing to do but get it over with. Lots of people hated their job. It was the human condition. Probably the hunter-gatherers who painted the mastodon hunts had bitched about the shaman and the tribal leader.

He pulled his legs out and turned around and fell back into the moon.

The yard was cold but lit. They were not allowed to linger, once Ms. Facon, the yard boss, had logged them present they grabbed a bike and took off for the site. He envied the real fish jocks, the ones who worked the fish pens; the two mechanics were almost always in the yard doing something. It was nice to be a mechanic, you could be anywhere and as long as you looked busy people assumed you were supposed to be there. He couldn't be a mechanic, he couldn't really fix things. Besides, the mechanics and the jocks that worked with the fish were permanent and the construction crew was all temporary. When they got the building up they'd be done.

He didn't think he'd be here for the two months that the project was scheduled.

The dark was always bad, the long ride out to the site. But he felt strong with his two pyroxin. He felt full of energy. His head was clear.

They were putting up sheeting to pour concrete. He hoped he'd be working with Patel, she didn't talk much, just worked, and he liked that. But MacKenzie, the foreman, put him with Lopez and Antoine. Antoine was all right, but Lopez talked all the time.

"Dese keed," Lopez said, and something else that David couldn't understand. "Dese keed is estupeed."

David thought maybe Lopez was talking about the new kid, but he wasn't sure. He always had trouble understanding Lopez' English. He usually just made agreeable noises.

The site was full of silt. He could see the separate particles, suspended. Stirring up silt brought the wrath of the foreman down on you, but no matter how careful they were they stirred it up. The filters were working, but as they went up the superstructure of the building the fog got worse until the lights were dim and far away.

They went up on the structure, prepping for putting walls up. Better than pouring cement, David thought.

He took a deep breath, his telltale said he was breathing fast, but not too fast, not hyperventilating. He felt eager to start, ready to be doing something.

The first hour flew. He was surprised to glance at the time and see he'd been out here that long. He was starting to feel a little cold, but not too bad. Mostly on his back and in his fingers and toes. The silt hung around them, defined their helmet lights so that he could see the sweep of Lopez' beam as he turned his head. Lopez' vision. Where the light was, that was what Lopez was seeing—in a way he could see Lopez' sight.

The silt drifted, sometimes in clouds, sometimes just particles. They didn't shine like dust particles, they were heavy and absorbed light.

But once in awhile one winked back at him, a flicker of reflection.

Once he started to get cold, he got cold fast. Like he always did. And time slowed down, began to creep. An hour and a half left on shift. An hour and twenty-six minutes. His fingers were getting clumsy.

But somebody must have stirred something up, or maybe he was just noticing more, because the silt was flashing more often now. Flickers bright as crystal—maybe mica or something in the silt? Was there mica on the ocean floor? He didn't know. Didn't know who to ask.

The recycs were able to deal with some silt, but he couldn't remember the silt ever being so heavy. It had to cut down on the recycs' efficiency. Maybe they would call off the rest of the shift? (In the fog around him, something winked bright. Like ice.)

His fingers were cold, he was getting clumsy. The water felt thick. There couldn't be so much silt that the water was turning to mud. It wasn't possible. Still, the water made it hard to move.

(Ice. The bright bits looked like ice. He tried to keep his eye on it but there was nothing to mark where the flash had been, just the silt, swallowing the light.)

It was colder than usual, too.

"Take a break," Lemile said. So they stopped a moment. The site lights at the base of the structure were huge, like spotlights, and he could see the way they warmed the water so it rose, curling like smoke. There were lights in that, too. Bright bits. They looked so much like ice. The water here couldn't get cold enough to freeze, it was too deep, there was too much pressure.

The bits of brightness were like snowflakes, only they moved up the beam of light rather than down. This wasn't right, he should tell someone that it was snowing. It was so goddamn cold.

He had drifted off the beam, he hadn't been paying attention, but he was so cold that he ached and it hurt to move his arms and legs, so he didn't do anything about it right away. He would start to drift down. Then he'd do something. He should tell the American woman, what's her name, that it was snowing, because the snow was starting to get thick. He was freezing to death, he felt so sleepy. He closed his eyes.

"—downside pyroxin," a woman said.

The wind was rushing past. And there was a vibration, like something mechanical. "Downside pyroxin." What a strange thing to say. David couldn't quite assign meaning, he got stuck at "downside" which should have made sense but didn't.

Downside pyroxin . . . downside pyroxin. The woman's voice was soft and sibilant. Downside pyroxin, soft and sibilant music. Almost a little song. He was laying on his back on something vibrating.

"Facon is going to be angry."

He liked the voice. Opened his eyes but everything was black. Night sky, no stars, just wind.

There was nothing to watch but he lay there with his eyes open, and then he sat up. The world was unsteady and he clutched for something. His legs were secured by a sack so he wouldn't drift in the wind. He felt light and yet thick.

He was on the sled.

There were two people at the front of the sled. One of them glanced back. "Park," she said. "Good. He's sitting up."

It was Patel. He couldn't see her face but he finally recognized her voice.

"You've had a pyroxin reaction," she said. "We're taking you back."

A pyroxin reaction. "Downside pyroxin," he said.

The sled came into the yard.

The other diver was Rosa. Rosa and Patel moved the sack. "Come on," Patel took his arm.

It was hard to swim, he felt stiff and awkward and woozy. The moon pool glowed ahead of him and he felt grateful, but once they broke the surface he was too heavy.

Patel pulled herself out. "Hand me your recyc," she said. He tried to hand it up, but he couldn't get it much above water. She heaved it out, and then she took his arm and helped him heave himself out. The weight of things, he thought. He could barely sit up for a minute.

"Come on," Patel said, "hurry."

For what? He was so fucking tired. But she kept at him and he got to his feet, got his balance. She walked with him into the men's locker room and sat him on a bench.

"Take off your mask," she said. She took his mask and his flippers and gloves. Then she matter-of-factly undressed him, skinning his tunic over his head, helping him pull his tights down. She ignored him when he protested, as matter-of-fact as a mother with a toddler.

He felt as if he was half-witted or something, not an adult. She didn't seem angry, though. "You have to hurry," she said.

"For what," he said.

"Before the shakes," she said. "You need to get warm."

"I don't feel cold," he said, although his skin was white with chill. But he didn't feel cold.

"You will," she said.

She made him pull off his long underwear. He was more embarrassed by the scars on his knee than he was by his nakedness. His nakedness just didn't seem to matter in front of Patel.

He was cold. But he couldn't stand up, didn't feel as if he had the strength, and his legs were shaking from the cold. He just wanted to sleep.

"Get in," she said.

His teeth were chattering. He was cold, so cold, and so tired. "Want to lay down," he said.

"Get in and sit on the floor," she said, grabbing him by his upper arm and hauling him to his feet. She was strong, and there he was, swaying for a moment, and then she propelled him into the shower. The sound of the water ricocheted off the white tiles. When she let go he sat down, skin against the bare tile.

The water was hot, too hot, but he didn't have the energy to get up and turn it down, so he sat, letting it beat against the top of his skull. Rain on the boneroof.

After a few minutes the water began to cool, and he had to palm the wall to get to his feet. He was surprised to find that the water was only set for lukewarm, and he turned it up hotter and sat back down.

He dozed, dreaming of a flat he had lived in, only the room was dark—and jerked awake when he heard voices. Fish jocks. He managed to stand up and turn the water off. He was red and wrinkled. The air was cold and he shivered.

"Kim? Hey Kim!" Santos was still in dripping gear. "Hey man, you okay?"

"Would you get my clothes?" David asked.

"Sure man. Patel tell you to take a shower?"

David nodded.

Santos disappeared, came back with a towel and clothes. "Go on and sit down. You okay, man? *Park!* I said, you okay?"

"Yeah," David said.

"Okay."

Getting clothes on was tedious, but he managed, and then while Santos was still showering, he made his way back to the bunks and crawled in. He was cold, and he—

"Parks. Come on, man, wake up. You gotta get up."

"What?" He sat up and tried to run his fingers through his hair but it was ratted from lying down on it wet. He was glad he'd had it cut.

"Come on," Santos said. "You gotta wake up. You gotta eat."

He wasn't hungry. He'd skip dinner.

"No man, you gotta eat. You don't eat you'll feel worse tomorrow."

Santos badgered him, getting him out of the bunk. God it was cold out from under the blankets.

Santos herded him down to the dining hall, chattering a mile a minute about how after a pyroxin reaction you had to eat. "Carbos," he said to the cooks, "give him some spaghetti, and refrieds, and a roll, yeah." Spaghetti and refried beans. But it smelled good. Santos got him a bowl of stew and a piece of cake, too.

"Yeah, I been downside three, four times," Santos said. "Once time I had a seizure, you know? I mean, I don't remember it or nothing. If I throwed up in the mask, like I coulda died, you know? This guy used to be a diver here, Carlos something, Carlos, Carlos, I forget his last name, anyway, he did that, choked on his own vomit, died before they could even get him to the yard. Eat some of the stew, too. Stew sucks today, I hate the fish stew here, my mama makes great fish stew."

Santos ate and talked and badgered him until he had eaten a lot of what was on his tray. David couldn't believe how much he ate.

And then he could barely keep his head up. He was afraid Santos wouldn't let him sleep, but Santos told him that sleeping was the best thing he could do. "You'll be okay tomorrow. You take two? You and me, man, we don't be big enough to take two. Big Andre, he got all that fat, he can take two. Facon's pissed, but Facon is always pissed. She'll dock you two shifts' pay, but it's your first time. People ask you if you take pyroxin, like Facon, you say no. She know you be lying, but if you say yes, then everybody gets in trouble, okay?"

David let the talk wash over him as he climbed back into the bunk. He remembered lying there for awhile, hearing something on the vid. And then he slept.

The alarms started going off at the usual time the next morning. He sat up. Everything ached and he still felt tired. But he stumbled out of bed.

Coffee helped and by the time they had to suit up for first shift, he didn't feel too much worse than a hangover. He looked at his pyroxin, wondered if he should take one.

He had to take one. Everybody took them. How the hell could anyone dive without them? So he tossed it back, like always.

Another day in the dark.

12

Gone to Earth

Each morning there was Sophie from the security agency who drove Mayla to work. Sophie was a young, narrow-faced girl from the fourth level. When Sophie opened her mouth it was possible to hear her whole history—a girl from the second or third level, whose good Catholic parents had sent her to school where she got an education that prepared her to work for a security agency. Mayla suspected that Sophie had earned the honorable C.

Sophie talked about her boyfriend as she drove. Her boyfriend was Haitian and his name was Albert, and he was looking for a job. Apparently Albert had been looking for a job for as long as he had been living with Sophie, and Mayla suspected he would continue to look for as long as Sophie would put up with him. Mayla listened and tried not to think about the fact that Sophie seemed even less competent than Tim.

She was not treated badly at First Hawaiian, despite the Marincite buy-out. People said "Good morning Mayla." Sevrin Parker even said good morning to her. Sevrin Parker never said good morning unless you said something to him first. Sevrin was a bastard who everybody suspected had something on the CEO because everybody hated him. He was good with figures but horrible with people. Having Sevrin be polite to her made her feel as if she had some sort of terminal disease.

Which was probably true, least as far as her career went. Marincite Corp. owned the bank. They would leave the name, First Hawaiian, and they were reviewing to decide if there would be any changes but for now they said there would be no firings.

Her desk was clean when she came in the morning, and it was clean when she left. Before the sale, the Marincite deal had become most of her work. Now she should have been establishing new accounts, but Alex Morel, her boss, had suggested that she not worry about that until they knew what was going to happen. So she went to work about nine, looked through her existing accounts, maybe wrote a renewal note, and at about three in the afternoon Sophie picked her up and took her home.

After three weeks, she walked into Alex Morel's office and handed in her resignation.

"I'm sorry," he said. But he didn't say, "Please stay."

She signed a non-compete clause that said she could not work for another financial institution in either Caribe, New York or the Pacific Rim for two years. She received a reasonable cash settlement as a partner.

And she was free. Sophie came to pick her up. Sophie thought her job was first rate. "Usually, the people I work for, they have to work all these hours, unless they're with the government. Do you work at home a lot?"

"No," Mayla said. "I just quit."

Sophie didn't know what to say about that.

"I guess I don't need security," Mayla said. Then she added, because it was the one day in her life when she knew she could, "Albert is a parasite, you ought to get rid of him."

Sophie didn't look at her. Mayla thought that she'd gone to far; anglo ladies didn't really have much right to be commenting on Sophie's life. Then Sophie grinned. "Yeah, I'm knowing, but sometimes you just do." And she chattered all the way home about what a no-good Albert was, but how'd she met him when he was a life model for her drawing class. Sophie really liked art. Which proved that there were parts of people you never guessed. "You take care of yourself, Ms. Ling," Sophie said, when she let Mayla off. "You're good people."

It was a day for speaking her mind. Which was good, because she had to tell her grandfather that she no longer had a job. She had to tell her grandfather what had happened to his bank.

"Grandfather," she said. "First Hawaiian has been taken over by Marincite Corp."

He blinked at her, an old Chinese man with a skinny wattled neck and very thick glasses.

"They haven't dismantled the bank," she said. "Everything is the same as before, Ives Istel is still head of the board, he just reports to Polito Navarro."

Her grandfather didn't say anything, which frightened her. Domingo waited, holding tightly on to the back of a chair. Tim stood in the doorway with Jude. They had all agreed he had to be told.

"Polito Navarro," she explained, "is CFO of Marincite Corp."

He cleared his throat. "You work for Marincite Corp?"

"The bank belongs to Marincite Corp., but I resigned," she said. She didn't know what she was going to say when he demanded to know what she was going to do. She didn't know what she was going to do. She didn't know how she was going to explain what she had done, how she had caused his bank to be swallowed up.

"You resigned?" he said.

She nodded.

"Good," he said.

He didn't ask any questions at all.

Mayla stayed in her room a great deal. It was bare but still full of the fine dust that comes from concrete. The house felt as if it would never be clean. She was in her room when Jude said that the police were calling. The moment Jude said "the police" she knew it was about David Dai.

The woman calling was a uniformed officer: a blue and white with a pinched square face that made Mayla think she had grown up poor. "Ms. Ling," she said, "we'd like you to come down and make an identification."

"Identify who?" she said without meaning to.

"Ms. Ling," she said, "if you do not come down voluntarily I will have to send an officer to pick you up."

"I'll be there," she said. She knew from the vids what it meant to identify someone, someone was dead. She would be looking at a body, not cleaned and made to appear asleep. She had never seen a body except for her grandmother and her grandmother had died in a hospital, her death only a continuation of her decline.

Domingo drove her down. There was no reason to assume it was David, but she couldn't think of anyone else it might be.

Maybe he was just arrested, was still alive. She'd have to have a lawyer then. Her lawyer wasn't a criminal lawyer. She tried to think of who she might call if David was in custody, who did she know who had any pull? Maybe her grandfather could call Enrique Chavez, but she didn't know if that would do any good. If they had David in custody a few days they would need a doctor. (Horror stories, electrical shocks, burned testicles, sometimes the old methods are best.)

If he was dead, maybe he had been killed "resisting custody." Or maybe he had committed suicide. A lot of people committed suicide when they were interrogated. She wondered how many of them really committed suicide, if given the opportunity to stop interrogation, wouldn't some people kill themselves?

She didn't know how she felt. Nothing was real. When she saw the body, would that make it real? What would the body look like? Would she get sick? Would it change her to see a body? Would her life turn at this moment?

Rehearsing, she was always rehearsing. It would be nice to have a genuine, unselfconcious moment that didn't involve being shot at.

Domingo walked in to the station with her, which she appreciated. The sergeant told him to take a seat but he said, "I'm staying with Ms. Ling, her grandfather told me to."

She was surprised, her grandfather had done no such thing.

The sergeant just shrugged and pointed to a set of double doors.

"Room 154," he said. Through the double doors was a wide hallway with a concrete floor. Domingo's soft-soled shoes didn't make any noise.

The hard-faced blue and white was waiting in Room 154, which turned out to be something like a reception office. "Ms. Ling," she said, "sit down." She looked Domingo up and down, raised an eyebrow and did not offer him a seat. "Bhagat," she called into the next room, "get the viewer, would you? And get Ms. Ling a cup of coffee." Then the hard-faced blue and white went back to something on her desk.

Domingo was pale. She was grateful he was here; she hadn't always been nice to him and she didn't deserve his loyalty. People went into police stations and never came out again.

Officer Bhagat brought a viewer and put it on the desk. Then he brought her a cup of coffee.

The blue and white nodded at the console ignoring the viewer. She was scanning something. "Okay, let me see the next one. No. No. No. Okay." Mayla looked at the viewer and wondered what it would show. David with a noose around his neck, his hair in his face. Or crushed by a skid. Or drowned and bloated.

The blue and white cut the call. She picked up the viewer, flicked it on and looked in it for a moment. The she flicked it off and handed it to Mayla. The plastic case was cold and the lens was a blind reflective eye. Mayla flicked it on.

It was a body. It was a black woman.

It wasn't David Dai.

"Who is it?" the blue and white asked.

She hadn't been looking at who it was, she was looking at who it wasn't. She didn't know who it was. She didn't know the woman. And then it came to her who it must be. "Anna Eminike," Mayla said.

The im had been taken in a morgue. Anna Eminike was nude to the waist, from there down she was covered by a sheet. Her skin was the color of clay, a strange inhuman color, but she didn't look badly used. Did bruises show up on the dead? Surely they did? Her mouth was flat, too wide, a grimace, and her chin was tucked down. Her left breast was small and whole, spread flat. Her nipple was shriveled and pointed, as if she was cold or aroused. Part of her right breast was gone and the muscle exposed was curiously pale. It was both too large and too innocuous to be a gunshot wound. There was something bluish white on her chest and Mayla peered at it for a moment and then zoomed in on it before she realized it was the exposed bone of a rib.

"Your employee, David Dai, identified her in a deposition," the blue and white said. "She approached him in the parking on Merister St." She meant at the bank. Mayla nodded. "Do you know where David Dai is?" the blue and white asked.

"No," Mayla said. It sounded so rhetorical she expected the blue and white to answer: "he's in jail," or "he fled the country."

Instead the blue and white said flatly, disappointed, "He hasn't been in touch with you?"

Mayla shook her head.

"Please let us know if he does contact you."

"What happened to her?" Mayla asked, lifting the viewer. Too late she thought maybe she wasn't supposed to ask.

But the officer just said blandly, "She was resisting arrest. They prefer death to arrest. It is definitely Anna Eminike, the woman your employee saw." She tapped the console and a piece of paper printed smoothly out. "Sign this please."

"What is it?"

"A form," she slid it across the table. "Sign at the bottom." The paper had Mayla's name and her grandfather's address neatly printed at the top, followed by a couple of file numbers. There were a couple of long dense paragraphs of single-spaced text and then a signature line at the bottom.

"I'd like to call my lawyer," Mayla said.

"It's not necessary, sign the bottom please." She tapped the signature line.

"I haven't read it yet," Mayla snapped.

The text was a description of the shooting in the parking naming

Anna Eminike as the person who had shot at her and David. "I can't sign this," Mayla said, "I couldn't see who was in the car."

"The woman is dead, it doesn't make any difference," the blue and white said.

"I couldn't see anything," Mayla said. "I was behind a pillar. It's in my statement. I'd be perjuring myself." To her own ears she sounded oddly prim, as if this were some sort of breach of etiquette.

"Fine," the blue and white said nastily and took the paper back. "I'm afraid there may be a few more things we'll need to ask you. You'll have to stay here." She turned off the monitor and walked out, the door clicking behind her.

Mayla looked at Domingo. He tried to smile and shrugged.

She should have signed. Why did they want her to sign? What difference did it make? Anna Eminike was dead. If she signed they would have her perjuring herself, was that why they wanted her to sign? Or did they care if there were inconsistencies?

Mayla checked her chron, it was 7:57 p.m. Were they being monitored? Were they hoping she would discuss it with Domingo? If so they were going to be disappointed, she didn't know what she would say to Domingo. She thought about picking up the viewer and looking at the im of Anna Eminike again, but she decided it would be better not to touch anything. Better to do nothing, to wait. The blue and white would have to come back eventually.

At 8:15 the blue and white had still not come back. She thought about getting up and trying the door. But if they were being monitored, what would that look like? On the other hand, if the door were unlocked, wouldn't it be ironic if they could have just gotten up and left?

They couldn't leave, even if the door was unlocked. If they left, they might as well simply leave Caribe, because no one ever ran out on the blue and whites.

How long should she wait before she did anything? She wondered if the monitor had security on it, if it didn't require a password then she could use it to call her lawyer. Surely it had security on it. Systems at the goddamn bank had security on them.

"Do you think you should have signed?" Domingo asked.

"I don't know," she said.

"Who is the dead person?" Domingo asked, nodding at the viewer.

"The im? Her name is Anna Eminike. She's a member of *La Mano de Diós*. She tried to recruit David Dai, my driver."

"The one who ran away," Domingo said.

"Right," she said. David had run away. The blue and whites had not been able to find him, either. Maybe she could run away? But David must have known how to disappear because they hadn't found him yet. She wouldn't know how to disappear.

"He is a member of *La Mano de Diós*," Domingo said.

"No," she said, "he's French."

"Oh," Domingo nodded, as if this explained everything.

Everybody thought David was part of *La Mano de Diós*, maybe he really was. Like the old saying, when three people tell you you're drunk, lie down.

Nothing to do but wait. She couldn't leave, she couldn't call her attorney. Oh Christ.

So they waited, curiously silent, as if talking would get them in trouble. Maybe it would, anything they said could be taped and then edited, made to say anything the blue and whites wanted said. But the blue and whites could make up anything they wanted, nobody would say anything. So the fact that they were being made to wait meant that the blue and whites didn't want to just throw her in a cell, didn't it?

At least she was wearing comfortable clothes. Imagine if they decided to keep her overnight and she'd been wearing a suit. Imagine if she had still been working at the bank.

The body in the im didn't look like that much had happened to it, there wasn't so much damage, but Anna Eminike was dead. It occurred to her that Anna Eminike had been shot from the front, so she knew she was going to die. What was that like, to die? To know you are going to die in this mean place and that no one cares and that is that? But anyplace anyone dies is finally a mean place and death matters most to the person dying, right?

She didn't want to die, but at least if she died it would be over. And everybody died, and in a hundred years, no one would know what awful things had happened. Did anyone care that in what was now eastern Europe they turned the Moslem invaders by, among other things, impaling thousands of captured men on poles, standing the spears in rows like armies? It didn't really matter to anyone but the two of them that Domingo was brave enough to be here.

"Ms. Ling," said the blue and white, a different one this time, "will you come with me?"

"Where are we going?" she asked. It was after ten. Domingo stood up cautiously, and she felt stiff in the knees and hips.

"Just Ms. Ling," said the blue and white.

Domingo looked at her, not volunteering this time, hoping that she wouldn't make him go with her. She wanted him to stay, didn't want to be alone. "Go on home," she said, moved by what impulse she couldn't say. After she said it she realized that if he left he could call someone, do something. It made her feel a little better.

The blue and white didn't seem to care if Domingo went home or not.

At the door Domingo looked back over his shoulder, as if he wasn't certain of the propriety of what he was doing, but he went. The blue and white jerked his head for her to follow and they went into the hall after Domingo. Domingo glanced over his shoulder again, his fine silhouette floating ahead of her. I won't forget, she thought, I won't forget that people can be like this, that people can walk into the police station with you even when they are afraid.

The blue and white took her left, she saw Domingo stutter step when he realized that they were no longer following, and she leaned back watching for as long as she could until the corridor cut off her view. She could hear Domingo's shoes, hesitant, and then she thought a little faster but she was too far to hear the squeak, and this corridor was meaner than the one they had come in, the walls yellowed as if by body oils, stained from hip to shoulder height as if people had rubbed along it as they walked. They went through a door with wire in a tiny window and the moment the blue and white opened it she could hear voices, crashing and echoing off of concrete floors and block walls. Creole and Spanish. There was the strong smell of vomit and beer and her stomach lurched. The left side of the room was holding pens full of people in street clothes, mostly men but two of them with women in them: patient women, in divers' vests with goosebumps on their arms—prostitutes coming off of their pyroxin—or women just dressed like anyone on the street. One with a cut down the side of her head, and her hair matted back away from her face as if lacquered with hairgel instead of blood.

The blue and white walked Mayla across the room towards a door on the other side.

The men were calling her "pollo," chicken, and laughing. *"Polito,"* someone said and for a moment she thought he was from Polito Navarro, that it was some sort of code that she was not alone, that the Uncles were here watching her, help—but then she knew again that the Uncles weren't on her side. But she had jerked her head around, staring into the brown face of a man in a Guatemalan vest. He looked like a fish jock, with his bare arms. He had a big bruise on his cheek. *"Politico,"* he said again. Politician, a political prisoner.

The door opened on a small office, two desks and filing cabinets and paper and barely room to turn around. She smelled incense. (Didn't people use that to cover the smell of marijuana? The blue and white wasn't Haitian, but that didn't mean they couldn't use marijuana.) The blue and white gestured to a chair.

He didn't say why he had brought her to this office, he just sat down and printed out a sheet of paper and handed it to her. She read it again but she didn't really connect the words to meaning.

"You should sign," he said.

And she did.

At the office of foreign services Mayla requested permission to go abroad. The application was familiar, she had been abroad before.

She wondered why they gave people pencils. She filled out her passport number. *Reason for Trip*. For the last ten years she had been putting business.

Reason for Trip. She could say it was to see her family in the States. She could buy a plane ticket for Hawaii, pretend she was going to visit her cousins in Honolulu. She just needed to get to the States, she could apply for a conversion from a tourist visa to a resident visa once she was there. She couldn't do it here, if she went to the U.S. Consulate in Caribe the government would know. They monitored people who applied for visas.

Reason for Trip. "Vacation." Never explain a lot when you are lying. It's a clear sign that something is not right.

She stood in line behind an overweight woman whose back had rolls of fat at her shoulder blades. The woman's hair was artificially straightened, a curtain of shining black hair. Mayla wondered where she was trying to go, was she trying to visit family in the islands?

She wished the U.S. were like other countries and she could have applied for a visa through the mail, although her mail might be monitored for all she knew. Or she might just be paranoid.

The office was too small, too crowded. There were only four windows open. It was damp. People had to crowd because there wasn't enough room for the lines to form.

She could just leave the application and go back to her grandfather's.

Getting permission to leave didn't mean she actually had to leave. It just meant that she could. And she could go, take a vacation and come back.

The big woman in front of her was at the window, but Mayla couldn't see around her to know what she was doing. Not that it mattered.

Waiting. Waiting was getting harder. She wished she could do something, these days she had too much time to think.

The big woman turned, her application still in her hand. The big woman was scowling. There was no place to get out of her way so she shoved against Mayla to get past.

Time to get out, Mayla thought, but she wasn't sure if she meant this office or Caribe.

"Identification?" the woman asked.

Mayla handed over her temporary ID. (The regular one had gone with the house. The replacement hadn't come yet.)

The woman in the window said something inaudible and pecked out the information on the temporary. If it had been a regular card she could have scanned the information. Of course, in the U.S. it would have been tied to her thumbprint, no card at all.

"Application," the woman said and Mayla handed it to her.

She pecked that information in, too. *"Diós,"* she said, after a moment, exasperated. She pecked the information in a second time. Then she sighed. "Your application is turned down."

"It is?" Mayla said. "Oh. I'm sorry. Um, why?"

"Your file is flagged, in order to travel you must clear it with the Security Office. You'll need to forward all queries to this address." She handed Mayla a sheet of paper.

"Thank you," Mayla said.

There was no place for the people behind her to step aside so she had to push her way out through the crowd. She wasn't going to query, it was probably bad enough that she had even tried. Someone in the Security Office would probably notice that she had tried to leave the country.

She didn't know what any of this meant.

Maybe it was just routine. Maybe her file had been flagged because of the bomb in the house. She sat down at the console in her grandfather's office to compose a letter of inquiry but she couldn't think of any way to word it that wasn't incriminating.

She addressed the letter. She stared. *I am writing to inquire about a permit to visit family in Miami.* That seemed innocuous, didn't it? Or would it draw attention to her? She had already drawn attention to herself by filing for permission. If she just let it drop, would the note just go in her file somewhere? Maybe they wouldn't pay much attention, after all, her name probably just went on a report. There was data coming at them from all directions and she probably just got lost in the sea of information. But if she wrote the letter she might raise another flag. Too many flags and someone would notice her again. Best to lay low, hope that they had other things more interesting going on. Wait, and eventually she could leave. On the other hand, maybe the fact that she had applied and wasn't querying the security office would be read as a sign of guilt—

The console rang a call and she jumped and slapped the receive. The console was set so it could be heard from the hall and it was amazingly loud, if she'd thought she wouldn't have hit it.

No video. "Hello?" she said, she could not hear anything in her voice, but her heart, her heart, was her heart pounding in her voice? No video. She put her finger on the record and pushed it in. The indicator came on the screen, silent numbers clicking the seconds.

No answer.

She sat, thinking about cutting it off. Blue and whites playing mindgames? *La Mano de Diós*. She reached out and almost touched the cutoff. The air sounded open, like a seashell without the sea.

"Hello?" a man's voice said.

"Yes?" she said. She waited at the cutoff. *La Mano de Diós*, surely. Leave me alone, she thought. The call would be monitored, the seconds clicked on, 12 . . . 13. . . . The blue and whites would think her an accomplice—

"May I speak to Mayla?"

Strange accent, familiar. "This is she."

"Mayla?" The video came on and it was David Dai.

For a moment she was stunned. He was dead. No, she thought, it wasn't him, it was Anna Eminike who was dead.

"Hello," he said, wary. He'd cut his hair. It made him look different, younger.

"Hello," she said. "Are you okay?" Oh God, were the blue and whites monitoring?

"I'm okay," he said, "are you okay?"

"I'm fine."

"Okay," he said.

Where are you? she wanted to say, but if the blue and whites were monitoring she didn't want him to tell her, but she wanted to know. They sat looking at each other. There were no real clues behind him, just a wall. He was sitting, wearing a diver's top, but a lot of people wore those. The wrist fasteners looked like the heavy ones, not the ones people used for everyday swimming. "I quit the bank," she said.

"You quit?" he said.

"It was sold, to Marincite. It was taken over, actually. It was my fault, partly."

"What are you going to do?" he asked.

He was the only person who had asked that. She felt suddenly and profoundly grateful, and her eyes welled. But she wasn't going to cry. "I don't know."

He sat silent again, but a different silence, the silence of someone trying to think of what to say about something.

How did you hide? she wanted to ask. *I need to get away.* She couldn't even ask him if he was in Caribe, although she supposed he was or he would have told her where he was. The blue and whites couldn't touch him in France, could they?

"I can't really talk," he said.

I need to escape, she thought. "Wait," she said, her mind racing, wanting to ask him something, if the blue and whites asked she could always say she assumed they were monitoring and wanted to give them time to establish a trace, "are you really all right?"

"Kim," someone called, another man. "Is this the spawning info?"

"I am on a call!" David snapped.

"I need to know about the salmon trays, what is the biocompatibility, where is the rating?"

"I have to go," David said to her.

"Are you working?" she asked, desperate.

"I'll call you again," he said, but he was lying. And he cut off the connection.

The screen blanked except for the indicator, which recorded the time of the conversation, one minute, ten seconds. It had seemed longer.

She played it back. It went fast when she played it back. She watched him, adjusting her memory to his image, she had not remembered exactly the way his eyelids were, without creases. Memory was important, untrustworthy. Tim had seen him get on the bus, and he had disappeared.

Where was he? Some place that they used salmon trays, whatever salmon trays were. And spawning. Probably a fish farm.

She called up a listing, printed out all the fish farms. She looked at all of them, but didn't know what to do next. She didn't know if the blue and whites were monitoring or not. They couldn't monitor everybody on their lists, could they? Or maybe they recorded it all, but how could they screen it? Even with some very sophisticated screen they would get more than they could look at.

Or they would be here.

She picked up the list and went up to her room. She pulled a couple of tights out of her drawers and a couple of sweaters and underwear. No suits. Strange not to take suits. What are you going to do, Mayla? You are going to run.

She took her cards, her account access, her temporary work ID. The good one was gone with the house, but that was good because it had ID, work history, med insurance information coded on it, this one had nothing but her name and old address.

She didn't take much, just a few things. She walked out of the house with a shoulder bag with the list of fish farms stuffed in with her clothes. Outside she had to walk awhile, but unlike David she didn't have to catch a bus to get to a bank machine. She wondered if her account would be frozen.

She dropped her card in, if it took it she would keep going, but it just asked her for her name and she said, "Mayla Ling."

"Read this code phrase," it said.

On the screen it said, "Talk so people will listen, and listen so people will talk." Which was a new phrase. She read it. At the bank they bought all their voice recognition equipment from the States, and quarterly they got updated codes to make things more difficult for counterfeiters.

"Please repeat," it said.

They had denied access. She repeated the phrase, wondering if she should just run.

But the screen asked her to pick a transaction.

"Balance check."

She had a pretty decent amount available.

"Withdraw."

She took all but 100cr.

Then she stood for a moment, looking all around. She caught her reflection in the window of a shop and saw herself standing out, tall anglo woman, looking. So she walked. She needed to find a place to make a call. She needed a public exchange, even if it was to make just local calls. She should have known where one was, she'd seen them all her life, places where people who couldn't afford service in their own place went to make calls. She needed to go down a few levels.

Right, she had something like 12,000cr stuffed in her shoulder bag and she was going to go *down* a couple of levels. A white woman. Might as well just get herself a jacket and paint a big bullseye on the back.

She walked to the shopping plaza and waited for a bus. David Dai had gotten on a bus. She would bet he had gone down, too. So she would go down. Wasn't that the instinct of animals, to go to earth when trying to hide?

She waited a long time, standing in line with women who came to the plaza to work—girls with elaborate hair and jewelry and women with string bags with fruit in them. The bus that chugged up to the edge of the plaza was a taptap, sky blue and swirling with serpentine lines of neon colors and dots. They looked as if they had been painted on with a broad paintbrush. She'd seen them all her life, but she'd never gotten on one.

She paid her coin and sat down in the middle. The bus started sluggishly and the driver pulled on something, some lever, and the engine roared. She smelled the stink of petrol. Petrol was supposed to be restricted bu the taptaps had been running her whole life. She looked out the window.

The taptap ran behind shops so she saw concrete and doors and garbage dumpsters. Sometimes the way got so narrow that people flattened against the wall to let the taptap pass.

She wasn't in a hurry, not really. She wasn't going anywhere. But she wanted to get to a place to make some calls, so she could figure out what to do next. She tried to watch the backs of the shops to see an exchange, sometimes a door was open and a heavy brown woman would stand impassively, leaning against the door frame, one foot up. But inside was always darker than the lit street and she could never see.

The taptap turned onto a thoroughfare and it took her a moment to identify Revolution (which her grandfather still called Walter—if the blue and whites came would her grandfather think it was her fault?) They lumbered a few blocks on Revolution and then the bus heeled like a sailboat and U-turned into an interchange, a steep descent like a parking garage, rumbling in low gear against the transmission. Making their way down a level.

She rested her forehead against the glass, even though it was cold. She wished she could just find a place to stop for awhile. She had to be smart. She had to use her head, make herself do things her body didn't want to do. She wanted to go back to her grandfather's and go to bed.

The taptap didn't have any stops on the second or third level, but rumbled down to the fourth. She didn't know anything about the fourth level, she thought she had been there but she couldn't remember what for.

She got out at another little shopping plaza because she thought there had to be an exchange there. The neighborhood was Spanish, she thought from the mainland because people didn't seem island, but she wasn't sure.

"*Excusa*," she tried—oh God, she wished her Spanish were better. "*¿Un central?*" The first person she asked just looked at her. A man pointed off and rattled directions at her. She understood straight, *derecho, derecho,* so she walked for awhile, out of the plaza, and then she stopped and asked someone else. She could feel the sweat running under her sweater.

She finally found an exchange and got change. She took a booth and pulled out her list of fish farms. She called the first one. "Hi," she said, "I'm with Julia Aquacultural Supplies, I believe I was talking to someone out there about some salmon trays? An Asian named Kim? I'm afraid I accidentally cut him off."

The first call the girl couldn't help her, no one named Kim there. The second call was answered by a Haitian girl who didn't speak English. She shook her head a lot, and Mayla didn't know if it meant that there was no Kim there or if she just wanted Mayla off the line.

There were thirty-one numbers on her list. She called fourteen. "Kim Park? *Si, está aquí, un momento por favor.*" The young man transferred the call and Mayla killed the video.

"Park." There was a moment's pause. "This is Park. Hello?"

It was David Dai. She cut the connection. She knew where he was.

She had found him. The blue and whites couldn't, but she had. She was thinking, she was using her head. She was going to be all right.

She didn't know where to sleep. Any place where she paid anything but cash would leave a trace. She had never stayed in a place that took cash, criminals stayed in places that took cash. That thought made her perversely pleased with herself. She paid for the booth and asked the old man taking money where she could find a place. "*¿Donde esta un hotel?*" She couldn't remember the gender of nouns, couldn't remember when to use *ser* or *estar.* But the old man answered her in equally broken English.

"Go," he said pointing with his hand out the door and then left.

"*Izquierda,*" she offered, the word rising out of some place she didn't know she remembered.

"*Sí,*" he smiled, "*izquierda,* and go two, ah two, *calle, y a la derecha,* one."

"Two," she motioned left out the door with her hand, "and one," she motioned right.

"*Si, señorita.*"

Being a criminal might turn out to be pleasingly easy.

The plaza was small, but the air felt better than it had inside the booth. Until she got outside she hadn't even realized how stale the air had seemed inside.

People were outside, shopping, walking around. A lot of people for a work day. Maybe some of them worked second shift somewhere. Maybe a lot of them simply weren't employed.

She wasn't employed. Strange to think that.

At the second street she turned. She didn't know what kind of place to expect. The side street had a roof much lower than the plaza and it was narrow, the kind of place a skid would come through, but too small for a taptap. All along the street were warehouse doors. At the end of the block was another primary, wide and well lit. On the corner was a coffin hotel.

It was completely automated, of course. Put a debit card in the slot and rent herself a six by five by three. She needed to pay cash. Was there a human operator? No number listed on the console. If she put her card in, it would give her a number to call for problems, but that would just be some management company, and besides, she didn't want to leave a trace.

She tried to think of what to do. She hated walking around here with a shoulder bag carrying over 12,000cr. But she didn't want to stash the thing, she'd just need to find a place where she could stay. She tried to think of the word for room. *Cuarto,* she thought, as in *¿Dónde está el cuarto de baño?,* but she didn't know if that meant the same room as "room for rent." Maybe she could find someone who spoke English. They were all supposed to learn English in school.

She turned onto the primary, which was called Sorrento, and walked. Maybe she would see a notice for a room for rent or she would pass a place. But she walked through neighborhoods, past little shops with steel grates pushed up for the day's business. Places that rented medical supplies like wheelchairs, hospital beds and crutches, their windows full of dusty bedpans and a chipped anglo mannequin, smiling in her nurse's uniform. That might be a way to make herself invisible, if for some reason her description was given out. Get a pair of crutches and people would only see the crutches, not her face. She had read that, or seen it on the vid. Hardware stores. Yellow signs with red hands—palms covered with zodiacal symbols—advertising reader-advisors. Places where you could get coffee, and fish sandwiches on Jamaican coconut bread, and stew.

She walked a long time without seeing a place to stay. She was on the wrong road, but she didn't know where to look.

She had no idea where she was, but that wasn't so bad. If she didn't know where she was, neither did anyone else.

What was she going to do after she started hiding? *What are you going to do?* David had asked. She didn't know. It didn't make any difference. The blue and whites wouldn't give her much in the way of options; maybe she would have come out of the police station the next time, and maybe she wouldn't. This way she wasn't in.

She stopped in a restaurant that served Cuban black beans and rice. She was running out of small change, pretty soon she would have to break one of her 500cr notes, and she didn't want to do that where other people could see it.

But the beans and rice made her feel better, and after that she started taking side streets. Residential streets, where people's flats looked out and people were coming home from work. She stopped a young man and asked if he spoke English. He shook his head.

"*¿Dónde está un cuarto?*" she asked, "Where is a room?" But he just shook his head, smiling uncomprehendingly. Afterwards she thought she should have asked for *un cuarto de hotel* but by then it was too late. She didn't want to talk to too many people, she was conspicuous enough.

It was the fact that she was so conspicuous, and that it was after seven and there were fewer people on the street, that convinced her to take a side street that took her behind shops. She found a dumpster and sat against the wall behind it. Her legs were so tired that they ached.

She planned to sit for awhile and then keep looking, but she just kept sitting. Her mind felt curiously empty. Eventually it was after eight, and she didn't really want to be wandering around with a bag full of money after the lights went to night. She took out two more sweaters and put them on, since once she wasn't moving she felt cold.

Some people lived like this, she could do it for a night.

Through the night people came through the alley, sometimes just one, sometimes two. Once, at a little after one there were four or five; she heard their feet and heard them talking, soft Spanish voices, just boys, laughing and kidding each other. She wasn't even really afraid anyone would find her, her biggest problem was that her neck was stiff and she couldn't really sleep. Her thoughts would wander and she would be dreaming but then she was awake again. She was so tired, she would ask someone about a hotel. She'd find someone who spoke English.

At a little after two she had to go to the bathroom so badly she couldn't stand it. She tried to ignore it, but she couldn't.

She came out from behind the dumpster and looked until she found a drain. If someone came they would see her, but she didn't know what else to do, so she pulled down her tights and crouched. The air was cold on her bare skin. She was careful and didn't get any on her shoes. She didn't have any paper, hadn't thought even to bring a tissue, but the relief was incredible. Still, she felt better when she was back out of sight behind the dumpster.

At four-thirty in the morning she got up and went back out to the street. Someone would come before too long to open up the shop and she didn't want to be found.

She found a place to have breakfast, a safe place, full of people dressed as if they were going to work. The front window was steamed and the place was warm with the heat of bodies and the flat fry table. Her hips ached. She had a pastry and coffee.

The bathroom was tiny, a toilet and a stained sink crowded together. She ran water until it was warm and cleaned her hands and face. She still felt filthy, but not so bad, and she didn't think she smelled yet, although sometime during the night she had stopped smelling the dumpster. It was still only five-thirty, and she wasn't ready to go back outside so she went back to the little table and had some oatmeal and fruit.

The waitress spoke some English. She came, refilled coffee and took empty plates. "Do you need the table?" Mayla asked.

"No," the girl said. "It's okay."

"Can you tell me someone who would rent me a room?" Mayla said.

The girl shook her head.

"A hotel?"

The girl thought and then nodded. "I write you map, miss," she said. She drew carefully on a napkin, ink lines blurring into the paper.

"Also, an exchange?"

The girl nodded and said, "Here," adding a street to her map and drawing an X. "Is here."

"Thank you," Mayla said, and she was so grateful she left a huge tip.

She felt better when fed. The map helped. It gave her purpose. She followed it carefully and found the exchange, but it was only a little after seven, there was no sense in calling the fish farm.

No sense in getting excited yet about the hotel since it was probably a coffin hotel like the last one. If worst came to worst she could sleep behind her dumpster again.

She didn't know what to do with herself so she thought she'd at least check the hotel and see if it was a place where she could stay. The farther she walked, the more she worried she was going to see another coffin hotel. She had all day to find some place, so if it wasn't a hotel where she could stay that didn't mean she would have to sleep behind the dumpster again.

She almost turned and walked the other way, but there was no other way to walk.

But it wasn't a coffin hotel, it was a string of flats that someone had bought and painted pale pink, with dark-green trim around the doors and windows. The paint was peeling and mildewed, and the place didn't look very well kept. The owner was an overweight Indian wearing a housecoat who lived in the pink flat on the end, next to a *bodega* run by a man as slight as she was overweight. Mayla wondered if they were husband and wife or brother and sister. The flat where Mayla paid her money smelled of cumin, but the woman seemed to think nothing strange of an anglo woman with a 500cr note.

She did not ask if Mayla wanted a receipt.

Mayla felt strange sitting in the bar in Saucone Street. People were staring at her, she knew. There were other women here, but they all had a thick-skinned look. Not coarse, just thick. She was the only anglo there, not even the reps ranged along the bar were white.

Ah, but David had to have been the only oriental. If he could do it, so could she. Besides, women were supposed to make better divers than men, better able to stand the cold. She just had to figure out which was the rep from the fish farm where David worked and then she had to get him to give her a job.

The reps were flashier than the divers; one wore long burgundy braids, a *maroon*. The one next to him wore a broad-brimmed khaki hat, the front pulled low over his eyes. She didn't like him, didn't like the way he rested his bare elbows on the bar and laughed into his fist.

She didn't like the *maroon* either. Or the one with the belly and the walrus moustache, or the one with the white hair and goatee. She tried to decide who she'd have the best chance with, but didn't feel as if she had much chance with any of them. She couldn't talk to them, she didn't know how.

She asked the bartender who was the rep for David's fish farm. He indicated the bare-armed one in the hat and she thought she should have known. But she bought him a rum. Carrying it down the bar felt a little inappropriate, as if she were soliciting him. He was listening to something the *maroon* said and didn't seem to notice her, although the *maroon's* eyes flickered across her.

No more interest than if she were a barstool.

She went back to a table to wait. The tables were filling, people saying hello to each other as if they knew each other. No one sat down at her little table.

She watched the rep, she didn't care what happened as long as she got this job. If she got the job it would give her a place to hide. The blue and whites hadn't found David, no one would ever think to look for her on a fish farm.

No one would ever think to look for her where she was now, either, but staying in that room was making her crazy. She didn't even dare call her grandfather and tell Jude where she was. She had been gone five days, did her family think she had been kidnapped? If so, they had probably called the blue and whites, who probably thought she had gone underground with *La Mano de Diós* which meant she couldn't go home now even if they hadn't been planning to pick her up.

So it didn't matter. What mattered was that she needed a place to go. And David had found a place to hide.

She watched her rep for an hour and ten minutes while he sipped from a glass and a jock approached him and they retired to a side table. He finally picked up a glass and sipped it and she started to get up and then realized she wasn't sure if it was hers. She waited, afraid that if it was hers and she waited too long that he would decide on someone else. No one else stood up, so she got up—and then someone did get up and she froze, but they were headed for the back, for completely different purposes.

He jerked his head and she followed him to the side table where apparently negotiations went on. "I'm not hiring right now," he said.

"Oh," she said. She had never thought of this. What was he doing here if he wasn't hiring?

"I'm looking for a couple of handlers, are you a handler?"

She thought about saying yes but she didn't know what a handler was and that wouldn't work.

"I, ah, I need some experience," she said.

He smirked. "Yes?"

She knew what he was thinking, that it was obvious that she wasn't a fish jock. "I can maybe pay a learning fee?" she said. She had rehearsed this in her head. "I need the work and I need to get some experience, but I know that you shouldn't, or, I mean, the farm shouldn't train me for free?"

"How much?" he asked.

Madre de Diós. "500cr," she said.

He shook his head.

"1000," she said.

He said. "Let's see some papers on who you are. I don't hire people in trouble."

She pulled out her workcard.

"It's temporary," he said, suspicious.

"I was robbed," she said. "They took my purse, everything. It's taking forever to get a new card."

"Why do you want to be a fish jock, lady?" he said. "You no fish jock."

She didn't know what to say. "I need to get out of the city."

He studied her for a moment. "You got man trouble?"

She looked down at the little table. "He beats me," she said, her voice cracking with the lie. "He said if I ran away he'd find me." Jesus, she couldn't act, and her face flooded red with embarrassment. *He beats me?*

But the rep nodded, his face suddenly softer. "Okay, lady. 1000cr."

She reached down for her bag but he had already stood up. "Tip the bartender," he said. "Be at the shuttle dock Sunday night.

She went back to her table and carefully folded the 1000cr into a 5cr bill. It looked too thick to be a tip but she kept it hidden in her hand and walked back to the bar. She was even more embarrassed, now. She couldn't wait to get out, to go back to her hotel. The bartender was busy so she had to wait a long minute, but finally he came back down to her end. "Yes, ma'am?"

"Thanks," she said, and handed him the money.

"Good luck," he said.

13

Transfer

Y ou were in the war in South Africa, right?" Santos said.

David nodded. Sunday night, and they were hanging around in the men's bunkroom after dinner. The television was on at one end, but they were all in the space between Santos' bunk and the next bunk.

"Did you ever kill anyone?"

Too many weekends spent playing war games. They had been logged in five hours today and David could still feel the phantom weight of the helmet. But it had been Argentina again and the light was so wonderful.

Had he ever killed anyone? He remembered firing into the face of a startled Prot across a city street. In Durban. The Prot had seemed right there, so close to him, but he had not stopped running and he didn't know if he had hit the man or not. "I don't know. It is not like that," he said.

"I guess you can't tell in a firefight," Santos said.

David shook his head. Even firefights were not what Santos thought.

Everyone was watching him, even Roland, who was sitting on the concrete floor between the bunks, playing solitaire. Roland was a new *maroon*. Santos fancied himself a ringleader, a streetcorner boy, and he recruited people to his *société*. Roland was a thick, sweet boy who was happy to be in anyone's *société* and who couldn't have been a wild *maroon* if his life depended on it.

"When you are fighting a war, it is not like the game," David said.

"When you are fighting a war, you learn that all the things people do, a lot of things that they believe in, are not real. They do not matter. When the police give you a citation for crossing the street in the wrong place, what does it matter? You have to go pay a fine, but you are still alive, you do not hurt. It is not real, that the corner is this place to cross, and that the middle is not a place. You are not hit by a car, nothing happens, the citation it is not about whether you are hungry, or you are hurt. People just do it because they don't think about how if everybody stops obeying the rule it is gone."

They didn't understand.

"But you see," he stumbled on, "things do not work if people don't believe papers and laws and all those little stupid rules like what is fashion and how short your hair should be." He swiped at his, it was getting long and he should get a trim. "War makes it hard to ever belong to anything again. You have to forget what you know. War makes you learn too much."

Santos nodded, but he didn't understand. "Is that how you hurt your knee? In South Africa?"

David nodded.

"What happened?"

"A man I was with, he stepped on a mine."

"Did he die?" Roland asked.

"Of course he died," Santos said, worldly wise.

Of course he did. So easy. Of course.

"Did you know him really well? Was he a friend of yours?" Roland asked.

"No, I was . . . how do you say, he reported to me. I was, like his sergeant."

Santos looked thoughtful. "Did you feel like it was your fault?"

He shrugged. It was hard to remember now what he had felt. He had been so surprised. Had he thought about whether he should have done things differently? He supposed he had, in the hospital in In Salah, but he couldn't remember that now. He remembered he had been waiting for so long, expecting a bullet or a shell or something, that he was mostly astonished at how unexpected it was, mostly astonished that he was surprised, because he would have thought it was almost a relief to get it over with and to know that he wasn't dead.

He had been a little relieved. Once he knew he wasn't going to die, at least. He had hoped he wasn't going back although he hadn't been sure until they told him in Algiers.

That was before he realized that the war had derailed him and that he couldn't step back into his life. "Roland," David said, "play the red seven on the black eight."

Roland looked down.

Santos started talking about a new girl. "She's Chinese, although I don't think she looks so Chinese, she looks anglo. But she's got some sort of Chinese name, and there wouldn't be an anglo fish jock."

"MacKenzie is anglo," Roland said.

"She's a foreman," Santos said, dismissing Roland's comment. "Kim, maybe you should meet her, might be a good thing, you and her."

"Right," David said.

He had thought—and he had not even realized it—that if he came to Caribe he could get away from the war. Even at home the war had been everywhere, all around him in the way his life after the war was so different than his life before. But the war was more here than it had ever been at home. Anna Eminike was here, and the violence, and Santos' games of war. All around him was the dark. Surrounded by the night. The dark had never bothered him until after the war. So he had come to a place where it was night all the time. Stupid.

He sighed. Anywhere he went, half the day was night.

He spent so much time trying not to think about the war, what would happen if he gave up and just let the thoughts come?

But he couldn't imagine letting himself think about it. Once he started thinking about it, he might end up one of those sad hulks who live the war every minute.

He shook his head. Think about things here. About a job, about the moment, that is what most people did. He could wonder about whether Naranji would have work for him in the lab. Twice now he had spent eight hours in the lab, helping Naranji with the new salmon project: running titrations on water samples to check for contaminants. There was a leak in the system and they were getting trace amounts of lubricant in the water. The salmon fry were sensitive.

He could, by dint of constant vigilance, keep himself distracted. But there were thoughts back there, like a toothache.

He bought two bottles of beer from Lopez, who kept a cooler under his bunk and charged twice what a bottle would cost in the store. But they weren't supposed to have beer on the fish farm, so Lopez was charging for risk. Lopez also sold pyroxin. The beer helped him relax. Meph showed up and he opened a can of catfood. He thought he had controlled things quite nicely.

At ten he turned in, listening with one ear to the Spanish station on the vid at the other end of the bunkhouse with the words too far away for comprehension, not trying to understand, just listening to the rise and fall. Meph was curled up on the bed, and he put his hand on the cat. Meph purred and butted his head against David's hand, hard bone under fur. Meph grabbed David's hand in his teeth but did not bite hard, just watching, tail twitching. Ready to play. "No," David whispered, pulling his hand away. He waited, sometimes Meph got it in his head to attack, but tonight Meph stared for a moment, then closed his eyes and sat, sphinx-like. The long bunkroom was almost empty, Sunday night a lot of the jocks got together for some sort of *société*, not like Santos' group, but something else. Santos was part of it. He said it was like religion, but he wouldn't say *voudoun*.

David didn't care. In the stillness he drifted off, riding out on his thoughts, more and more distant from being really awake. The Spanish station became people talking in a group, but not paying any attention to him, which was fine with him—

Something came out from under the pillow beside him and for a moment he was frozen, he could see it there in the half light. Dull dark composite, flat like a plate, a man-made thing. Then it went off the bed and as he jerked up he caught a glimpse of it scuttling across the floor on hard crab legs and he heard the clitter of the feet made for sand and he almost cracked his head on the bunk above him.

A wandering mine. Like in South Africa. He couldn't find it. It wasn't real. A nightmare, he had done this before. He had felt it, but it wasn't real. No one would have set a wandering mine loose in a bunkroom. It was a dream, he had had them before, dreams that were like hallucinations. Think, he told himself, what makes sense for reality. What would be true. Use your head, not your perceptions. If there were a wandering mine under his pillow when he lay down he would have activated it. Therefore, it couldn't be here. And it made no sense for one to be here, anyway.

So it was a dream. *Hypnogogic hallucinations*, that is what they had called them in the hospital in Algiers. They didn't mean he was crazy, lots of people had them, children had them. Night terrors. Dreams. They seemed real, he always felt as if he was awake, but he wasn't.

The problem was he had experienced it, and even though in his head he knew it was a dream, he still felt the experience. He strained to listen for the sound of those crab feet on the cold floor.

Carefully he got out of bed and looked under his bunk and under the bunk on the other side. There was nothing there.

He climbed back in, and Meph jumped off and disappeared under the bed.

Don't chase it, he thought, listening for the sound of it, picturing it crouched, trying to burrow into the concrete. Knowing it wasn't real. But the cat would be attracted, like the bomb at the house. Only wandering mines moved, how much more attractive for Meph.

It was all the talk of war today, it had started him thinking and now he could not get the war out of his head. Nothing to do but lie down and hope he could sleep, hope he had no more dreams.

Wandering mines, you took them out on the edge of the desert, set them down and activated them, like in a sandy wash. And they settled down in the sand and rock, burying themselves, till sand covered them. And then you went away, and the enemy entered the area. And after a preset time, if nothing had crossed them, they dug themselves up, scuttled across the Kalahari on their crab legs, found a new place and buried themselves again. You could preset the range, bury a beacon to keep them fairly close—but the beacon could alert the enemy, so mostly they were set at random, set so as not to wander more than a couple of hundred meters from where they were first buried.

Once, one of his men had been sleeping out on patrol, and he had woken because he heard a scuttling. He'd thought scorpion, and froze. And out of the sand rose a wandering mine. Faceless little thing on six legs, with sand trickling off it like water as it rose. It had stood, and he had known that if it came towards him, he might set it off by being an obstacle. He was afraid to call out, some of them homed in on noise. He couldn't even warn the others.

And then it had scuttled out into the desert.

That is what had caused his dream. David hadn't thought of that story in years, but now it had risen out of his memory like the mine out of the sand.

It took him a long time to get to sleep.

He was stupid and sleepy the next morning, following Santos into the cafeteria. Santos had been up half the night with the *société*, but nothing bothered him. He was nineteen or twenty and he could do without sleep.

"You know, Kim, if you going to be a jock, I think you should at least come. I'm not saying you need to be an initiate or nothing, just come and see what it is, you know?"

"Maybe next Sunday," David said.

"Oh fuck," Santos said. "No coconut bread. They always have coconut bread on Monday, what the fuck is this?"

David got his tray and looked for a place to sit. He saw Patel, and then he saw Mayla.

"Yeah, that's the new woman, the Chinese one," Santos said. "See, she don't look Chinese, but she got a Chinese name. She's way too tall, man. And Big Andre say she's pretty, but I don't think she's so hot. She ain't bad or nothing, you might still want to get to know her."

"I already know her," David said.

"Yeah?" Santos said.

David walked over to the table, because he didn't know what else to do. Mayla was sitting with Patel, eating, and she didn't look up, didn't see him. Still, she had to be here looking for him, unless she was here because of a loan? No, he couldn't believe she would be here to make a loan.

He stopped, trying to decide; if she was here because of a loan, then the best thing to do would be avoid her. Just because she was here didn't mean that the police knew where he was.

Then she looked up at him.

So he had to walk over.

"Hi," she said.

"Hi," he said.

"Sit down," Patel said. Patel had never acted like she even remembered stripping him in the locker, but he remembered and it always made him flush.

"How are you?" Mayla asked.

"I'm fine."

"You look good," she said.

"You know Kim?" Patel said.

"Did you come looking for me?" he asked.

Mayla shook her head and her hair swung. "I got a job. I'm working as a jock."

He didn't know what to say to that.

"I lost my job at the bank," she said. "There was a takeover, Marincite Corp. bought out First Hawaiian."

"Are you working in the accounting, here?" What would she be doing, running the accounting department here? But that would not be a very good job for someone like her, would it?

"No," she said, impatient. "I'm working as a fish jock. But I need to talk to you about some things."

"This is crazy," he said.

"I needed a job," she said, with peculiar emphasis. "And I needed a job like you have. I *needed* to do what you did. I *needed* to get away from the bank and everything. You remember all the trouble." She said it as if he should understand something, but he didn't.

Patel started out of her seat, "I need to look for my husband—"

"No," David said. "We'll get together, after lunch." He needed to get away, before she called him David. "I'll talk to you then. But I have to eat in a hurry, then get some things done, okay?"

He needed to think.

She nodded. "That's okay," she said.

He expected to talk to Mayla, but MacKenzie, the foreman, found him and told him Naranji wanted him in the lab. Working in the lab meant an eight-hour shift, with no time after lunch to talk.

He spent the morning helping Naranji dismantle the freshwater recyc system for the salmon project. Naranji joked about how they were doing engineering instead of chemistry. In the U.S., where he got his education, someone else would have done this.

David wondered if it was safe to go to Port Authority and buy a ticket to Miami. He could head up to Virginia, to his aunt and uncle in Blacksburg and they would loan him the money to get home to France. He would be safe. Or maybe he could stay in the U.S. for awhile. They would sponsor him, he could get a job. But with Mayla here, could the police be far behind? He'd probably be arrested.

If he could just get out of this country. This little trap of a country.

Should he quit and try to hide in the city? He could leave Meph, he thought the cat would be okay. But he didn't know when he could catch the sub back to Julia and he was afraid to ask Naranji how often the subs left. It sounded like such a suspicious question. The fish farm had seemed perfect, because it was isolated. He should have thought that it was like the city, only one way in and one way out.

Usually he and Naranji waited until after the jocks ate to get lunch, when it wasn't so crowded, but he needed to get to Mayla. "I need to talk to one of the jocks," he told Naranji.

"You want to eat now?" Naranji said. "Okay."

The dining hall was loud and busy, he could hear the noise as he walked down the hall. It would be too crowded to talk. He wouldn't find out anything. But he could tell her he was working until 5:00, that he'd see her after dinner. Maybe he would be arrested by then, he would see what her expression was when he told her. See if he should run.

He didn't see her for a long moment, then he did, in tunic and tights, like all the jocks. She was sitting with Patel again.

"Mayla," he said, and she looked up from her food.

"Hi," she said, tired-sounding. Her hair was wet from the shower and she looked drawn from the morning's dive. It was then that he realized she really was working as a jock. Which made no sense as far as he could see.

"I'm working in the lab today," he said. "I can't meet you until after dinner."

"They told me out at the site," she said.

Had she called him David? She had to have, she wouldn't know to call him Kim. His stomach clenched. He would have to leave, have to get out of here. People would be wondering, it wasn't good when people wondered.

"How are you," he said lamely.

"Tired," she said and smiled. "I feel like I've already worked a whole day and it's not even half over."

He nodded. Why? Why are you doing this? But he couldn't ask, not in front of Patel. He didn't know what she had told people.

"I'll see you after dinner," he said.

He got a tray and went to sit with Santos.

"Hey, Kim," Santos said, "how well you know her?"

David shrugged.

Santos and the jocks around him grinned.

"I worked with her, before," David said.

"Yeah?" Santos said. "She work good?" Everybody laughed.

"I don't know," David said.

His stomach ached. He couldn't taste his lunch. Maybe he would go back to the lab and tell Naranji that he didn't feel well, but then what would he do for the afternoon, lie in his bunk? After lunch the jocks would all be back, he could talk to Mayla.

Why was she working as a fish jock? He couldn't understand.

He went back to the lab.

She was running, like him. He wanted to scream at her. She was telling him what she did the day she left. "I slept behind a dumpster," Mayla said. She looked ragged after her dive, washed out and exhausted. She had slept before dinner (new jocks always slept between second shift and dinner) but she still looked drained.

"Why do you become a fish jock?" he asked.

"Because it's safe," she said.

He laughed, a sharp bark. "There is nothing safe here," he said. "People get hurt, get killed. Pyroxin is bad for you."

"I didn't mean safe that way, I meant that they haven't found you."

He shouldn't have called her. He had done it, regretted he'd done it, then put it out of his mind.

"So now you are here because you think we can both hide?" he said.

She nodded, "I had to get away, and I knew you had."

"So you are Mayla Ling, here? You use your own name?"

"My workcard has my name on it—oh," she rubbed her face with her hands. "It's not my regular workcard, that was destroyed with the house. They can't just read everything off it. So they just fill in some information and wait for the real workcard to come through, only I'll never get the real workcard."

"So they report your name to the government, for air tax and income tax and then the blue and whites come knocking, eh?" he said.

"The government is too big, it's too much of a mess," she said, "they'll never connect it." But she sounded uncertain.

He did not say anything. She would get more frightened the more she thought about it, and then they would have to leave. Maybe Santos could suggest another job? No, better not, Santos talked too much, always talking. Santos would tell someone.

It had been stupid luck that he had found this, how would he find something else? Maybe they should go to another city? To Del Sud? But that would mean Port Authority.

"How did you get this job without a workcard? Or do you have a fake workcard?"

"No," he said. "They pay me off the books."

"What do you think we should do?" she asked.

He shrugged. "I think you should have stayed at your grandfather's."

"I didn't want to go to jail," she said.

"You have money, you could get a lawyer. You could get away."

"They turned down my request to go to Miami," she said.

"What do you mean?" he asked.

She told him about trying to get permission to leave. He didn't know what to make of that.

"Still," he said. "You didn't know."

"You didn't know when you ran away," she said.

"So, I was wrong."

It was strange to be her equal.

"You are here now," he said. "We have to think."

She chewed on her lip.

"We need different jobs. Or maybe not a job," he said, "maybe we should just hide. I have some money, you have some money."

"We need to get out of Caribe," she said.

"Is there another way?"

"We need documents," she said.

He sighed.

"No," she said, "we need documents. Is there someone here who might know someone who could get us documents?"

He shook his head. "I don't think so." He thought about Lopez, who sold contraband beer. Lopez wasn't exactly a criminal, but would he know someone? It was not safe to ask.

"I know someone," she said.

"Who?" he said.

"I have to think about it," she said.

The next morning David waited for Mayla at the lunar pool. She had been here for a whole day. He felt that there was a clock ticking, the longer she was here, the more dangerous everything got. Time to go. He sat with his legs in the water so the pyroxin wouldn't make him too hot.

He knew her the moment he saw her, she was as tall as MacKenzie, and her diver's suit was too big around the waist. It bunched around her weight belt. He felt himself curiously glad to see her.

"How can you stand that?" she asked.

"What?" he asked.

"Sitting in the water that way?"

"You don't want to get too hot," he said.

"Oh, right," she said, sarcastic. "Big problem. God, this sucks." She sat down next to him but didn't put her legs in the water.

Was she taking pyroxin? Maybe nobody had told her. If Santos hadn't told him, he wouldn't know. He thought about getting into that water without it and shuddered.

"If you're cold, get out," she said. "We've got a few minutes."

"I'm okay," he said. "Did anyone talk to you about, eh, keeping warm?"

"Not specifically," she said. "What?"

He looked around, there were other people coming to get on shift. He felt funny talking about it in front of people. "I'll tell you later."

"Okay," she said.

He watched her at the site. She was awkward with tools. He would be better off if he took off without her. An anglo and an oriental, they would be obvious. Foolish to think they could disappear together. Maybe it was foolish to think he could disappear at all.

It would be easier not to be alone, though.

He would have to find out how she thought she might be able to get them documents. This was her home, she had been pretty well connected.

Maybe she could get them out. Maybe he could go home.

Mayla found David in the bunkroom after dinner.

Women were allowed in the men's bunkroom until ten, men were never allowed in the women's bunkroom. But there was no sense trying to talk in the bunkroom. There was no way that they could have talked in the dining hall during dinner, either.

Santos said, "Hi." Friendly, a little respectful. His face was carefully neutral. Meeting some guy's girlfriend.

Mayla said hello. "You still have Mephistofeles," she said. She fondled the cat's ears. Meph sniffed at her fingers curiously and David couldn't tell if the kitten remembered her or not. It had not been that long ago, really. Just weeks since the house was blown up. It seemed like a long time, that was all.

"After all the trouble you went to," Mayla said, "I guess I shouldn't be surprised." She smiled, making the connection between them.

Santos looked interested. Shit, there would be questions later. "Come on," David said.

He took her down to the dining hall. It was too bright, brighter it seemed because it was nearly empty after dinner except for some jocks playing cards. The chairs were loud when they pulled them out.

She sat across the table from him, leaning on her arms. "You said you can get documents?" he said.

"I don't know," she said. "I know someone to try, but you may not like it."

"Who?" he said.

"Saad Shamsi."

It took him a moment. "The guy with the slave bracelets? In Marincite?" he asked. He remembered the partner, the crazy man on drugs. And the girl.

She nodded.

"That's crazy," he said. "He is a crook."

"Who do you think is going to sell us documents?" she asked. "A nun?"

"You would not work with him," he said. "He will not want to work with you now."

"Money is money," she said. "He wants money to immigrate to the U.S."

No. No, no, no. Craziness. "We don't have enough money for him to immigrate. And he is in Marincite, are you going to call him? You think in Marincite they don't record every call?"

"I wasn't going to call him," she said. "I could go there."

"Right," David said. "Go to Port Authority, buy a ticket for Marincite."

"You can pay cash for Marincite," she said. "Go the way we did, second class. They don't care what your name is, they don't even ask if you buy your ticket at the terminal. It's like taking a bus."

Too crazy. Marincite, the spider web. He didn't like it, remembered the sullen security force. Like going to a military base when you are on the run from the police, stupid. "There are people here that I can try. Let me try first."

"Like who?"

"Lopez," he said. "He's a jock. He sells pyroxin."

"Some jock who sells pyroxin isn't going to be able to get us documents," she said.

"But he might know someone who can," David said.

Now she shook her head.

He partly agreed. Lopez wouldn't know anything about documents, but he bought his pyroxin from someone, and someone above him would know how to get documents. How many layers up before there was someone who could get them documents? But it was better than going to Marincite. "In Marincite there will be Uncles."

"The Uncles aren't the blue and whites," she said. "They don't like each other. The Uncles won't care about us."

"You don't know," he said.

"You don't know about Lopez, either," she said.

He tapped his fingers on the table. Sighed. "We were not meant to be criminals," he said.

"Fugitives," she corrected. "Criminals have done something wrong."

Maybe the distinction mattered to her. If he had done something criminal, it was to be criminally stupid. "Lopez will not get us in the kind of trouble that Marincite might."

"There's no way that Lopez is going to be able to come up with documents," she said.

"I said that he might know someone who could."

She shook her head. "It's a waste of time. And the more people we talk to here, the more risk."

"We do not have time to wait until the weekend to go to Marincite," he pointed out. "If we leave here, we lose this job." It was true, if they took a day off, they might be told not to come back.

"Is that so bad?" she asked.

Was it? The fish farm had been a place to hide, but now that she was here and using her own name, it wasn't anymore. He wondered, too, how much of her refusal to consider Lopez was because it wasn't her idea. In her head, he suspected, she was still the boss.

"If we are going to quit, then let me try Lopez first," he said. "If we have trouble, we can just leave."

"I don't think you should," she said. "Maybe we can get a day off, go to Marincite. If we can, then we can try Shamsi and if it doesn't work out we can still come back here."

"It was safe here," he said, "until you came."

"I'm sorry," she snapped.

"You said you come here, you came here, because I know how to hide," he said. "So this time, we will do it my way, okay? And if it does not work, we will try your way."

"If it doesn't work, we may not be able to try it my way."

He didn't bother to answer her. In his mind, if they tried Lopez, they might lose their money, they might have to leave the fish farm, but Lopez was not going to turn them over to the blue and whites.

Shamsi's partner was a crazy man, a drug man in a way that Lopez was not. Maybe Lopez' connection was as bad, but it was better than going to Marincite.

She did not like it, he could tell. But she couldn't stop him, and she knew it.

He smiled to himself. It was good for her not to be in control. Let her learn what it was like to take the orders.

Lopez was *société;* on Sundays David had seen him dressed in white for the meeting. But he couldn't wait until next Sunday, it was already Tuesday evening and he felt that the longer they waited, the shorter their odds.

He sat on his bunk awhile, then finally got up and walked past Lopez' bunk, but there were jocks around. There were always jocks around Lopez, usually in the evening they were drinking beer. Lopez' bunk aisle was the local bar. The bottom bunk across from his was kept empty, and David figured it was because so many people sat there.

Lopez was stocky and dark; somebody had said sometime that he was from Guatemala but David had only a hazy idea of where Guatemala was.

He tried to think of ways to get Lopez so he could talk to him. People were always pulling Lopez aside so they could talk to him— to buy pyroxin. But he felt strange just walking up to Lopez and asking him to come and talk. Better to wait until morning.

In the morning, Lopez was late out of bed. In the dining hall his table was full of jocks. And out at the site it would be impossible to talk to him, because anything David said would go over the mic and everybody could hear it.

David got to the locker room early and suited up, then watched for Lopez.

Lopez came in, rolling on short legs, grinning at something someone had said.

"You need pyroxin?" he asked David.

David shook his head. "Not yet. I need to ask you some things."

"So ask," Lopez said.

It was late, they were supposed to be in the yard soon. Mayla would be waiting and wondering where the hell he was. "I have this problem," David said. "You see, it is my ex-wife."

Lopez nodded, frowning.

"I cannot use my own workcard, so here I am paid off the books. Do you know what I mean?"

Lopez knew.

"I am looking for someone who can help me get a new workcard, maybe some more identification." David paused, waiting to see what Lopez would say.

Lopez shrugged. "I can't help you."

He opened his locker and started to suit up.

"Do you know someone who could help?"

Lopez thought, dumping his tights and tunic onto the floor, pulling his boots out of the bottom of the locker. "I don't know. I'll think about it." Lopez turned "think" into "theenk."

"Thank you," David said.

"For what," Lopez shot back, "I haven't done anything yet." And he grinned.

David smiled and nodded, and backed away.

And then there was nothing to do but wait for Lopez to answer.

14

Out of Water

Mayla pulled her suit out of the locker. She thought she could have handled the cold and the mind-numbing tiredness if she only knew what she was doing. Not that it mattered if she didn't know about construction, she wouldn't be here long. If David could get something out of Lopez, they might be gone tomorrow.

The suit was bulky and there was never enough room in the locker room. She tried to keep her elbows in, fighting into the leggings. Everybody else had to have the same problems, but she felt exceptionally stupid.

They were going to be putting up walls again today. The interesting part was that she had never seen how things were built. Things like light fixtures and all the parts of buildings that looked so smooth. It was surprisingly obvious.

The seals on her suit resisted her efforts to close them. No one else had trouble, but the suit was so much thicker than the ones she was accustomed to, her fingers couldn't get them to do what they were supposed to do. Christ, how was she supposed to use tools when she couldn't even seal the fucking suit?

Luz, next to her, was chattering in rapid Spanish. Luz intimidated her. Luz had coffee skin and brindle hair and wore eye makeup even when she was diving. Streetsmart. Which Mayla knew she would never be. She also knew Luz knew she was incompetent, even though Luz had never said so. "Here," she said suddenly in English, "let me help you." English was taught in school, but some of the women didn't speak it.

"You remind me of my daughter," Luz said, unexpectedly.

Mayla smiled, not sure what that meant. She hadn't even known that Luz had a daughter.

"She's fourteen, she stays with her father. I miss doing things for her, you know, brushing her hair in the morning and helping her get ready for school? Not that she would let me anymore. There you are, all sealed up." Luz patted her shoulder.

"Thanks," Mayla said. "I feel like such a klutz."

"Everybody has to learn," Luz said. "Anybody willing to work is already ahead of all those bums that sit at home and moan. Like my sister's boyfriend, he is, you know, a waste of breathing space. My parents, when they came here they were so poor they didn't have a corner to die in, you know? But they worked, and they kept us together, and even during the revolution, my father had money hidden and my parents kept us fed."

Luz gathered up her gear without stopping. "They lost everything they had during the revolution, but they started all over again. And my mother runs the *bodega* all day, and my father works. See, when it's time for my father to retire, they'll sell the *bodega* so they have money for their old age, and this way they get groceries for cost."

Mayla nodded. She'd seen the little *bodegas,* just a narrow little grocery that sold *masa fina* and rice and all the basics.

"So someone like you," Luz said, "I mean, you can tell that, you know, you come from better, and you lose your job at the bank, and you don't give up, you become a fish jock. I admire that. 'Cause you're working. So if people give you a hard time about learning, fuck 'em. They weren't born knowing how to run a sealer. Somebody had to show them the first time, too."

What would Luz think when she quit? "How long have you been a fish jock?" Mayla asked.

"Eleven years," Luz said. "Now, though I don't work all the time. I do a lot of construction work, 'cause the pay is good, then when the project is done, I go back and spend some time with my husband and daughter. Then I can pick up another job. I could be a foreman at a couple of places, I had offers, but then I never see my family but two weeks a year. And Rafe won't live on a fish farm, even if he could get a job."

At the lunar pool Luz stopped again, popped something in her mouth then shrugged her recyc on. "You're smart not to take pyroxin, too," she said. Then she pulled her mask on and sat down and fell back into the water. Just like that, no hesitation.

She sank away for a moment, down through the clear water of the pool, and then turned and flicked her flippers.

Mayla didn't feel as if she could just get in; she knew that just going straight into the water could shock your heart. You were supposed to sit half in and half out, let your body acclimate a little. She sat down and dropped her legs in the water and waited for David.

Luz took pyroxin. David had said that Lopez sold pyroxin, she wondered how many of the jocks took it. Chasing the dragon. It was supposed to speed everything up, and make you feel warm. It wasn't worth it though, not if she wasn't going to stay here long. Last thing she needed was to get in trouble for illegal substances.

Keep your nose clean, she thought.

A couple of jocks came and sat down, one of them was David's friend, Santos. Her chron said she had only about five minutes more to get into the yard. Was David working in the lab today?

"Santos?" she asked, "is Kim diving today?"

"He's coming," Santos said. "He's talking to Lopez."

Was that a good thing? Lopez could be saying anything, he could be saying that he didn't know about anything like that—but if so, why hadn't he said something the night before? Maybe he had gotten in touch with someone?

She couldn't help hoping. She was afraid of going to Marincite; she didn't know what Saad would do and she was terrified of meeting Saad's partner again.

She just wanted to get through this.

David came with Lopez but they weren't talking. She watched David for any sign, but he just said hello and sat down. She didn't know whether she should say something in front of Lopez or not. Better to be safe and say nothing. Better to wait until the dive was over and she could ask. There was no sense in risking anything.

Her stomach turned on itself, acids devouring.

Better to do something rather than sit here. She pulled her mask down and pulled her legs out. Turned around and fell back on her recyc unit, on her back, into the pool, pushing off the side with her legs. It was cold. She thought she would never get used to it. Patel said she needed more fat on her.

That wasn't something she was inclined to do. Certainly not since she didn't expect to work here the rest of her life.

In the yard, Ms. Facon barked, "Ling."

"Yes ma'am," she said. Ms. Facon should have been a sister in a Holy Order. She reminded Mayla of the heavy-legged middle-aged women who taught her at the convent and who used the Church as an excuse for a kind of sadism. Ms. Facon would have been disappointed if they were to all behave and be on time. It contradicted her view of essential human nature.

Mayla's muscles were clenched and her teeth were chattering. She grabbed a bike off the rack and let it tow her out to the construction site. Streaming along behind it she consciously loosened her muscles, made herself relax against the cold.

It was only a couple of hours, then the shift would be finished. Anyone could get through a couple of hours. And if Lopez had come up with something then this might be the last day she had to do this.

At the site she reported to MacKenzie, the shift boss.

"MacKenzie," Luz called, "I'll show her the sealer, put her with me."

"Okay," MacKenzie said.

The walls were already halfway up, and the ceilings were in on the first floor. They swam through the cave of a building hanging work lights, and then Luz showed her how to spot bond stirrups. Mayla had seen them before. Luz also showed her how high off the floor to put them and where. "We need them when we run the sealers," she said.

People used the stirrups as footholds when they did stationary work; they were all over the frame. The spotweld was a tube of stuff, Mayla squirted some on the stirrup and then used a little heater like a gun to touch the junk until it just started to glow. As soon as it started glowing—the water would be steaming around it, a stream of bubbles rising in the cave of the building—she touched it to the wall. Luz had told her to touch them straight, where she put them they stuck. If she really screwed one up, she went and got Luz who put some sort of paste around it and worked it and worked it until it came loose. She screwed up two the first half hour, but then she got the hang of it.

It wouldn't have been so hard if she didn't have trouble with the cold. Her hands got so cold that it was hard to keep coordinated. She thought about hypothermia a lot. Lots of the divers came out of the water with blue lips, particularly after second shift. When she had been learning to dive, that was one of the signs of hypothermia. It was hard to tell if their speech was slurred, because nobody talked much after the shift was over.

She didn't see David, but he might be working above her, putting up walls. In the chatter of the divers she didn't hear him, either, but he didn't talk much. She wondered about Lopez. It was best just to assume that Lopez couldn't help them, she wouldn't be so disappointed then.

Working with the heat gun should have made things better. She kept heating little pockets and trying to put her hand in the ghost of the heated water. (The water rose so fast she couldn't really catch it.) She could feel the difference in the water temperature when she did. That should have helped her hands, but it didn't, maybe because she had something to compare to so she felt the cold worse than if there was nothing warm. She was afraid to do it too much, it was wasting time and she'd get in trouble.

They were on two hours in the morning, David said that they did short shifts in the morning for two weeks and then switched to short shifts in the afternoon. She thought she'd like short shifts in the afternoon better because she was so tired in the afternoon. But right now, she was glad when the shift was over and MacKenzie sent them back to the yard.

David was at the moon pool, but Santos was there so he just said, "After lunch we can talk."

After lunch. She took a nap after lunch. How was she supposed to do a three-hour shift without some sleep? Unless maybe he would tell her something that meant they could quit. But he could have let her know somehow, couldn't he? She didn't know, he could be so deadpan. Son of a bitch. She didn't think he knew anything. Even if he did, it would be best to do second shift, to not draw attention to themselves, wouldn't it?

Maybe she could say she was sick.

She was too tired to know that she was hungry but she knew she'd be hungry as soon as she started to eat. But stripping off her gear was tedious in her exhaustion. A hot shower made her muscles feel soft, particularly in her legs. Luz was coming out of the shower at the same time she was. Like most of the women, Luz was heavy, and the fat collected under her arms and in her thighs. She was tough and muscled, but her stomach still looked soft; and stripped of her make-up her nose and cheeks showed a fine tracework of red lines, a spiderweb of broken capillaries. The people who'd been diving awhile all had them. Was it the cold or the pyroxin?

Diving did not make you pretty, even if it did make you strong.

David wasn't in the dining hall when she got there.

The smell of food made her stomach contract and suddenly she was empty. She shouldn't eat so much, she'd end up like the other women, with that layer of fat. It was good to have it if you were going to be a diver for the rest of your life, but she wasn't. Still, she piled it on; enchiladas, fish, a bowl of soup, a slice of cake, some beans. Cheap food, filling food. Nothing expensive like vegetables, mostly complex carbohydrates. But she was too tired to resist getting anything that looked good. For dinner she'd do better.

Maybe she and David should just quit and get out of here, after all, David acted as if they were in more trouble the longer they stayed here. As soon as he told her that Lopez couldn't do anything, she'd suggest they leave. She had money, they could find a place to stay for a couple of days, she'd get in touch with Saad Shamsi. But she didn't want to think about that.

It was all too much to think about after a dive.

She saw David come in with Santos and another diver, so she sat down at an empty table and when they came out of the line she waved them over. She half expected David to ignore her, but they tromped to the table, Santos chattering away about some game they played on the weekend.

"How was your morning?" she asked David, hoping for some clue about Lopez.

He shrugged. "The same."

The same. What did that mean? Goddamn it, couldn't he have arranged to meet her before lunch and tell her what was going on? For one thing, she was so goddamn tired.

She decided if he wasn't going to talk, she wasn't going to waste time talking, either. She dug into her soup. Her effort was wasted, though, as Santos chattered through the meal, and if David noticed her silence he probably thought she just couldn't get a word in.

Santos walked with them as they left the dining hall.

"We need to talk," David said politely. "I'll be there in a few minutes."

"Oh, sure," Santos said, unoffended.

David watched Santos walk on. "He is really very young," David said.

Mayla thought it was obvious and at the moment she really didn't care. "What did Lopez say?"

"He'd like us to meet someone tonight," David said.

"Someone who can get documents?" She couldn't believe it. She didn't dare.

But he was shaking his head anyway and she felt it in her stomach. "No, this is the guy who supplies Lopez. But maybe he can take us to someone who can supply documents. Lopez, ah," David shifted. "I have to, you know, have some reason for the documents, and I do not want to give Lopez an idea, so, I tell him, I mean I told him, that I was trying to get away from my ex-wife. He thinks I am really still married and that you and I are, you know, like boyfriend and girl-friend."

He was embarrassed. "That's okay," she said. "Actually, I think it's pretty smart."

He looked down and nodded, unwilling to meet her eyes.

"So how are we supposed to meet this guy?" she asked.

"Lopez will take care of it, but he said it would be late, like after ten, so you have to get out of the bunkroom after ten."

She would be there.

She had never met a drug dealer, besides Saad Shamsi's partner the Argentine with the moustache. She lay on her bunk, attempting to read, until ten, but all she could think of was Saad's partner and the girl in the slave bracelet. The girl who had called her sister. She suspected that people who went into drug trafficking had to be a little crazy.

At ten she got up and walked out of the bunkroom, past the vid and found David waiting in the hall.

"Where's Lopez?" she whispered.

David didn't know. "He said he would come find me." David handed her a beer. "I bought it earlier."

She didn't want a beer—her stomach was hurting and a beer would probably make her sick—but she opened it and sipped it. She wished this were over. She wished that they knew what they were doing.

Maybe David knew what he was doing, he had gotten this far, had gotten a job without a workcard. She didn't even know how to do that.

Oh God. What if David were right and she should not have left home? What if she could be home, safe, right now? If she went home and never left again, became a recluse. She could do it, the government would leave her alone if she never did anything. Then, maybe in a few years, she could leave. Or maybe she could stay at her grandfather's house, become a dotty old lady, the daughter of the banker, who never left her house.

She could stop this now, she could say to David, "I won't meet him." She could walk away, this was a mistake. It was a serious mistake. What was she doing caught up in something illegal like this? Buying forged documents was a crime.

She would tell him. But she couldn't bring herself to open her mouth. Oh Christ, she would die because she was too embarrassed to say stop.

Remember, she thought, that before you knew this was the best way. It's either this or Saad Shamsi. Now that she had run, surely she had indicted herself in the eyes of the blue and whites. Only the guilty run. But it seemed impossible that she hadn't been playing some elaborate game, that she couldn't just quit now and go back to regular life.

A couple of jocks came out into the hall and walked past them towards the dining hall.

She studied the label of her beer bottle, she studied the floor. She wished David would say something. Who were they going to meet?

At ten-thirty Lopez still hadn't shown up. "He's going to stand us up," she told David. She was tired, and they had to get up for first shift.

David just shrugged.

Which was not an answer. It occurred to her that he never answered, never explained, never even asked. And he always thought he was right. He was so self-contained. Really it was arrogance, thinking he was always right, not caring about what other people knew or thought. It was very male, very macho of him.

And who was to say that he was always right? She thought this was wrong and she thought this was stupid and she had told him that, but she had let him decide and now here she was waiting for some two-bit pyroxin seller who was supposed to be able to get her documents out of the country.

She was angry, scared and angry and she was beginning to think that she had had enough.

"I'm going to go to bed," she said.

"If they come," David said. "And I can't go get you because of the curfew." Because no one was allowed in the women's bunkhouse this late.

"No one is coming," she said. "Lopez can't get us documents."

"He said he is bringing someone who can help us," David said.

"Why would he know someone who can help us."

"It is all we have," David said.

"Saad."

"If Saad could get documents, he would be in the United States."

"No," she said. "Saad wants to immigrate legally. I have family in the States, you and I just need travel documents. And if Saad can't get travel documents, what makes you think *Lopez* would be able?"

"Wait," he said.

She thought it was a command and for a moment she was so angry she was speechless. And then she heard feet and a quiet voice and realized that someone was coming and he had really meant "wait a moment."

They were not coming from the dining hall or the moon pool or the yard, but from the other direction, where the fish ponds were. Where the fish were spawned and tended until they were old enough to go out into the pens outside. The jocks weren't supposed to go back there. Mayla had never even seen the ponds.

The lights were down, although there were supposed to be jocks on watch at the pens. She thought it was probably two jocks coming off watch. The regular fish jocks stayed four to a room in farm housing, not bunkrooms like the construction jocks. But the farm housing was back the other way. Maybe they were headed for the dining hall?

But it was Lopez and a fish jock she thought she recognized and someone not dressed like a diver.

He was Haitian, tall and lanky and moving like a street corner boy. As they came into the light she could see that his hair was all deep blue braids, velvet, midnight blue. He wore a sleeveless white vest and the light curved across his biceps. He looked like the cliché of a drug dealer. A wild *maroon*.

He looked straight at her and smiled: a wicked, appreciating smile, a barracuda smile. His eyes were funny but the light was not good enough for her to make out why, and she looked away.

How had he gotten here? She couldn't imagine that he'd just gotten on a sub with a bunch of supplies and ridden out to the farm.

Lopez said, "This is a friend of mine. You can call him Henri."

"Hello," David said.

Henri nodded. He acted as if he was swimming, every motion slow. He turned his face up into the light and his eyes were the same unnatural color as his hair. Slips in his eyes.

"I know you before," Henri said to her.

"I don't think so," she said.

"I remember you," he said. "Where are you from?"

"Costonos," she lied. She wasn't going to say where she was from, and she wasn't going to say her grandfather's neighborhood, and she didn't know any drug dealers.

"I swear you are familiar," he said, stepping towards her. "I think I see you before. Did you ever live in Marincite?"

"No," she said. On the floor where it met the wall there was a spider, soap pale and still. She watched it rather than look at him. She wanted to say that she didn't know any drug dealers.

"It's nice beer you have," he said.

It was just beer.

"That is my favorite beer," Henri said.

Lopez was grinning as if this was some sort of joke.

"You're not drinking your beer," Henri said.

"I don't really want it," Mayla said.

"It's good beer," Henri said. "You shouldn't waste it. You don't want it?"

She shook her head.

"Give it to me," he said.

She handed it to him. She tried to hold just the neck of the bottle so that he didn't touch her but he did, anyway. Deliberately, she was sure. His fingers were hot. The beer was warm, she'd been holding it all the time they were waiting, but he didn't seem to care. He took a drink, unconcerned that he was drinking after her, and she looked away again. It felt too intimate. Her eyes went back to the spider. She wasn't even sure it was a spider, it might have been just the empty husk.

"You need some help," Henri said.

"We would like to talk to you," David said.

Henri ignored him. "What do you need, sister?" Patronizing. Apparently polite.

I am not your sister, she thought, but she didn't say it. She looked from the spider to David. He was watching her but she didn't know what he thought she should do. "I need to get to the States," she said.

Henri nodded, thoughtful. "The States is a good place, in some ways. In some ways it is not. It is not a spiritual place."

She nodded as if she understood. She felt as if he were testing her.

"I have been there," he said.

She doubted it, but she nodded again.

"I have been to New Orleans," he said. "It is a strange, strange place, sister. It is almost underwater, now. You know? It is almost like Caribe. The cemeteries are all above ground. Little cities. When you go to the States, maybe you will go to New Orleans."

"Maybe," she said.

"I am sorry, though, I cannot help you."

She should have been angry, they'd waited all this time and now he couldn't do anything, but she just felt relieved.

Lopez was still smiling, and now David was watching Henri.

"That is too bad," Henri said.

Everybody waited, although she didn't know what they were waiting for.

"I have a friend," Henri said. "Maybe he could help you. Maybe tonight you come back with me. You think you could do that?"

"We have to work tomorrow," Mayla said.

"You want to be a fish jock or you want to go to the States, woman?" Henri was suddenly sharp, contemptuous.

She couldn't look at him, but when she looked at the floor the spider was gone. She peered up and down the corridor, but there was no sign of it. It couldn't have gone very far, she had just been looking at it, but the fact that it was gone felt as if it meant something. Her knees were trembling. "I want to go to the States," she said.

"So you come with me," Henri said.

Mayla looked at David. Was this what people would normally do? Was this some sort of trap?

"Okay," he said. "We need to do some things first."

"No time," Henri said.

David shrugged. "We don't have money here."

Henri thought about that. "We talk to my friend, you and he work out the money." Then he held his hand out to Lopez, who grabbed it. "See you next week."

Nobody had paid any attention to the other diver. He stood behind Lopez, watching. Not like a guard, like a bystander. Was he buying something?

"Come on," Henri said.

She looked one more time, but she still didn't see the spider. She wondered where it was waiting.

The sub left at about eleven-thirty. The pilot explained to her that docking fees were less at night, so most of the fish farms ran all their supplies after ten. The pilot knew Henri but didn't seem to care much for him. Henri said hello and the pilot nodded and turned his back on him. But he was willing to talk to Mayla, offered her a seat behind him and started to explain the controls of the little sub. There was no partition between the body of the sub and the pilot's area, since this was a cargo sub, although there was a partition that the pilot could pull. When she had come out to the fish farm the first time the sub had been full with people who had spent the weekend in Julia and the partition had been pulled. Now she could see the monitors and the console.

"Sister," Henri called, "come back here."

The pilot shook his head a little in sympathy but didn't say anything. She got up and went back, winding her way through sweating coldboxes. She assumed they were full of fish. David sat down against the wall and she pretended not to notice when Henri patted the floor next to him and instead sat down next to David.

"How long does it take to get to the port?" David asked.

"About an hour," Henri said.

An hour trapped looking at Henri. She had sat down so close to David that she was touching his thigh, but she didn't want to move. Besides, David had said that he'd told Lopez he was trying to get away from his ex-wife. So she was supposed to be his girlfriend.

She thought about taking his hand, but David wouldn't know what she was doing. It would have been nice. He had put his arm around her once, in the car, after the shooting.

"How do you like being a fish jock?' Henri asked her.

"It sucks," she said.

He laughed. "It sucks," he said, savoring the phrase, delighted to be surprised. He was drugged, she was sure. "That's good, sister."

He leaned his head back and closed his eyes.

She thought she could faintly smell fish, but it could have been her imagination.

David leaned his head back, too, and closed his eyes. She knew she couldn't sleep. There was a faint smell, not of fish, but a faint, dry, musky smell. It was Henri. It wasn't a real body odor kind of smell, more like some sort of oil, maybe slightly rancid. It was somehow associated with his hair, with those velvet blue braids. They didn't look dry. They didn't look exactly wet, either, but they were shining, clean looking and deep blue.

He opened his eyes and caught her looking at him and smiled at her.

She felt the heat in her face and leaned her head back as if she could sleep and closed her eyes. She was afraid he'd get up, she thought she'd hear the sound of him getting up, even over the vibration of the sub, but she was afraid she wouldn't and that he would touch her.

She opened her eyes, because she couldn't stand it anymore, even though she knew he'd be waiting, watching her, and he'd smile again. But his eyes were closed.

She sat, not looking at him, but aware. She didn't understand how men could sleep anywhere.

The sub vibrated behind her head. She was tired. She wished this was over. She closed her eyes for a moment, opened them again, but Henri still had his closed. So did David. David was no help at all. She closed them again.

She jerked awake, realized she'd been somewhere between dozing and dreaming but couldn't remember exactly what she had been thinking. She felt more stupid and tired than if she hadn't dozed off. She drifted again.

The sub ride was like a fever dream.

The docking startled her awake. Henri stretched and stood. David stood slowly and worked his bad knee for a moment. It seemed to her that she should put off getting out of the sub, but there was no way.

Beyond the municipal dock everything was dark and shut down for the night, the lights on half.

They followed Henri. She had no idea where they were and didn't know if she could have gotten back to the sub or not. The street was full of shuttered shops. One place was open, the lights inside bright, spilling fluorescent light onto the street.

"Dinnertime," Henri said to no one in particular.

She smelled something fried, cumin and curry, Indian food. She didn't have any money on her, they didn't have any money at all. No one carried money on them at the farm, you had the foreman lock up your money, hid a little bit if you wanted to buy beer or something.

Most of *her* money was in a storage place on the third level, where you paid for a lockbox.

Henri didn't ask them if they wanted anything to eat, but she couldn't have eaten anyway. He bought curry, yogurt and cucumber and poori bread like pillows. He brought it all back with a big cup of sweet/tart tamarind drink and sat down across a scarred plastic table from them. "This is my favorite place to eat," he said. "They know me here, always give me the best food."

The restaurant was empty except for two boys behind the counter who paid no attention to them. Were they going to meet Henri's "friend" here?

"You like spicy food?" Henri asked David. It was the first question she could remember him addressing to David.

"Some," David said.

"Here the food is spicy, but not too spicy," Henri said. Around the midnight-blue slips in his eyes, the whites were red and inflamed. The smell of spices made her queasy. "Sometimes, my stomach bothers me," Henri said. "I have to be careful, eat right. This friend of mine, he is a bit political. You should remember that, not insult him."

Political? What did he mean, political? She looked at David. He was tense, his fingers drumming on his thigh, making careful patterns.

"He is not *La Mano de Diós?*" David said.

"What?" Henri said.

"If he is *La Mano de Diós,*" David said, "we cannot deal with him."

The curry was almost the same yellow as the plastic table. She wondered if she'd ever be able to eat Indian food again without thinking about this place, this moment.

"You are political, too," Henri said. He shook his head. "Everyone is political, except me. I am just a poor man, making a living, and all around me this one will not deal with that one will not deal with the other one."

"Is he *La Mano de Diós?*" David said, insistent.

"There are politics like there are shrimp in the sea, everyone has a different one. Everyone thinks of *La Mano de Diós*," Henri said. "Because they are on the vid, because they are on the news. You say political and people are saying," he hiked his shoulders and minced his words, girl-talking, "*La Mano de Diós, La Mano de Diós*."

David did not answer, did not rise. He waited.

Henri's shoulders dropped and his voice was suddenly different, no make believe, "If you think it makes any difference which politics it is, you are as stupid as they are, but no, it is not *La Mano de Diós*."

David relaxed and then sighed.

"Sometimes," Henri said, his voice once again the voice of a tour guide, talking for their entertainment, "my job, it is stressful, I think that why I got to be careful. But this place, they treat me right. Make it special, I always tell them. I been having stomach trouble since I was twelve or so. Run in my family, my mother, she's the same way."

Henri didn't seem to care that they weren't saying anything back, he chattered on about the foods he could eat and the foods he couldn't. "The doctor, I went to the doctor, he said eat more fruits and vegetables. Shit, I try that, and you know what? It make me more sick. So I don't go to the doctor anymore. Henri know what is good for him, hey?"

It was after one in the morning when Henri finally took them back out on the street. Mayla felt twisted with tiredness, her stomach sour.

Henri was quiet, too. He simply walked, head down. He stopped at a street corner. "Wait here," he said.

He loped on down the block.

"This is crazy," she said to David.

He nodded.

"What do you think we should do?" she asked.

"Wait," he said.

"You don't think we should go somewhere, maybe get a room in a hotel?"

"You think he is going to do something to us?" David said. "You think we are set up?"

"I don't know." Henri stopped at a storefront. She couldn't tell if he was knocking or unlocking the door, but he went inside.

"You work with people," he said. "What do you think?"

She was awful with people; it was numbers she was good at. She had gotten the damn bank sold because she couldn't read people. But she thought. Henri was keeping them off balance, not telling them where they were going, taking his time. But that didn't mean he was setting them up. Did it mean he was trying to establish some advantage before negotiating? Or that he couldn't take them to his contact too early? Or that he was just hungry?

"I don't know," she said.

"It is Henri or Saad," David said. "And Saad has a grudge against us."

"But we know Saad," she said. "Saad is after money. This guy is a drug dealer. He's crazy."

"Saad's partner is crazy," David said. "And Saad may not be able to get us documents. I think we must take this chance."

She felt made of glass.

"This is bad," she said. "This is crazy."

He agreed. "This country is crazy," he said.

She wanted to say it wasn't, that she had lived here all her life, but she didn't.

"We will get out of this," he said.

Hollow comfort, he didn't know any more than she did. But she smiled at him.

Henri was gone for about ten minutes, long enough for her to begin to think that maybe he had just ditched them, but then he came back out with a stocky guy in tow. He sauntered back up the street. "Okay, we'll go see my friend," he said. The stocky guy didn't say anything and Henri didn't introduce them. He was dressed like Henri, in a white vest, but he wore a long-sleeved shirt under it. His hair wasn't dyed either.

Henri took off, and she and David followed Henri and the stocky guy followed them.

Henri was full of energy, swinging his arms, singing to himself.

He seemed to have forgotten about them completely. Maybe he'd taken something in the storefront? Popped a pyroxin?

She expected to wander around another hour or two, she'd about decided he was waiting until morning. He took them down a couple of residential streets, zigzagging through a neighborhood of narrow ways and graffitied walls. It was the kind of neighborhood that normally would have scared her to death, but tonight it just seemed to be part of the evening. Besides, who would bother them while they were with Henri?

She wished they could stop somewhere and sit, her legs ached.

And then Henri did stop at a door. He buzzed and waited impatiently, unable to stand still. He shook his hands at his thighs, dancing in place, jittering, the streetlights shining off his velvet hair.

He buzzed again, muttered, "Come on."

She was standing outside a tenement, waiting for a drug dealer to make a sale. This was crazy. It had to be crazy.

Henri buzzed a third time. The stocky guy was looking down the street at nothing in particular, and Henri was jittering, and David was tapping out cadences against his thigh and she was just so tired she couldn't think.

The door finally opened and somebody said something she couldn't hear. The voice sounded male.

Henri leaned into the doorway to talk.

She looked at her feet. She didn't want to be part of this, didn't want to see anything.

"Okay," Henri said, "come on in."

The light was dim and yellow in the flat, a little two-room tenement that had the musty odor of a bedroom, the smell of sleep. The guy who had answered the door was wearing a pair of diver's tights. He was young, and he didn't look like she expected someone who used drugs to look. He looked plain. She didn't want to remember him, so she looked around the room.

It had a couch, a table and plastic shelves full of books. Rows and rows of paperback books. Like a student's place.

"These are my friends," Henri said. "They are having some trouble and they are looking for documents so they can go to the States."

The student answered Henri in Creole, although he didn't look Haitian. Mayla spoke no Creole but the man was clearly unhappy.

"It is time to do business," Henri said, aggrieved. "Business comes when business comes, it knows no hour."

"I can't help you," the man said to Mayla and David.

"No," Henri said. "Don't believe him, friends." He said something to the man in Creole. They talked for a minute. Mayla tried to listen, but she was mostly aware of the smell in the room: of bedsheets slept in, the musky smell she had come to associate with Henri's braids, and another sour smell she could not identify. Politicals were often students, perpetual students. This man probably didn't worry about things like laundry.

"Okay," the man said. "Tell me what you need." His English was only faintly accented.

"We need documents to be able to get tickets for Miami," Mayla said.

"They will just deport you when you get to the States," the man said, tired. "They'll just send you back here."

"I have family in the States, and Kim is not Caribbean," she said.

"They are in love," Henri said. "Isn't that nice?"

"That's nice," the man agreed. "Why don't you just leave then?"

David cleared his throat. "There is my ex-wife," he said.

The man rolled his eyes. He said something sharp to Henri.

"It is money," Henri said soothingly, "money for your cause."

"You will get your money," the man said.

Henri spread his hands. "I help you, right? I bring you business. I like to help you." He smiled, a big threatening smile.

"Can you get us documents?" Mayla asked.

The man nodded. "It will cost you, though. You have money?"

"How much," David said.

"Five thousand apiece," the man said.

It wouldn't leave her much, but she could do it.

"We did not bring money now," David said, "we did not know we were coming here. We will have to make arrangements."

"I have to get the documents together," the man said. "First though, before I start, I want half. When can you get it?"

"Today," Mayla said. "We can bring it today."

"Good, we'll take the ims and get started when you bring the money."

"I will bring them," Henri said.

The student frowned but said nothing.

Mayla wished it was all over.

"You stay with me," Henri said when they were out on the street.

"I have to go get the money," Mayla said.

Henri shook his head. "Send your boyfriend, you stay with me. I make you a nice breakfast."

"I can't," she said. She covered her mouth with her hand. She couldn't stay with him, not without David there. She was afraid.

Henri reached out and took her wrist, pulling her hand away from her mouth. His palm was hot and dry, almost not like skin, and his fingers had an almost gritty feel although his hands didn't look dirty. She wanted to yank her hand away but she was afraid to make him angry.

"I cannot get the money," David said, his voice bland. "It is under her ID."

She nodded, too eager.

"I will go with you," Henri said.

She didn't want him to go with her, but she didn't know what to say.

"You don't trust me," Henri said, his voice mock-sad. "Haven't I been a friend to you? Didn't I help you? You are getting your documents."

"We're g-grateful," she said. She wanted him to stop touching her, she could feel his smell creeping into her skin. Like rancid perfume, the smell of Henri.

"You see," Henri said, "I have spent all night with you, I get no business done. I am a nice guy, don't you think? I help you, I help my friend, and his cause, and I even help Henri a little bit. But now, you are not so happy, you are not so grateful, so I am wondering, maybe these people will go away and not come back. Maybe then I lose all my time. My good friend gets no money for his cause. You do not get the documents you need. No one gets what they need."

Henri was going to make her stay or he was going to come with her. She could not imagine walking into a place on the third level with Henri. "You can't go there," she said, but it came out a whisper.

"What?" Henri said.

"I can stay here," David said.

"No, I think she should stay," Henri said.

"But I cannot get the money," David said.

"Then I should go with her," Henri said.

"No," David said. He crossed his arms and stood, one hip thrust out the way he did so his weight wasn't on his bad knee.

"You need me!" Henri shouted. "I am trying to help you and you are distrusting me!"

David shrugged. Mayla looked up and down the street.

"I will go with her!" Henri shouted.

David shrugged again. "We will not go get the money, there will be no deal. So if that is the way it is, then this is over and we will go away."

"You cannot leave!" Henri shouted. He was enraged, the veins and ligaments in his neck stood clear, an anatomy lesson. He towered over David and she waited for him to lash out. The stocky man who had followed Henri looked anxious. He was armed, surely. "YOU CANNOT LEAVE! WE ARE MAKING THIS DEAL! I CAN HURT YOU! DO YOU HEAR ME?"

David said nothing, did not uncross his arms.

Henri swiped at him, palm open, and David ducked and threw his arm up and out so that Henri's palm only hit across David's shoulder.

"*Stupide*," David hissed and said something rapid in French. Henri stopped, startled by the language, so close to Creole. David continued talking, fast and low and angry, and Henri, astonished and then frowning to follow, listened.

Henri said something in Creole.

David shook his head. "No," he said in English. "Listen to me, *écoutez*, if she does not go get money, there is no deal. If I am here she will come back."

Henri was breathing heavy, like a winded runner. He did not say anything.

"So," David said, "we all go get some breakfast, eh? And when it is time, she will go get the money. And we will finish the business."

She wasn't even sure Henri was really listening, he seemed just to be watching David, just watching what he was doing. In a minute he would turn to the stocky man and say something and the stocky man would shoot them.

Instead he turned and started walking.

David beckoned to her to follow and they trailed him down the street, the stocky man behind them.

Henri walked fast, long legs making her have to half-skip every few steps to keep up. She had a stitch in her side, she couldn't even pay attention to where they were going.

Henri stopped. "This is a good place," he said.

She jerked around, expecting to see the stocky man armed, and ready to kill them.

But they were standing in front of a restaurant, and Henri meant that this was a good place for breakfast.

It took her almost three hours to get to the third level by taptap. The psychedelic bus was the cheapest way to go and she had to ask bus fare from Henri. He was amused. He put the money in her palm, fingers sweeping her skin in a caress. He seemed to have completely forgotten the argument, talked all through breakfast while the three of them listened to him and ate and waited until it was late enough that the place where she was going to get the money would be open.

In the taptap she thought about going to her grandfather's. David had said that if he was with Henri then she would come back. She was afraid. She couldn't go to her grandfather's, either. She wanted to go home, to her house that was gone.

She got the money that they would need for the documents and a little extra, but no more. They could get it when they were leaving, it would be foolish to go back to Henri with extra money.

Nothing to do but hope it would soon be over.

When she got off the taptap, the stocky man was waiting for her.

She would have to trust David. David was getting them through this. David was thinking.

It was ten-thirty in the morning. She was so tired. Normally she would have been diving by now. She wondered what Luz was thinking. She hadn't even given notice. Luz would think she had been wrong, that Mayla was the kind of person who would leave without giving notice. When she was in the States, she would write a note to Luz, explain that it was a life-or-death matter. That she had to escape. Her stomach hurt, hurt and hurt from no sleep and the aching, disoriented feeling of being too tired.

Henri didn't look tired at all. His eyes were still red around the midnight-blue slips, but he was laughing and gesturing. David looked tired. Like her.

"Ah," Henri said, "you have come home. You have your money?"

"The half," she said.

He nodded, smiling, and she noticed for the first time that when he shook his head his braids didn't move. "Okay sister, let's go."

Maybe his hair was a wig?

They walked again, but this time the streets were full of people. Children watched them when they knocked on the door of the man who made documents.

"Hello, Leo," the man said tiredly to Henri. Henri didn't seem to care that the man had called him "Leo" and she wondered if that was his real name, or if they were all fake names.

The young man was dressed now. He had a sheet on the wall and he put David in front of it and took an im. Then he dropped the im into a reader. "My contact can't get a slip for the port reader until Saturday," he said. "Stand there."

Mayla stood in front of the sheet and had an im taken. She hoped it was better than the last one. As if it mattered, she would use this im once.

"What do you want the documents to say your names are?"

David said Kim Park. She tried to think of a name. "I don't know," she said.

"I'll put something down," the man said. "Do you have an ID I could work from?"

"Not with me," David said.

"I have my workcard," Mayla said. "It's a temporary though." She carried it in a clear sleeve in the pocket of her tunic. She handed it to him. "Okay," he said and glanced down at it. He frowned. "Mayla Ling?" he said.

"Yeah?" she said. She shouldn't have given it to him.

"Okay," he said, still frowning at it.

It seemed to be all right. "Mayla" was an odd name. A lot of people had trouble with it.

"Put the money there," he said, meaning the table.

She put it down. It was a lot of money, a lot of cash. He sat frowning at the reader and entering information. She waited for him to look up.

"Okay," he said, "see you Saturday."

"You want to count it?"

"If you gave me too little, then you get a document that won't get you out of the country," he said, still not looking up.

"Okay," she said.

On the street, Henri was waiting. She didn't want to deal with Henri.

But Henri looked right past them, as if they weren't there.

"We should find a place to stay," David said.

They walked down the street, towards the main street where Henri's place was. "I know a place," David said. "In Dedale. I've stayed there before.

"We'll be safe," he said.

15

Hegira

At night, with Mayla asleep in the other bed, David thought about Meph. Somebody would be taking care of the kitten, maybe Santos. A lot of the fish jocks had kept an eye on Meph and fed him scraps. But he had let Meph down; Meph had depended on him, and once more he hadn't been responsible.

During the day, he and Mayla watched the vid and waited until Saturday. The only time they left the room was to get cheap take-out food.

They talked about the deal. "How do we know that the documents will work?" Mayla said.

David shrugged.

"Why should they even bother to make them work?" she said. "All they have to do is give us something that makes us happy, and we go to the port and get arrested. They have their money, we are out of their hair."

It was something he didn't want to think about. Being at the port, handing over the documents and having blue and whites everywhere because the documents were just bits of plastic, pieces of paper, just nothing, without the information to fool the systems. He remembered the man in the casino, remembered him saying, "It's a mistake." He didn't want to be the one saying that.

"What can we do?" David said.

Mayla chewed on her thumbnail. "Arrange that they don't get their money until we get out of the country."

"How?" he said.

"Give the money to someone else. Then we call the person who has the money and they make the payment."

"And who will make this payment?" he pointed out. "Santos? Patel? Lemile? Henri?"

"Tim Bennet," she said.

"No," he said. "That is crazy."

"Yes," she said. "We should get in touch with Henri. Tell him we have to renegotiate. If they refuse, we can tell if the documents were phony or not."

"You are risking Tim Bennet," David pointed out. "Besides, maybe he is not even in the country, maybe he has left."

"Not Tim," she said. "Tim won't leave until he has to. Tim doesn't act, he reacts."

David shook his head. "You cannot do that to someone. You cannot get him in trouble."

She wasn't listening.

"It is not responsible," he said. Which sounded stupid. Besides, she had grown up exploiting people, her family had servants. She couldn't help it, she thought of people as hired.

She got up and looked out the window. The condensation on the outside of the glass made the world outside distorted. "We can *ask* Tim," she said.

Tim would probably love the idea. Tim would think it was macho, dangerous. All the more reason not to use Tim, he would get in trouble and it would be on their heads, on their hands. "How do we contact him?" David asked.

"We call him," she said.

"What if the phone is, how do you say, they are listening?"

"They weren't listening when you called," she said.

"That was a mistake," he said flatly.

"We could call from a public place. Talk to him. I could tell from talking to him if someone was listening."

He didn't even bother to answer.

"Seriously," she said. "Tim can't hide anything, he's like a big child."

"He is like a big child," he said. "You are thinking of bringing a big child into this. It is foolish. It is wrong."

"If we don't do something, we won't get out," she said. "Do you want to disappear?"

He shook his head. It was still wrong.

"Then I won't go through with it," she said. "And without my money, you can't."

"You are using him," David said.

"Not if I ask him," Mayla said. "Then it's his own free will."

"You have always used him," he said. "Until you didn't want him anymore."

"I am trying to survive," she said.

"That is what every tyrant says."

Ugly words. But she just shrugged. "Too bad," she said.

In the end she won. He had known she would, she had the money. They went out and called Tim.

They took a taptap up a level and just wandered for a couple of streets until they found a place where they could make a call. As they walked he found himself thinking over and over, "this is not a spy vid." The words fell in time with his footsteps, until he was marching along to "this-is-not-a-spy-vid." It was stupid to play games. It was stupid to think they could get out of here, they had no friends and they didn't know what they were doing.

He watched her make the call. She flicked the monitor off and used the handset, her finger in her other ear to block out noise.

When she spoke he almost jumped. "Eess Teem there?" she said, "this is Leesa." She was talking in a hard Spanish accent and it sounded too artificial to be believed. He wanted to take the handset from her and hang it up. He could, too, just reach up and take it.

He found himself curiously embarrassed.

"No," she said, her voice still stilted and hispanic, "I am a friend, he will remember me." And she grinned, not at David but at who-ever was on the other end, even though they couldn't see her. Falling into her role. "Hello, Tim? This is Lisa, do you remember me? This monitor, it is broken, but this one is near my house."

He could not hear Tim's answer over the handset.

"Can we talk, you know, I mean, no one is listening, right?"

Tim must have answered affirmatively, because she reached out and flicked on the monitor. "Hi Tim," she said in her normal voice.

Tim blinked in a moment of surprise. "Oh my God," he said. "Where are you?"

"Have the blue and whites been looking for me?" she asked.

"We called them when you didn't come home," he said. "Are you all right?"

"I'm okay," she said.

"What happened? Let me get Jude."

"No," she said, "don't. If you go get Jude I'll cut the connect."

"Is someone there?" he asked.

"David is here," she said. Habit made him tense when she said his name. It was okay, he reminded himself. No one knew him as Kim.

"David?" Tim said neutrally.

"I found him," Mayla said. "It's too long to tell here. But I need to meet you somewhere."

Tim was silent.

"I can't talk to you like this," she said, exasperated, "Jude or Santos or someone is going to walk in."

"Are you okay?" he said again.

"Yeah," she said. "But I applied for a visa to leave the country and they denied my application. You know what that means?"

Tim shook his head.

"They think I'm involved. They were going to arrest me."

"Arrest you," Tim said. "You haven't done anything."

"This is Caribe," she said. "You don't have to do anything, you just have to be in the wrong place at the wrong time. Don't tell anybody, just meet me somewhere, okay?"

"Okay," he said. "Where?"

"I don't care, someplace you know. In the Warrens or something."

He named a place. "Sure," she said, "where is it?"

* * *

The place was in the Warrens, a little bar/sandwich place. It was long and narrow, with a bar running the length of it and dark-green plastic booths, like a fast-food place, down the other side. The benches were nicked and scarred, and the plastic tables were graffitied, but the place was clean. David expected blue and whites waiting when they got there but there was only Tim. Tim looked bigger than David remembered. And . . . neutral. Not friendly.

"What's going on?" he growled as Mayla slid into the seat across the table.

"You want something to eat?" Mayla asked. "A beer?"

"A beer," Tim said.

"I'll get it," David said. While he stood at the bar, they waited, silent. He felt them waiting. The bartender was a bronze-colored man with skin so dry it looked dusty. David felt itchy.

He brought the beer back, the glasses already condensing, the water running down like tears.

"I'm really scared, Tim," Mayla said.

Tim kept his face still, but David felt a shift in tension. A little sympathy, maybe?

"I think that the government is going to use me, as a scapegoat."

"Mayla," Tim said, "they blew your house up. How can the government use you?"

She shrugged. "Then why did they deny my visa to leave? They set me up that night, at the police station, when I signed that statement I perjured myself. They can use that anytime they want because they've got me on record saying I couldn't identify who was in the car. And I don't have the bank to protect me anymore."

"That's paranoid," Tim said. "Why didn't you tell someone you were leaving?" Meaning, David thought, why didn't she tell Tim? He didn't understand Tim and Mayla.

"I've got to get out of here," she said. "David has got to get out of here."

"How did you find him?" Tim asked.

"It was my mistake," David said. "I gave her a call, you know? I was working at a fish farm, so she tracked me down, from the call."

"You traced the call?" Tim asked. As if she had some sort of secret equipment built into her console and she could do that.

Mayla shook her head. "Somebody asked him a question about salmon trays, so I just started calling fish farms and telling them I had lost the name but the guy I wanted to speak to was oriental. There aren't a whole lot of oriental fish jocks."

Tim grinned, and Mayla smiled, too, relieved.

"I need a favor," she said, and she outlined the deal they had made.

She left out Henri, and all names.

"Wait a minute," Tim said, "you met this guy at a fish farm?"

David shook his head. "This guy, he sells pyroxin, he knew of someone, who knew someone, you know, like that."

"No," Tim said. "No goddamn way. It's crazy. You don't know these people. Politicals? Half the time they're blowing themselves up and getting themselves caught, and you think they can get you out of the country? No."

"What else can we do?" Mayla said.

"Come home," Tim said. "Nobody can believe you're guilty, they blew up your fucking house."

"Then why did they deny my visa?" she asked.

"They don't want you to leave until the investigation is finished."

"You don't understand," she said. "I tried to leave. In their eyes that means I have to be guilty of something."

"How do you know," Tim said.

"Because I've lived here all my life, and I know how this place works!" she said, too loud. David glanced at the bartender who was ignoring them.

More quietly she said, "And what about David? They're looking for someone to pin this whole thing on. Anna Eminike was Anzanian, David served in Anzania, ergo, there's a connection."

Tim shook his head.

"That's the way it works," she said. "A connection, so they can arrest someone, so they can say they've done something."

"Then you come home and I'll help with David getting the documents," Tim said.

"You already reported me missing to the blue and whites," she said.

He shrugged. "Tell them you couldn't handle the stress and you went to stay with a friend."

"They'll want to call the friend, or the hotel, or wherever. And if I tell them I found David, they'll arrest him."

"I've gotta think about this," Tim said.

"We don't have time," Mayla said.

"When do you have to have an answer?"

"We're supposed to get the documents on Saturday."

So they sat and drank their beers.

"You didn't even ask," Tim said after a minute. He waited, but when Mayla didn't say anything he went on. "About your grandfather, you didn't even ask."

"Okay," she said. "You're right, I'm sorry. Is he all right?"

"Well two days ago he was terribly confused all day, and Santos finally took him to the doctor. They said he had like a mini-stroke, and that it could be the first of a lot of strokes or that he might never have another. But he's okay. They just sent him home."

"He's okay?" she said in a small voice.

"Yeah," Tim said.

"He's mad at me?" she said.

"He was worried," Tim said, "but since the stroke thing, I don't know if he always remembers that you are gone. I think he forgets that you live there."

"Okay," she said.

Tim left first. They would call him the next day and meet again. David and Mayla walked back to the exchange to catch their bus.

"He'll do it," Mayla said confidently.

"You are so sure," David said.

She nodded. "We have to get in touch with Henri, set up the deal."

"What if Tim won't do it?" he said.

"He will," she said.

David thought, she likes this. It's like the bank, making deals. And he felt cold.

Henri was waiting on the street where the political lived. He was standing on the street corner, blue braids shining in the fluorescent streetlight. He was whistling and drumming on his thighs, and something in the way he stood reminded David of a cop. As if this was Henri's beat, his neighborhood. Which, of course, it was.

"Happy to see you both," Henri said.

Mayla shrank. She was reduced by Henri's presence, she pulled in, and her shoulders came up.

Henri liked that. "Good morning sister, have you been well?" he boomed.

"Fine," she said in a small voice.

Henri would ignore David, so he didn't say anything. Henri didn't like that, he wanted David to try and be big so he could put David in his place.

He should let Henri put him in his place, because things could only go better if Henri was kept happy, but he couldn't. And it wasn't Henri that mattered anyway, it was the political.

The room smelled just the same, musty and personal, as if the political never left. Maybe he didn't. Maybe the room that he and Mayla were staying in smelled just as intimate and they couldn't smell it anymore.

"They aren't ready yet," the political said.

"We didn't think they would be," Mayla said. "But we came to talk."

"There's nothing to talk about."

"You understand that we're trusting a lot to these documents," she said.

The political looked at her, blank. Not inquisitive, just stiff, uncaring.

"I have done some business before," she said.

"I'll bet you have," said the political and for the first time, smiled. It was a little, ironic kind of smile.

Mayla shrugged off the innuendo (if that's what it was). "In business, I would normally ask for a guarantee."

"Fine," he said. "If you're not satisfied, return the documents in thirty days for a complete refund." He sat back on his chair. He was wearing a long shirt like divers wore under diving suits and when he leaned back, David could see that he was thickening around the waist. For the first time it occurred to David that maybe he wasn't a student, maybe he was older than David thought.

"We have made a different arrangement," she said briskly. "We will take the documents, and when we have left the port, and it is clear that they're good, then you'll get the rest of our money."

"No," said the political, flat and uninterested.

"Yes," Mayla said. Would she be so tough if Henri were in the room instead of waiting on the street?

"Go somewhere else for your documents," the political said.

Mayla stood up. "I'll tell your friend with the blue hair," she said. The political shrugged.

"Come on," she said and started for the door.

She was bluffing, he thought, and the political wasn't. Or else she had decided they stood a better chance with Saad. He followed her because he didn't know what else to do. They had lost so much money here. They wouldn't have enough for Saad.

He could stop, force her to stop. He couldn't think fast enough.

"Wait," the political said.

She was at the door, one hand against it.

"Listen, bitch," he said, "the world doesn't owe you a damn thing."

What did that mean? If Mayla knew what it meant she didn't say anything. She just stood, waiting.

"Money can't buy you guarantees," he said. "You may think it can, but it can't. No matter how much money you've got, there are things you can't buy off."

"Okay," she said, and pulled the door open.

"Wait," the political said, coming halfway out of his chair. "Close the door. How do we know you just will not pay us?"

Outside was Henri, probably wondering why the damn door was open. David wanted her to close the door, too.

"This friend, the one we will call, the one who will give you the money, he will need documents to leave, too. This is his way of seeing if your product is any good."

The political didn't like that word, "product."

"It's a referral," Mayla said. That was her hook, she had explained that the hope they would sell more documents would make them more likely to agree. But he didn't think they really cared if they sold more documents. Henri had some debt on this man, but that didn't mean the man wanted to go into business. Politicals always needed money, he understood that.

"I have to check with some people," the political said.

Mayla didn't close the door but she didn't open it any farther, either. Any minute, David figured Henri would be pushing it open the rest of the way, and saying "Hey little sister, what are you doing?" and then would she be so tough? Henri could fuck up everything.

As if everything wasn't already a mess, with Mayla getting Tim to do things for her.

"Close the door," the political said.

She finally did.

The political sat back down in his chair and rubbed his eyes. "Okay," he said. "Let me think. Okay. I've got to make a call. You should both wait in the bedroom."

The bedroom was small, impossibly crowded with printouts of newspapers and magazines lining the walls, and smelled more strongly of old sheets than the front room did. There was very little place to stand and David didn't want to sit down on the bed. Neither did Mayla, she stood right next to him—there was no place else to stand, studying the cover of a magazine.

The bed was a tumble, the sheets were all brightly patterned children's sheets covered with jungle animals with big bright eyes. He studied a black panther with almond-shaped green eyes. The panther had a red dot in the middle of his forehead. The elephant did, too. And the peacock and the tiger, they all had bright red dots as if each had been shot in the middle of the forehead. It made no sense, no one would print sheets like that—had the political marked them all? Was it some sort of obsessive thing, some mental disturbance that manifested itself this way?

He got a cold feeling, that they were dealing with a psychotic. If the political was that crazy then they were dead.

And then he realized they were caste marks, the animals were all marked with Hindu caste marks. They all had long eyelashes. They were a child's sheets, a little girl's.

He didn't think the political was Hindu, he looked hispanic. Maybe he was Hindu. Maybe he had converted.

The magazines were all news magazines and political journals. Some were in English, some were in Spanish. There was a wooden crucifix on the wall, which struck him as very Catholic, so the political wasn't Hindu after all, probably he had gotten the sheets cheap, they were overruns or seconds or something, or else why would a grown man have children's sheets? The sheets made him uncomfortable, even more uncomfortable than the crucified Christ, twisting in agony on the cross.

The agonized Christ. The exaggeratedly agonized Christ, like the crucifix that Anna Eminike wore, like the crucifix of the South African Catholics.

"*La Mano de Diós,*" he whispered.

"What?" Mayla said.

"That's the same kind of cross, the same as Eminike had."

"How can you tell?" she whispered.

"The Christ," he said, "the way it looks."

"Maybe they are just, you know, a fad."

The ebony Christ writhed on his cross, ribs and hip jutting like the bones on a starved gazelle. A fad, could it be that this was something this man had bought with his Hindu sheets?

The political opened the door. "Okay," he said.

David and Mayla turned, twisted actually, since there was so little floor space.

"I've talked to my comrades," he said. "They say they understand your concern." He waited a moment, to see what they would say, then took a breath. "They are willing to accept your conditions."

"Are you Catholic?" David said.

"Yes?" the political said.

"What do you believe?" David said. It wasn't what he meant to say at all.

"What do I believe?" The man laughed. "Do you mean as in the Apostles' Creed? 'I believe in God the Father Almighty, creator of Heaven and Earth'? Why, are you Catholic?"

"You are a political," David said, "what group do you belong to?"

"All groups are the same, in the end, united in the same struggle," the man said. "It doesn't matter really which group I belong to." The words were rote.

"It matters to me," David said, but he already knew. "Were you going to wait for us here when we came for the documents? Or were you going to give us bad documents and let the blue and whites arrest us? Or did you care once Mayla did not have a job at the bank?"

"I don't know what you are talking about," the man said.

Too many vid shows, the words sounded artificial.

Talking too much, they should have just left. "So we will come back when the documents are ready?" David said.

"Yes," the political said, "when the documents are ready, but we need to talk about how this transfer will be made. About your friend and the money."

"Let us go in the other room," David said. He wanted to be out of this claustrophobic little place, he wanted to be able to move his feet. In the other room he could no longer smell the scent of habitation;

he'd gotten accustomed to it, he supposed. But he still had the panicked feeling.

"My friend will meet you after we call," Mayla said. "We'll call as soon as we're in Miami. My friend might need documents, too, if ours work."

"Where will we meet the friend?" the political said.

"On the mall, on the first level, in front of Gautier. There's a bench there." Mayla was caught up in all this, she thought she was in control.

It was too easy, David didn't know what to think. Why wouldn't they think that he and Mayla were going to just skip them?

"We have to go," David said.

Mayla frowned, started to say something.

"No," the political said, "we need to discuss this."

"We have to go," David said.

Someone knocked on the door and everyone in the room jumped. But the political stood up so fast that his chair clattered over, but his face, his body was expectant. The door opened, and it was Henri. "What is it?" he said.

"We're still talking!" the political said. Henri wasn't who he had expected at the door.

"We are done!" David said.

Henri was too big, blocking the door. "What noise is this?" he asked.

"It is a set-up," David shouted. "It is a set-up! His friends are coming, they don't care about the money!"

"No," the political said, "it isn't true, we need to talk!"

"Get out!" David said.

Mayla was too afraid of Henri, blocking the door.

The political pulled open a drawer and David knew the gun was coming before he ever saw it, knew it was all too late, that they would not get out—

Henri shouted, "Fuck! You owe me money motherfucker! I get you business and you screw around!"

The political brought the gun out of the drawer but it was aiming at Henri. Henri was coming through the door, all enraged. When the gun went off it didn't seem to make any difference, except that Mayla screamed.

Then Henri seemed to fold a little towards them. But he just kept coming, not falling, but coming, but David didn't know if he was shot or not. David grabbed Mayla, and the political fired again, and some of Henri's forehead and blue braids misted in a fine fog of red. And then, he stopped and for a moment rested his hands on the table, looking down at the political. Then he started to fall, curling up as he fell, but David was dragging at Mayla, getting her out the door while there was still Henri between them and the political.

He heard the gun again, and they weren't clear, Mayla was behind him, and then they were out on the street. So he ran, because there was nothing to do but run. And Mayla ran with him.

"Are you all right?" he asked after a moment, because at first he couldn't think of the words, not in English or in French.

"I'm okay," she gasped.

On the main street they turned, "Just walk," he said. "Just walk and shop."

But she was crying, crying and crying in great gasps. And he was shaking.

"I'm going to be sick," she sobbed.

"No," he said. "Just walk."

"I'm sorry," she sobbed, and he thought she meant she was going to be sick anyway, but she wasn't, and she said, "I'm sorry," again. So he guessed she meant about Henri and the political.

Or maybe she meant about everything, he didn't know.

16

Deep Water

They should have been dead. There was no way Mayla could see around it, except that maybe people were harder to kill than she thought. Both harder and easier, because it seemed as if people were always miraculously surviving or being killed without effort. She wondered if Henri would survive, but she thought not. If she closed her eyes she could see the fine spray of red misting across his blue braids, but she could not remember his forehead rupturing.

So she sat in the waiting area for the shuttle to Marincite and did not close her eyes.

They weren't dead, but somehow they had disappeared. When David bought the tickets, the ticket seller had paid absolutely no attention to them. They were surrounded by men and women with flat mestizo faces and sharp, dark Haitian heads and they were invisible. Just a couple of people in fish jock tunics. She needed a shower, but so did some of the people around her. Maybe part of the reason she had always stood out before was more than just being an over-dressed anglo, maybe part of it was pheromones. She washed hers off, these people didn't because water was too expensive to waste on showers every day. So now she had found a key to good camouflage, stink a little.

"We have to call Tim," she said.

David frowned at her. "Tim is out," he said. "There is no deal."

"We still have to call Tim." She wasn't exactly sure why. "We said we would call him. And I have to ask how my grandfather is doing."

"Do you want Tim involved in all this?" David asked.

"No," she admitted. But Tim would be waiting for them, she should at least tell him that she and David were all right.

She wondered if there was anything in the paper about the shooting, if they had been implicated. "I'm going to buy a paper," she said.

The papers available were mostly Spanish and Creole, but the Julian paper was listed. She asked for the last update, it had been updated less than an hour ago, which meant that the shooting might be there. She requested a copy of the whole paper, it would give her something to read, and took it back to the bench.

There was nothing about the shooting, which may or may not have been a good thing, she couldn't tell. Maybe it hadn't been reported? That was impossible to believe, that even someone like Henri could have been shot and it wasn't reported.

But it gave her something to do until the sub came in. It gave her something to think about other than Henri, or meeting Saad and his partner in Marincite. Because if she started thinking about contacting Saad, she started thinking about how they really didn't have much chance. And she couldn't think about that.

In a way, if they were dead, at least she wouldn't be so scared anymore.

She and David almost had to sit in separate seats on the sub. This very nearly panicked her. But David asked some men to move together and sat her down by the window. She nodded off on the trip but she was so tense that her dreams were like fever dreams, endless dreams of walking through city streets trying to get somewhere. The dreams started almost as soon as she closed her eyes, as soon as she started to drift.

They took the chute to Cathedral. She wasn't sure how to get to the loft where Saad and Moustache had their jewelry-making operation but she thought she would know it when she saw it. None of the streets looked familiar, and it all felt like glass. Slippery. Unsafe.

"This way," David said. He was good at getting around. She remembered how he had gotten them to Tumipamba's funeral. She was sure she'd remember the door because they'd had such trouble finding it. This was daytime, there would be people going in and out. But she would have passed it if David hadn't stopped them.

If she had to save herself she didn't think she could. David had all these skills, he thought of things like not using his name, and noticed things. "I'm no good at this," she said.

He looked at her, that sideways look he sometimes gave her when she made no sense to him, but he didn't ask what she meant.

No one answered the bell. Were they out of business? Maybe they never found a loan? (Maybe she had not been so crazy to say "no," maybe no one would touch them, even with Polly Navarro's offhand recommendation.) She stood there, listening to the swirl of Indian music from across the street. What next, give Saad a call? Call Marincite Corp? The Uncles had to monitor every call. She could wait outside the building. But someone would know her.

She looked at David. "I don't know how to get to him without telling the world we're here."

"Maybe we can pay someone to take him a note?" David said.

"They won't let just anyone in," she said. "And we don't want to write on a note. We need to call Tim."

"For what?" David said, sharp and irritated because she was harping on it.

"He can get in, Saad has met him."

"He is connected to you," David said. "What business does he have going to Saad except you?"

She thought. "He could say he was looking for a job."

"No," David said. "It is crazy."

"Then you think of something," she said. She would trust him, everything she had done so far had been wrong, except for getting away from her grandfather's. So if David could think of something else, that would be fine. David's instincts were better than hers.

They found a place to stay. It had brilliant pink doors and smelled strongly of cumin in the halls. She wondered why so many cheap hotels were owned by Indians? Not that it mattered.

Another cheap hotel. Another vid.

David found a soccer game on the vid and sat on the end of the bed, tense. "I wonder if they are taking care of Meph," he said.

It took her a moment. "A lot of people liked him out at the farm," she said. "Santos would take care of him." Which made her think of Luz—Luz thought Mayla was hardworking. Luz probably thought she was a quitter. Stupid to care what somebody thought when you were trying to save your own life.

"I can't think of any way to contact Saad," he said. "Except Tim."

The first thing she noticed about Tim as he came off the sub was that he was so white. And so clean. Even though she had showered and bought a new pair of tights and a new diver's tunic (not a real one, just the kind everybody wore on the street) she was amazed at how scrubbed Tim looked.

He looked pleased with himself, too. Elaborately casual, as if he was on holiday. Big blond anglo, he stood out. An advertisement of presence.

That was why David didn't want him around.

"Hi Dave. Hi Mayla," Tim said. "Are you losing weight?"

The diver's tunic was big but she didn't think she was losing weight. She needed a haircut.

It was conspicuous walking with him. She must have looked like that all the time, no wonder David hadn't been thrilled to see her at the fish farm. Were the Uncles watching? If so, Tim would certainly attract their attention, he had everybody else's.

"So what happened?" Tim said.

"The people who were getting us documentation were connected with *La Mano de Diós*," David said. "Things went wrong."

"What do you mean?" Tim asked.

"Things went wrong," David said. "We had to think of another way. So Mayla thought maybe Saad Shamsi would know a way to get false papers."

"Shamsi?" Tim said. "Why would Shamsi know?"

"Because his business, the one that needed the loan, was a slave bracelet business," Mayla said.

"No," Tim said. "Well, fuck."

David was right, Tim was enjoying this. He didn't understand.

"His partner is a psychotic," Mayla said. "An Argentine. The last time we went to turn him down for a loan he pulled a gun on us."

Tim shook his head. "Then why are you going back to Shamsi now?"

David shrugged. "Do you know someone who can make us false papers?"

Tim thought a minute. No, he didn't. Wouldn't even know where to start. "I knew someone when I was in Indonesia," he said, "but I don't think his documents were very good. But then, you didn't need very good documents in Indonesia."

Tim had to be worldly-wise, had to not be surprised by anything. She wanted to scream at him, to tell him he didn't understand, that she had seen a man shot in the head and that Marine Security would turn them over to the blue and whites in the blink of an eye and that they may never get out of here. But he wouldn't understand.

"We can't call Saad, Marine Security must monitor everything," she said. "But you can go in and tell him that you're looking for a job since Mayla disappeared and ask him if you can take him to lunch. We can meet you at lunch."

"Okay," Tim said.

"Remember that his office may be monitored, too."

"I'm not stupid," he said.

She looked at David, expecting him to roll his eyes, but he didn't seem to find Tim nearly so exasperating. Or maybe he just hid it well.

They caught the chute to Central, and she felt compelled to sit next to Tim. She didn't want him to get miffed and do something stupid. Be nice to him, she thought. This is your life you are worrying about.

"Been a rough ride, eh?" he said.

She nodded. She hadn't known how to talk to Tim before, she knew less now. "How's my grandfather?" she asked.

"He was doing okay when I left."

"Did you tell him you were going to see me?" she asked.

"No," Tim said.

"Good," she said. Her disappointment was irrational, she'd have been furious if he had. "I'll get back in touch with him as soon as I can."

"I just told Jude I was taking some time," he said. "I didn't say where, although I think he had an idea."

"He knew where you were going?" she said, her chest tightening. Not that Jude would tell anyone, but the more people that knew. . . .

"Nah, I just think he suspects I've been in touch with you."

That would be like Tim to hint around. Not exactly hint but to let you know he had a secret. But she couldn't get angry, not now. There was nothing to do about it now, Tim was all they had.

The chute slowed and they were in the corridors of Central.

They found a luncheon place. "He probably won't be able to come for lunch today," Mayla said, "so just come back here and find us. But make it clear to him that you really need to have lunch with him."

Watching him walk she could only notice the jaunty way he moved, his sweater, his goddamn boots, for Chrissakes. Everything about him foreign, noticeable, wrong. Everything screaming to the Uncles to follow him back here.

"It's a mistake, isn't it?" she asked David.

"It is all a mistake," he said. "But, it's all we have." And they went inside to have coffee and wait.

Mayla didn't expect Tim to bring back Saad. And Saad clearly did not expect to find her sitting there with David. She looked up in time to see him come in the door, and then he checked, startled.

Tim was behind him, visibly pleased with himself.

"You didn't make the connection?" she asked.

"No, I really didn't," he said. "When Tim told me you had disappeared, I thought you had really disappeared." He looked quite corporate in maroon and white.

"Marincite Corp. colors," she said.

"What happened?" he asked.

"They denied my permit to travel to the U.S. and," she hesitated, because it sounded so thin, "there were other signs that I ought to disappear, so I did."

"What do you want?"

"We need travel documents," she said, "David and I, to get us out of Caribe." He would sympathize, he'd gotten involved with Moustache so he could someday get to the U.S. "We can pay, it's a pretty good wad of cash towards the capital you need for a residence permit in the U.S."

"Documents? You mean that will get you through the port?" He shook his head. "I don't do documents," he said. "I do jewelry, remember? And you didn't want to do business with me."

A boy stopped at their table, "Do you need more time or are you ready to order?"

It gave her time to think, while they all ordered enchiladas.

There was nothing to say but the truth. "I was too afraid," she said. "I was afraid of your partner. I'm still afraid of your partner."

There was nothing else to say and she didn't think it would be enough.

Saad didn't answer her. The burn of slow anger, she was certain.

Then he said, "I was sorry to hear how Polly set you up."

She felt the color rise in her face. "I should have seen it coming."

"Polly does that to people," Saad said. "I don't know a thing about documents, but I'll snoop around. Ask some questions."

She couldn't believe it.

"Hey," he said, "I can't guarantee anything, I don't even know where to start. But you're going to have to tell me how much you've got so I can shop, you know?"

"I've got 7,000cr, about, and I might be able to get more," she said.

"7,000cr, for documents for all three of you?"

"No, no," Tim said, "I don't need documents, I can leave anytime I want."

She wasn't sure but she didn't correct him.

Saad shook his head. "You'll need more."

"Can you get it if it's in the U.S.?"

"Sure," he said, "if you give me an account number."

She was thinking, thinking. "I think I can, my grandfather has accounts in the U.S. But I'll have to get in touch with Jude."

"No," David said, "you cannot."

"I know," she said. "But Tim is going to go back there eventually, isn't he? He can talk to Jude for me."

Tim was nodding. "I can go back tonight," he said. "I'll be back tomorrow."

"I can write a note," she said.

"Nothing written down!" David said.

"Quiet," Saad said, but he nodded, "Nothing in writing."

"Okay," Tim said, "okay, I can remember. I know what you need anyway, you need money from your grandfather."

"*No*," Mayla said, "I need access to his North American accounts. Jude will understand. Grandfather put money in the North American accounts after the second liberation."

"Okay," Tim said, "access to the North American accounts."

"And I'll need an account number," she said. "You'll have to write that down."

David was shaking his head. "Nothing written down."

"Look," Mayla said, "if they pick up Tim that means they know something anyway, so it doesn't matter."

"No," David said, "they may pick him up just because he used to work for you and he is going back and forth from Marincite. He must just remember the account numbers."

"Can you get 75,000cr?" Saad said.

"75,000?" Mayla said. "I don't know."

"It'll cost you 50,000 for my services."

"Fuck," Tim said.

Everybody glared across the table.

"I'm risking everything," Saad said, still keeping his voice quiet. "50,000 would allow me to collect enough capital to go to the U.S. If I'm going to screw around this way, I ought to at least have a chance to get out, too."

"I'm not paying you 50,000cr without knowing if the documents work," Mayla said.

"Half," Saad said, "and half in the U.S. And if I don't get my half remember I can implicate your family."

"The blue and whites aren't going to do anything to my grandfather," Mayla said.

"Maybe not," Saad said. "Think of it as insurance."

"Bullshit," Tim said. "Think of it as blackmail."

"Look," Saad said, "I don't like this, I don't like this country, I don't like working with Galvez and I don't trust Polly Navarro any more than you do. Less, because I've seen what he can do. And he knows too much. I want out."

"Okay," Mayla said, "ask Jude for 50,000cr. Tell him I'll pay it back."

If he could get it from her grandfather. If any of this worked. But she was full of excitement, full of possibility. Saad would try, she trusted him. It was stupid, after the way she had been taken by Polly Navarro, but she could understand Saad's motives. She could feel his wanting. She had had this feeling before, dealmaking. This was a sweet deal. This was good to go.

Lunch came and she was hungry. She wanted to smile at everyone. It was going to be okay.

The feeling of rightness didn't last. There was nothing to do after Saad went back to work and Tim left to catch the sub back to Julia but go back to the room and think of things that could go wrong.

"I can't stay in here," she told David.

"It is crazy," he said, "we should not leave. We should stay out of sight."

"I know," she said. "I just can't. I know I should, but can't we go do something? See a show?"

"We could find a Reality Parlor," he said.

A Reality Parlor? She hadn't done that since she was in middle school.

He mistook her surprise for hesitation. "We should not go anywhere," he said. "This is not a game, we should be smart."

"I know, I know, I just can't sit here. I just can't."

"Okay," he said. "We will go look for a show."

"A Reality Parlor would be okay," she said.

He stood up and stretched and she thought of the endless evening and night ahead of them and sighed. Whatever they did she would not be able to concentrate and the show would make no sense or she would be awful at the game and she would wish she was back here, because the truth was she didn't want to be with herself.

"I don't know," she said. "You're right, we should stay here."

"I don't think I can sit here either," he said.

"Yeah?" she said. "Except will it be any better to be out and doing something?"

He shrugged. "Probably not."

She laughed. "We're like an old married couple, you know? I think I know you better than any man I ever had a relationship with."

He grinned and nodded. "Foxhole buddies."

"Is that it?" she asked.

"After this is all over," he said, "we will find out that we are really strangers. That we only know each other in moments like this, that we do not know each other's everyday lives."

Glossing over the fact that when this was all over, everything may be much worse instead of better. "Like sex," she said. "Intimate but not."

He sat down next to her on the bed and the mattress inclined her towards him. She could feel the heat of him next to her. It was what she had said. She had brought up sex. After days of living in the same room with him, sleeping in her clothes and he sleeping in his, keeping chaste in separate beds. He had been so distant and polite.

And it wasn't what she wanted. But she didn't not want it either.

And she did really feel closer to him than she had to any other man in her life. So he leaned forward and she closed her eyes and kissed him back, a kiss with lips closed. He was hungry but careful, respecting her need to accustom herself. They kissed for a few minutes and then he drew back.

"Do you want to go do something?" he said.

Would this moment disappear then, as if it had never been? Or would it hang between them awaiting consummation?

She shuddered, and he pulled farther away, mistaking it for a denial of him.

She didn't know what to say, only that men always said women talked too much, so she turned her face towards him wordlessly and after a moment, he leaned back towards her and she closed her eyes.

After a little while he put his arms around her. He was small, narrow around the chest, but all hard bone and muscle. It wasn't helping, she was still self-conscious, aware of the time. But it would have to work at some point, wouldn't it? It would have to overwhelm everything, at least for a bit.

He unzipped her tunic. "Is it too cold in here?" he said.

"Let's get under the blanket," she said.

He stood up and she did to, thinking she was supposed to get undressed now, but not exactly sure, and watching to see if he did. He unzipped his tunic and pulled it over his head without fuss, but he sat down on the edge of the bed with his back to her to take off his tights.

She undressed as quickly as she could, checking only to make sure he had taken off his underwear, and then got into bed, too. She didn't feel sexy, she felt trepidation.

He waited, looking at her. He had interesting eyes, she had never gotten to stare at someone with oriental eyes except her grandfather, and David's eyes were not like her grandfather's. They tilted or appeared to tilt and her grandfather's didn't. And her grandfather had creases in his eyelids, but David's were smooth, like curtains.

She stroked his eyebrows and he smiled. "That's nice," he said.

"I'm a little nervous," she said.

"Me, too," he said.

He kissed her again, and traced a circle around her nipple, which felt playful and almost ticklish. She touched his and he flinched and smiled again.

"Touchy," she said.

He took his time with her, he was considerate, and it helped. And briefly, she did forget about everything. So it was worth it.

Waiting for Tim to get off a sub she wondered if he would be able to see any difference in her. She didn't really think so, she didn't feel that much different, just tired because she had had trouble sleeping with David. She couldn't go to sleep and worried about keeping him awake tossing and turning, and then she had kept waking up, it seemed as if every time she needed to turn over she woke up.

Tim was not on the eleven o'clock.

"What do you think," she asked David.

"Maybe he missed it?" David said.

Or maybe he was detained. Maybe he was detained last night when he got off. Ironic that she might have been in bed with David while Tim was being interrogated.

"If he's not on the twelve-fifteen then we need to get word to Saad," she said.

David didn't say anything, so she didn't know if he agreed or not.

She looked for the Uncles. As if she would know a plainclothes officer if her life depended on it.

So she looked for anyone who looked as if they didn't belong, or anyone who looked as if they were watching her and David.

"Sit still," David said under his breath.

"What?"

"Sit still," he said.

What, she looked guilty? Well, she probably did, she felt guilty.

She wanted Tim to get off the sub. She pictured him getting off the sub, wearing his bright blue sweater, blond and shining, screaming anglo. She pictured it. Pictured it with everything she had, as if she could construct him with force of will, with the strength of her wanting.

When he got off, she was so grateful she could have hugged him.

"What took you?" David said, sharp.

"We had to wait until after eight to make some transfers," Tim said. "The money is in a bunch of accounts. But you have three accounts, two with 30,000cr, and the third with 45,000cr. So you'll have a little money when you're in the U.S."

"What did my grandfather say?" she asked.

Tim shrugged. "We didn't ask him. Jude just took the account numbers out of your grandfather's files. The encryption key authorizations were right there with them."

It was too easy, it was all falling in place, it was too sweet. For a moment she thought it was a set-up, and she stared into Tim's face looking for guile, looking for some sort of proof that the blue and whites had set him up to it. But it was Tim. It was just that the deal was sweet and she knew from banking, when the deal was sweet it just went and all the obstacles just fell away. You worked and worked on the ones that went sour and the sweet ones just fell into your lap.

It was an omen, it was all going to happen.

Tim recited the account codes, long meaningless strings of letters and numbers, and she wrote them down. It was one thing if Tim got picked up with them, but if she got picked up it didn't matter if she had anything incriminating on her or not. She was with David, that was enough.

"Okay," she said, "give the first 12,000cr account to Saad, and tell him that's for the cost of the documents. The second 12,000cr goes to him before we leave, and the rest gets paid to him in Miami."

Tim nodded. It wasn't the agreement, but Saad would have to understand that it was the best she could do under the circumstances.

"Are you going back tonight?" David asked.

"Yeah," Tim said.

"Okay. We'll meet you at the diner where we had lunch," David said. "You know, I think you should leave Caribe. Before we do."

Tim nodded. "I've been thinking about that."

"In case something goes wrong, you know. You might be, you know how this country is, what do you say, involved."

"You're right."

Tim would be leaving. Scary, even though it didn't really matter, since she would be leaving, too. All that time she had wanted him to leave.

"I think I'll try Belize," Tim said.

"Do you need any money?" Mayla asked. "I could give you some, I'd have to send it after I got to Miami—"

Tim was embarrassed, "No, no, that's okay, I've got some put back. You always paid pretty good, Mayla."

"Okay," she said. "Okay." Because she couldn't think of anything else to say. She didn't know if all the debts were paid up, she wasn't even sure what all the debts were. "Okay."

It was an awkward way to say goodbye.

"We should go with you to the sub," she said.

"No," Tim said, gruff. "The less time you're with me, the less likely something can go wrong."

"Okay," she said again, feeling stupid. "Well, get in touch with Jude when you have an address, someplace I can get in touch with you, okay? So that once I get to Miami I can make sure you're all right."

"I'll do that."

In front of the restaurant they stood there, all four of them, and no one quite knew what to do. "I've got to get back to work," Saad said. He stuck his hand out to Tim. "Good luck to you."

"Thanks," Tim said.

Watching Saad walk off gave them something to do for a moment.

"You know," Tim said, "it would have been better if I didn't work for you."

Regrets? Maybe now he saw the mistake it had all been?

"It killed our relationship," Tim said. "Money does that. If I hadn't taken the job from you, the relationship might have worked."

"It might have," she said, smiling warmly through the lie.

"Yeah," Tim said.

And then he walked away, too.

"Okay," Saad said, "I've talked to somebody, he says he can do it. I've set it up so that he gets half the money when he gives us the documents, and the other half twenty-four hours after I leave the country. He can guarantee them but he can't withdraw before that."

That was what she had needed to do all the time, but cut off from the banking system, she couldn't do it.

"When do we get the documents?" David asked.

"Friday," Saad said. "Traffic will be busiest Friday, there'll be a bunch of people going out of the port. I've got three tickets reserved. We decompress on the Miami side. It's more expensive then decompressing here, but I thought you wouldn't mind." He grinned.

Nobody minded. Decompression, more days in a room. But it would be different, she could stand to be bored when she wasn't so afraid.

She would call her cousin in Hawaii, maybe go out there for awhile. She had never been to Hawaii, she had heard it was hot and bright. Then she would look for a job, maybe finance with a corporation.

It was almost too much to think about. Maybe eventually she could come back? The government would change eventually, she would come back to Caribe.

She couldn't eat her enchilada this time.

She couldn't think what they would do for two days, either.

"Thursday night you need to get ims taken and have some bio info put on the card, okay? We can do it at the loft."

"Is this through your partner?" Mayla said. Alarm bells, if the Argentine, Moustache, was involved, then she had to think.

"No," Saad said, "Galvez is in Del Sud for two weeks, making connections. I don't want him to know I'm even doing this, he'll kill me if he finds out."

Set-up. She looked at David.

But David was nodding. David was agreeing to everything. He had been since they got in touch with Saad. Before he had always been worried, but now he just nodded, allowing events to take him.

Or maybe the deal was really this sweet, maybe he felt it, too. She was being paranoid, they either trusted Saad or they didn't.

She needed to be clearheaded. She hadn't suspected Polly Navarro, and she'd thought that Henri's political could be guaranteed.

"Thursday night," Saad said. "At seven."

On the street again she said to David, "I wish I could go to sleep and wake up on Thursday."

As soon as she said it she wanted to take it back—it sounded as if she wanted to spend the next two days in bed. And she didn't, not at all.

"Better than that," David said, "how about waking up in the U.S.?"

"Yeah," she agreed. Relieved. Still not sure what he would expect, but relieved.

"Do you want to go do something?" he asked. "Go to see a show or something?"

"Sure," she said. Meaning, she supposed, instead of going to bed together. So he had felt it, too, that it was a one-time thing. Unless, she thought he felt that he ought to take her on a "date." Which given the present situation was ludicrous. But he had said that they should stay in the room, so why change his mind?

But if she said they should stay in the room, would he see that as an invitation?

"Look," she said, "why don't we just go back to the room and watch the vid or something?" She thought of the "or something" and it flustered her. "I mean, watch the vid. I mean, I don't regret last night, but it was a one-time thing, okay? I mean, it's not you, it's just that this is all so awful—"

"Okay," he said, "I understand."

She had insulted him.

"Really, it's not you," she said. "It's just wrong, like what Tim said about hiring him. Anything we do now is just craziness, we don't know what we're doing."

"It's okay," he said. "It is okay, Mayla. I thought it was for one time, also. I did enjoy it, but it is what happens when people are afraid. Yes?"

Yes. Yes, yes, yes.

"We will go back. We will wait for Thursday."

By Thursday she was glad to be doing something, no matter how afraid of Saad's partner she was. She could not get the fear that it was a set-up out of her head.

"Maybe," David said. "We will just have to see."

"How can you be so calm?" she asked.

He laughed a little. "I am not so calm. But there is nothing I can do. We just have to see."

She stood up and looked around the room. Now that the time had come she was afraid to leave it.

It had all gone so wrong before, with Henri and the political.

"Do you think it will be okay?" she asked.

"I hope," he said.

"You do the talking," she said.

"You do better than me," he said. "You convinced Saad."

She shook her head. "Saad wanted to be convinced. I make too many mistakes, I don't know what I'm doing."

"No one knows what we're doing," David said. "Come on, this is just talk. We have to go."

"I talk too much," she said.

"Some people talk when they are afraid," he said. "Some people can't say anything."

They walked down to their chute station. "Their" chute station, she thought. Two days in a room and this was "their" neighborhood. The human capacity to make alien places "home."

She wondered if Tim had left Caribe yet.

Her thoughts flitted and she tried to be calm. Only one more night, she thought. Only one more night in the room lying there wanting it all to be over, wanting to be able to sleep without being afraid.

It would not go wrong. That was the only sensible way to think.

The chute ride was longer than she remembered, so long that she wondered if they had missed their stop.

The chute station was full, but Saad wasn't on the platform when they got there. That scared her. A set-up, she kept thinking. Saad had betrayed them, to Polly Navarro maybe. Not to his partner the Argentine, the Argentine wouldn't call the Uncles. Although he was paying the Uncles, so maybe he had.

So why weren't the Uncles here?

The station cleared leaving them alone on their platform.

"This is crazy," she whispered to David, to keep her voice from echoing. She hated standing here, it would have been better to have told Saad to meet them on the street. At least on the street she and David would have had some place to go if they saw someone.

"It's like the parking, all concrete," David said. So she knew he was afraid, too.

Every time the chute came in she tensed, thinking Saad would be on it. The chute would come in, rumbling the concrete under her feet, and people would get off. Rush-hour traffic, for a moment the station would be full of feet and voices. The chute would rumble out and she would scan the crowd frantically, looking for Saad. Beside her, David rose on the balls of his feet, trying to look. No Saad, unless she had missed him. And in a couple of moments, the platform would clear.

There were four more chutes before she finally saw Saad get off, but when she saw him, she wondered how she thought she could have missed him.

"Sorry," he said, "I couldn't get out of work."

He couldn't get out of work? He didn't sound like someone who was leaving the country the next day. What were they going to do, fire him?

She looked at David, wondering if they should run now. But after Saad, what did they have left to try?

It was not good to be desperate.

The streets were full of people coming from work. Lots of women with string bags. Never men, why don't men ever shop, she wondered.

Saad was nervous, he chattered about work, about someone named Septiem who had wanted him to stay and help with something even though he kept saying he had an appointment. She found it hard to follow so she didn't try.

She remembered the way to the loft this time. Saad pulled on the door. She wanted to say, "Wait." She wanted to talk to David.

"It's early," Saad said. "The night people aren't here yet."

"What about your partner?" she said, hanging at the door. "What if he's here?"

"Galvez is in Del Sud," Saad said. "You think I'm crazy? I wouldn't bring you here if Galvez was here, he'd kill me."

The doorway at the top of the stairwell was dark, as if no one was there, but still she hung back, unwilling to climb the stairs.

"What?" David asked.

"I don't know," she said. So she climbed the stairs, listening, straining to hear the sound of people.

The loft was dark, and when Saad palmed the lights, the lines of benches were empty.

"Where are the people with the documents?" she asked.

"They're coming at seven," Saad said.

Now it was coming. Now the Uncles would come up the stairs, that was why Saad had been late, some sort of last-minute procedural nonsense.

She thought David would react, the way he had when he saw the crucifix in the political's bedroom. David would put it all together, get them out of here.

David sat down at a workbench.

Saad said, "I'll make coffee."

It sounded exaggeratedly normal. Everything was extraordinarily normal. Saad went into the office and she held her breath, but after a moment he came out with the carafe from the coffee maker and ran water in it.

The sound of the water was loud.

They drank coffee and waited for the people with the documents to arrive. The coffee was sweet and bitter. Tim had always said that coffee in Caribe tasted funny. Assuming she did leave tomorrow, the coffee would never taste this way again. How could she already be homesick and she hadn't even left?

At seven minutes after according to her chron, someone beat on the heavy door at the street. Saad got up too fast.

It would be so strange to be sitting here drinking coffee when the Uncles came in. But on the other hand, it would be over.

She heard Saad say hello, waited for the Uncles to rush up the stairs, but instead she heard the sharp sound of voices. They came up slowly, someone walking heavily.

But it wasn't the Uncles, it was a stocky Indian woman and an old hispanic man. The old man was leaning heavily on the bannister, his body bent forward and his arm ahead of him as he pulled himself up the steps. The woman had a camera bag around her neck and a big briefcase in one hand.

The woman looked hostile, she would not look at any of them. The old man was too busy recovering from the stairs to look up from the floor.

It was her luck that Saad's document forgers were bargain basement. She found it hard to believe that these people could hack the security system at the port and create the necessary authorization to get them through. Hackers were usually kids, soft feral boys who looked as if they never got any exercise.

"Stand against the wall," the woman said to David. There were no introductions. How nice it would be to be back in the world where people said, "hi, I'm—"

David didn't look comfortable standing against the wall. The command had an ominous ring to it. But all she did was take some ims.

"Now you," she said to Mayla.

Mayla brushed her hair with her fingers, trying to get it to lie flat. Who cares, she thought, but she did it anyway.

"Okay," the woman said. She heaved the briefcase onto one of the benches and took out what looked like a printer. She found a power source. While she was scuttling around, the old man slowly lowered himself into a chair.

"Here," she said suddenly, turning back to the camera which had been steadily spitting out ims. She dug into the briefcase again and pulled out a reader. "Pick out an im."

They were all awful, but document ims always looked awful. In the light from the loft she looked flat-faced and kind of Chinese, which was a surprise. She picked one out, handed the reader to David. He put one of his in the reader and—she was pleased to see— grimaced.

"I look ghastly, too," she said.

"I hate my ims," he said.

The Indian woman looked irritated. "You do not want too good a picture," she said. "Pictures look a little different from the card-bearer, because time has passed."

The Indian woman took the im and slipped it into a fold in a blank ID card. She fed the card into the printer.

For a moment they all stood looking at the printer. Mayla was holding her breath. Then the card fed out. The Indian woman glanced at it and handed it to Mayla. It was still warm.

The card looked like a regular card but the name on the card was Constanza Rodriguez. The Indian woman did the same for David and his card said Luis Chen.

"Now," said the Indian woman to Mayla, "I cut your hair."

"Pardon me?" Mayla said.

"Women never look the same as their card, always a bit different, because their hair is longer or shorter. At the port, they will be looking for things like that. So I will trim your hair so it will be different." The woman smiled maliciously, "Don't worry, I am not expensive."

Okay, so she could get another haircut in Miami. "Not too short," she said, feeling foolish.

"Okay," the woman said.

The old man started to get up.

"Baba," the woman said, "stay quiet." He blinked at her but sat back down.

"Would he like some coffee?" Saad asked.

She shook her head. "It isn't good for his heart."

"Coffee?" the old man said, his voice a rasp.

"No, Baba," she said loudly. "There's no coffee." She took scissors out of her briefcase. "He cannot be left alone anymore," she said, matter-of-factly.

He wasn't Indian, maybe her father-in-law? She wasn't wearing a wedding ring, and Mayla thought Indian women did wear wedding rings but she wasn't sure.

The woman cut her hair briskly, with practiced movements. It was strange to have her hair cut without a mirror to look in. She wondered what she was doing. Mayla wanted to say not too much again, but she didn't dare, so she sat, listening to the snip of scissors.

"What about David?" she finally asked.

"Men do not change so much," the woman said. "Just do not wear the same clothes that you wore in the im." The scissors snicked. She seemed to be taking off a lot around the ears.

"Okay," she finally said.

"It looks nice," David said. "You look different."

"I think it is a good look for you, Constanza," the woman said. "Okay. That is all, you have your cards."

"What about the port system?" Mayla asked. "What about hacking it?"

"My hacker works at the port. The cards have an access code that the technicians use to check the equipment, they will come up green," the woman said. "Then the system don't even check your information against the base, it just repeat the information on your card. But use them fast, the port changes the codes sometimes."

"Will tomorrow be okay?" Saad asked.

"Should be," she said. And then loudly, "Okay Baba, let's go."

Mayla wished she had a mirror.

She hated her haircut. It was short on the sides and hung longer and flipped under in the back. Her bangs ran across her forehead. It was too young for her, for one thing, a middle-school girl's haircut. For another, it looked, well, cheap. It made her look hard. And old. Or maybe the last few months had made her look old. Or maybe she was just tired. But she didn't like the haircut at all.

"I like it," David said.

Men liked things like that, though. Men didn't recognize class, they liked flash. This haircut was all flash, like a tight gauzy blouse.

It would grow out. If it got them to Miami then she'd have nothing to complain about.

David was sitting on the bed. He had a duffel bag. It was mostly empty: a toothbrush, a change of clothes. She had a little suitcase that was just as empty, but they thought it would seem strange if they didn't have any luggage at all.

She sat down on the bed. Nothing to do but go, but she was afraid.

He sat down next to her. He had been so good, not pressuring her about sex, just letting that one night go as if it had never happened.

"You're a good man, David," she said.

He smiled and the creases ran away from the corners of his eyes. "I am not so good," he said.

"If it wasn't for you," she said, "I'd have been arrested."

He shrugged. "If it wasn't for me, you would never have been suspected. Because I walked away from the house."

"Maybe," she said, "maybe not. The blue and whites can make strange decisions."

"They are crazy, the institution, because the country is crazy. Now we have to go."

But she still thought it, following him out of the room. He was a good man, he tried to do the good thing. Maybe he shouldn't have walked away from the bombing, but he had called her, when it would have been smarter not to. And he had stayed with her since she found him on the fish farm.

A good man. But that sounded like a judgment, it sounded final. A superstitious shudder walked up her spine. She shouldn't be thinking about him in final terms.

She tried to think of Miami, but there was nothing, she couldn't force her mind in any direction at all.

They were on their way to the port. Saad would be at the port.

She was leaving Caribe. That should have been good for some emotion but it wasn't. She did hope, in an abstract sort of way, that Tim had left. She should call her grandfather—

What an amazing reflex. Call her grandfather. Absolutely. Just as soon as she got to Miami.

They got off the chute at the Marincite Port Authority and walking up the ramp she saw an Uncle. All in black, like at Tumipamba's funeral, with a headset. He was watching the crowd come through the entrance. She half-stepped and David said, "Keep walking."

Of course, if they turned around that would call attention to themselves.

David drifted away from her and then back until there was a couple of meters between them so they did not appear to be walking together. Maybe her haircut would hide her. Nothing could hide the fact that he was oriental. Was he going to allow them to pick him up so they wouldn't see her?

No, she thought, if they were looking for a couple, there was no sense in being a couple.

She passed the Uncle, her eyes on the concrete ramp, her shoulders tense, waiting for him to come away from the wall, to glide through the crowd like a barracuda—

But he didn't move, not when she passed, not when David passed. She thought maybe he said something into his headset, but she wasn't sure, and it didn't necessarily have to be about them. Or maybe they were just going to be picked up farther in.

Her stomach hurt and she had to go to the bathroom.

She saw the ladies public and ducked in. It smelled, publics always did, but she felt a little sheltered.

She had cramps and she took a long time, and all the time she was sitting there she expected the stall door to be kicked open and the Uncles to come in and rag her out with her tights around her knees. She had her hands clasped together, she felt as if she were praying, but she didn't really know what to do except think, please no, please no. But the Uncles didn't come.

They weren't waiting when she came out of the public. Across the concourse she saw David reading a newspaper but she pretended not to see him. She checked her gate on the monitors and saw him fold the newspaper and start walking. So she walked to.

At the gate she would find Saad and get their tickets. Then she would leave David's on the seat so he could pick it up. If he got to the gate, if she got to the gate—

Two more Uncles in black, standing outside a stall that sold coconut bread hamburgers and beer. And two more a little beyond them on the other side of the concourse. Uncles everywhere. For her and David, for Saad? Had something happened and Saad's partner figured out what was going on? Were their documents okay or had the Indian woman betrayed them?

She saw their gate, full of people. She saw Saad waiting just this side of the departure check. She started for Saad, better if she got the tickets from Saad than if David did, she was marginally more disguised than he was.

And she saw, standing between her and Saad, Polly Navarro. He was impeccable in his suit, holding a newspaper.

Business trip. *Madre de Diós*, let it be a business trip.

The carpet was Marincite maroon, heavy duty, and she thought she was past him when he said, "Mayla?" with just the right amount of surprise. Completely natural.

She realized after she looked up that she should have just been deaf. But he was here, he was waiting for them. And it was all over.

She looked around but didn't see the Uncles.

"Polly," she said.

"Going to Miami?" he asked.

She nodded. "My grandmother was from there. I have cousins there." She didn't have cousins there, they were spread across the country, and she shouldn't justify.

"You remember Saad Shamsi?" Polly asked.

David was drifting towards Saad, who was not watching anyone, who was blank as a stone, watching into the concourse. When Polly turned David turned and found a seat.

The instinct to live, she thought. It is all up now, but he is still going through the motions.

"Saad," Polly said, "you remember Mayla Ling."

"Yes, of course," Saad said.

Polly put his paper on the counter. "I'm going to Miami on business," he confided. The confidence sounded awkward, of course he would be going on business. "I hate the decompression, though."

"Are you decompressing on this side or on that side?" Mayla asked. The instinct to survive, pretending everything was normal while she waited for Polly's Uncles to come get them.

"Usually I decompress on this side, but this time I'm decompressing on the other side."

A small part of her that had not yet given up the belief that they would get free thought about being stuck in decompression in Miami with Polly.

"Oh," Saad said, "so you're on our sub." He was so stiff.

"You're on the 10:30?" Polly said.

Something was strange about Polly. She remembered him from the take-over. He had been different. He was in control here, why wasn't he riding high? Why was he perspiring?

"Are we served lunch?" Polly asked vaguely, but his eyes drifted away, across the concourse.

She glanced across. They were there, finally. Uncles, three of them in black and one in regular street uniform maroon. *Les Tontons.* Where they crossed the concourse there was space, people were gone.

Polly had a funny half-smile.

She wondered if they would pick up David. If they didn't, he would still be stuck, Saad had the tickets. He would still be hiding. Better to be in hiding.

She was going to be arrested, turned over to the blue and whites, but she couldn't feel anything. Time was so slow. She felt suspended. This were the last few moments of this life, and she didn't know what was coming.

"Have a nice trip," Polly said.

The uniformed Uncle said, "Mr. Polito Navarro?"

"Yes," Polly said.

"I'm afraid we need to talk to you."

The black-clothed Uncles were cutting between Polly and her and Saad, cutting him off.

"I'm supposed to be meeting some people in Miami, I really need to get there," Polly said and she could see the sweat on his upper lip. "Can this perhaps wait until I get back?"

"I'm afraid not," said the uniformed Uncle. He was older, every fitting on his uniform polished to high gloss. "You'll have to come with us."

"You don't want to do this, Marat," Polly said.

"No sir," the uniform said. "Come with me, sir."

Saad whispered, "Oh shit."

Blue and whites on the concourse. A lot of them. Blue and whites weren't supposed to be in Marincite. But they were there. "Sir," the uniform said, "Do you want to come with me, or go with them?"

Polly nodded. "The President," he said.

"Yes sir," the uniform said.

Polly took a deep breath. "All right," he said.

She handed her card to the woman at the departure gate. Saad was waiting on the other side. The light flashed green. The woman at the departure gate chattered in Spanish, something about the ticket and her name. She called her Señorita Rodriguez. Mayla nodded and took the ticket and her card.

Behind her David went through the same routine. She couldn't help watching to make sure that the light flashed green.

The sub was nearly full. She waited, thinking they would still come, that the Uncles would pull them off the sub, that their documentation would not stand up. But the sub pulled away.

She dozed and dreamed of being in a cathedral. Along the walls were people she thought were blue and whites, and she was getting married, but she didn't know who to. Once she thought it was Tim, and once Saad, but most of the time she didn't know.

17

Daylight

David found that suddenly he was tired, so tired he wanted to do nothing but sleep. They climbed out of their seats, his knee was stiff. Sitting still a long time always made his knee stiff.

"I guess we have to get our luggage, eh?" he said, smiling.

Mayla looked startled. "Wouldn't it look suspicious if we didn't?"

He laughed. "We are in Miami. There is no suspicious anymore."

He would call his aunt and uncle and make arrangements to go there when he had decompressed.

The sub had surfaced, they could feel it riding buoyant and it did strange things to his equilibrium. Up the debarkation tube and out into a hallway full of light. Bright hard white sunlight. He wanted to laugh.

Behind him Mayla stopped in the doorway.

"What?" he asked.

"It's too much," she said. She was blinking and tearing.

She was still in Caribe. Caribe was all she had, and she was still there. A refugee.

He went back and took her hand. "Come on," he said. "We will buy you sunglasses. It is okay. You will get used to it."

She shook her head, the tears were more than just light. David waited, polite.

"It is like after the war," he said. "At first you bring the war home with you. You can never forget the war, but finally you can leave it behind."

He didn't know if she understood him or not, he wasn't sure if he believed it or not, but he was sure going to try.

"Come on," he said again.

And this time she came.